UNFINISHED
BUSINESS

UNFINISHED BUSINESS

by
CONRAD WILLIAMS

To my beloved Sue and David
Enjoy!

BLOOMSBURY READER
LONDON · OXFORD · NEW YORK · NEW DELHI · SYDNEY

This edition published in 2016 by Bloomsbury Reader

Copyright © 2016 Conrad Williams

The moral right of the author is asserted.

Bloomsbury Reader is an imprint of Bloomsbury Publishing Plc

50 Bedford Square, London, WC1B 3DP

www.bloomsburyreader.com

Bloomsbury is a trademark of Bloomsbury Publishing plc

Bloomsbury Publishing, London, Oxford, New Delhi, New York and Sydney

ISBN: 978 1 4482 1552 2
eISBN: 978 1 4482 1551 5

Visit www.bloomsburyreader.com to find out more about our authors and their books.
You will find extracts, author interviews, author events and you can sign up for
newsletters to be the first to hear about our latest releases and special offers.

You can also find us on Twitter @bloomsreader.

Printed and bound by CPI Group (UK) Ltd, Croydon, CR0 4YY

For Rod Williams, Pip Torrens and David Sherwin

Contents

Chapter 1

I am a literary agent.

It sounds excellent, I think, impressive. 'Literary' has a dig-
nifying ring, a gentlemanly air. I represent authors, edit their
work, and get them publishing deals.

Writing can be a long and lonely game. Many are called, but
so very few succeed. If after years of endeavour a writer hits the
jackpot, he needs at his side a dedicated partner who can turn
kudos into cash. He needs a fearless chevalier to shout at accounts
departments and 'nice' foreign publishers, at poorly dressed film
producers wanting something for nothing, and at 'immensely
gifted' publishing editors bobbing in a marinade of mid-life crisis, booze and self-pity. A good agent makes a writer rejoice that
not every close reader is 'creative' and not every business brain a
bloody banker. A good agent is an author's comrade-in-arms
and confidant; and the gratitude we agents get from our authors
is the reason we love to agent. We relish the deals, we enjoy the
cut and thrust, but it is the emotional wealth of serving talent
that rewards us the most, if I am honest.

Or so I thought until my best client sacked me. A morning in
May: unforgettable.

1

I had walked in to work under a blue sky, come through reception with a smile for the intern, and slipped into my office at the end of the corridor. Sunlight blazed from a high sash window and the fragrance of coffee wafted from Sheila's room. It was a fine morning to be thirty-four years old and in love with my job, and as I flicked on the monitor and tossed my case on a chair, I saw a letter someone had left on the desk.

The envelope was addressed to me in ink and marked 'private'. It is hard to say why exactly, but as I drew out the sheet, I felt a sense of disquiet. This was a letter from Ophelia Jamieson, a client of two years' standing. She had sent me hundreds of emails in recent months but never a *letter*. Her handwriting, I remember, was rigidly neat.

I will never forget the first time Ophelia came into the office. I was eager to meet the author of a first novel that had landed in my inbox a few days before, and kept me reading all weekend in a blaze of interest. Her writing had style, buckets of it, and presence. There was thrust to her manner, her language, as though a powerful intelligence were shoving all before it. She possessed that essential and mysterious quality in an important new writer: an authority beyond her years.

She was shown into the room by my assistant, Helen, and sat herself down on the sofa; and as I reached back from a first, friendly handshake, nodding, listening and laughing at her charming, nervous attempt to amuse me, it was all I could do to conceal the effect of her appearance. The young woman I hoped to sign as a client was a striking, theatrical proposition of oval face and pale skin, of pursed noble eyebrows and auburn cascades of perfectly twirled hair, like a reincarnated Pre-Raphaelite muse. She made vital expressions – furrowed thought, faraway longing, impish smiles, and a wide open I-agree-with-you-with-all-my-heart

2

kind of look that seemed to drink the essence of my thoughts and store them in a precious, secret place. Yes, Ophelia was a personage alright, very compelling to a literary man, and I admit I found it rather intoxicating that someone so gifted should also be beautiful. I was as charming as hell, and after half an hour of praising her novel to the skies and asking about her interests and plans, and impersonating gravitas to the limits of credibility in an agent, I offered to sign her, and she accepted instantly. From then on, when I ushered her out of the office and revolved in the lobby with a little jig of excitement, I felt a loyalty that was both properly professional and keenly personal.

'Cripes,' said Steve, my faux-cockney colleague in Film/TV, as he walked into the after-waft of Ophelia's scent and leather-care product.

'Don't say it, Steve.'

'Very promotable!'

'Well, very talented, actually.'

'You're telling me. What's the name?'

Steve was too cynical by far, but I proved his imputation wrong: by selling Ophelia's book to an excellent publisher for a grand price. From then on everything went perfectly and there was unstoppable momentum. The novel made friends of everybody and the legend of its excellence spread and burgeoned until Ophelia was shortlisted for the Orange Prize and I was caught up in the career-gilding excitement of having a hot client whom I liked very much.

I now held her letter in my hand.

She had signed with Marjorie Stone at Intertalent Agency 'for this next most important stage of my writing life'. She hoped 'very sincerely' that we would remain friends. I was thanked for my hard work and dedication and she 'hereby gratefully' terminated my representation 'with immediate effect', referring to a clause in the agency agreement that was normally used for *firing* clients.

I gazed at the dazzle of the sash-window, mouth opening and shutting. The humiliation of being fired by a top client – absolutely monstrous! As I stood there, breathless and faint, Sheila Acbe, the company's founder, leaned into my office.

'Mike,' she said. 'Can you pop across the corridor in a minute? Colin's got some ideas he wants to discuss.'

Colin was Sheila's assistant.

'Colin?'

She was all smiles.

'Can it possibly wait?'

'He's absolutely *dying* to tell us his "vision" for the agency. Come over when you're ready. Bella's made some coffee.'

I bathed my face in my hands then grabbed the phone, looking for Ophelia's number. But even as I dialled, sick to the pit of my stomach, I knew it was pointless. Her letter was cold and final. The author I had served with such utter commitment had put me down like a rat in a ranch-house – with a single bullet.

Minutes later, I was sitting in Sheila's grand office. My eyes were smarting but I managed to present a listening countenance to the twenty-five-year-old juvenile on the sofa. Sheila invigilated from behind her desk, sipping a coffee and lightly sorting papers from her in-tray. Colin had been talking up a whole range of dismal subjects – interns, the website, foreign-rights policy – and wanted me in on the discussion. I stared at him, abjectly. I was badly shaken up.

Colin Templar was a short man with clunky spectacles and buoyant hair. There was a Joe College air to his look that advised: 'bookish young fogey, disdain and avoid'. When he joined the firm two years ago, I didn't give him a second thought. His mission in life, it seemed, was to add a mousey librarian presence to the assistants' mess room and that was it. But within weeks of his arrival, Sheila had noticed Colin's zeal. Very early on I sensed a difference in her tone with the new boy. Supremely adept with computers, Colin's nosy brain craved the grown-up stuff. He offered Sheila a gleaming, super-keen interest. 'Tell me everything you know,' he seemed to say. 'I will feed it back to you paradigm-shifted by my mint-fresh perspective.' Soon Sheila was taking Colin to lunch as a 'reward' for his 'marvellous' work. He would accompany her to meetings with publishing honchos and sit in war councils with big-shot novelists; and as Colin's cancerous interest spread into every recess of the agency's business, he became more of a 'familiar' to Sheila and less of an underling.

The man's body language was a master-class in deference. He would enter her office with a light knock, speak quickly and efficiently, enabling her to hold a train of thought while taking his brief. Sheila would acknowledge him with an aside, Colin would reverse humbly, but then be drawn back when some casual quip suggested she fancied a chat, and then his posture would mould itself to the moment, an easing of gait as he prepared to laugh promptly at a joke, or nod in gleeful assent as Sheila lambasted some publisher twerp, while remaining on lithe physical alert to pull a contract, or whip down a finished copy, or find an email for his boss. Colin was brilliant at those non-intrusive questions that seem caring, but are just a knack for toeing personal stuff into touch. Around the practicalities of Sheila's family life he manufactured endless empathy and interest.

It was a Michelin-starred performance, and I found it appalling, and to see him afterwards, sitting in his lair of an office like some empowered chancellor gaining dominion as the queen's favourite: oh, that was something to behold.

The young thruster now had things to say to us from the wisdom of his *two years'* experience, and Sheila was giving him the floor at a time of day when any decent agent wants to be blitzing out emails and lining up skittles and burning off a blood-rush of caffeine and almond croissant.

Sheila had a new scent on the go, a bit strong. There was a celebratory air to her manner that morning. She had the presence of a leading lady, the power to hold attention when others were speaking because of an aura of 'class' – so rarely convincing in our profession. She was bright, she was sunny. Her cheekbones were fabulous. One of her clients had just won the Nobel Prize for Literature, and reflected glory doesn't get brighter than that.

I was holed beneath the waterline. Shock goes through stages: astonishment; a sense of sagging defeat; recognition of the bitterness to come. Was it something I said? Some trick I had missed? Or was I just a stepping stone for an ambitious client who never gave a damn about me despite all the vulnerability and anxiety I had mopped up? One thing was certain, I thought, wiping my nose with a hanky and staring at the spotless vistas of Sheila's office: no prize-winning author had ever booted her.

Colin was talking away.

He sat bullfrog-perched on the sofa opposite, his spectacles catching the window-light, his big hands helping to mould ideas. For a short man, his voice was deep and beefy. His intonations rose in waves of volume that followed the spurts of his thought. Colin lacked experience, but his enthusiasm was a force to be endured, and some part of my bruised, flummoxed mind registered a threat. He had been poring over bestseller lists, and collating *Bookseller* articles, and interviewing top retail chiefs for some online magazine, and at last his 'big idea' came to the fore.

Literary fiction, he said, was too rarefied a commodity to be the stock-in-trade of a leading agency. Sheila's list of distinguished authors and Booker laureates was a false premise for future success. Publishing had transformed in recent years and our corporate reputation for the very best fiction and non-fiction was a handicap and a liability.

'I hate to say this, Mike,' he pushed up his spectacles, offering me innocent eye contact. 'But your old Booker longlisters are probably dead wood.'

'There's no dead wood on my list.' I said quietly.

'No offence!'

I closed my eyes, feeling absolutely shattered. I had really admired Ophelia Jamieson. The personal side had worked so well and I counted her a true friend. She had come to a dinner party at my flat and I had been to her New Year's Eve do, for goodness sake. This was just so painful.

'There's dead wood on every list,' he said reasonably.

'Is there dead wood on my list?' said Sheila, all eyes, all ears.

Colin smiled. 'Well … you know, Miriam Carrero is slow, and needs too much editing. Daniel Sears is bogged down with childcare. And June Clementine seems to have written her best book thirty years ago.'

She looked at him levelly.

He hesitated.

'What do you suggest?' she said.

'Axe the lot.'

She raised an eyebrow.

'We are not a charity,' he said.

I hated the 'we'.

Sheila was oddly serene. 'We owe our living to the endeavours of writers. We can hardly put them down when they go off the boil.'

7

Colin smiled tightly. Sheila's dry common sense could be very diminishing.

'Actually,' he said, 'I think they all need a boot up the arse.'

There might have been some low-level verity here, some kindergarten point not worth my time. Even the best authors go through fallow periods. Not every head-start brings lasting success. So what? Any client prepared to go the distance and keep trying had my support, because writing is a long game and faith counts for more than anything.

'I really don't think anyone who's been nominated for the Booker deserves a *boot up the arse*!' I said.

Colin became agitated. 'In a winner-takes-all market second prize means very little.'

This was so tiring. 'A nomination is surely an achievement!'

'With a very short half-life.'

I groaned.

'We shouldn't be wasting time on writers who've had their chance and missed the jackpot. We're too attached to a crew of literary B-listers read by three people in Hampstead.'

'And Ophelia Jamieson!' I said suddenly. 'For whom I've done half a dozen translation deals since the Orange nomination!'

They looked at me closely.

I flushed. There was an unbearable silence. I don't know why I said that.

'She's a very good client,' said Colin slowly.

He swapped looks with Sheila.

'I ...' I felt suddenly queasy. 'Literary fiction is what I do, Colin.'

For a moment it seemed the debate was over. Sheila would understand the standards I aspired to and Colin knew the value of the world's McEwans and Rushdies, but the obvious truth of this was somehow crushing, because finding real talent, God, real, promotable talent, was a matter of incredible persistence and luck. Writers like Ophelia didn't grow on trees. Her departure, I realised, was like an amputation. I looked down, fingers touching my temple distractedly.

'Your Jim Fielding is a bit of a spent bullet,' said Colin.

I glanced dizzily up at Sheila, my heart beating hard.

'The staff think he's a pest. He's got the hots for Karina, and won't leave her alone. You spend hours on the phone, servicing his neuroses. We can't be full-time psychotherapists for that level of client, surely!'

I stared at Colin in abject amazement. How dare he traduce one of my clients and question my professional judgement? I controlled my indignation as best I could and tried to stay calm because the last thing I needed now was an inquest into my frigging client list.

'Colin, if you can't hack the personal stuff, be an accountant. It'd be utterly unprofessional to ignore a writer going through a major creative crisis.'

Sheila nodded. 'I wish it weren't the case, but talent and neurosis often go hand in hand.'

Colin shook his head irritably. 'Fielding isn't having a crisis! According to Karina he's been kicked out of the house by his wife for boffing a waitress from Strada restaurant, and he's lost twelve grand on the greyhounds. He's a talentless prat, and you should get rid of him before our staff resign in protest.'

Sheila looked at me.

'He's a very fine writer with a cult following,' I said softly, almost inaudibly.

Colin was extremely dissatisfied. 'I'm sorry, Mike …'

'I'll say something to him.'

'No, Mike. Listen,' he glanced in appeal at Sheila, who smiled her encouragement. 'I want to be frank. Quite a few of your clients could go.'

'Excuse me!'

'Basil Squires, Kit Casterbridge, Selina Ford ...'

'What!'

'Time-consuming, mid-list ...'

'What!'

'I think they're a waste of space. Squires is a hack. Casterbridge a has-been. Nobody takes them seriously. I'm sorry ...'

'Stop saying sorry!'

'Because I respect you as an agent. You're marking time with these guys.'

I glanced in amazement at Sheila. What licence did Colin have to shoot down my clients? What entitled him to address an older colleague like some new broom manager from head office? Yes, OK, there were issues with Casterbridge's latest blasted book. Yes, Selina had not fulfilled her early promise (despite a very lovely author photograph), and Basil Squires was a name from the past, yes!

'I accept,' I said bitterly, 'because I'm not defensive ... that Selina's last book was ...'

'Piss poor.'

'Not of the first order. And sure, Kit is still on trial. Both of them are on a learning curve and, I think, show considerable talent. Colin, one has to edit assiduously and get the best ...'

'Where's your Dan Brown?'

'Dan Brown?'

'Where's your Katie Price?'

'Katie Price!' I ejaculated.

'If it's not happening on the literary side, where is it happening?'

Sheila looked at me with raised eyebrows, and for a moment I found it hard to tell whether she was backing Colin or offering amused solidarity with me.

This was hideous, completely dreadful. I was too winded to fight back off the cuff, and, for a moment, hesitated as if actually absorbing his challenge, as though maybe yes, sure, there had been disappointments recently, body-blows and soul-searching, and any casual commentator would see a discrepancy between Sheila's might and glory and my more relative standing. I was no stranger to the concept of frustration, believe me, but I also believed in comparative success. I had not entered the book biz to flog celebrity memoirs or mass-market women's fiction with its larding of cliché and wish-fulfilment. I was utterly bored by the book-a-year gravy trains of the blockbuster scribes. Like Sheila, I admired our best novelists and biographers, and was driven to add to the wealth of our literary heritage and not its disposable airport turnover. Extracting financial success from the quality end of the market was always a waiting game. But already I had earned respect as an agent, worked hard and in good faith, and I was fucked if some bright-spark little shit-face was going to use his freshman licence to have a pop at me.

'Know what, Colin?' I said with sudden edge.

He looked at me distrustfully.

'A little less arrogance, if you please.'

He ate the remark with a bitter smirk.

'Now if nobody minds,' I said, 'I'll get back to the office and do some work.'

'OK,' said Sheila, suddenly. 'Let's recruit you, Colin. Start as an agent tomorrow.'

Colin's face lit up.

'What?' I spilt coffee on my trousers. 'Sheila, I ...'

'Why not?' she shrugged. 'Let Colin put his money where his mouth is. If he thinks we need more chick-lit and crime and supermodel memoirs, go for it. I don't care whether you're humble or arrogant if you can pull in the deals. Find me a new assistant and one for yourself.'

I stared at Sheila, incredulous. This should have been a board decision.

Colin seemed as surprised as I was.

His face transformed from within, happiness rising intensely to the surface. His eyes widened in pleasurable amazement. 'That's just fantastic. What can I say?'

Sheila was a picture of benevolence.

I remember sitting on my seat, as though stuck between forward and reverse gears. What stunned me in retrospect was Sheila's nonchalant embracing of a luridly commercial ethos when for years she had embodied the best taste.

Later, after Colin had tripped from the room and I was getting to my feet, utterly dazed, Sheila said, almost as an aside: 'We need somebody doing that kind of biz. It's not your taste and it's certainly not mine, and if Colin walks as big as he talks, it might give us all a fresh lease of life.'

I felt a profound unease. Though work would resume, the daily round, this meeting showed a glimpse of something I had never seen, my professional self as others perceived it: not the well-spoken, intellectually adroit man of the world with excellent taste and social grace; but a second-division also-ran, whose aspirations were naïve and standards pretentious – a depiction that seemed horribly unfair but almost infectious as I crossed the corridor back to my office and thought how damning the news of Ophelia's resignation would look in the light of that meeting. As I entered the office, I saw my assistant, Helen, standing by my desk and holding Ophelia's letter. She glanced up suddenly, guiltily, and her pained expression said it all.

'I'll get you a coffee,' she said, quickly.

The sympathy in her look brought moisture to my eye.

Chapter 2

Madelin Farrell was an artist with gleaming black hair, a marvellous mouth and a sense of purpose. I had met her three weeks before in a pub (for a drink with Steve from the office). I took to her instantly and decided she was very attractive and noticeably nice to me, and I wanted to see her again. Steve released her number a bit cagily, as he nurtured fantasies of his own, but Steve had known her since college days and I persuaded him that he was too much of an old friend to switch tack now. So here I was, sitting on the sofa in my north London flat, working myself into the right state of mind and crafting a text.

These mini-declarations require confidence, even via text, and mine had evaporated. Ophelia's betrayal – there was no other word – had left me reeling. I was in no shape to be making an advance on a really interesting woman and, anyway, the text approach seemed too cool, too digital, too derivative, not what she would expect from me, *if* she remembered me.

As I sat there alone in my one-bedroom domicile, a book-lined, third-storey flat in Crouch Hill, with hand-me-down furniture and all-too-familiar prints on the walls, and an atmosphere of jaded respectability that I resented but could never quite evade, I knew that I was at a watershed point in my life. Too easily I could drift into career bachelordom when what I needed was an abiding relationship. Too easily I could fall into a liaison that would unravel over three to four years, and postpone the next chance until my sinister late thirties or toxic early forties. I had to discriminate and do justice to my own best feelings. It meant being perceptive and risking more, putting everything on the line, and, if necessary, taking a hit. And Madelin, there really was something about her … though I hardly knew what – something valuable, rare, and my thought was this: early days, but you have to pursue it. True love was a moving target. A chance for happiness and fulfilment might come and go in the blink of an eye.

With the first whisky of the day a maudlin tiredness kicked in. I could admit to myself the devastation of Ophelia's departure. I was hollowed out inside. She had been my badge of success, and now that was torn away. My aura would certainly need a makeover before I could go on dates and talk enthusiastically about what I loved and cared for. A man of my age had to offer a future, a place in the world, some kind of command; whereas it seemed that even sending a text like 'Dinner on Friday?' could be tainted by this dreadful feeling of chagrin. You can't woo a woman with black and blue balls. Chagrin has a digital smell all of its own transmissible by wireless or telephony.

That evening I started a diary. I went to the alcove desk in my bedroom, found a notebook and pen, and almost involuntarily began to write. It was probably an unconscious exercise in self-repair. The agent mind is too easily a gad-fly mind. Intellectual bottom is so easily eroded by the formulae of salesmanship, the knack and knockabout of negotiation. I wanted to stand outside all that and know who I was independently of work, and, if work was going to trick with my pride, recover myself as an articulate

15

person whose mind could be of interest to a woman like Madelin. I wrote with a fevered, harried hand: great reams of roiling prose. There was need, evidently; copious need.

I remember thinking, later, that horniness is so much worse over thirty. Every night alone on a king-size double bed, every erotic self-dalliance steals something from the future.

Some of what I wrote came out in the third person, as if it helped to get outside of myself. Mike de Vere was someone I could leave behind if needed, going into other points of view, giving versions of myself and other people which might have been truer than I sounded in my own voice. Somehow I wanted respite from the tone of being me, from the tunnel vision of personality. Writing in the third person and imagining events through other eyes discovered something I could not see otherwise. And so it was, bit by bit, in the evening hours, I pulled myself together and came back to a sane state. I had taste. I had integrity, and the correct approach to a shitty day in the office was to erase it from the mind and to strike into work next morning full of confidence. Colin would *not* steal my thunder. Ophelia would *not* trash my self-respect. I would stick to my guns and to hell with the pair of them!

After a second whisky, I fell back on the sofa and texted Madelin.

Instantly the mobile throbbed back.

'Love to have dinner. In Paris till 27th. Catch you when I'm back. Xx.'

***

He stares at that text, Mike, for long moments, feeling the contact, the presence in the cup of his hand. It is as if Madelin is in

16

the room with him. For the first time he sees her name incarnated on his screen, the emblem of her being around in the digital ether, responsive.

'Paris, eh?' He knows so little about her.

The future has returned, and with the thought of a dinner *à deux*, the wheels start rolling again. A plan is afoot. He rises from the sofa and grabs his glass for a refill and reckons it is time to start reading Camilla Guardian's manuscript, which he knows won't be good, but which couldn't be worse for a third whisky, now sloshing from the bottle.

Chapter 3

Within six weeks Colin had grabbed an office next to Sheila's. This seemed like an annexation. Yes, my office was opposite Sheila's, but his was next door. Colin was determined to insinuate himself as the heir apparent, an absurd presumption, but Colin was gifted at presumption. Audibly close to the boss, he became super-industrious, as if his every deed and saying might be a way to impress her.

From the lulled order of my desk I heard his pushy calls, his rush to succeed. Colin's zest sucked energy from us all. He was so muscularly on top of the job, so gung-ho on the swivel of his seat like some cowboy tank-commander ripping into battle, that quieter styles were made to look effete. I heard his excited exchanges with Sheila, the shared laughter; I heard him tread the corridors as he throbbed down the passage to boss the IT people. The film agents he lion-tamed and got working. Interns were drilled, secretaries subjugated.

Boisterously present in the agency he was bumptiously out in the world, skimming through the Groucho and Academy Clubs, maxing his entertainment allowance at media-biz restaurants. A man I had written off as a bluestocking was contagiously sociable and only too thrilled to present himself to the party of publishing. With a sinking heart, I noticed his verve at book launches, his tendency to bob up before editors and marketing heads, and his relish for nodding and grinning in a toxic blaze of zeal at whatever publishing grandee or editorial diva he had managed to trap in the fluorescent glare of his enthusiasm. I remember him at a client's birthday bash homing in on Nicholas Clarence, the room's most famous writer. Colin was stocky, Clarence tall, and I wince to recall Colin's flashing, radiant spectacles and the air of assiduous sycophancy that hung about his spryly deferential body language. I could never do that, I remember thinking, could never abase myself like that; and yet Colin was getting in front of loads of key people and big names, and his combination of enthusiasm and shamelessness seemed to work.

He was hungry, so hungry, and better at it, too. His type of success I just couldn't emulate. Probably naively, I believed in culture. Like many who wind up in the arts, I had read English at university and wanted a career that involved me with authors and books. Perhaps it was a kind of vanity, believing I could make a mark. It seemed like a worthy cause, adding to the literary heritage in some useful way. But after the Ophelia debacle, it appeared that authors were rather less interested in a kindred spirit handling their affairs than a brutal old trout like Marjorie Stone, who could squeeze publishers' goolies till the money gurgled out, and keep editors on their knees like a row of gimps in PVC panting for the lash. Unnerved by Colin's progress, I tried to think commercially. Colin told me, in one of many patronising exchanges, about the rule that twenty per cent of your clients earn eighty per cent of your revenue, which meant you should spend, max, a fifth of your time on the majority of your authors. How writers could be so efficiently managed, I had no idea.

Colin knew the answer: 'Only lunch as a reward for deal success. Only do lower-case unpunctuated emails and keep them short. Remember that authors do the "humanity" product, not agents; that pleasure in reading is not in the skill-set, because you must agent what sells.' Colin claimed that writers don't really like their agents. 'Why should they? We're cunts,' he laughed.

'Cunts?'

'Yes!'

'Why?'

'It's in the job description. Get the deals, screw the publisher, tuck up everyone in sight. We are meaningless to authors unless we get them more money than they deserve. Those schmaltzy acknowledgements in books, you know: "Thanks to my dearest Michael, true friend and agent." What does that really mean?'

'Um … appreciation, respect …'

'It means: "I love this fucker. He made me rich. Be nice to him while he's useful." Agenting isn't about impeccable taste and discerning literary judgement. It's about salesmanship, leverage and bluffing. It's about money, power and clout. It's about …'

'Oh please, Colin!'

'Seriously, Mike!'

'I am not a cunt. I don't want to be one.'

'Try. You'll like it.'

'I'm going to eat my sandwich now, if that's alright with you.'

Followed closely, Colin's philosophy would turn you into something between a cynic and a psychopath. One rule of the trade I did get, however: you only need one big client. A big client could redeem years of work. A big client was a magnet to other big clients and told the world you were a player. I only needed one big client and the likes of Colin could be made to FUCK OFF. Galvanised by Ophelia's departure I redoubled my efforts to find the Next Big Thing, working the slush-pile, patrolling book launches, sounding as articulate and smart as I could, and perspiring more urgently wannabe vibes. If nothing succeeds like success, you have to *seem* successful at least. I resolved to hang out, name drop, network, get up early, look the part, do more face time, have cachet, press flesh, iron my shirts better and edit my clients with true acumen. The aura of all this industrious purpose would surely attract genius from the ether.

It wasn't quite me, of course, this desperate keenness. I had always feared, vaguely, that I was a poor businessman, maladapted to commerce, and probably I should blame my dad. My late father was a vicar in a Hampshire parish. He loved so many things beyond his Lord, but especially old aeroplanes, motorbikes and country ales. We grew up in an Edwardian house on the edge of the village with a drawing room just big enough for Dad's beloved Blüthner on one side of the hall, and his study on the other. In this book-lined room I spent the days of my youth reading everything on his shelves, from Cold War thrillers to Victorian adventure yarns, from books about birds to dusty old second-hand hardbacks of the classic novels, with their tiny print and mottled endpapers. I remember neat shelves stocking the civilised essential volumes: the complete Shakespeare, Milton and Wordsworth, an *Oxford Book of English Verse*. Dad had all these staples at an arm's reach from the desk where he wrote his sermons. The Word was present with him, running through the daily round, constant in his musings, resonant in his heart, and so were the words of a literature he habitually read and imbibed. The study was cosy in winter, with its coal fire and wing-backed chair, and if our family was at times too modestly decent for teenage horizons and the propriety of the church-round a bind, Dad never seemed narrow to me. Books were his window on the world, his capital, the very lining of his mind. He was active and industrious and loved to blast about the country lanes on his motorbike, but always he returned after parishioners' meetings or evensong to a place where books signalled freedom and the companionship of other minds.

Was it genes, then, or example? Was it a very English, bookish, dated model of domestic life that led me as an adult to feel that people were more important than trade, books more valuable than 'units sold', and that the value of a thing and never its cost should determine my course? 'God feedeth the ravens also' says the Gospel. Was this my undoing, then, a deficit of ruthlessness?

I worked harder than ever. I spread my bets, chucking more mud at the wall, whilst searching all the while for that 'new voice' whose genius would cast golden light on earlier endeavours. I had to survive, obviously, but I had to hold out for achievement on my own terms. Unnerved by Colin's rising commission income, I watched my list turn into a graveyard of mid-list fiction tryers struggling to get airborne; of alcoholic biographers light years behind on their delivery dates; of literary pups kennelled at Faber or Picador, the soon-to-be pelts of road-kill in the retail sector's turf wars; and just one lucrative anomaly: Melina Fukakowski, the bombshell TV presenter, acquired as a client by the guys in Film/TV, and passed my way to handle her tie-in tome. ('Handle' is too loaded, too teasing a word to describe my fraught navigation of Melina's mouth-wateringly buxom but bossy personality through a deal process that put the curvy prof on BBC Two, and then saw two hundred thousand copies of her book mince sexily from the stores.)

And then the worst thing happened. Something so terrible, it turned me to stone for a week.

Vincent Savage.

***

The public has an exalted view of authors, and rightly so. Great writers impact deeply on our imagination. And yet, behind the kudos, there sometimes lurks a person at odds with the nobility of the author photo or the 'sheer humanity' of the prose style. We agents are well placed to 'note' (and resent) that difference.

Vincent Savage is a case in point: a festival favourite, a mordant broadcaster; a man whose books strut their stuff and flex their pecs in the window fronts of Waterstones. On Sunday mornings his loveless eyes glare from arts sections. Those stern monochrome portraits of him seem loaded with inquisitorial severity. It is a public face that proclaims stark independence and a hint of tonic mockery, as though Savage has seen something which we don't understand but need to for our own feeble betterment. Not to like his writing would be stupid. His fictions are there to disturb and disrupt, to put the mainstream on special measures. It seems widely accepted that we need this discomfiting figure in our midst and that his public image is the deriding mask of genius.

But I knew him well before the celebrity and success. I was the first to talent-spot Vincent bloody Savage.

I met him at a party of Madelin Farrell's.

It was a Saturday night in Archway – a council flat with stripped brick walls and spotlighting, and gaggles of Madelin's old art-college friends smoking and plotting and gently twisting out of denim or leather as the place warmed up. Madelin swooped in from the kitchen, necklace swinging as she lowered vistas of canapé and cleavage over a table around which people were chatting. Men in T-shirts with muscled arms stood squarely by, clutching beer cans. I hunkered down with a group by the fire and fixed my regard on the multiple ear studs of a girl called Ceri, who exhaled great gouts of cigarette smoke as she disagreed with Avril, and wrung her hands, and laughed jaggedly, and saw me listening, but was too trippy and into her theme to share the conversation with a newcomer. I could hear the deadbeat drawl of a bloke called Bone, going on about a gig – 'Yeah … Aldershot. Yeah … Sundee, Satdee … Yeah …' – and in the opposite corner of the room I saw a man with cold, blue eyes and oiled hair sitting moodily on an armchair. This was Dmitri, Madelin's 'new' boyfriend, someone told me, which came as a shock. The previous week I'd taken her to the cinema, and there was never any mention of a boyfriend.

I waited uncomfortably, trying to blend in. Madelin's set were new to me, and it took a while to get a fix on their wavelength. As I sipped at my glass, wondering how long I could stay on the sidelines without looking like a wall-flower, I saw her loitering with two guys in the kitchen area, glancing encouragingly at one, and touching the other lightly on the forearm. Her radiant smile and swept-back flow of hair and testing gaze with its provocative bedroomy aspect that said 'you sexy bullshitter, open that wine bottle and make yourself useful' kept both men on their toes and competing for her laughter. Madelin, it seemed, could never ration her goodwill to the opposite sex. She was witty and sassy, meaning to make you work for those rewarding hints of sexual availability; but very warm and generous, too. Her hug of hello reassured any man that he was lovable. Tonight she would be kept busy by her friends and I could almost feel sorry for Dmitri in his armchair tomb. The bullet of his possessive gaze went towards her, a beam of love that had no impact at all. Her body language almost mocked the notion of a boyfriend with rights and needs. I considered going over and giving

24

him a bit of conversation, but his dark, throttled look as he watched her soak up the attention and love every lascivious minute of it was hardly a come-on. The truth was: I wanted Madelin's ravishing attention, too. I wanted to clear the room of people and have her to myself, though I did think she might have invited me to see how I fitted in with her friends. I suppose I was still circling, working her out, interested, but not quite sure of myself. In recent weeks we had met a few times and I liked her a lot. There had been a boyfriend, Patrice, she said, but Patrice was in Paris and that had 'sort of' ended and the hint was she was free again. Madelin was good at hinting.

She had described herself as a flower rising from a back patio. Her parents were staid provincials living in a culture-free bubble in Swindon. Dad was a former airline pilot, mum was in corporate catering, and there was a married sister living in Hove. 'I'm a refugee from middle-class banality,' she declared, smiling brilliantly. 'Was I adopted, or did mum have a fling with a gypsy traveller?' She got help with her studio rent from a 'rebel aunt', and worked part-time at anything that would allow her to paint three days a week. A Korean businessman with London dealings kept her on retainer as PA, and paid her over the odds 'without laying a finger on me'. Meanwhile she used all her charm to persuade people whose faces she wanted to paint to commission a portrait from her for a couple of grand.

In a period when the art schools had been all installation and conceptual art, Madelin arrived on the scene as an exultant figurative painter for whom colour was an endless source of almost carnal delight.

She was, I had come to reckon, the essential artist: contemplative, unpredictable, free-spirited. Aged twenty-nine, she had clearly done much business with the male of the species but was pretty unimpressed by the emotional results, tending to regard her boyfriends with affectionate frustration to begin with and then despair. She would move on smartly, willing to be charmed anew, while developing a fundamental independence. Certainly, she knew how to relish male company, and also had the need – through conversation – to plumb depths and figure unsettling emotions; but whatever the intimacy, Madelin remained strange in some way, never seeing things along familiar lines. Though I found her fascinating, I was definitely perturbed by Dmitri, who looked like a poser to me (and a bore as well, judging by his refusal to talk to anybody). A woman of her calibre needed more than magazine good looks in a man, surely?

It was getting noisy in the flat; people were streaming in; music was throbbing up. I eased out into the entrance hall with half a mind to go home. I had just found my coat in a pile on the floor when I heard the words 'Nabokovian hauteur' coming from the end of the corridor. I looked up, alert.

'… spectral Kafkaesque parables … swingeing satires …'

The voice seemed to hail from Madelin's bedroom.

'… super-transparent minimalism …'

I blinked, dropped my coat and slipped along the corridor.

'The whole stylistic train set. It's pure sorcery. Shouldn't be allowed.'

As I entered Madelin's boudoir with its Venetian blinds and futon and rack of dresses shoved against a wall, I saw a man leaning against the wardrobe, his hand raised to shape another point.

'*Vacuum*. Start with that. Read the Perec monograph. Look at his essay on Nabokov in Russian. Don't miss the art and music stuff: Bonnard, Alkan, Sorabji. Then do the novels chronologically and when you finish start again.'

I later learned this was Vincent Savage. He was lecturing a fat chap in a buttoned jacket.

I lurked as Savage kept talking, semi-frozen by surprise. He was talking about Julius Straker, one of my literary idols, an extraordinary writer whose fiction I had read insatiably in my twenties. It was odd and rather exciting to hear him spoken of by a stranger at Madelin's party. Straker was off the margins these days, more like a rumour than a reputation, a secret tip even for die-hard literary bookworms. Someone like Ian McEwan described him as a 'writer's writer's writer' – enough to put off the general reading public for years, which was probably Straker's devout wish. It seemed that only literary professionals had the measure of his confounding brilliance.

Savage kept talking. He was in the middle of extracting a thought-process from a point in the wall just above my head. My presence did nothing to deflect him from articulate pronouncement. He had a nasal, resonant voice, the voice of a cab driver who has seen everything and smoked more; but the content was riveting, a word-perfect soliloquy which ended with a sip from the beer can. His companion nodded reasonably, as though intelligent thoughts were always welcome even if he could think of nothing to say in reply. It turned out the fat guy was a drummer in Bone's band, an amiable bloke, but not a big fiction buff.

'Tell you what,' said the drummer, 'can I get you a beer?'

Savage leaned against the wall with a blank expression – the familiar sense of squandered brilliance, I supposed. The drummer puttered off and Savage turned his gaze on me. His eyes were deep set, but flashily bright and searching. He gave me an animal-checking kind of look.

'*Vacuum* was remarkable,' I said, 'but *Hypertrophy* distilled Nabokov to his essence.'

If he was surprised, he ate his surprise in a wink. It took him just a moment to compute and proceed.

'But Nabokov is there in a way Straker never is. The voice is biographically unaccountable. A Babel of stylistic registers skittering around the periphery of a black hole. He can do everything without being any of it. Magical realism, the Hampstead novel, European dystopia. Any style: demotic, Mandarin, stream of consciousness, fancy prose narrator modes to make Banville blush and Nabokov raise a "Who *is* this guy?" kind of eyebrow.'

I laughed. 'I think he's absolutely the best.'

'Pissingly so. The Americans stub their toe on his sheer superiority, though he *is* half-American. There's a sort of conspiracy of silence around how good he is.'

'Strange that he hasn't published in years.'

'Hence the quasi-posthumous stature. Straker's silence defines his output more eloquently than the sausage-strand bodies of work put out by our brand-name authors.'

Straker had lived in Paris for years, well away from the London or New York literary scenes. He was a remote figure, saturnine, reclusive and solitary, by all accounts. There was an equivalence, I had often felt, between Straker and the Canadian pianist Glenn Gould, who abandoned concert giving for a life of nocturnal recording and pill-taking eccentricity.

'So …' I said, cutting to the heart of the conundrum. 'Seminal?'

Savage's eyes hit the ceiling: a quick extempore judgement required.

'We're not going to get a lot of little Strakers. He's too complex to imitate. The best authors can only proceed by reading him and desperately trying to forget how good he is.'

'A Nobel Prize, maybe?'

'I think he'd regard it as reputationally damaging. Who wants to be aggregated into the reading group and desperate Christmas present lists?'

'Hi. Mike de Vere,' I said.

'Vince Savage,' he nodded. 'Which leads us to the case of Martin Amis.'

'Oh ... Indeed.'

'Now there's a prose style whose balls dropped hard and fast.'

We spent an invigorating twenty minutes correlating Amis's 'twin peaks' (Bellow and Nabokov) to his stylistic development. Vince was a brilliantly original thinker and kept spouting prize epithets with a tall man's throwaway aplomb. I took it all in thirstily and tried to keep up, not missing the bobbing Adam's apple, the thong on his wrist and the industrial-width forearm veins. He wore denim and Doc Martens and was romantically haunted-looking, as though kept awake all hours by a furiously active mind. The agent in me was absolutely twitching to know what he did for a living, where he came from, how he applied this impressive body of ideas. To have asked him crudely 'Are you a writer?' would have broken a kind of pact and the premise of our talking like this – that you didn't need small-talk, that good minds just hit the ground running, that what counted was the state-of-the-art intellectual position on a given subject, not personal trivia. I got this and was very happy to play along, though my patience was rewarded later. Vince let slip (to my utter delight) that he was working on a collection of stories 'in answer to Baudrillard' and had two novellas in the bottom drawer: 'non-publishable divertissements'. Now I'm not the kind of agent who is always pushing a business card at strangers, but I did of course hint at my considerable professional skills and interests, though Vince was slow on the uptake. The practicalities of publishing were probably too mundane for his powerful brain and beyond his ken anyway.

Even then, I knew in my bones that Vince was the Real Deal. Here was a natural-born talent from outside the mainstream with a first-class brain and a blinding use of language. He would offer no allegiances and promise no loyalties, and this I embraced. His failure to pick up that I was an exciting young literary agent who should have been patronising him, not the other way round, was only moderately irksome. Such distracted otherworldliness proved the need for good practical representation, and on that score, I was the man.

In due course, Madelin appeared in the bedroom. She came over with a 'Hello, boys', linked arms with me, and whispered so that Vince could hear, too, that Dmitri was 'maybe on the way out'.

'Really?' I said.

'I think he's insane.'

'Oh!'

This was very welcome news.

Vince's head rocked round curiously. 'What would have been the original attraction?'

'Standing between you two hunks, I can't think,' she said.

'Was it the brooding good looks or the electrifying wit?' he queried.

She burst into laughter.

'The Slavic intensity is obviously intoxicating.'

'Don't be unkind,' she said beautifully. 'He's a very sensitive boy.'

'And a prodigiously athletic lover?'

She snuggled into my side. 'Not telling. Mike, would you go out with me if Dmitri had an accident?'

'My pleasure,' I said, heart racing a little.

'Is there some kind of queue or waiting list?' asked Vince.

Madelin smiled at me, as if deflecting the enquiry. I must say, she looked very beautiful in the soft bedroom light. Her hair was a river of dark sheen, her neck slender, her collarbone fine, somehow queenly.

'You have to apply, Vince,' she said, suddenly leaving us.

Vince offered me a minutely inflected eyebrow as she dinkily waited to get through the gathering by the door. I watched her departure very closely. That was the first time she had flirted with me. It was like swimming into a patch of sun-warmed sea.

I later sussed that Madelin's flirty style kept a lot of men on the hook. There *was* a kind of queue, though it moved pretty fast. A prolific artist, she was breathtakingly fast and loose in the 'get me a man and peel me a grape' manner of the silver-screen vamps, and ranged freely for her pleasures over a bewildering sequence of pub hunks, Hungarian tilers, fashion photographers and bouffant refugees from the British upper classes. She later admitted to accomplishing five one-woman shows and forty one-night stands by the age of thirty. It was a little hard to see how a more serious suitor might fit with this scheme, but I do remember indulging in a delicious fantasy that night in bed. My problem, I realised, was the depth of my need to be loved. The male heart can be a dead weight at times.

Shortly after her exit Vince upped and left. He gave me a parting shrug.

'Good luck with the novel,' I hazarded.

'How did you guess?' came the reply, ironic.

'Because I'm a brilliantly astute literary agent,' I *nearly* said.

By chance, I saw him a few days later in a pub in Dartmouth Park. He was lodged in a corner of the bar with a couple of mates. I could see him listening tolerantly to the opinions of others and then lobbing in some laconic grenade that blew up all previous arguments, leaving an intellectual Ground Zero where Vince could whop down his latest theoretical edifice, blotting out the heavens. At one point, I raised my glass and smiled at him, thinking he had seen me. There was no observable response.

'People', I realised, didn't really grab Vince. 'People' were at best disembodied voices whose attempts to keep up with him conversationally might rarely yield a scrap of intelligence that he could weld into the superstructure of his argument. At worst, we were just middle-brow twits.

I have to say, this was somewhat challenging. I mean, I could have really liked the guy. He was so interesting, so well-read, but so difficult socially. He would never be the first to greet. Only once did he cross a room to say hello to me. It was a 'poetry' evening organised by a friend of Madelin's, and when he clocked there was no one conveniently on hand to electrocute with his über-brilliance, he came my way, fag ash crooked, and said: 'How's it going, mate?'

'Oh!' I was spontaneous. 'Actually, I've just finished reading an incredible manuscript.'

'Yeah?'

'Very talented novelist. Sheila Acbe's most impressed.'

My zeal was inescapable.

'Sheila what?'

'Probably the top book agent in the country. Close colleague.'

Now he knew. 'How is your book coming along?' I smiled.

'Sorry?'

'Your novel, Vince?'

I don't think I had his full attention.

'Tell you what,' Vince nudged me. 'Madelin Farrell's rather a dishy little numero, isn't she? I'm liking that frock.'

'Yes, well …'

I had spoken to Madelin already, and Dmitri, too (still on the scene alas). He lurked like a guard dog while she greeted friends with a tight hug and sparkly eyes. I wondered if she expected a George and the Dragon-type rescue whereby Dmitri's successor seduced her and slayed him simultaneously. I was still interested, of course.

'You do know, Vince,' I said slowly and clearly, 'that I am a literary …'

'I do know that my eyes are undressing Madelin Farrell faster than a dozen Casanovas on coke.'

I gazed at him steadfastly.

He frowned, as if vaguely remembering something.

One of Colin's pet themes was the need to hang out in artistic circles because the personal connection is so crucial when a writer starts looking for an agent.

'If you'd like a reaction to your novel, I'd be delighted to read it.'

'What's your line again?' said Vince.

'I am a literary …'

'Hang about. Madelin!' he called, and shot across the room to intercept her. She gave him a smile as he craned in for a kiss.

'… agent,' I said.

***

Vince signed with Colin Templar.

Colin auctioned Vince's first novel to three contesting publishers and extracted a monster advance from Cheshire and Paulin.

I lie awake at night thinking about this.

The sense of missed opportunity was shattering. Losing Vince to Colin was absolutely crucifying. Why Colin, not me? Could Colin talk about Baudrillard and Nabokov and catch references to Henry James? No. Was Colin sensitive, judicious and tactful? No. Did Colin have taste? No. Was Colin the second senior agent at Shelia Acbe Agency admired as much for his editorial flair as his negotiating skill? No, he fucking wasn't. I was flabbergasted and deeply depressed, but absolutely nothing could prepare me for the sheer hell of Vince's critical success. His reviews were incredible, everything that an arrogant author and his uppity agent could have prayed for, a cavalcade of superlatives. Colin was beside himself with glee and kept emailing everyone in the agency quotes from the abominably proliferating raves. He'd run into my room with a cutting. 'Read this, read this. Just incredible!' sliding a *Times* profile under my nose with reams of Adventist froth about the Savage phenomenon. 'The biggest thing in ten years' said *Prospect*, and soon enough Vince was everywhere, on radio reviews and TV shows and at the festivals maxing his moment and acting the part of cultural seer to the hilt. There followed a green wave. Every foreign publisher lay down before Colin, deals were popping up right, left and centre. He was jetting to New York, whistling over to Munich, and ducking and pirouetting and leaping like some tennis pro at the net collecting every shot and socking it home to victory and kudos.

Why? Why had Vince avoided me when I worked at the same agency and was so evidently interested in his project?

The answer was unbearable to contemplate but no amount of huffing and puffing and bigging up one's trampled ego, no amount of denial or angry disavowal could mask the fact that Colin was more successful. Colin was hot. Colin's nose for a bit of business and shrewd weighing of a book's commodity value had started to attract not just genre writers but literary heavyweights. A man with no interest in the literary project beyond a few handy platitudes that he could use in meetings to lull serious novelists was the fashionable option. Vince had circumnavigated my genteel and solicitous overtures because Colin checked out bigger and better.

This was a mortifying development and one that left me lame and bereft. Even with a head-start I'd lost out to Colin, and was daily to be reminded of it. Colin's binged up confidence burgeoned horribly as he clutched the supersonic tailcoats of Vince's success, like a cheesy playboy on water-skis zooming flashily past. Every prize nomination, every clutch of foreign reviews accustomed him to prestige. Commercial success was all very well, he now advised, 'but what really counts for the agency, Mike, is literary stature. It's made a real difference. I've never met so many stellar novelists.'

It was bad enough walking into the office during the months in which Vince's success played itself out; it was hardly any easier that I knew him socially and was forced to celebrate his transformation from pub sage to shameless self-promoter. Savage was launched like a flaring rocket, and acquaintances who had regarded him as someone at a similar level had our faces soiled by the soot of his success. We were just an entourage of well-wishers, of gawping peons, of slobbering stooges nodding him to victory; and then, fuck it, the Somerset Maugham Award rubber stamps it and the heavies move in: D. S. Henson, Celia Burberage, a welcoming ovation of literary doges all clapping their hands and raising their glasses as Vince lopes down the Avenue of Kudos, his knuckles grazing the dust. One twit critic wrote him up in *Great Novels of the Noughties* and, hey presto, Vince was gathered to the woollen skirts of the Literary Establishment as its new glowering mastiff.

It took a long while to read that first novel of his. When eventually I did, sick bucket at the ready, it gave me a hearty surprise. Vince, it seemed, could not go at a book through the human side. His big ideas ran his characters' lives off the page. Was this novel really 'a bracingly alien view of the human condition that strips away our clichéd perceptions and replaces them with a merciless vision of how things are'? I persevered and tried harder, skipping a few pages every now and again, but came away with the indelible thought that this international event in contemporary fiction was a load of cobblers, and that success in publishing terms could represent something that meant nothing to me as a reader.

Shockingly, Vince's success had made Colin attractive to women. Colin now surged in a debonair waft of smart-casual elegance. His shoulders seemed broader, more athletic, his jaw-line cleaner and cooler. The meringue-effect hair and Gauloises-styled gesticulations and Jonathan Franzen-referenced designer stubble conjured a whole world of Left Bank chic. Colin's spectacles were mysteriously less Brains than before and much more Jean-Paul Belmondo; and young literary belles cottoned on fast. Here was an ambitious young man who might care to place the first novels of chick-lit wannabes, or assist publishing lovelies with networking steers; and faster than we could follow, Colin had moved from sheer eligibility to actual betrothal. He was momentously engaged to the deputy literary editor of *The Times*, the pale-perfect Violetta Pritpen, who was well-born, well-connected and set a very classy seal on his social ambitions. His confidence burgeoned all over again, as did his address book, and then, when Violetta's surplus heirloom furniture arrived in his office, the image of doyen agent was complete, to the detriment of his peasant co-workers.

I had, through gritted teeth, to endure it. Mercifully, I was soon to be distracted.

Madelin Farrell was single. At last.

My source: Steve Bartholomew in the Film/TV department.

'Dmitri's out on his ear. Madelin's gone Ramadan on boys,' said Steve. 'Working hard, apparently. She's got some big commission. "Operation No Shagging for Six Months", we're told.'

I was very intrigued by the sound of this.

'Hard to imagine, isn't it?' said Steve, looking at me over his glasses.

It *was* rather hard to imagine.

***

By a coincidence I bumped into her two days later, on the street outside Boots the Chemist. She seemed genuinely pleased to see me, said she was in a hurry, but maybe we could get together, and I said what about doing a film at the Arts Cinema next week, and she said 'Great, have a bottle of wine afterwards', which made me feel very happy.

The film was average. We were out of the cinema and into the pub by 9.45 pm and all I need say was that it went beautifully, it converted an idea into a possibility, and although at the end of the evening we went our separate ways with a kiss and a squeezy hug that could have meant something or could have meant nothing, I had already extracted another date from her. She had a client who lived opposite our offices and was coming to see him on the Friday, incidentally her birthday, and so I offered to take her out to lunch afterwards. 'What a treat!' she said, with a dazzling smile.

Prior to that Friday lunch some part of me was churned into being: the part that feels deeply. Such trysts, however casual, are stages in a precarious path that can lead to something life-changing if things go well, but their going well is ambiguously in your hands and not at the same time. You give off something special, hoping that it will be taken up – the distillation of deep desire into a personable intensity that friends never see. I already knew that Madelin meant something to me because I felt this kindling.

Madelin surely had something extra in reserve for the right man. It is true that her allure was in part the holding out of a possible drunk fuck or lusty affair based on the freeing need to transgress when it suited her, in contrast to the composure of a woman who may well feel attracted but doesn't want to spend three years going out with a draft-dodger. But how tempting it was to believe that this beautiful, independent intelligence might suddenly discover, in a sympathetic man, an emotional climate that enabled her to thrive artistically *and* be faithful.

***

She had arrived surreptitiously in the restaurant, like someone not on offer to the general public, in her black leather jacket, scarf and leggings. If she wanted to be glamorous she would truss her hair up, put on a frock, and then the effect was of cabaret sleekness, all concavities and shoulder blades and luscious dark hair, and a fragile, gazelle pertness. All this was wrapped up on the street. On the street she was the observer, the purchaser. You could miss her easily. But once incarnated across a table, seating herself with a nifty lateral parking of the derrière, once she and the environment were in accord, Madelin's beauty materialised in a way it was hard to imagine in advance. Though she was slight, the pools of her brown eyes seemed to grow larger as she looked at you, drawing in essences. Her responses were subtly physical and involved. You could almost drown in the sight of her thinking. She listened in deep, empathic stillness and then came back from the depths of her being. Madelin's mouth was a great succulent pad of a bouche, and when she smiled, her lips retracted around her teeth in a winning, bright, joyous way, like sun bursting through. The eyes and the mouth formed an invitation that was almost hypnotic and soon the inclination to kiss her pulled on my nerves like the force of gravity.

She ordered, finger on the menu, smiling at the waitress. It was a smile that said 'I've been a waitress, too' – and it hinted at her charm for the same sex, as the waitress melted a little. Madelin was a ready valuer of prettiness in women. She identified with the 'sexy' and with all the feminine touches that combined in allure.

She had told me that she liked my willingness to go into things layer by layer, till the onion was in shreds. No derivative thoughts, no comfort zone, the adjacency of serious talk and high mirth, because the profound and the hilarious are a Rizla-width apart. Definitely, I endeavoured to fascinate her, to be full of life and insight. Mainly what she liked, I sensed, was that I had passions and that my passions were bound up with my work. Work really mattered to Madelin.

We chatted away combustibly over the Viognier, and she was focussed and quick, and I faced, I realised, an executive decision: succumb and go into free-fall, or wait for a sign, and don't mortgage heart or hope till you get it. The dilemma had barely presented itself when I heard myself say:

'I'd like to cook you dinner.'

She knew immediately where I was coming from and reacted with an instant smile of surprise.

'That would be lovely.'

'I know you're working flat out.'

'I am working horribly hard. It's completely obsessive at the moment.'

'Your current commission?'

'Yeah,' she was thoughtful. 'Well, where I am generally with life and work. There's a lot of figuring out to do.'

This sounded pertinent.

'Well, these are matters that are best discussed in the right environment with good home cooking and fine wine,' I said, smiling.

Suddenly, I was staring at a plate of glistening pasta, then a side salad, then a confection of squid, trussed and sauced, sailing into place, as though all this were the perfection of my happiness.

'Thursday any good?' I swallowed. There was something almost pushy about just saying it.

'What are you having there?'

I forked up some pasta and gave her the fork and watched her slide it into her mouth.

She chewed slowly, lingeringly, her eyebrows fraught with pleasure. 'Hmmm. So tasty!'

'Thursday's good,' I said.

'There's something about Thursday,' she frowned.

'When's the painting got to be delivered?'

She shook her head, bad subject, don't go there.

'Doesn't have to be Thursday.'

'I've just fucked up a commission. Royally fucked it up.'

'How's that?'

'Because I can't concentrate. My concentration is in tatters.'

'Friday's also fine.'

'Actually, I may have done something very stupid.'

She swallowed, dabbed her mouth with a serviette and gave me a flirty look, a not-quite-sure have-I-got-news-for-you kind of look, with a hint of figure-me-out glamour.

40

'I've ... um,' she tapped her fingers on the table, looked askance. 'I've got engaged.'

I felt the colour leave my face.

She nodded, a near barmy nod, confirming the reaction.

I set my fork down, took a sip of wine.

'Bit of a conversation stopper,' she laughed, apologetically.

She gave me a steadying almost humorously challenging look.

I was completely overwhelmed and unable to conceal it. I found it impossible to manufacture a response.

'It's all very sudden, Mike.'

Emotion coagulated and lay thick and heavy on my chest. You know the intensity of your longing when it is futile.

I smiled weakly, a dying attempt to fake pleasure for her good news.

'You'll never guess who,' she said.

Well, actually it hardly mattered who. I hardly cared to know. I already knew the essential thing about him because he had fallen for Madelin and made her feel a need to commit, and snatched from before my eyes a woman who was developing into one of the loveliest, most sympathetic creatures on the earth. How absolutely excruciating that another man had spotted the change in Madelin and got her half-way up the aisle before I'd got her through lunch!

'Vince,' she said.

'Sorry?'

'Vince Savage.'

Her expression was very focussed, discovering and intent as she followed this statement through the backs of my eyes. Get your head round that was the thrust, because I'm having to.

Later, there followed a surreal conversation which I can hardly piece together about Vince's 'incredible' writing, his career, his

41

'huge' house in Dartmouth Park, what I thought of him as a writer. Madelin seemed dazed, still putting it together, and excited. She had taken the plunge, out of character, and was adapting as the ground moved under her. She even looked strangely different, her aura more open, as if suddenly she were a woman in the mainstream of life, aimed at a social, domestic future that would require a new way of being.

It was such a twist, so appalling really that it was as much as I could do to nod and listen and soak up her disjointed musings on a man she saw in a light so utterly different to mine that he might have been somebody else. If I thought their union utterly bizarre, I could tell that she regarded Vince as a big catch. Vince was going to take her all the way. He was the passport to a new identity.

This was one to take back home and be alone with, to know what it meant really. I was so absolutely going through the motions but I tried to seem interested and even did my best to be generous about Vince.

'It says a lot for him that he's had the good taste to fall for you,' I managed, after a third glass of wine.

If I was to keep my friendship with Madelin, I would need to dissimulate *some* respect for a man who had pissed on my chips from an enormous spattering height.

She caught this suddenly. 'Mike … this is really different! I just don't know what's hit me.'

She gave me a piercingly beautiful look, the look of a woman madly in love and struck with feeling. She flushed with the sense of it and then gradually her colour came back, as though she were recovering from the usurping force of an emotion I had never seen before.

My heart plummeted. Jealousy, yes, but also the effect of a friend in love coming out with it, transformed, grandly

42

transformed, and the pang of my deep, envious longing to be the cause of so much feeling in a woman.

'You'll come to the wedding?'

My mouth was dry.

'Promise! I'll need moral support,' she said ardently.

***

She had to rush off soon after, so I waved goodbye and stayed to pay the bill, and sat there for several minutes having no energy to take myself back to the office. My feelings didn't surprise me. I expected to be gutted, and took it like a sick man, with kyboshed inertia. What surprised me was a rising sense of how much I had already invested in Madelin and my hopes for a romance, and how desperately I needed something to succeed for a change, and how diminishing it was to have to endure *another* setback.

Later, back home with my diary, I wondered whether it was just life having a go at me, ordinary bad luck, and whether keeping on would pay off in the end. Crushing disappointments were supposed to be character-forming. But then it seemed so wrong that Colin had got Vince, and Vince Madelin, and I honestly wondered whether I was failing in the competitive human marketplace. How could my desires and ambitions be so powerless? Desire and ambition are life forces that I felt keenly, and yet the need for success and happiness – a passionate core in any person – were useless without perception, and without the ability to adapt emotional needs to reality's terms and conditions. Was I hampered by romantic, old-fashioned character traits, and if so, how could I reconcile my need to be wholehearted in love and work with the need for trading power and competitive edge? You turn over such ideas as an exercise in self-rebuke, and they lead you nowhere. Probably I knew myself too well to believe in strategic reinvention. It seemed that feelings were the only thing I could hold on to. Feelings were a kind of asset, an opportunity, an insight even. I had to believe that all these feelings, all this commotion, would someday lead me to happiness.

Chapter 4

The wedding. A grim reckoning: registry office job in Marylebone Road; lunch at a fashionable restaurant. The prospect
of a book-world party caused the inevitable rash of status-
anxiety, something I could see in my complexion. My only social
resource, it seemed, was a kind of demoted geniality. It absolutely didn't help that this literary wedding of the year, attended
by publishing grandees and Vince's new famous friends, would
have at its centre the grinning superintendent of all that was successful in the world, Colin Templar. I debated whether to go, and
felt sick at the prospect, but the radioactive core of my agent-
being knew it was better to be seen than not; better to be mixing
with the fast set than moping it alone at the pub.

After fifteen minutes at the bar of Verdi's, unease had become
paranoia. In the corner of the restaurant stood Madelin's parents looking uneasily conventional. On the other side of the restaurant, almost in an annexe and shielded by a screen, sat Vince's
parents (grisly), and an entourage of mutton-dressed-as-lamb
aunties, all reading the menu, lips moving, and taking it in turns
to shout at a small boy who was exploring under a table. Between
these rum poles Literary London smugly scintillated, and at the

centre of all celebration, brimming with confidence, was Colin. He smiled at everyone like Success's maître d'.

I warily took in the faces around me: slope-shouldered reviewers and literary dames with puckered lips opining about the latest Booker shortlist; gliding wannabes from the publishing-industrial complex photosynthesising the brilliance about them into personal cachet and cool; Madelin receiving congratulations from a queue of admirers, and looking painfully gorgeous in her wedding dress (and slightly fuller in the bosom than I had conjectured, ye gods), and then in the sea of faces I saw 'famous' people, and every time it shocked me to spot a Whitbread winner, or a TV presenter, or a renowned artist amidst the sunny haze that flooded the restaurant.

My attendance amounted to a brushstroke of colour, I knew, a glint of beaming ingratiation in the canvas of Vince's celebrity. I was beginning to feel rather ill when a chap with a pointy nose and greasy hair slid up.

'Quite a bash, eh?' he said.

'Oh! Yup. Sure.'

He looked at me encouragingly. 'You with the bride or groom?'

'Bit of both. Hello, Mike de Vere.'

'Cheers, Kevin Savage. I'm one of Vinnie's rustic relatives.'

'Oh, yes!'

'Romford way. Bit much all this.'

I nodded tightly. 'Well, you know, the *glitterati*!'

'Some nice birds, 'n' all. What's your line?'

'I'm a … um … ah …'

I was staring at Gilbert Baines, the novelist. It was quite a coincidence because only the previous night I had finished his latest novel, *A Far Away Place*.

'Sorry?' I said.

Despite everything, it remained a tactical must to befriend important authors like Gilbert who might one day be looking for a new agent, and anyway I was enormously keen to talk to him about his book. I glanced back at him anxiously, as if fixing his position in the room.

'Do you know many folk here?'

Without a doubt, Kevin was not the right level of person to be seen chatting to at the literary wedding of the year.

'Indeed.'

'What's your line, then?'

I exhaled tensely. 'I'm a book agent.'

Baines was surrounded. Vince wasn't introducing anyone. A wall of relatives stood beyond Kevin. I couldn't see an easy out.

'Tell you what,' said Kevin. 'I been lookin' for an agent. Got a card, like?'

I had read every one of Gilbert Baines's novels. I was actually something of a connoisseur of his work. This was a great chance to say hello and make a mark. I needed to get in there and strike up a conversation – without looking like a sycophant obviously.

'Cos I've taken a leaf outta Vinnie's book.'

'You what?'

'Yeh, 'n' all.'

I nodded, heart tightening. I felt slightly short of breath.

'Done this synopsis gizmo and a chapter outline.'

Suddenly, I saw Colin coming over.

'Hi, Mike,' he said, engulfing me in a bogus comrade hug. 'Talking to the relatives?' He patted my arm as he passed, leaving me with the certainty that Kevin was a much-avoided bore in Vince's family circle and that I had really distinguished myself by latching onto him in a room full of the illustrious and the poachable.

'It's about a bloke, well it's actually based on … it's based on … like, *I'm* the hero. Which is great, cos the psychology, well I know that from my own brain, innit. Cos you gotta write what you know, ain't you?'

'Well, actually …'

'Can't believe you're a literary agent! D'you look after Vinnie?'

'Perhaps just email me your chapters?'

'Can I pose three frequently asked questions?' He smirked.

I thought I was going to have a heart attack. I glanced over my shoulder in panic.

'We're in the world of the stamped addressed envelope?'

I was blinking. I had just seen Martin Amis.

'Yes,' I said.

'And how many chapters would you be wanting?'

The waiter came by.

'A glass for this gennerman, please,' said Kevin.

'I'm OK, actually.'

'Have another on me.'

Martin Amis! I had no idea that Vince knew Amis. Seeing his live presence had a stiffening effect on the sense of occasion. I felt a bridal flush at the very possibility of meeting him.

'Must be a gas, repping writers.'

I squeezed out a smile. I didn't want to be rude or look like some rubber-necking shit, but this was networking prime time, and soon we'd all be trapped in our placement, and God knows where Madelin would have shunted me.

'So who d'you represent?'

Martin Amis's face was framed by the slender arms and concave backs of three good-looking girls. Gilbert Baines was listening in creased concentration to the brilliant playwright Jezebel Banham Cleaver.

48

'I look after Geraldine Shaw and Camilla Guardian and …'

'Don't mean nuffing to me. I don't really read. I actually find most books quite boring.'

'Well, you know, if you're going to write …'

'Some of the things I see on telly, I think, I could have knocked that off in a lunch break.'

Out of the corner of my eye I sensed movement. I looked round.

Gilbert Baines was moving towards me, his wife on his arm, with Julian Hopwell bringing up the rear. My heart started to race. This was a chance.

'Will you excuse me a moment?'

'Like to say, you know, as a way of sellin' the book …'

'Excuse me,' I turned. 'Mr Baines!'

Gilbert Baines looked up, startled.

'How do you do?'

Moving forward, my foot missed the edge of the step. Everything lurched sideways and somehow the back of my fist thwacked the springy mass of Mrs Baines's considerable and disorganised bosom.

'Oouph!'

And the remains of my champagne spritzed over her shawl.

'Ahhg …'

'I *do* beg your pardon. Allow me …'

I tried to dab her down, but the poor woman was winded and shaken.

'Goodness gracious!'

'Steady, dear,' said Baines.

'I am terribly sorry. Are you alright?'

She caught her breath.

'Forgive me … I wanted to say to your husband …'

Baines looked at me suspiciously.

'I *must* sit down,' she said, flushing.

Julian Hopwell glared at me; Jezebel Banham Cleaver was all ancient dismay, as if some lower-order brute had burst into the club. Other guests looked on, at Mrs Baines sympathetically, coldly at me. Her recoil had nudged a waiter, whose tray wobbled as he swerved, saving the day, but drawing more attention to the cause of the bother.

'Mr Baines, I'm one of your greatest admirers. I finished *A Far Away Place* last night.'

He stared at me, nonplussed.

'Gilbert, our table is there,' said Mrs Baines, drawing him on.

'I loved the evocation of pre-war Germany and the scene with the pigs. So sorry,' I extended a hand, 'Mike de Vere.'

'There's *Annabel!*' exclaimed Julian, pointing at a bright young thing.

I smiled fixedly, seeing out the moment, as if there were some dignity in holding the posture, but as Baines shuffled on, I could feel myself colouring. This was dire.

'That went nicely,' said Kevin.

I glanced at him, heart pumping, and then I saw another department of the room on the move. The three very tall girls with elongated supermodel bodies were gliding my way like a trio of beautiful horses flicking their manes and twitching their tails.

Just beyond them was Martin Amis, directing his trademark frown at the table placement.

I decided: this was my moment.

As I headed towards Amis, time slowed down. Only twenty feet ahead of me, he seemed impervious to the throng, an aloof figure, who would acknowledge what impinged (like a wine waiter tuning his glass) without surrendering his self-possession for a moment. Hemmed in by peers and colleagues, by wannabes and star-struck strangers, he seemed undiluted by company. Indeed, as I moved through the crowd towards him, hoping his avoidance of eye contact might be the maidenly modesty of fame, I sensed an air-thickening buffer of resistance to strangers; and yet *not* to connect with an author I admired, *not* to pay tribute in some way, was to treat myself as a passive consumer of fiction and not a participant in the literary discourse. All this had nothing at all to do with being an agent and everything to do with the passion behind the career choice. I *had* to engage. I *had* to feed back. What I would say to him was, of course, worrying. He could field my compliments graciously, but on an occasion like this the exchange could hardly amount to more than a few pleasantries, which would hardly be gratifying and might even be a come-down; so the very premise of me introducing myself was misguided, sapping it of conviction; and indeed, as I drew close to Amis, and saw him sitting down, he appeared to glance up with a look that said: 'Who the hell are you, and don't you know this is a waste of time?'

And then I saw Julius Straker.

I stopped in my tracks. He was sitting at a table by the window with his coat on the back of a chair. It was him without question. He was stooped and uncomfortable-looking, his grey hair pulled back over an ear. The sight of him was absolutely startling and bizarre. A man of genius had sidled from Paris into the broad daylight of a Saturday morning in Marylebone.

This seemed like a revelation. Had Vince risen so high, so quickly, that he was on personal terms with the great novelist? Was there some kind of stratospheric discourse between them based on mutual admiration? Whatever the cause, this was an incredible coup … Vince had drawn a legend into the heart of his social and professional world.

'Sorry to butt in,' I said. 'I'm a friend of Vince and Madelin's, and I just wanted to say "hello".'

Straker was startled.

I had to do this.

'I've read so much of your work, enjoyed it so much, it seemed silly to pass up the chance …' I smiled, '… to touch the hem.'

He was not quite in the zone for this. It took him a second to muster the wherewithal.

'Well, thank you.'

'May I?' I indicated the chair next to him.

'I believe there's a placement.' The accent was gently American.

'No, of course, I … I wouldn't …'

He stared at me, as though he had no conception of what I might want to say to him.

'My name is Mike de Vere.'

He watched me sit down. I must say, slipping into the personal space of a great novelist was unsettling. There was no question that I had his attention now, or was the object of it, and might be found wanting pretty quickly.

'Lovely day for a wedding,' I said.

Intelligent thought had flown from my mind.

Either nobody else at the party knew who he was, or knew him well enough to leave him alone. As I settled in, I noticed his eyes, evasive and dart-like, and the way he took me in side on, as if to preserve his self-containment. It was the posture of a man who observed by avoiding eye contact.

'Mike de Vere?' he said.

'Yes.'

'Are you some kind of literary agent?'

I flushed, astonished. 'I am!'

'With the Sheila Acbe Agency?'

52

This was just remarkable. 'Yes. Do you know Sheila?'

I couldn't conceive of Straker having a social life, of existing somehow in the same dimension as other people. Perhaps Vince had mentioned me.

'I know her as Vernon Lovecraft's agent.'

'Oh!'

Lovecraft was a cantankerous old litterateur, super-snobbish, egotistical and vindictive. He lived in Montmartre.

'A friend?'

'Not really. He haunts the streets of Paris, and once you know Vernon you can't un-know him. He says Sheila is a wonderful lady.'

I was racing to adjust. A writer I had thought to be unapproachably great and on a superhuman plane was connected to agency clients. There were so many questions I wanted to ask, but the reality of his presence was somehow confusing.

'I know your client Camilla Guardian, too,' he said.

'Camilla?'

'Her mother was a New York heiress with a literary disposition.'

'Gosh.' This was incredibly fortuitous and pleasing. 'Well I hope she said something nice about me.'

He gave me a pleasant glance. 'She has spoken of you.'

I found it hard to take it all in. My reputation had preceded me.

Straker smiled warmly. 'She said you were terrible.'

I managed a laugh but felt the colour rise to my cheeks. For a moment I was completely tongue-tied.

Straker glanced over my shoulder as though his comment was a truth imparted for the general weal of mankind.

I felt a bolt of nerves. Things had been tricky with Camilla recently. I had been tough on her so-called novel.

'Camilla's delightful and very good,' I said.

It was awful to think that she had trashed me after I rubbished her lousy book.

'I really doubt she's good,' he said. 'Her mother declares her a basket case.'

Straker was not at all how I imagined him.

'Well, I ...'

I certainly didn't want someone of his stature to think I represented mediocre writers, though Camilla was mediocre, as it happened, and annoying, too.

'Camilla is not a literary novelist,' I tried to explain.

'What does that mean?'

I stared at him, completely flummoxed. I was desperate to convey how a really good agent might occasionally represent clients who were not of the highest order.

'There is room in the world for less demanding fiction ...'

'Is that the kind of work you handle?'

'No, no! My tastes are very literary.'

'I see.'

I found it impossible to tell whether he was being ironic with me. If I'd known that Camilla knew Julius Straker I wouldn't have put the boot in so hard. How come she never told me about him?

'Anyway,' I resumed, 'I really enjoyed *Vacuum* this year, and all the fiction going back to *Saturn* and *Reality Estate.*'

He was looking at me now, but seemed faintly distracted. It was almost as though he had the measure of me, had sampled me somehow, taking in more than our conversation had suggested. I had to ramp it up to engage him properly.

'It's interesting to see how your voice has evolved. The confluence of Flaubert and Nabokov. Hints of Pynchon and DeLillo.'

I paused for effect. 'Milton. Even Chaucer.'

Straker was intrigued. Writers regard 'voice' as a deep and abiding mystery. To hear it pronounced on by an agent must have been quite novel. Agents do deals not content; trade talk not insight; buzz not passion. Agents 'love' the books they read and that's usually as far as it goes. Well, I was determined to prove the exception.

'Chaucer, I think, is …'

'It was actually me that influenced DeLillo,' he said.

'Oh … hah … well, I do find the question of voice utterly fascinating.'

'I probably also have *some* voice of my own.'

'Of course! Goodness, yes.'

'All voice and no trousers,' said a person behind me.

I turned to see Vince look our way before sliding into the crowd.

Straker's eyes swivelled in the direction of the voice.

'But surely,' I persevered, 'every writer's stylistic DNA is drawn from the writers they love most?'

He was following Vince's departing figure.

'Voice has to be subservient to subject matter and character,' I said. 'Voice is … is …'

He raised an arm suddenly, turning in his seat.

'… a hangover from the days …'

'Let me introduce my American friends.'

'… of the omniscient …'

I was surprised to see the tall girls gathering around us, like suppliant graces.

'Chelsea, Petronella and Felice,' he smiled cordially.

'Oh,' I said.

'Hi!' said one of them

I rose uncertainly until I was on a par with their glossy streaming hair and brown eyes. I had no idea they were Straker's friends.

'Mike de Vere.'

The girls were amused by the overkill of their triple-glamour
bearing down on a non-famous person.

'So how d'you know Julius?' breathed Felice.

I looked over my shoulder, as if to keep Straker in on the conversation. He was rising from his chair and peering across the
restaurant.

'D'you work for Colin?' said Chelsea.

I glanced behind me. Straker was moving towards a group at
the far end of the table. Martin Amis was headed in the same
direction with Vince.

'I ... Mr Straker ...'

Felice hung on my words as if we were playing parts. I just
needed to say *something* to her and she would reply. The content
was irrelevant because she was uninterested in talking to me, and
knew I only wanted to be talking to Straker. Who were these girls
anyway?

My heart was sinking. 'Listen, I don't *work for* anybody,' I said.
'It's more collab ... excuse me. Mr Straker!' I called.

Straker had reached the far end of the table where he was
leaning forward to kiss Madelin, placing a hand under her elbow.
She glowed in response, like a glimmering deb before a
monarch.

'Yes?' said Chelsea.

'More ... um ... collaborative than that.'

Felice gazed at me, lips parted.

I inhaled.

Chelsea smiled. 'Shall we find our places?'

'Time to sit down, I think,' said Felice.

The girls moved off and left me staring at Vince and Martin Amis as they converged on Madelin, who stood in the middle of the group, like a bride in a famous painting, with its light-shot celebration of legendary personages. Colin slid in from the right, all teeth and burning spectacles, and Straker struck profile in the golden mean area, offering a hand to Amis while proceeding to amuse all at court with a quip that had Vince on the back foot, and Madelin glowing with loveliness.

I could not leave it. I made my way towards them.

It was time to greet the bride and groom, time to join the inner circle and show Colin that Vince and I went back, because I was a close friend of the couple, and entitled to acknowledgement.

'Hi, Madelin, hi,' I said, as I drove myself into their midst, aiming to take her hand and kiss my congratulations, and proceed to the bear hug with Vince, and a high five with Colin; but Madelin did not yield, she was fixed on Amis and wouldn't break eye contact, and Vince and Colin were competitively listening to Amis, and Straker had done his bit with me and had no more time for the public; and as I ground to a halt, my presence ignored, my proximity screened out, I realised that everything I might have meant to Madelin, my personal relations with Vince and Colin were worth not a mote of courtesy or fellow feeling to any of them, because I wasn't famous, not the agent of a famous writer, not meaningful to those in the premier peer group, and if anything, not even noticeable because at this moment none of them wanted to dilute the A-list exclusivity of the conversation by including me.

I was dying on the spot. My failed greeting gave me nowhere to go. The longer I lingered, the worse it got. To reverse was impossible, a body-language give-away, and for too long I stood with a fixed grin, as though included in the conversation while invisible to all; and then, when I turned, I could see the American girls smiling at me across the tables, and I knew my humiliation was complete. They had cottoned on to Straker's move to give me the slip and were now lapping up the spectacle of my second try and absolutely loving it, their eyes sparkling with amusement.

'Mike,' came the cry. 'Over here, mate!'

I could barely sense the direction of the voice.

'Mike!'

Somebody wanted to talk to me. Dejected, I turned.

Kevin.

It was Kevin.

'Hi, Kevin.'

He gestured for me to come over.

I took the life-line and waved myself off, as if torn between two groups of friends. Everything went slow-motion, as though I were struck by a tranquillizer dart and each step and every faltering breath took unbelievable, limitless effort.

I headed towards Kevin, heart in my boots.

'Stroke of genius,' said the welcoming Kevin as I staggered to the table and arrived at my placement. We had been seated next to each other (NEXT TO EACH OTHER!) at the end of the family table.

'Aunty Sal,' Kevin indicated the blue-rinse old heap on the other side of me. 'She's an author, too,' he said with a gargolic laugh.

I put my face in my hands.

'My new agent,' declared Kevin to all at table.

I tipped forward, as though vomiting my soul into some terminal mire of the spirit. When at last I looked up and saw Kevin's smirk, I realised that I was thirty-six years old, and still, in the world to which I had dedicated all my hope and ambition, an utter nonentity.

58

Chapter 5

Chagrin beats out its pulsing radioactive half-life and still you persevere, outstripped but keeping on, because a working life lasts long, and who knows what change of fortune lurks around the corner? We agents are salesmen *au fond*, and the salesman must keep on smiling, and shooting cuffs, and looking the part, masking what lies within.

In the weeks that followed the wedding I could be heard saying to colleagues 'Martin Amis was telling me the other day ...' or 'Gilbert Baines is a charming, delightful man ...'

A good agent exploits everything, even humiliation.

After the honeymoon, Madelin and Vince returned to the marital mansion in Dartmouth Park with its bespoke luxury kitchen and en suite Jacuzzi and five bedrooms with original fireplaces and distant views over the heath.

To begin with I was invited to their parties as a stalwart bore and industry backbone kind of guy you need to have as wadding. I policed the periphery of those glam-bam book launches, and joked with second-tier functionaries in the entourage around the Savages. Even this diminished role was worth keeping for the sake of appearances. Vince entered the fame domain on a birthright basis. He reserved the right to be rude, aloof, moody, but Madelin propelled him pretty efficiently to the No. 10 drinks and London salons, where talent flatters power. Not content to clean up as a novelist, Vince wrote reams of pungent journalism. Many things excited his ire, not least the direction of the book trade and its notorious structural changes, the discounting, the knackering of the indie bookshops, the rise of genres, the glorification of brands and the hard selling of merchandise in bookstores. Vince's periodic diatribes made him many enemies and changed nothing. More often than not I agreed with his sentiments whilst resenting the polemical overkill.

They had a baby very early, little Holly, and as the parenting got the better of them, I gradually saw less of Madelin.

I worked on and on, with moderate results and always in the lee of Colin and Sheila's power-house careers. It was through a haze, really, that I witnessed Melina Fukakowsky's success – in the shops, on the telly – and despite the fact that this quickened the tills at the agency and brought more tie-in business, it wasn't the high ground I cared about. My main concern was to stop Steve in Film/TV referring to her as 'Professor Fuck'. 'It's all very funny,' I said, 'but one day she'll come to the agency and you'll call her Professor Fuck by accident, and we'll lose a great client.'

'Bet she goes like a juggernaut with a carrot up its arse,' said Steve.

'For God's sake, show some professionalism!'

I nearly called her Professor Fuck myself when she phoned in one day. Bloody Steve.

But then something so out of the blue and extraordinary happened that I am still struggling to comprehend it. Eighteen months after Madelin's wedding I found her, the love of my life, and for the first time in years was blissfully happy.

I expected a girl from my own world. True love was to be found somewhere far grander. It was Melina who introduced me to Brian Barrow, the *Spectator* columnist, and through Brian (stuttering and mannered) I met Philip and Bolly Grieves, and was invited to join their reading group in Holland Park. Philip, like many barrister parvenus, saw himself as a country squire at the weekend and a patron of the arts in the week (when not jawing the House of Lords on some silly insurance law appeal – from which he had made an absolute jagging mint).

The reading group was a bit of a stretch for me. With my genteel vowels and English degree I could just about pass muster with the likes of Patrick Blenheim Bodbury and Annabel Charteris and actually, despite their Kensington and Chelsea airs they were really quite nice. Don't knock the Sloanes, I say, it's a good brand – unlike those nouveau hedge-fund cunts (although some of them *are* hedge-fund cunts – the cunts!). I could play my part whilst never expecting anything from the females of the set (with their Rule Britannia jaws and Clytemnestra profiles and braying G&T welcomes) and I even remember thinking that Nadia Lazenby, the first time I saw her, was a mirage of privilege, rather like a Monet on a boardroom wall, proving wealth's entitlement to beauty.

You ham it up with this brigade, vowels ripening, a bit of crust in the delivery. They like character in a chap, and they like a good opinionated spat, a chance to bang out core Tory values on the dining-room table once the claret's in the bloodstream, and some of the uncharitable views play well for a second or two (shock value) as a form of candour, of 'right, gloves off, send 'em all back' humour; and there is surprise in the fact that our multi-ethnic, multi-racial polyglot world city is, to this lot, a sort of accident or aberration, not really there in any meaningful way, not like the Farrow and Ball wallpaper and the prints in the loo, and the silver cigarette cases on mummy's divan table, or the weekends in Scotland, or the Abruzzi.

But even in this posh world Nadia Lazenby seemed on loan from somewhere far grander. Her very name was a metonym for sheer debutante panache. She made a party, and bejewelled an anecdote, and middle-class persons were deemed invisible in her presence.

'Oh, Nadia was there!' they'd say. The myth of her lingered in the languid vowels of that name. Nadia's grace and poise, her sparkling eyes and teeth and knowing look and bright laughter seemed the finishing touches to the purlieus of excellence. In that fabled dress, which squeezed forth neck and shoulders like a bursting rose, that slid glove-like around those elegant hips and slender waist and the offering of an ideal bosom, in that figurine of black velvet she embodied a *Belle Époque* kind of beauty so redolent of the *fin de siècle* as to revive for her hosts a bygone age of privilege and opulence. She seemed the incarnation of a Henry James upper-class heroine, or a Singer Sargent heiress – a central casting quintessence more desirable than any pert foreground Bobo or Camilla. When Nadia stood by the fireplace in Geoffrey Venables's Holland Park mansion, the mirror capturing the fawn-like back of her neck, the rolled-up hair, the shoulder straps on her dress, her earrings trapping candlelight and fire-blaze; when you saw the elbow-length party gloves, and the flickering play of hands that might culminate in a twirled cigarette that she would draw on with such delicate strength, enhancing her bosom; when you watched her lilting ascent of Michael Soames's Devonshire Place staircase, or caught her in one of those fabulous guest bedrooms deftly checking a fallen strand of hair, you had for a moment the illusion that a hundred years of British social history had not actually happened. It was as if the old order still existed, secretly and supremely, if you knew where to look, and were invited.

Such beauty would have many admirers. She seemed instinctively to need grand mirrors, flower-filled vases, a huge wardrobe. The very look of her spelled high maintenance. *Noli me tangere* – I concluded – unless you're titled or loaded, or both. And Nadia took a while to notice people. On a first introduction she could present beautifully, but that brilliant smile could pass without a winning distraction. Her eye contact would falter if a more familiar person reared behind you; and so at a party her attention flitted rather, and although that gloved hand might fall on your jacket sleeve, almost in apology, as she prepared to shoot quicksilverishly around you to Kitty or Camilla, her lieutenants in pulchritude, one felt at a loss as to how to trap her interest and make an impression.

Nadia resisted impressions. Like a cat, she needed security of habitat before leaping on anybody's lap. Amongst the old furniture of her peer group you were required to blend in and then from that sub-fusc state that made you accountable to the people who loved her, the tribe, you could gradually differentiate yourself. Once Nadia had seen you were sort of *appellation contrôlée*, she could begin to shift a little and start to annex her attention to the idea of you; and thus it came about that sooner or later, in my case later, Nadia would grant an audition. You might be sitting on the sofa, nursing a post-prandial drink, thinking it was just about time to go, and suddenly she would flop down beside you. 'Got a light,' she would say, and the ritual would commence: the studiously zipped match, the mating of flame and tipped cigarette, the full-mouthed exhalation of smoke, the quick smile, the cat-like settling on the sofa cushions, the sense of readiness and expectation as if I were bound to be witty or urbane because that was the deal. She did captivating, you did witty; and if all went well and Nadia laughed, one was flattered with a sense of equality, even intimacy, because that was her gift. She was not particularly a person who wished to be known. She preferred diverting statements to searching questions. One created oneself anew to talk to her, and I suppose in my case I adopted a 'talent to amuse' type persona, hints of Noël Coward, yes, mildly camp, crisp and darting, which I think she knew was an impersonation and enjoyed as such. I have to say, it came easily. Nadia seemed to curl around the thread of one's sentences, poised for the punch line, which she consumed with a bright laugh that sparked dimples in either cheek. Her eyebrows elevated expectantly. 'I know whom you remind me of,' she said once.

'Whom?'

'Laurence Olivier.'

I was pretty pleased to hear this.

'Really?'

She seemed to think it was very funny. The penny dropped.

'Oh, I see. Laurence Olivier as Richard III?'

She burst out laughing.

'Piping voice, interminable nose, girly haircut. Hmmm, flattering.'

She waved her hands. 'Not at all. Not at all.'

'Left the hunchback in the car, actually.'

Nadia patted me on the shoulder, begging me to stop; she was almost convulsed with laughter.

'What are you two guffawing about?' said Kitty Pemberton.

'I've just realised,' said Nadia, recovering herself. 'Mike's the dead spit of Laurence Olivier.'

'I'll take it as a compliment.'

'You should be pleased. Vivien Leigh fell in love with him,' she said encouragingly.

'You're very up on all things Olivier.'

'I adore those old films,' she said, almost wistfully.

I took care not to suggest that I could play Olivier to Nadia's Vivien Leigh.

Conversation with her was a matter of sidestep and deflection. She came alive when she saw you were completely unthreatening, and my faux debonair playfulness kindled in her presence really because there was no other way of being with her. She was too skittish, too social, too distracted and too perfect to pursue. She knew all men were shareholders in her beauty and she could flirt with us as she liked. What I didn't see was the disarray behind the beauty, or the simplicity of heart behind the manner.

She was thirty-one back then and not about to slip up. She knew the value of her feelings and the power of her love. Too much was at stake at this high hour of her loveliness, before the biological alarms started drilling, to risk herself on the louche cats that circled in Holland Park, or the banker-types with specs and pates who wanted to die spending money on her. A romantic prince would surely materialise from somewhere if she just kept her head, leading on a few bachelors for practice in the meantime.

I met her one evening on a street in South Kensington. I was strolling along after a drink at the Society of Authors, admiring the icing-white villas in Onslow Gardens and the lanes of mews houses, the picture of the church behind flourishing lime trees, and there, coming in my direction, was a familiar face.

'Mike!' She was startled.

'Hello there.' I kissed her cheek.

She wore an elegant navy blue coat with big buttons. Her hair was up.

65

'What are you doing here?' She seemed amused.

'Oh! Just trundling home from a bit of biz round the corner.'

'Really?'

'Society of Authors.'

'Gosh!'

'Lots of old poets and a few shaggy authors having a drink.'

She nodded, following my eyes. She seemed fascinated by the spectacle of me out and about in the world at large, as though it were always difficult for her to imagine what people did in their working lives.

'Are you ...' she hesitated, reaching into her bag. 'D'you want to come in for a drink?'

'You live here?'

'Sort of. Well, my parents live round the corner and I ... live with them sometimes.'

'How nice.'

She smiled.

'I'd love a drink.'

'Ma and Pa are in Rome, jolly conveniently. Gosh, fancy bumping into you here.'

She seemed a little flustered as we went along the street towards Drayton Gardens, with its huge brick terraces. We crossed the road, and she took me to the door of a mansion block.

I followed her into the substantial hallway and up the communal staircase, noting the chandelier, the stained glass lozenges in the landing window and the air of well-appointed Edwardian space; and as Nadia surged ahead, somehow quickened by the turn of events, I realised that I had no manner for being alone with her, or she with me. We were acquaintances rather than friends. Coming into her parents' home was like going behind the scenes. We entered a door on the second-floor landing and

66

Nadia conducted me quite briskly into the vestibule of a maisonette, with a staircase leading to the floor above and smart entrance hall going to the drawing room one way, and the kitchen the other. It was all immaculately Brompton, high spec, radiators behind grilles, prints, lamps and gilt. The drawing room was a paradigm of conventional good taste: the sisal, the Chesterfield, the drapes and pelmets, an oil painting of a young woman in blue taffeta dress above the mantelpiece. I learned later that Nadia's dad had been a Foreign Office high flyer who retired early owing to a heart condition. He became a Lloyd's name to boost his income and lost around half a million in the mid-eighties, poor chap.

I hovered uncertainly. She seemed to be rushing around, hanging a coat, fetching this and that, glasses from a corner cupboard, wine from the kitchen. She wasn't quite poised, as if it were slightly irregular having a guest in her parents' flat. I didn't know then that she lived here. She had a pair of rooms on the upper storey – a boudoir, and a little bedroom with a double bed in it.

She asked me whether I had seen Annabel since she got back from California, a place-holding question that neither of us was much interested in. Until Nadia was able to sit on the chair opposite, wine glass cupped in her hand, Chinese crackers at the ready, she did not really know what to say.

We talked for an hour, not every subject of conversation quite taking off, but all the while I felt the immediacy of her attention, as though she were trying not to miss anything now we were alone, and although it was a bit staid at times – Nadia was tense – she was lightning quick on the uptake too, and her eyes were engaged and attentive, and she wanted to listen carefully.

We were talking about David Probert and his interest in Sally Johns, a saga of unrequited love.

I reached out, a gesticulation really, hand turned up, offering the idea of something, and as she sat there, elbow on the chair arm, finger at the corner of her mouth, she took my hand and gave it a little tug, a playful grabbing, which I reciprocated by holding on tight, as though this were a little tussle.

'And so you see,' I said, still holding her hand. 'I think what David should do is …'

I came forward, as if to give more.

'What should he do?' she said, pressing my palm. She gazed at me urgently wanting to know what more David should do.

'Oh, there's no question, he should …'

I placed my other hand over hers.

'Go for it?' she said suddenly, watching me.

I came off the sofa into a kneeling position by the arm of her chair. Her hand was compressed in mine and gently pulling on me.

I watched her eyes switch between mine, the play of a half-smile on her lips, then I drew close, my head tilting, and her lips pursed and her eyes grew large and dark as I hovered and then kissed her, and her grasp was tight, and it was done. And then a second welling took place and we came together again and I was, in the gravity of that moment, calm, and her eyes, up close, were wide all the way. I saw the filaments of her irises, the reflection of window light, the fine stitching of her eyebrow, those thick lashes as I leaned in to kiss her, and felt the soft, forward pressure of her mouth as she responded.

We were enthralled by the momentous nature of that kiss, and we held the silence, the endless, slow-motion suspense of a delicate revelation. Something was known for the first time at this dilating point, something you could never know beforehand, though I wondered, as I held her still and close, who was Nadia? Who was this person?

68

***

Nadia's friends accepted me as though I had always been destined for the role of boyfriend. She was an incredible prize and my going out with her was cause for deep respect and the prompt for many a confidence. 'She's a very special lady,' admitted Rodney Wyatt over port, somewhat wistfully. 'You've got the prettiest girl in all London,' opined Katie Beale, like a faithful lady-in-waiting.

Nadia was invited to everything and I was her invariable consort: orangery parties, Home Counties weddings, hunt balls in Gloucestershire. To arrive on her arm at a private reception at The Ritz or The Ivy, to sail under the flaps of marquees on summer lawns with Nadia at my side was to seem thunderously eligible and intriguing to a swathe of unmarried women in their early thirties, and I guess it boosted my confidence no end to be the chosen one; but it never went to my head. I was happy, grateful to be happy, and so committed to my girlfriend that the glorious vanity of being her 'man' meant nothing.

Our romance became a relationship and our relationship an institution, and although at times I felt a slight impostor in this top-drawer world, everybody was so decent that I soon relaxed. I could do the manners and the small talk, and most importantly, I could handle the odd set-up of having a thirty-one-year-old girlfriend who lived with her parents.

Her parents were charming and withdrew tactfully whenever I came to the flat, leaving us alone in the drawing room, though more often we went upstairs. I would arrive in my best coat with felt trimmings in the collar: a mirage of well-tailored presentability. Always it was necessary to say hello to her dad, usually desperate for male conversation. He knew better than to detain me. 'Daddy, don't bore Mike to death,' Nadia would call lovingly from the landing. Mr Lazenby would smile benignly – still amazed to have sired this miraculous daughter – and I would nod and head upstairs. Nadia would speak in a quite deafening voice to begin with, as if to convince her parents that nothing furtive was going on. She needed a pretext for my being in her boudoir and usually had some ruse for getting me upstairs ('Help me with my computer, Mike' or 'It's so chilly in the sitting room' or 'Mum, just going to watch a film'). Later, it amused me how she could make love without even locking the bedroom door. She worshipped the proprieties, but was recklessly passionate when it suited her.

I frequently wondered what Nadia saw in me, or rather how she saw me. Did I really look like Laurence Olivier? Was that the archetype? Olivier might have seemed many things, but was never quite what he seemed. Did Nadia recognise a fellow actor in me, someone who navigated life's ironies with subtly transmuting facial expressions only intelligible to a kindred spirit? Looking at myself from her point of view I could see that Mike's gallantry, his opening of doors and helping with coats, was the reflex of an actor who knows what the leading lady needs to accomplish her effects. It was a style that said things must be done in a certain way because that is how appearances work. Such sleight of hand was liberating. Nadia could wear what persona she liked in company, because Mike knew it was a kind of performance, and backstage they could both relapse into whatever mode lay behind the actor's mask. Mike, of course, reads. He sits in her room, whilst matters of toilette are finessed, a book cupped in his hand, and then his face becomes fixed with concentration. She loves his ability to step into other worlds. His self-containment at such times intrigues her. His short bursts of reading are like quick intervals of prayer. Mike, it seems, is not

70

bound up with the here and now, and this gives her breathing space, which she likes, because Nadia finds it tiring to be as perfect as she looks, and her occasional lapses (a violent whispering he hears from the bedroom, a hoarse shriek down the stairwell at her sister) he ignores or tunes out, so deep is his concentration, so disinterested is he in the quirks of her domestic life. And Mike is liberating in another way. He tries to be a force for good in the world but occasionally he spouts something so poisonous it is absolutely hilarious, and then she'll screech with laughter and recognition. Nadia knows this transformation. She feels similarly compressed herself: by people, her mother, and stuff. She is quite brittle, because Nadia has learned to put herself across in a way that leaves little room for manoeuvre; she has tempered herself to appeal. Her manner is a mask, and she is dead sure that nobody wants to see what feelings rage behind the mask, what claustrophobic turmoil, because she is not quite this poised, beauteous anachronism that everyone wants to keep in aspic. And yet, what avenues offer her true self-expression? She is too highly strung (and too proud) to hold any desk job for longer than a few weeks. The arts she enjoys as a listener or reader, but her talents were never given a chance at that beastly ladies' college. She is fascinated by other lives, but has lost all confidence in catching up with professional girlfriends. It seems her only vocation is to wait for marriage, but the roles of wife and mother seem like a different chapter in life to the one she is living, a stage that is not quite real at the moment.

***

I remember a dinner party with her friends in Chelsea, a typical crowd, her City chums and fruity barrister amigos and posh girls with hair bands and horsey laughs. We were at the liqueur stage, talking about movie stars, and the women were taking it in turns to name their favourite screen idols whilst the men listened and laughed. 'I'll take James Dean, any day,' said one. 'He was gay, old girl.' 'Can I have Paul Newman?' said another. 'Another shirt-lifter, I'm afraid. If a star's that good-looking he's bound to be queer.' 'Well, I just think Mike's the most handsome man in the world,' said Nadia all of a sudden, 'and he's certainly not gay.' She smiled, blushing at the inadvertent giveaway. There was a loud 'hooray' and I got a nudge in the ribs from Kitty. 'That's an endorsement,' said Kitty. I smiled back at her with a mixture of embarrassment and emotion, catching Nadia's eye as I did.

Nadia may not have understood me profoundly, but her loving nature had adapted to the idea of me and made that her ideal. To her, I *was* the handsomest man in the world. We were different in many ways but somehow iconic to each other.

I was gliding into my late thirties; Nadia was thirty-three. After the second anniversary of our first kiss I knew I wanted to marry her. Of course there were differences between us. Nadia was posh and well-bred and her friends undeniably Sloanes, compared to whom I was a middle-class offering from the Home Counties with amphibious social skills who never invited any of her friends back to my flat.

If our relationship wasn't the universe, what relationship was? Nadia was a particular kind of person and the intellectual side of things was not her bag. When I asked her, half playfully, half in earnest, if she thought she understood me, she replied 'Oh good heavens, no!' Hers was not a class that made windows into the soul. Psychological insights: not the done thing. 'What you see is what you get' was the pertinent adage. Thus certain kinds of conversation – the sort of conversations I used to have with Madelin (freer, more speculative, inevitably more intellectual) were not going to happen with Nadia, because Nadia accepted appearances. Nadia might have thought it not quite cricket to query the personality of her friends, or see the underlying impulses and anxieties that combined in character. 'He's a very sweet boy,' she would announce, as if that settled the matter without quite explaining why Phillip Case was such a crashing bore or Jasper such a rubber-necking socialite. If I sensed there was something essentially lifeless and anaemic about Hugo, she'd say 'Don't you just love his shoes!' as if a man with three-toned suede shoes was bound to go far. If I were to note that in Pippa Handley's family, with whom we had stayed the weekend, nobody seemed to have cracked a book open in three generations, Nadia would say 'We can't all be intellectuals like you, darling' which was perfectly true. Not all the world needs books or bookish conversation, and one of the great liberations of Nadia and her set was the social acceptance and respect I got irrespective of my fucking client list (as I now called it) or my standing as an agent. Love did not insist that each partner in a couple had identical interests and capabilities; rather love showed that the greatest blessing in life was to be loved for oneself.

I couldn't imagine Nadia moving into my flat. NW2 wasn't her stamping ground. I could hardly move in with her parents. Something had to happen that would smooth the path from romance to marriage, probably involving heavy borrowing on my part, and some compromise on hers, and always I felt that something needed to click in my career, a break-through, a supernova client, new levels of confidence that would give me the balls to load up the mortgage and put to Nadia not just bended knee and proffered ring but a vision of the future. If this

73

wasn't happening in a hurry, Nadia seemed in no great hurry. There was perhaps a Peter Pan aspect to her nature that preferred liberty to domestic routine. Perhaps she baulked at having children. These conversations did not happen because neither of us was ready for the answers. Our happiness worked with things as they were.

***

Meanwhile, there *were* developments on the career front: something of a breakthrough, indeed.

I had decided to go commercial and dip a toe in the waters of women's mass-market fiction. Every literary agent needs an Aga saga, or a chick-lit bandwagon to pay a few bills. My solution was a glossy chocolate box of a numero written by Janine Samuels (good name) with mild literary pretensions that hit the sweet spot at Venus Press and was vouched for by one of the young interns. Personally, I found it unreadable – the wish-fulfilment, the preposterous male characters (duds, cads, studs), but this deft exercise in applied cynicism got a great advance and suddenly the whole project was looking sort of plausible. We had that happy thing: a commodity. We had Janine's 'looks' (made over to the hilt in the fly-leaf photo – whose eyelashes were those? Whose hair?), a super cover, and a story of 'happiness and heartbreak, of tears and triumph, of love and loss' care of the quote we had blagged off one of Sheila's fading clients. The supermarkets were ordering in, and for once in my life the publishers were actually doing something. This was success of a sort.

Until Vince Savage clocked in. One morning, reading the Saturday *Guardian* Review, I had a nasty shock. Vince had decided to make Janine's innocuous debut the subject of a scathing diatribe against the fatuousness of commercial fiction and the laziness of modern publishing. A novel that had been justly praised in *Belle* magazine for 'bursting with feeling and tenderness and love' he dismissed as 'blubbering hormonal tosh, with less spine than a used tampon'. I was appalled – and absolutely furious that one of the agency's authors should be traducing another of our clients. The following Monday I stopped Colin in the corridor and told him that it was a major own goal for one of our clients to be slagging off another in the national press.

'He was purifying the dialect of the tribe,' said Colin.

'Bollocks, he was envious she got a bigger advance than his latest unreadable novel.'

'What do you want me to do? Smack his wrist?'

'Yes!'

'Mike!'

'I think it's uncollegiate. It's bloody bad form. Why not allow others a little success?'

'Listen, if you go downmarket, don't expect to drag the world with you.'

'You were the one who told me to go commercial!'

'Well, there's good commercial and there's tosh.'

'It's not tosh! Janine's novel is a superior piece of popular fiction.'

Colin smirked. 'I love it when you talk rough.'

'What?'

'She's a hack, Mike. Jewish mother of two knows all about sex and money and gets it down between trips to Waitrose and the hairdresser.'

'She's not a hack. She's a great storyteller.'

'Listen, every woman's magazine journalist has a couple of cracks at conning an advance off some menopausal editor who has lost her touch, and Janine got lucky. She knows the score.'

'That's disrespectful. Why …'

'Janine's readership don't take the *Guardian*. It doesn't matter!'

'I don't care about her readership.'

'Now you're confusing me.'

'Vince should know better than to trash his agent's colleague's client.'

'This is ridiculous. You're personally offended?'

'I am personally very offended.'

'So now you're the patron saint of mass-market women's fiction?'

'No. Rubbish. I think it's fucking bad manners.'

'I agree. So what?'

'He's pissing on the doorstep and biting the hand that feeds him.'

'Steady, Mike. Vince is the one feeding us. His books pay a load of salaries round here. Far as I'm concerned he can say whatever he likes to get his big brain through the day. If he wants to piss on your clients, let him power-shower the lot of them. You know what? They'll lap it up. Bit of tough urinating love from a literary star is more than most hacks deserve.'

'"Less spine than a used tampon" is NOT ACCEPTABLE!'

'Well, form a new fucking agency and take the moral rant with you.'

He stalked off down the corridor.

'Colin,' I called after him.

He turned.

'Don't be a complete tosser,' I said.

He looked at me coldly and then shrugged and went to his office.

In the days that followed Colin was the same as ever: indifferent, busy, unperturbed. We both had our office way of rubbing along with colleagues and my complaint about Vince would have given him absolutely no cause for reflection, just as the word 'tosser' was a word he ducked and forgot instantly. Meanwhile the episode boiled in my thoughts. What value could I ascribe to a person who talked of urinating on clients? The sentiment was disgraceful and made a deep, distasteful impression. I would have to watch my lip. Previously I had been cowed by Colin's success, and on the back foot and somehow quarantined into thinking that he knew best which values an agent should have. Now I could imagine myself speaking up. I could imagine myself telling him that, actually, he couldn't be a complete cunt all the time – and if he didn't like hearing it, maybe he should fuck off and set up *his* own agency.

***

In Nadia's arms, I managed to cool down from all this. It was Nadia, I realised, who had enabled me to turn the other cheek and let Colin wash over me; and it was in Nadia's embrace on her vast double bed that something extraordinary happened. We were lying under the duvet, propped against pillows and watching television, when Nadia said that she wanted children. She muted the TV with the remote and just said:

'I want babies.'

Even to this day I don't know what came over her.

I was, of course, so startled as to be speechless. My fantasies of a romantic proposal were completely pre-empted.

'But then we should get married,' I said simply.

'Of course,' she said.

'Shall I propose to you?'

There was such tenderness in her gaze. 'Only if you want to.'

She looked at me with the deepest feeling and I knew then that Nadia loved me more than I ever realised.

I remember her touching my cheek and delivering one of her softest kisses to my mouth.

'Actually, Mike … before you propose, I want you to do one thing for me.'

'Get the champagne?'

She smiled, and then she looked aside modestly.

'Would you have a fertility test?'

I was a little embarrassed and slightly surprised.

'Of course. If you like.' My heart was beating hard.

She ruffled my hair and looked at me sensually. 'I *so* want to have a baby.'

I had never seen such longing in a woman's eyes.

'So I shouldn't propose till I've checked out OK?'

'D'you mind awfully?'

Emotions are appalling things. I felt as though I was dissolving inside.

'Mike, it's a doddle,' she said, reassuringly. 'You think of something saucy and do it into a cup.'

'Oh … OK.'

'You're really quite clever at that, aren't you, darling?'

I was a little taken aback.

'Good at what?'

She raised an eyebrow teasingly.

'Masturbating?'

'Good with your hands, Mikey! In every way.' She leaned towards me for a kiss. 'Apparently … Now this is the only tricky bit …'

I looked at her suspiciously.

'Before you do the test there's a three-day ejaculation ban.' She smiled.

'Is there, indeed?'

'D'you think you could do that for me?'

I laughed coarsely. 'Three days off sex just to get married!'

She laughed. 'I'll make it up to you! I promise.'

'Oh yes?'

'Let your imagination run wild,' she said, looking at me in a cute way and raising her eyebrows meaningfully.

'Right. Well I suppose I might just stretch to three days of abstinence in the interests of marrying the woman I love.'

'My hero!' Nadia kissed me hard and fell back on the pillow, hair fanning around her head. 'Then we can go somewhere expensive for dinner and you can do the ring bit and we can drink champagne and spend a lovely night in the Ritz making mad, passionate love.'

I smiled at her indulgently, stroking her hair, and cupping the back of her head in my palm. I well knew what it was to be wrapped around a woman's little finger. It was like this, and it was actually OK.

It had never honestly occurred to me that her feelings would be so simple that we could agree to get married sprawled in front of the telly. But that was the way with Nadia: she always sprung these surprises. I kept blinking to conceal the moisture in my eyes. We had been dating long enough and now marriage would follow. My life had been blessed with overwhelming happiness.

***

The business with the fertility test was sort of odd. The very next day I set up an appointment at a family clinic.

I was in a daze of excitement. I couldn't tell anybody but already I felt different, as though some bomb of happiness had gone off in my head. Getting through a day's work at the office was virtually impossible and I remember feeling distracted and none too bothered as I scrolled emails and stared blindly at contracts, and navigated around the W-drive like a junky in a maze. I wanted to pounce on the world and tell everyone.

On semen-test day, I did my sample into a special cup at home and then taxied it to the clinic. The cup was graciously received at the desk, and I was told by a lady in a white coat to make an appointment to see Doctor Iverson ten days hence. I slipped off to the office with a sense of mission accomplished. At the end of the following week I pitched up for my 'sign-off' with Dr Iverson.

I knew from the start that something wasn't quite right. As I sat by the desk in his consulting room I could see the doctor's face as he printed off the test results and put the sheets before him. He looked calm and professional, but I saw his eye catching something in the sheet and the preparation in his look of a special manner for his patient.

'I'm glad you've had this test,' he began, forefinger on the bridge of his nose. 'Have you been trying for a baby?'

'Uh … No.'

'You're married?'

'I … I'm engaged.'

'OK.' He nodded, looking at me carefully.

'I should say that your kinds of results … are very common these days and it's far better to know what's what, so you and your partner can move forward in an effective way.'

He showed me the sheet. The tests, he explained, measured sperm density, sperm morphology and sperm motility.

'In the average ejaculate sample you might have 40 million sperm. Sub-fertile men can have as little as a million per sample.'

'A million?'

'Sounds a lot, but there's morphology and motility to consider. In your case there's a high level of dead and deformed sperms. Factor in the low count, and you're looking at functional infertility. I'm sorry, but better you know, really.'

He looked at me directly.

I stared back at him.

'So pregnancy through sexual intercourse is unlikely, because this kind of sperm never reaches an egg.' He smiled kindly. 'You're firing off blanks. We'll run more tests to be sure, but there are three solutions. There's adoption, obviously. Or assuming your partner is fertile, the sperm-donor route. You pretty much select characteristics, racial origin, eye colour, etc., but it won't be your child and there's an element of chance about what you end up with. The first option would be *in vitro* fertilisation, using one of your sperm, injecting it into the egg, and injecting the fertilised egg into the uterus.'

I gazed at him, not really hearing what he said.

'You and your partner need to be ready for this course of action. The oestrogen boosters used to harvest eggs have an intense emotional impact. It's a bumpy ride and often takes a number of tries to get lucky. We're confident here about our ability to get results. But the process is expensive and you've got to be ready for it. Some couples decide, OK, we're not going to have kids.'

He looked at me candidly.

'Certain clinics have rather over-sold the virtues of *in vitro*. You need to go into it with your eyes open, and prepare for the possibility that it might not work. The main thing is that you're not going to waste years trying to do it naturally. When do you plan to get married?' he asked.

***

I remember standing in the street outside the clinic. I blinked at the bright light that glanced off windscreens and blanched the pavement. There was no use thinking too much, because this bit of bad news was beyond my control and would worm its way into my mind and make me suffer all kinds of devastating emotions. I remember feeling unmanned and foolish, and somehow disgusted with myself, but also horrified by the timing of this discovery, which opened up a corridor of terror about what Nadia would think and how I could break it to her. I told myself that there were ways around it, that having babies was still possible. But in the pit of my stomach I could already feel her disquiet.

I had not wanted Nadia's love to be tested at such a critical moment. Why take the risk you may never have children by marrying a man you know to be infertile? Why should anyone have that choice inflicted on them?

These thoughts leaked in like poison. Nadia and I were an odd couple, refugees from the contemporary, old-fashioned and rather mannered. She could be wilful and highly strung. I was not quite the *homme d'affaires* I seemed, but more a character in search of a play that nobody could be bothered to write anymore. Our relationship was a triumph of affinity over social background, of chemistry over intellectual interests, of romance over practicality, and yet how unbearably intense was the love I felt for her as I walked through the afternoon streets to my office, preparing to put on the mask and go back to my desk.

I knew it then, like having something torn away. This was a direct hit.

Chapter 6

He sits on a bench outside the cottage, tightening the laces of a walking boot, tensioning and hooking, looping and threading. The boot holds his foot tightly: reassuring, fit for the purpose. The shoe leather smells good.

Sunlight sprinkles through branches, dappling his face and hands. The air is fresh. Birdsong plays in the heights above – local tweets rising from crowns of hawthorn beyond the bridge, more urgent trills harking from trees above the cottage: limes, sycamores, beeches with mouldering bark and serpentine limbs that unfurl majestically.

Mike has a headache and feels slightly pinched this morning, not quite focussed; but the air is good, almost drinkably clean. He has a plan, and his mood will fit around the plan.

Up on the heights it will be windy and fresh and, if the clouds blow in from the west, it could get cold. He wants to be buffeted by that wind. He craves its overwhelming mineral freshness, its heartening might. The climb will take an hour or two. He is bound to be puffed, but energy is there in his limbs and he is dying to feel the ground pounding under his legs and the burn in his thighs and the miracle of elevation as the valley falls away under him, trees shrinking, fields veering off, cottage roofs dwindling to spots of grey, while the brightened flanks of the mountains loom like shoulders of beckoning altitude.

He must take possession of this habitat and let the scenery act on his mind.

Then, Crickhowell. Bacon, bread, tins of soup, firelighters, matches. The shopping list is in his pocket.

The cottage is his redoubt and he will make it cosy. Despite the broadband connection and fridge-freezer, the place is basic. Damp from the path-side ditch has invaded the stonework. The smell of mould lurks in every room. The window frames are stiff. Plaster bulges over the skirting boards, leaving fine dust on the carpet. There are surely mice under the landing boards and birds' nests in the chimney. The building is under siege from nature and has acquired an organic texture over the centuries: ivy clenching the outer walls in decorative veins, roof tiles mottled by exposure. The cottage seems half hostage to the big trees behind it and the mossy boulders that, in times past, have slipped from the paunch of the hill. This hideaway he adores: this stone dwelling with its low ceilings and woody prospect snuggled in the crook of the valley.

Here in the valley his mobile is off-network, though there might be a signal in Crickhowell, or on higher ground. The world cannot hector him now. He will determine the agenda. More than anything he needs perspective. He will saunter in old churchyards, browse antique shops, savour the timber-frame villages and pubs. He will lose himself in the old, quiet, rural world, and will learn not to care about what happened in another life.

The landline rings just as he is about to leave.

'They want to buy you out.'

One enemy had become many.

Kate was direct, well-spoken, a stone wall of hard common sense. She ran an employment law practice from the annexe of her home in Wiltshire where two children and three dogs were forever tumbling out of a four-wheel drive.

He stood tensely by the sideboard in the living room. 'I can't believe Sheila would let this happen.'

'In exchange for relinquishing your shares,' she began, 'You get a hundred K.'

He snorted, supported himself against the sideboard.

'Framed as an ex gratia redundancy payment for tax efficiency. After due consultation your post is terminated,' she said. 'In effect three months' gardening leave.'

He had come here as a fugitive from London-based toxicities and fury. Danny Shyter, acting as broker, asked him to vacate the office whilst tempers cooled and everyone picked up the pieces. Sheila agreed it was for the best. He had kicked around for two days in his flat, found that unbearable, and decided to make a break for the hills: a time-out salving of the nerves that would stave off madness.

Now he was being written out of the script, airbrushed into a non-person.

'The offer also has a condition. You cease practise as an agent for two years and agree not to solicit former clients.'

She left it hanging there.

After a moment, he spoke in a bodiless voice, like a Nuremberg Nazi in the dock, stunned by verdict and sentence. 'Will the courts support a restraint of trade clause that long?'

'They'll support a reasonable period.'

Murderous thoughts passed through his mind.

'I see.' His temples strained. 'They want my shares *and* my clients!'

'For a price.'

Mike roared. 'That heap of shit!'

He was to accept money as a quid pro quo for being rubbished. Either Templar thought him a pusillanimous negotiator, or his lawyers were telling Colin to break his back while he had the advantage. And Sheila? Sheila was not going to play God. Sheila would stand back and let the best man win. Shyter backed Colin, obviously. Obviously!

He inhaled deeply. The process was so painful. 'What do you advise?'

'Shake and run. Put the cash somewhere safe. Sit out the two years and start your own agency. You can represent old clients, but you mustn't solicit them. They'll all flock back.'

Meanwhile Colin keeps his best authors, takes over Sheila's list and bags an asset worth a million or three.

'I think the correct answer is "Fuck off".'

'Rashness got you into this situation. It won't get you out of it.'

This remark seemed unsupportive. 'What's that supposed to mean?'

'That it was not maybe a brilliant idea to slag off Colin to his sister-in-law *and* a leading publisher in a restaurant where everyone could hear.'

She left it there, starkly.

'It's slander, Mike. Prima facie actionable. You've just put a big gun in Colin's hand.'

This statement was unacceptable. Nobody, not even a solicitor, was allowed to say this. That kind of talk could get somebody killed.

'I didn't know she was his sister-in-law.'

'Ignorance is no defence. Nor is stupidity, for that matter.'

His blood pressure surged at the memory. There had been a

lunch with Patrick Dooley from Penguin and his assistant editor
Lucy Berridge. Mike was talking about clients and everything
was going fine until Patrick decided to embark on a pretentious
speech about which literary agents were worth listening to, which
of them understood the import of an author's work and could
articulate it in ways that were helpful (to poor dunce editors
caught between the booby-traps of their mid-brow taste and the
blandishments of marketing departments), and after a tour of the
usual suspects Patrick alighted on 'brilliant' Colin Templar and
waxed lyrical on the theme of his genius, whereon Lucy joined in
fervently, the two of them working themselves into a lather of
adulation, until Mike suddenly snapped. He wasn't going to hear
this crap. He was going to rebut every word of it, and tell them,
actually, what a tosser Colin was, and how 'fucking useless'. Patrick was surprised at first, and then he laughed with embarrassment as he caught Lucy's reaction. Mike was going on and on,
getting more worked up. Everybody in the restaurant could hear.
He seemed to brim with pent-up feelings, speaking in an ever
louder voice. He said Colin had utter contempt for writers, was
cuntish towards colleagues, had piss-poor professional ethics and
was completely mercenary. Colin was the dirty face of agenting,
couldn't edit for toffee and was as ugly on the inside as he was on
the outside, and that publishers should stop licking up to him and
inflating his toxic little ego. This was all repeated several times
with a venomous intensity that dismayed Patrick and horrified
Lucy. When Patrick did his best to calm Mike down, and get the
bill in, Lucy stared at Mike with cold fury. Mike had traduced her
brother-in-law and she was not going to let him get away with it.

Lucy later told her sister, Violetta. Violetta told Colin.

'I was drunk.'

'That's no defence.'

'Kate, everything I said was the truth.'

Colin spoke to Sheila the next day, and then he confronted Mike in his office. Mike erupted defensively and many people in the agency overheard what he said to Colin.

'Lucy's deposition,' said Kate, 'is littered with four letter words. And so is Colin's.'

'This is publishing for fuck … for … God … for goodness sake.'

'"Cunt" is a term lady judges have difficulty with. Female jurors, too.'

'Wait till they see the little fucker in the dock!'

'Oh really, Mike!'

'Listen, Kate, please. I am a mild, well-mannered, well-spoken person, and EVERYONE BLOODY WELL KNOWS IT!'

He was finding it impossible to concentrate. Somehow it was unbearable to accept that he was the author of his misfortunes. The destruction of his career was like a nightmare that refused to end.

'Now is not the time for rhetoric,' she said, firmly.

Colin's nerve was breathtaking. He was disingenuously suing a former colleague for slander whilst hypocritically offering him an exit deal.

'Colin Templar is a serpent, a conniving little …'

'Mike, I know how you feel! The statement of claim quotes everything you told Lucy: "a fat-lipped snake, a duplicitous toad, a conniving little turd, an incompetent blow-hole". You slate his looks, his honesty, his acumen. But Colin is rated by his clients and backed by your boss. I can see that your outburst puts a weapon in his hand, but I can't see us persuading a jury that he provoked you into slandering him so he could somehow use a litigation threat to extort your shares. Mike, you've shot yourself in the foot.'

There was a long silence.

'"Fuck off",' summarised Kate, 'is going to be a mite low-tech for our purposes.'

***

On the map, the lanes were like tiny vessels branching off the B-road. They forked and looped, feeding hill farms, isolated cottages, or turned into the dashes of a footpath. He would drive to the limit of one of these lanes and park against a dry stone wall, and walk from there.

An hour later, he was over a gate and pressing up the pitted track that led to the first field. Sheep wool was attached to thistles and snared on barbed wire. Tree roots were stitched into the ground like awkward steps. Wind-grizzled trees set the limits of the field, and beyond them lines of hawthorn marked the rising levels he would have to climb in a warm-up for the treeless heights above. Here were the last steep hectares of grazing land, organised centuries ago into a patchwork above farmstead and dingle, a tenacious realm where the trees were gaunt, and the fields littered with branches cracked off by high winds. Sheep huddled in far corners. Wild horses stood proud in the contrasty light as he progressed along the field's edge, taking in the cinema-vision splendour of the ridge and the features of a landscape you could never remember in all its grandeur: the ash stands and decrepit field-gates, the collapsed stone walls clawed at by tree roots, the bunkers where half a tonne of soil and rock had loosed and spilt down a gulley; and there, high above – visible through the grizzled beams of a sycamore – a preview of the drama to come: a ravine that seemed to plunge from unseen heights to disastrous depths, covered in scree, and fringed by escarpments of fir half torn away by the cascade.

He pressed on under the final canopy. His legs were strong. He was determined to conquer this mountain, to command great reaches of spectacular solitude, to rise above the slings and arrows and brickbats of outrageous fortune, and as he began to pant, and felt the rhythm of the walk jolting him, and kept in his sight the magnitude of what opened out beyond that canopy – an immensity of bracken sheering off to unseen heights – he felt a thread of joy he could grip like a cable that would haul him up those ankle-twisting ruts and slopes towards a fabulous panorama, a place of inordinate vantage occupied before and now to be reclaimed that would shiver his soul and leave him gasping; and as he climbed yet higher, he came to a knoll where a hiker could turn and gaze at the incredible view, a breathtaking moment in which landmark hills on the drive from Llanbedr subsided at his feet like stepping stones, and the fields he had crossed ran into each other and streamed down the valley, lapping at the sides of the mountains, veering and sinking in the grooves of hills; and as he stood there, flushed, the wind in his hair, light-fringed clouds apocalyptically lowering, the peaks of the Brecon Beacons rising in the west, the bottle-green undulations of Welsh farmland spreading as far as the eye could see, he felt the tears coming, an uncontrollable welling. He was wracked with emotion, riven with sorrow. He started to weep, and when the damp of the rain mixed with tears on his cheeks, he felt he had come to the end of a dismal phase of his life, and could bear it no more. Everything must change, he must change, and he sank to the ground and let the rain soothe his burning face and tormented soul; and then his mobile rang.

Nadia?

She had received his letter.

Nadia!

Where was she?

Nadia?

Was he OK?

A wash of feeling overcame him.

She had called him at last!

'Mike,' she said. 'Oh, Mike!'

The letter had arrived.

She had picked up the phone.

His heart was hammering.

'I'm …' He wanted to describe this cataclysm of heaven and earth as though it was part of what they shared.

'Listen,' she said. 'Mike. There's something I need to tell you.'

'Nadia, I'm always going to love you.'

He cradled the phone, moved his weight into a better position.

The line was breaking up.

Wind came in sidelong gusts against his face.

'Mike, I'm … I'm … I'm …'

A revolution of joy struck him in the heart.

'You're pregnant?'

'I'm engaged.'

The sky was wide and frightening.

'James Woodruff proposed to me on Saturday. I accepted. Mike, I didn't want you to hear this from anyone else.'

James Woodruff; thirty-nine; hedge-fund manager.

The line ran open.

'I'm really sorry,' she said.

He lay there, on the grass. Some bird was twittering in the sky above.

An age seemed to pass.

'Lots of love, Mike.'

She rang off.

Chapter 7

I had always liked Crickhowell – a well-appointed little town on the edge of Beacon wilderness. It nestled at the base of Crug Hywel – a flat summit of the Black Mountains – and faced the light-collecting warmth of the Usk valley. The Bear Hotel conjured a history of tourism at this last gatepost between anglicised Powys and the heart of Wales, and the elegant Georgian townhouses along the high street evoked a prosperity and respectability which, in the context of the formidable landscape beyond, was reassuring. I suppose I had remembered the Dragon Hotel, with its bay windows and boxed shrubs on cobbles; also the pillars of the Corn Exchange, possibly the white street shops with the characteristic black stripe between first floor windows; but nothing had prepared me for the bijou prettification of the high street with its cafes and galleries and clothes shops. The period fixtures of an historically elegant town – the clock above the town hall, pediments of Virginia creeper fanning beneath first-floor windows, black palings fronting townhouses – were now enhanced, if that is the word, by deluxe shops offering retail relief to the Bear's moneyed guests, and to second home owners who had bought cottages in the area after the property price crash and needed a Primrose Hill facsimile to absorb their spending urges and house and garden fantasies. I won't say all these observations came to me with crystalline clarity as I dragged myself out of the car and walked past the ironmongers towards the butchers – I felt like a car-crash victim – but I could sense something in the air.

I was trying to keep going, of course. Bits of me had been blown off, I was reeling between shell-shock and sharp pain, but had a plan and would stick to it doggedly – getting groceries and provisions for the cottage. The knowledge of certain truths is a cognitive blow first and then a slow-acting emotional poison. More sickness would unfold. Meanwhile, what remained of the functioning Mike had to get in new potatoes and streaky bacon.

In the butcher's I tried to think about French mustard and some local form of pork pie. Odd shapes of pasta struck me at eye level. There were blocks of cheese, cuts of meat, fine wines reaching for my palm. I turned in the bustle by the counter amidst brusque Welsh ma'ams with shopping baskets and crew-cut lads. There was a blur of service going on, much weighing and chopping, three aproned men smiling and serving, and lots of broad-fingered management of sausages and twirling of paper bags behind the counter.

I had waited years, I realised. Nadia's fiancé had betrothed her in weeks.

I stood outside the shop in the street.

I remember the taunting beauty of the light. In the prettiness of an old village was a gorgeous indifference. The hills beyond, even the sedate traffic, the empty pallets on the kerb, the spry accents and footstep echo signalled the cheery continuance of quotidian life. Crickhowell belonged to the light of heart.

The graveyard was set behind the high street on falling ground.

The church seemed to snuggle into the slope, allowing the sky in, casting open – beyond the west side – a view of the hills over the valley. Cow parsley flourished on the verge. Clematis ran up the wire of a telegraph pole. I pushed open the gate and felt the warmth of the sun on my face.

I sauntered along the paths between headstones, treading gently, carefully, as if soaking into my soles the blind quietude of the oblivious dead. Headstone inscriptions crossed my lips: '*Resting where no shadows fall ... The peace that passeth all understanding ... To have, to hold, to lose, and when God wills to find.*' On the grave of a nine-month-old baby: '*Jesus called a little child to him.*'

Was it the pathetic sight of a tiny grave that brought tears to my eyes or the straining for consolation in these stock phrases, known to every stonemason: the poetry of coping? Each grave memorialised an intense sorrow. How could one not be moved by the lying place of a couple separated by the husband's premature death for forty years and then, in 1916, on the passing of his widow '*Reunited Again*'?

The leaves of the trees were shiny in the afternoon light. Even the grass glinted. I sat down on a bench and closed my eyes.

The speed of Nadia's engagement was an absolute revelation. It was like the key to something not understood before. I had been thinking that it was wrong of her not to marry me, despite my problem. Anyone capable of real love would have stood by me. I had told her the results, all the doctor said, and then not proposed (in order to give her space and time). She was completely unable to manage any kind of spontaneous reassurance, though I could allow for that. I hoped she would weigh her feelings, realise that I was the most important thing and then, when the signs were right, agree to get married. I honestly expected redemption from this curse. Even when she broke it off – about two months later – I couldn't believe the finality. We were so used to each other that separation seemed the surest means to bring us together again; and besides, Nadia was not exactly easy. I was one of very few men that had figured out how to fit in with her. I accepted her foibles and loved her for what she was: an intensely feminine creature with bad nerves and a quick mind. She needed me, surely, as much as I needed her.

The truth was now glaring, like the stark reality of a firing squad from the prisoner's point of view. My years of devotion were written off, and a man who thought himself blessed and happily coupled had nothing. It seemed cruel and impossible, but this was the reality and, as I sat with my hands in my pockets, it felt as though the fuse of insanity had been lit.

I mean, had I just been some kind of scratching post for a housebound cat? Were Nadia's pleasurings of me just pretty little lollipops for being good? Was I only ever a man in tow, a playmate and fashion accessory and diverting convenience until something better cropped up? Was her love a kind of emotional trying on of certain lifestyle options and domestic postures?

I was struck by the beauty of the light in that graveyard. Every particular leaf and grass blade, every fissure of bark, every incised letter on every headstone seemed to have its own etched shadow in the falling sidelight, and at the same time there was a halo of gold, a late-afternoon radiance in the crowns of the trees and on the warm stone of the church. As I fastened on the pink spray of a sprout of valerian, its colours dissolved in a glaze of rage, till all was blurred, and I had to smudge the tears away with the back of my hand. I waited long minutes as the welling came and went and an ache spread through my back and shoulders, and the breeze dried my cheeks. I understood nothing, I realised, nothing at all.

It was time to head back to the car and off to the petrol station. I had no idea how things would go at the cottage. Probably it was stupid to be alone in the middle of nowhere at such a time. I would need to navigate the flack and junk and heartache with a routine: long walks on the mountains, pub visits, diary-writing. The world makes a fool of you and you just have to plod on.

I was plodding into the high street when I saw Madelin Farrell.

She was ten feet away, standing like an art-world Posh Becks before a shop window. Her attention seemed glued to a luxury item.

I checked myself and pulled back into the alley.

The feeling of dread was overwhelming. Vince had to be somewhere close.

I could escape down the alley and hang a right, or I could let her pass and slip off the other way. I felt queasy. What the hell were they doing in Crickhowell?

I hurried off down the alley, slipped along the cemetery path and joined a lane opposite the hotel. It felt very feeble to be sneaking away like this, but I was in no state to meet Vince. I dropped my shopping bags in the boot of the car and clambered into the driving seat. Then I saw her in the rear-view mirror; then in the side mirror. She was walking along the pavement towards the car.

With bated breath I watched Madelin grow larger in the wing mirror, her flowing approach, the groomed hair falling around her face, the shades, the cheekbones, and the hint of faint distraction or even aimlessness that went with being a metropolitan female in a Welsh village a million miles from her usual hunting grounds. As she drew closer and I gazed in suspense at the approach of her image, I could see she looked older, less vivid – due to a fading in the overall colour scheme.

Vince was nowhere to be seen.

She was reaching for her keys, a handbag moment. For a few frozen seconds I stared through the windscreen as she went between my bonnet and the back of her car, glancing over my roof to see if the road was clear, and then impulse got the better of me, and with a burst of energy I sprang from the Peugeot.

'Madelin!'

She looked at me in astonishment.

'Mike!'

Without breaking a beat we both declared: 'What are you doing here?'

Five minutes later we were sitting outside the Number 18 Café at a table in the alleyway, a pot of Earl Grey between us.

***

It was fundamentally good to see her again; just to look at her, actually. She was a more mature prospect these days, the skin a tad less perfect, but even so, her glamour, the line of her jaw against falling hair, the forbidden fruit of a mouth that offered itself like some edible treat between the tip of her nose and the curve of her chin all contributed to the sense of a woman going strong in the prime of her life, a woman with assets and attitude and enduring grace. What struck me afresh was the toughness of her thinking. She was so unsentimental where ideas were concerned. As a result, you never knew which to prize more: her originality or her honesty. Her presence was a merciful tonic, of that I was sure.

There was catching up to do. For example, I had no idea that the Savages had moved to the Black Mountains and were part of an emigré set based around the Hay Festival. The London house was rented out and cash-flowing a mortgage on a cottage in the hills. It was typical that Vince should get the dream he wanted, when he wanted it, and be able to snap up other people's lifestyle fantasies before they realised they couldn't afford them.

'How wonderful,' I said, with faux-worldly enthusiasm for other people's projects. 'I just can't believe you've left London.'

She sipped the froth of her cappuccino. 'Vincent wanted to get away from all the black people.'

'You're not serious!'

'Multi-culturalism and other nasties.'

I was surprised at this. Was the unsavoury Little Englander sentiment a new pose of Vince's, a kind of liberal-baiting honesty? 'I thought he was a junky for the urban experience.'

'Apparently some drug dealer cut him up on the Kentish Town Road and that was that.'

I nodded. The imputation of racism was striking. 'How does Vince cope without book launches and film previews and *Guardian* parties?'

'What was his last phrase?' She paused to remember. 'Oh yes. "The Tosseratti."'

'Ah.' It was a neat little coinage and it would doubtless include me. 'But Madelin, this is hardly *your* scene.'

'I'm fine with it. I applaud novelty,' she said, smiling gamely.

'Applaud' was very droll.

'He's bricked you up in a Rapunzel's Tower.'

'Vince has locked me away in the Black Mountains to stop me flirting with hunky young publishing editors.'

'I'm sure there are some lusty young Celts who'll appreciate your charms,' I said, smiling.

'Farm boys, bikers, shepherds, bartenders. The place is seething

98

with male talent. They don't call it Hay for nothing.' She nodded.

Already I was feeling better. I scrabbled out a cigarette and lit up, blowing away a few cobwebs. Yes, I had started smoking again. The equation still befuddled me. These guys thrived on party networking and entertaining, not rural retreat. 'What do you do for company out here?'

She pulled out a cigarette from the pack and held it, *trés chic* and debonair. 'Wild animals, sheep. A daughter in league with the devil.'

'You're not bored?'

'No. I love it. I run a life-drawing group. There are quite a few writers and painters who've done the same thing. Media refugees, alternative types, some quite groovy rustic lunatics and curmudgeons to spice things up. I just get on with the painting and pass the childcare buck to Vince whenever I can.'

Evidently, she was in very good form. It was nice to see somebody in good form.

'You are painting?'

She gestured at the cigarette lighter in my hand.

'I'm embarrassingly productive.'

I clicked and fired up for her.

'Thanks. I was just fixing up a show at the gallery next door.'

'I'd love to see your latest work.'

Madelin exhaled with cabaret élan and then addressed a certain look in my direction.

'*Female Bodies.*'

'Oh!'

'Why should Degas have all the fun?' she smiled.

'You're wresting the nude back from male artistic hegemony?'

'You bet.'

'Fascinating. Is there a sapphic subtext?'

99

She burst out laughing. 'Control your fantasies.'

'And pigs will fly,' I said. 'I expect you've got some ripe-bosomed, broad-beamed local girl who gets into positions for you.'

She looked thoughtful for a moment. 'I do.'

'Madelin!'

'She's lovely, actually.'

'She sounds delightful. Have you sold the film rights?'

'Don't be filthy.'

'God knows how you'd hire a life-model round here.'

'I found her in a pub.'

Oh, it conjured up a pretty picture this: some Renoiresque Sionid pulling the pumps before hearty labourers and local squires, Madelin perched admiringly on a bar stool with her half of bitter and wry smile as she slides a business card across the counter and holds the maiden's eye.

'I told her I worked with a group of artists and we were looking for a model and the money was good and would she give it a try. She said she'd never done anything like this but was happy to try. She came to the studio, saw all the pictures, really liked them, so that was that.'

'Doesn't hubby find it a little distracting to know all that's going on in the barn?'

'It would take more than a few pounds of shapely flesh to divert Vincent van Savage from the procedures of genius.'

I smiled.

'Besides, he takes no interest in my work,' she said.

I was keen to change the subject. 'And Holly? How's little Holly?'

She was momentarily overcast. 'Holly suffers no doubt from having two artistically preoccupied parents.' She tapped her cigarette. 'Quite a worry, actually.'

I was sorry to hear this. Madelin had never really concealed

100

that she found child-rearing a bore. She was averse to demands on her empathy and patience, and had to make a big effort with Holly. I could also see that in the politics of the home she would be determined not to let Vince escape the childcare burden just because he was a 'major writer'.

'And Vince? How's the great Vince?' It seemed impossible to avoid the dread subject any longer.

'Blocked.'

'Sorry?'

'Blocked.'

'He's blocked?'

'Yup.'

Her expression was complex, as if she had to sift and organise a medley of competing emotions before telling me more.

'He hasn't written anything usable in six months.'

I was extremely surprised, and of course very intrigued. I managed to play down my interest. 'Maybe he's gestating something new. He was never a contract writer.'

'Well, he needs to gestate some cash now. The cottage cost a fortune. We're pretty much running on empty.'

Set beside the woes of the world, a little splash of writer's block hardly seemed cause for concern. I was delighted that things weren't going swimmingly for Vince.

'He'll be fine,' I said breezily.

'He's in a grand old funk.'

I inhaled, as if bringing to bear the engine of my professional expertise in these matters, though there was nothing I wanted to talk about less.

'In a funk about the novel?'

'What else? What else is there in the universe but Vince's next magnum opus?'

It felt odd to be discussing his work with Madelin. She would know nothing of my feelings about Vince's signing with Colin all those years ago.

'Everything OK with Colin?' I managed.

Her expression clouded. I could see her making a decision to be indiscreet.

'Colin's fucked up.'

'Oh!'

She looked at me squarely. I could see reserves of irritation in that look. 'Vince's new book got turned down by Cheshire and Paulin.'

I rose in my seat. 'Really!'

'New editor. Didn't get it. Didn't like it. Didn't want to pay over the odds.'

Madelin's expression said it all. This was very bad news.

'I don't believe it.'

'Nor did Vince.'

Of course I was very surprised. Vince's stature seemed proof against that kind of reversal. 'I suppose you can hardly blame Colin for that.'

'Oh yes I can! He shouldn't have sent it out!'

I pondered this for a moment. Cheshire and Paulin were the option publishers, but maybe no longer the best choice for Vince. Colin might reasonably have wanted to move him.

'Some other imprint will snap him up. Don't worry.'

She looked at me with a beautifully poised smile that masked depths of frustration and annoyance. 'Six other publishers have already rejected it. Colin carpet-bombed everyone from Blooms-bury to Canongate. After six passes he recalled the manuscript and told Vince to "look at it again".'

My eyes met hers.

Yes, Schadenfreude was acting like heroin on certain pleasure centres in my brain. This was absolutely devastating news for someone of Savage's self-regard, but even I found the information disturbing. Had publishing come to this: that yesterday's literary lions could be superfluous today; that even eminent writers were vulnerable to the market's rationalisations? The idea that Vince, whatever you say about his writing, was dispensable to his publisher after all that acclaim was pretty sobering.

'Surely ...' There is such pleasure in these 'surprises', such rich, many-sided interest. I put it to Madelin with a hint of incredulity: '... the book can't be a total turkey?'

She seemed innocently astonished by this question. 'Since when have wives been entitled to express opinions about literary masterworks?'

It occurred to me that this was the first concrete evidence I had had of the existence of God. The most hubristic writer in the world had fallen on his face. I could feel my teeth clenching with furious pleasure. Vince must have been inordinately shocked. I imagined the blow as a demolishing punch that knocked the self-esteem out of the back of his head, and left him all dazed and migraine-ridden as he traipsed around the house, dwindling and tripping like a boxer and eventually collapsing in a heap. How could he have coped with such an assault on his sovereignty? How could he begin to understand or believe these rebuffs to his vanity: the polite, cursory formulations of letters that had the temerity to say no? To be suddenly inessential to the plans of a publisher, that must have been incognisable. His bludgeoned ego, like some two-bit gangster cornered by the boss for creaming off profits, would have motor-mouthed a dozen jabbering excuses and whinging denials, blaming, joking, pleading with his superego before it popped him like the stinky rat he was.

103

The whole of publishing he would have spat on as mediocrities and lowbrows, as a service industry of dwarfs whom he would crush with the heel of his shoe. All kinds of Zeus-like thunderous thoughts would rack his brain as he helped Holly with her homework, or washed up, or stalked around the garden tipping wheelbarrows and kicking over stinging nettles. A Chernobyl-like toxicity would hang in the air for days after each reject letter showed up in his inbox, reliably forwarded by Colin. And then what? Much hard thinking and second thoughts about the novel: frantic re-reading of favourite passages, which now seemed dull, lifeless, overwritten. A dizzy, half-lobotomised feeling as he re-ran various possible changes he could make that would not upset the structure, or require demolition of the house he had so carefully built for the reader; lots of loping over the hills and along the summit edge of mountains in chastened pursuit of solutions, ideas, the original well-spring. Lots of dodged housework and sloping off to the cabin where he would re-read time and again the blasted manuscript to see if he could recapture the narrative thread which he had understood to be there, if a little buried or obscure at times, but which his detractors presumably found absent, either because they were too shallow and mediocre to appreciate his design, or because the book still needed those finishing touches and edits which once applied would focus the material like overcast landscape set ablaze by sunlight.

Life is not usually so neat: that the overbearing and the contemptuous get their come-uppance.

Madelin asked after Nadia. I said we'd gone our separate ways. She accepted this easily. If I was cool, Madelin was cool. Nadia meant nothing to her. I was proud of myself for keeping it quiet and clean and giving so little away.

She asked what I was doing in the countryside. I said my uncle owned a holiday cottage in the Llanbedr valley which I used as a bolt-hole for reading clients' work and introducing myself to vintage clarets on a one-on-one basis.

'Where's the cottage?'

'Over that hill.'

'How lovely.'

'I like it.'

'And how's work?'

'Oh … um …' I shrugged. 'Very busy.'

'Mike … It would be really good if you could talk to Vinnie.'

I gazed at her very thoughtfully and seriously.

'Maybe you could help with his … book.'

Many thoughts crossed my mind. There were so many ripostes to this suggestion, so many ironic avenues to go down, such a melee of anger and rekindled outrage, that I must have looked absent for a moment or two.

'I think it's a matter for Colin,' I said.

'But Colin's editorially obtuse.'

'Well, that may be a long-term concern for Vince.'

'It's a short-term emergency.'

It was true of course that I no longer gave a toss about Vince's career. I was beginning to think I'd had it with writers. There had been so much snivelling from my client list in recent months (money crises, little ego problems, self-pity, pathetic railings against the state of the industry) I was beyond sympathy. What compassion I had left, I needed for myself.

'We should get you round,' she said. 'Would you come for dinner?'

'Well … that's very kind …'

'I could show you my pictures,' she said, smiling. 'I'd like to get a man's erection … reaction, I mean.' She laughed.

'Erection?'

'Reaction! Reaction!'

'Really?'

'I can't believe I said that.'

'Freud would be proud of you.'

'Please come and see us. Please!'

I drew breath. 'Won't Vince find it a tad irritating to have someone from the agency suddenly on his doorstep?'

'It'll do him good to see a person from real life.'

'He'll think Colin's sent me as a spy.'

Vince was the last person in the world I wanted to see.

'He's probably dying to bore on about the industry. I've stopped listening to his diatribes. You'd be a boost for him.'

'I'm always keen to be useful, Madelin,' I said, pointedly.

'You're more than useful,' she grasped my forearm. 'You're a source of inspiration and delight.'

She smiled one of her smiles, all teeth and dimples and feminine glow. 'Can't you see I'm desperate?'

I stared at her thoughtfully. This was an entreaty I should really turn down.

'Just think: *Female Bodies.*'

'Is that how you bribe people to come round and have dinner with Vince?'

She laughed at this. 'Pretty much.'

I smiled incautiously.

'Come tomorrow evening? I'll cook up something delicious.'

'Ah ... I ...'

'Your country needs you. Well, your friend needs you,' she said more softly.

'Only for you,' I replied.

'Thanks, Mike.'

I didn't want to see Vince, but Madelin's company was a cause for sanity and in the interests of sanity I wasn't yet ready to sacrifice her company in order to avoid his.

She gave me directions on the back of a paper napkin, pulled down on her jacket, and leaned in to me for one of those bosomy hugs and a kiss, and a moment later she was smiling at me over her shoulder as she capered off to her car.

Chapter 8

There was a black and white photograph of Nadia someone had taken years ago. She was probably about twenty-six at the time and resembled one of those Hollywood darlings, an Elizabeth Taylor or Audrey Hepburn in her prime. Here was a face greeting the world with such joy as if in the first flush of celebrity, a doe-like innocence in those wide eyes, a beautiful clarity of complexion, all of it offered up to the photographer, who snapped her on the half-turn (she was sitting with friends at a ball) capturing the bloom of a young woman with her whole life before her. I discovered it on her dressing table one day. She let me have it and I kept it in my wallet. The image seemed to prove that she could have been a movie star, or was akin to one in having a quality that bestows real glamour on that period in one's life, when everyone is dating and partying. An Oscar ceremony might have been glitzier, but a party with Nadia looking like this suggested the affinity between all peer groups of attractive young people going through the mating/dating rituals, finding a voice and a style for themselves, wanting to shine, to be loved, to be part of the nexus of desire and ambition. It seemed Nadia had found a way of being publicly true to herself, so you felt she was a lovely person, not just a photogenic brunette. The coming together of time captured, the hand in mid-gesture, the look on her face as she turned, the blaze of flash bathing her in celebration: all this split my heart.

Sitting on the armchair in my cottage, I tore the photo into strips and let them fall on the floor.

***

The afternoon had been restless. Kate had asked me to rack my brains for compromising facts about Colin. She said libel actions between people in the same firm were rare. Fellow colleagues usually knew too many spicy details, and if we could get Colin to think twice about the wisdom of suing me and bringing the Acbe agency into disrepute, that could strengthen our leverage in the secondary negotiations. I put pen to paper but found it hard to remember anything that would embarrass him.

Frustrated, hemmed in by the low ceilings and cramped kitchen, a little smoked by the fire, which drew badly and never got going, I found myself vacillating between the desperate sense of what was I doing here in the depths of the Black Mountains rattling around in this cottage, and sudden spurts of rage against Nadia and Colin that had me muttering out loud and going off into bankrupt trances of misery.

Kate had advised me to stay in contact with my assistant Helen, and to call my ally in Film/TV, Steve Bartholomew. I had to know what was being said, what the agency thought about Colin's coup d'état. I needed to stay plugged, have spies, a periscope. Instead of sulking like Achilles in fuming exile, my presence needed to be felt on the phone lines, perhaps in occasional emails, so that Colin might sense from office whisperings a ghost-like immanence pertaining to me and the threat of royal return. This all seemed very desperate, but it gave me the wisp of an agenda to cling on to as I sat in my armchair, gazing at the rain-flecked window panes and the objects in the living room, the circle of light beneath the desk lamp. It gave me something to put on my list as I sank through fits and starts of distraction and annoyance into a profound lassitude, a virtually paraplegic despondency based on an underlying truth, the ramifications of which were only beginning to strike home.

Infertility: what a terrible curse.

'It's like a bereavement without a body,' a married friend had once told me. How much hope and money do you throw at the belief that you will never be happy without a child … before deciding you *have* to be happy without a child? How do you compensate a fertile wife for failing to impregnate her? Wasn't it the essence of manhood that one's semen has magical power? If spunk isn't spunk but a bland soiling, an inconvenience, a damp embarrassment, where is the danger and excitement of sex? How could I go into any new relationship without arraying the anti-aphrodisiac truth about my condition? What kind of monstrous fluke would it take to fall in love with a woman whose love for me could endure the uncertainty without blaming me for the emotional hell of it?

These thoughts were a dead weight on the spirits. They filled me with rage against Nadia for forcing me to discover a truth about myself that she wasn't going to help me through.

I sat in my chair unable to move. The smallest action seemed to require the most incredible effort. Eventually I stopped thinking and just gazed at a spot on the floor. It was so quiet in that front cottage room you could hear the silence. Somewhere beyond the ridge of the mountain the sun was dropping to the

110

west and the mantle of cloud that overhung the valley was turning grey and casting an afternoon gloom on the slopes and trees
outside, which in turn made this dim little sitting room shadowy
and penumbral so that soon I could barely see the outline of my
shoe against the dark mists of the carpet, or the grey shapes of
my hands on the chair arms where they immovably rested.

Chapter 9

Fork left, open a gate, shut a gate, drive past a barn, clear the tree line, stay in low gear on the ascending pot-hole-ridden track that made my Peugeot bounce and grind, bear left when you come to the copse and proceed for a hundred yards along the edge of a ravine beside a Valhalla of rusted machinery towards the farm.

As I turned though the gateway, past sections of reconstructed dry-stone wall, I entered a zone of Gothic dereliction. This was a fabulously exposed plot, a desperate redoubt for an impoverished farmer who, years before Vince's arrival, had patched up outhouses and barns with makeshift struts and props and left agricultural debris all over the ground. The cottage faced the sky like a decomposing mask, its rendering peeled away to reveal brick, its roof faltering, its paintwork crackled. There were trenches and cables by the parking area – work in progress – and fifty yards down the hill, a new wood cabin. The smell of chicken shit wafted in from somewhere. A pair of goats lingered in a ramshackle orchard. The cottage was fronted by a strip of kitchen garden, cajoled into service by Madelin, no doubt. On the ground by the porch was a stack of rusted objects: brackets, hoe-heads, wrenches, little irons, nails – piled there like imprecations to the god of rusticity or mementoes of rural ways.

Wind gusted behind me as I stood at the door. The sky was slate coloured and blackening fast. It was cold.

Five minutes later I found myself on a sofa gazing up at the rafters of a galleried barn and feeling the warmth of a wood-burning stove and a fine glass of wine. There were people here, but I was adjusting to the shock of comfort and to the splendour of this room with its cruck beams and tapestries, and the light flickering from a huge candelabrum behind me.

Madelin had let me in and beckoned me through the cottage to this room at the back of the building.

Apparently Vince was 'finishing a paragraph' and would be with us soon. Meanwhile I could get to know the other guests, already arrived, and Holly, aged six, who was stationed by a bowl of crisps and feeding them mechanically into her mouth. Madelin looked lovely in a grey frock, and accomplished smiling introductions with her usual grace and charm before zipping to the kitchen where dinner was simmering on the Aga. She had help in the form of a neighbouring farmer's daughter, Jenny.

There was champagne, various knick-knacks on trays, an almost Elizabethan ambience: dried-flower arrangements, damask cushion covers, in fact all the luxury and good taste you would expect of a successful media couple. Yet even I could tell in the early moments of nodding hellos and plucking crisps and taking on light sips of wine that this was not quite the Hampstead crowd. Johnny Curlew, a local farmer, sat conservatively behind his jar of cider. He had a small-holding 'back Longtown way' and was clearly part of the local 'scene'. He nodded 'hello' and then looked away quickly. Beyond him perched a fine-featured woman in her mid-thirties, Valerie, quite posh and county, who apparently lived 'along the track' with her ex-copy-writer husband, Marek. They had a 'similar job' to this, i.e. a converted farmhouse with a view up Llantony valley, sheep, chickens, a couple of pigs for fun. To my left, blanketing the far end of the sofa, was an artist friend of Madelin's, Helena Gled-christ, a blousy collage of a woman with hair like a spider plant and extraordinary brooches and bangles on her fluttering arms. Helena seemed very well planted and at home in this setting, which in her presence became a spiritual outpost of the Chelsea Arts Club. Opposite, straddling a chair, and looking slightly muted was a familiar face with warm brown eyes, a handlebar moustache and an intent, listening look that seemed to be strain-ing for some sort of purchase on Helena's spurts of gabble and gesticulation. Meet Frank Jones, whom Madelin neatly, even tritely, described as a war reporter, as if that job description would put us all in our places, which it almost did until Frank shrugged it off and resumed conversation with Helena. Frank, it transpired, owned a bolt-hole in the Welsh Marches and was taking a break to edit a late friend's journal. He was low key and moderate, it struck me, for someone who knew so much of the world, but if I suspected him of a wish to take this group on its own terms and to omit all reference to world affairs in deference to local gossip – because you couldn't broach subjects like Syria and Afghanistan without taking over the whole dinner party – I was soon to be corrected.

The prospect of seeing Vince was darkly unsatisfactory. Vince was an eternal reminder of my not being allowed to be whom I wanted to be in life, and I was pretty sure that Colin would have told him about my 'outburst' as part of a campaign to discredit me with agency clients. It seemed anyway wrong to be accepting the hospitality of a man I resented. Maybe the bloody-minded core of my downtrodden ego wanted to be here as a gesture of defiance. Eat the fucker's crisps. Quaff his wine. Show that you don't care. The evening had to be lived through somehow, and why live through it in a cold cottage at the bottom of the hill when there was a square meal to be eaten in this 'lovingly restored and imposing' barn conversion?

My limbic system was churned to fuck, I realised.

Madelin kept sliding in and out, placing things on the table, asking Holly to circulate the crisps, and topping up people's glasses without joining in, as if even she could tell the social mix was misfiring. Valerie and Johnny's exchange was faltering. Frank and Helena were not a dream team. She was all chthonian, bedraggled instinct and bluster, and he was too mindful of man's inhumanity to man and the West's failure to control Israel in Gaza to engage with art-world small talk: and his expression confirmed anybody's hunch that Helena was not a prospect he found edifying to regard.

'Everything all right with Vinnie?' said Frank to Madelin.

Valerie smiled.

'Who's Vinnie?' said Madelin, with glittering irony.

'Your dear husband,' replied Helena.

'Thanks for reminding me. I sometimes forget I have a spouse.'

'You've done absolutely magnificently,' said Helena, gesturing at the room, the table, all the preparation.

'Is he inspired then?' said Frank. 'The muse and everything?'

'Deathless prose is pouring out as we speak.'

'Immortal prose, eh?'

'Literature in the making,' said Madelin brusquely.

I must say, Madelin did a pretty good job of playing the opulent hostess – her hair wavier, her frock more curve-finding than usual. You could be a mum, a wife, an artist and still look fabulous. It was a style that seemed to say: 'I have so much. Don't envy me. Adore me.' But if Madelin was indisputably the queen of this gathering and we her royal courtiers, the king's non-presence, which had already undermined our standing as welcome guests, was beginning to make Madelin look like a royal divorcée, demoting us into B-list groupies or worse.

I quietly asked Frank about his book.

'Oh, God!'

'Sounds really fascinating,' said Madelin, who already knew something.

'It is. It's unutterably depressing, too.'

He seemed to ready himself, to get in the right mood for an explanation. Valerie was listening. Helena was nibbling a crisp and gazing at him with round, schoolmistress eyes.

Frank explained that a great friend and colleague, the photo-journalist Damon McCabe, had died in Baghdad last year. 'He wasn't shot or blown up or beheaded. The silly fucker died of food poisoning. Fancy that. A man who had followed war his whole life dies of Montezuma's curse in a hotel bed. His luck had run out, I guess.' McCabe had left a clause in his will requesting that Frank pull into volume form a compilation of the pictures and diary extracts he had kept during tours of Cambodia, East Timor, Rwanda, etc. 'He mentioned it before he died, and I thought, that's your story, Damon, your testament. But him telling me was a kind of insurance, which turned out to be prescient, because he wouldn't quit going to these dangerous places. So anyway, he dies and it's very distressing because I loved the old bastard and he loved me and we'd been through a lot together, things you don't get to share with more than a handful of people, and suddenly I have this sacred duty to compile this testament, if you like, to go through a whole load of shitty history on top of

116

mourning the loss of a friend. And you know what – Mike will appreciate this – it's not coffee-table material. There's poetry and a beauty in those photographs, he was a real artist, but the cumulative effect of all the damage is almost intolerable, and makes me wonder what it was all about. We tell ourselves that it's a job, that the world needs to know, and always the big drive is to get the story, and actually it's unbelievably exciting living that close to the edge, but when you look at the sum of these pictures and realise it's the man's whole life, you feel kind of miserable.' He smiled suddenly. 'So that's what I'm up to. Can we talk about something else? Mike, what do you do?'

I smiled uneasily. He seemed to know already.

'Mike's a literary agent, nudge, nudge,' said Madelin.

I could hardly speak. I felt too ill at ease.

'Are you Vince's agent?' asked Frank.

Helena and Valerie were looking at me.

'No ... No ...' I said.

'Mike reps Melina Fukakowsky,' said Madelin.

'Have you a card?' said Frank.

'I ... I don't, actually.'

'That's alright. I think I'll probably need help from someone in the business.'

'You're still painting, Madelin?' asked Valerie.

Frank looked away, as if pocketing the world of human suffering he had alluded to.

I hesitated. I no longer wanted to put myself across as a publishing player. Moreover, it seemed second best to be the servant of other people's more interesting lives. Frank's brief description of his project and his friend's life filled me with envious fascination.

'Yah, I'm busy,' said Madelin. 'Frank, I'd love to see those pictures.'

'I'd appreciate a second opinion,' he said. 'You get punch drunk looking at all those images. You should read the notes, too. Damon was a good writer. Interestingly, he writes about himself in the third person, as if to get outside the maniac that's dodging around between sniper fire and mortar bombs. Mike, the thing is, there are so many choices to make in assembling it. D'you organise it by war, by chronology, as an art book with the emphasis on the vision of the photographer? And there's the banned pictures section: all the damning images governments won't let you see – you know, the turkey shoot in the first Iraq war – bulldozing bodies into trenches like the Final Solution, that kind of thing.'

I nodded. I *was* interested.

'Must say, I'd rather not know,' said Helena. 'I don't see what good pictures of death and destruction can do the world. It's all spilt milk.'

'Spilt blood,' said Frank.

'We're subjected to all these dreadful images, as if it's somehow our fault what people are doing to each other in Africa or the Middle East.'

Frank smiled. 'One hundred thousand dead Iraqis might just be our fault.'

Helena frowned disapprovingly.

Frank took another swig from his wine glass; allowed Madelin to top him up.

'What am I supposed to do with a picture of a battlefield strewn with corpses on the front of my morning paper?' persisted Helena.

'Are you still breeding pigs?' Valerie put to Johnny.

'Sold the lot,' he replied. 'Got two hundred head of cattle up Hereford way.'

'Another glass of cider, Johnny?'

'A'right. If you're offerin'.'

Frank caught my eye, a conspiratorial look at Helena's expense.

'Forgive me for saying this, but I think the media are too full of their own self-importance.' Helena brushed a bit of crisp from her lip. 'So many wonderful things do go on in the world, but we never get to hear about them.'

Frank could take this. He drained the glass Madelin had just refilled and put it down.

'How's the lovely lady, then?' he said, calling out to his hostess as she retrieved a log from the wicker basket and threw it in the stove.

'All the better for seeing you, Mr Jones.'

Madelin sashayed towards him, legs shimmering through the cloth of her dress.

Frank's eyes frolicked at the vision of her. 'Obviously, if Vince goes under a bus or anything, I'm next in the queue?'

She laughed brightly. Valerie seemed to enjoy this, too.

Frank's brow creased. 'Cripes, I hope he hasn't had an accident out there in the cabin. It's a dangerous life being a writer. Maybe he tripped over the chamber pot and bashed his brains out on the stereo.'

Madelin was most amused. 'Don't be too cruel.'

'Is Vince *suffering*?' said Valerie in a very knowing voice.

'We're all suffering,' said Madelin. 'Holly, will you stop eating those crisps and pass them around.'

Holly was not pleased to be spotlighted with her fist in the crisp bowl.

'And actually, darling, it's long past your bedtime.'

Holly had been a shadowy and darting presence throughout the conversation.

'Holly, would you be an angel and bring me an olive?' asked the whale-like Helena.

I turned to find the six-year-old standing at my end of the sofa.

The little girl seemed to have no interest in guests.

'Hi, Holly,' I smiled warmly at her.

'You're a bad man.'

This was something of a surprise.

Madelin gave her a stony look, but then turned her attention to Frank who was mumbling conspiratorially.

'So you're a literary agent?' said Helena in a velvet-smooth voice.

I glanced at her nervously. Holly was glowering at me – I had no idea why. (It later turned out that, thanks to Colin, she had an animus against agents – akin to bunyips, jabberwockies and other incarnations of pestering evil in the family mythology.)

'So Holly,' I said, as graciously as possible. 'What's your favourite subject at school?'

'Boring.'

'Holly!' said Madelin.

'Um … do you have a favourite book?'

'Mummy, when are the people leaving?'

Mummy was not to be diverted by this and studiously ignored her. Holly countered by plonking herself on the sofa between me and Helena, directing malevolent stares at all and sundry. She looked like a pocket version of the Mona Lisa on an off-day: centre-parted hair falling around a plump, pugnacious face with a sharp nose and a tight mouth.

'So …' I tried again.

'I'm not talking to you.'

Madelin later shared her worries about Holly – going through a 'dreadful phase' and beyond the reach of blackmail or bribery. She was a mistress of the monosyllabic answer, as in 'Fine' or

'Weird'. She made uncharitable remarks, walked past people without saying 'hello', avoided eye contact with moral superiors, resentfully misused cutlery, binged on tomato ketchup. And now, to cap it all, the six-year-old was writing horror stories. Holly was truly a charm-free zone, and yet I had some sympathy for any child growing up between the diverging agendas of Vince and Madelin. Alarming, annoying, shockingly rude – Holly had achieved the primary objective of any inconvenient child – to command attention. She was probably fundamentally cross with her parents. Seeing her in a room with Madelin, whose face changed subtly when addressing and dealing with her – to a sort of negative territorial glower as if Holly were a squatter or alien – made it clear that Madelin's former promiscuity had nothing to do with sublimated maternal drive or baby-making zeal. It was easy to read Holly's temperament as the outcome of a jagged mental space between Vince and Madelin: child in the form of war zone.

'You'll get beheaded,' she said to Frank, chiselling his attention away from her mum.

Frank laughed. 'Be careful what you wish for. It may come true.'

'Hope it does.'

Frank gave her a direct 'you don't impress me, young lady' type look which was moderately effective.

The other grown-ups struggled for a moment to overcome their embarrassment. We were mystified by her rudeness.

'Alright, shall we just get on with dinner?' said Madelin.

'We can't start without him,' said Valerie.

'That's turning into one very long paragraph,' said Frank.

'I'll bet Johnny could eat a horse,' said Madelin. 'You've been up since the crack of dawn.'

Johnny looked up at her with a good-natured smile. He was not going to deny it.

'Here's a thought,' said Frank. 'Holly, shall we bet the others that we can get your dad over here in less than two minutes?'

Holly was not opposed to the suggestion.

'Would you be part of the plan?'

'OK.' She was suddenly perky.

'Pop along to his cabin and stick your head in the door and say Frank's turned up with a couple of bottles of Château Legrandin 1972, 'OK. Can you repeat that?'

'Château Leglandin 1972.'

'That's beautiful. Off you go now.'

Holly shot out of the room.

Madelin was very impressed. She gave Frank a wide-eyed, almost grateful look. 'Did you really?'

Frank sighed regretfully. 'Sorry, love. Pair of Blossom Hill from the garage at Talgarth.'

There was wild amusement; even Helena slapped her thigh and guffawed.

Madelin's eyes glittered with a mixture of illicit mirth and embarrassment. Her husband had just been subjected to a public test of character.

'Guess we could decant the Blossom Hill,' said Frank. 'He probably wouldn't notice.'

'I think that might be going too far,' she said.

Seconds later, Holly shot back into the room. 'He's coming.'

There was plenty more laughter. Valerie gave me a complicit 'God, how awful' look, and Helena prepared to heave herself out of the sofa in order to greet the man of the house.

'OK, let's get going,' said Madelin, passing out to the kitchen.

I remained in my place, frozen. Frank looked about him with

a straight face. Valerie and Johnny moved across to linger at the table, as if somehow helping the proceedings to the next stage.

We heard the front door crunch shut, then Vince's voice. You could sense from his tone that he had not enjoyed the most fulfilling day's work.

His entrance was abrupt and suddenly he was at the other end of the room, casting quick glances our way to see who was here. 'Hi, Valerie, Johnny.'

'How lovely to see you,' said Helena, stepping forward.

She got the briefest of kisses.

He looked ungratefully at the magnificently laid table.

'Glad you could make it,' said Madelin, sailing in with a soup tureen, trailing Jenny in her wake, who set bowls on the sideboard and croutons on the table.

Vince removed his jacket. 'Holly. Bed!'

Holly had no interest in this at all.

'Want to read her a story, Vince?' said Madelin.

'We seem to have guests,' he said, flatly.

'Glad you noticed.'

I suddenly realised: Vince was not going to say hello. Frank seemed to pick up the same signal.

'Hi, Vince,' he said.

Vince's back was turned – he seemed to be rifling his pockets for something.

'I hear you had a great day in the cabin,' called Frank.

Vince disappeared off to the kitchen.

I took my drink to the table and waited tensely. The others stood around, hands on the backs of chairs.

'Everybody got a drink?' said Vince, popping back in and looking at no one in particular. He seemed to be scanning the table for the Château Legrandin.

'Everyone, sit where you like,' said Madelin. 'Mike, next to me, please.'

We took our places, and as I sat opposite Johnny, Helena to my left, I began to feel really pissed off. Vince was ignoring me point blank.

Frank got Helena in his sights, and the honour of Vince to his left. I could see him looking my way with a slightly diddled expression.

Vince returned with a corkscrew and surveyed the bottles on the table. 'What've we got?'

He was standing right behind me as though I did not exist. Why should I say 'hello' first when I was the guest? Madelin seemed not to notice this rudeness, but perhaps she was inured to it.

'Hello, there, Vince,' I said suddenly, unable to bear the tension any longer.

'Hi, Mike,' he replied, without even looking at me.

Vince dropped into his place at the end of the table and, before Madelin had sat down, started guzzling soup and pulling bread off the basket in front of him.

Somehow or other Frank's Blossom Hill seemed to be travelling up the table towards him. I saw him glance neutrally at the label and then pour from a bottle of white wine.

Soon everyone was seated and tucking in. We were all hungry so the sipping and nibbling was concerted and conversation was limited to one or two asides as though Vince's guests were intimidated by his mood and waiting for a cue. Presently Helena launched a couple of subjects, as if to drape the bedspread of her expansiveness over the sharp contours around her. 'I must say, you've done terribly well with this place,' and: 'The parking is dreadful in Brecon. What use is half an hour on the high street,

I ask you …?' Johnny managed some local tit-bit about hang-gliders on Alan Marsh's farm near Offa's Dyke. 'He went out there with two snarling mastiffs and frightened them off, cheeky sods.' 'Oh, I don't know how they do that,' followed Helena. 'I get vertigo just going down the stairs.' Valerie's two daughters were doing OK at the primary school in Crickhowell and Madelin had some positive reports about the state secondary in Abergavenny where Holly would be going 'unless Vince starts writing bestsellers'.

Throughout Frank made supportive comments, but seemed to keep a weather eye on Vince, who was too busy dredging up soup and wiping his mouth to join in. Vince seemed to observe us when we weren't looking, sharp little glances, always void of human warmth or interest, like some nocturnal military image-finder that can locate threats in the dark.

I was probably rather poor company for Madelin. There were too many subjects that I couldn't talk about candidly, and so little else to report that I felt not myself really, and of course was ill at ease with Vince, whose bad humour dampened even Frank's liveliness. Madelin was anyway preoccupied by Vince's taciturn mood. She held it together pretty well, but her earlier edginess had turned into something more festering, or so it seemed.

I remembered the paintings.

'Perhaps, after coffee we can have a look at your studio?'

'My sanctuary from married life,' she said into her soup. 'Wish we could escape there now.'

'Has Holly gone to bed?' I asked.

'Has Holly gone to bed, Vince?' called out Madelin.

Vince shrugged. 'Holly, wherever you are, go to bed.'

'Oh, for fuck's sake,' Madelin set her napkin down and shot from the table. 'Holly!'

She left the room.

Valerie smiled tightly, as if in sympathy, but she was clearly as embarrassed as the rest of us.

When Madelin came back, she brought a roast leg of lamb and proceeded to carve it on the sideboard, whilst Jenny went around the table collecting bowls. Vince was content to watch this labour without levitating a finger. Helena and Frank had a conversation going about the Hay Literary Festival, and Vince sat with a downward gaze, steadfastly trying to tune out. He looked exceptionally off-colour; completely averse to small talk, and strangely child-like. Whatever tumults were playing in his mind, he was powerless to set them aside in the interests of sociable good manners. We were obviously humdrum company for such a brilliant mind, I could see that. Oh, sure. But I knew plenty of writers whose sociability was an extension of their need to communicate and whose empathy for real people matched their interest in fictional characters. Vince's allergy to company was paradoxically putting him beyond the sympathy of a group of people who were probably interested in books and reading and the concerns of an author. There was something almost self-destructive in this.

Helena was gaining in momentum. 'Melissa Diamond, on the other hand …'

'Oh yeah?' said Frank, encouraging her to sound off about a popular fiction writer.

'She's supposed to be rather good, but I tried one the other day and it was absolutely dire!'

Vince blinked. 'Why would anybody be reading Melissa Diamond?'

'It's a bestseller. You sort of want to know what all the fuss is about.'

'Eat shit. Ten million flies can't be wrong.'

Frank nodded ambiguously.

Helena smiled uncertainly.

'I love a good thriller,' said Valerie with aplomb. 'You can't beat Dick Francis for sheer yarn. Or Grisham.'

'That's not *reading*,' said Vince.

'Johnny, do you read?' This seemed an ill-advised question from Helena.

Johnny, who was still masticating, laid down his knife and fork carefully. He cleared his mouth, swallowed and said: 'I 'ent read a book in near on twenty year. I don't feel much worse for it.'

Vince frowned.

'There are too many books published anyway,' said Helena.

'They're chopping down the world's forests for all this chick-lit stuff, aren't they,' said Johnny. 'Couldn't see the point of it meself.'

'Writers used to be a kind of elite,' said Frank. 'Now they're as common as teachers or journalists. Any old Tom, Dick or Harry can get between covers.'

'Including people who are known for having nothing to say whatsoever.'

'Like Vicki Masters and Dwain Smith,' smiled Valerie.

'Dwain Smith got four million for his memoirs,' said Helena. 'Horrifying!'

Vince's expression seemed to darken.

'Still that's the market at the moment,' said Frank. 'How d'you compete with that lot, Vince?'

Vince looked at him with barren interest, as if this were a non-question. 'I don't. That stuff will all be pulped and recycled in a twelvemonth. Not my readership.'

'So you can afford not to sell copies?'

Vince shook his head, trying not to be drawn into the debate, but it proved impossible. 'There's two kinds of reader. Grown-ups and infants. There's the addictive compulsive type reader who reads to fill a void, and puts up with paper-thin characters and clichéd writing for the sake of a wish-fulfilment plot that keeps them brainlessly huddled around an Agatha Christie, nibbling their fingers and wondering what's going to happen. Then there's the grown-ups, anyone who hasn't been infantilised by our culture, appreciates language, and wants to know what the hell's going on with this short, painful, mysterious business called Life. Reader One consumes and leaves in foreign hotels or on the beach. Reader Two discovers, re-reads and shelves carefully.'

I must say, I could hardly disagree with this.

He rubbed his eye. 'No serious writer goes to the market. A serious writer creates on his own terms and can take or leave the market.'

Madelin seemed not immensely thrilled to hear this.

Frank nodded equably. 'You can't make the Western canon without having a decent readership in your own lifetime, though?'

'I've got a feeling Agatha Christie's going to be around a lot longer than Vincent Savage,' added Madelin tartly.

'Oh. She's already a classic,' said Helena. 'I was reading one of her books the other day and the style is so marvellously crisp.'

Vince glanced at her darkly. 'The bestseller foreground collapses very quickly. Anything that is susceptible to rediscovery because of intrinsic worth will bob up again. The boom in reading is just like bad weather for the serious novelist.'

'What worries me here,' said Frank, with a gleam in his eye, 'is a creed of writing that licenses irrelevance, or obscurity, that turns its back on its contemporaries for being too vulgar. You should be writing to the concerns of a contemporary readership, not avoiding them.'

'There's no "should" about it. Any kind of prescription in the arts leads to mediocrity.'

'But if you despise the demotic culture that came into being with the mass media, shouldn't you be taking it on?'

'You take it on by ignoring it. Besides, it's not demotic. The people didn't produce their culture. They consume customised baby food made by professional hacks.'

Frank shrugged. 'Surely that's turning your back on the *Zeitgeist*!'

'I couldn't give a monkeys about the shitegeist.'

'You opt out of London, you renounce the *Zeitgeist*. What are you doing? Reading to the sheep on Hay Bluff?'

'There is no fucking *Zeitgeist*. Authentic experience has been muffled by mass-media cliché. There's a total disconnect between public discourse and inner space in so far as it still exists. The *Zeitgeist* is a completely ersatz, copy-written swill of ad slogans, blog blather and multi-channel brain death. The only arena for any kind of personal experience is in isolation from the miasma of cliché and bollocks or in serious fiction. The so-called *Zeitgeist* is just a supermarket where everyone wants your coin.'

'A supermarket that probably doesn't stock your book, more like,' said Frank.

'All the time,' Vince knuckle-rapped the table, 'I think how to write against this mass-media identity.'

'To quote Jonathan Franzen,' I said.

He gave me a strange look.

There was a pause.

'DeLillo,' he said.

'Quoted by Franzen ...' I inhaled. 'And reprocessed by Savage.'

'Oh, so are these not original ideas?' said Frank.

Vince looked vacant for a moment.

'Don't lose your thread,' said Frank.

Madelin seemed to find this amusing.

I had delivered a pre-emptive strike. I reached for my wine glass. My ears were burning.

Vince glanced absently at Frank.

'You were saying, Vince?'

Helena looked quite bored by now. Johnny had brought out a packet of cigarettes, which he cupped in his hand, and Valerie was huddled with her wine glass, cross-legged and fairly resigned.

Vince seemed to hesitate. 'The intelligentsia has to radicalise and cut away from the mainstream. Popularity is the biggest single enemy of quality in the arts.'

'Christ!' said Madelin, sneaking out one of Johnny's cigarettes and passing it to me.

'Gimme a brandy, someone.'

'I forgot to say,' Helena was out of her trance and suddenly perky. 'I saw one of your books in Oxfam the other day, Vince.'

'They turn up everywhere,' he said, flatly.

'Somebody wasn't re-reading that book,' mumbled Frank.

For a moment Vince seemed vulnerable, even haunted, as though the ideas he paraded revealed more alienation than arrogance. His was the rhetoric of the besieged masquerading as visionary soothsaying: a posture of extreme minority chic. Everybody else is wrong, I am right. Any more sanguine view of popular culture was a form of denial. Someone had to hold the line on what mattered in fiction. Aesthetic relativism equalled ignorance and indifference. Emotionally I could agree with all this, but there was something so disagreeable about hearing it insisted upon. Could someone as tricky and difficult as Vince really know enough about human nature to be justified in saying Melissa

130

Diamond was crap? I mean, obviously, she *was* crap, but even so!

'What are you working on now?' said Valerie, almost on a reflex.

'Can we talk about something else?' moaned Madelin.

'But this is so interesting,' said Frank. 'Real, intellectual table talk.'

'Mike can scribble it up in his diary and flog it in a few years' time,' said Vince, in delayed retaliation.

'I want to hear about Frank's book,' said Madelin.

'Oh fuck. Not another wannabe writer,' said Vince.

Frank was amused by this. He enjoyed Vince's glorious lack of fellow feeling.

'I've published three books, actually. Sold quite respectably.'

'Not novels, I hope.'

Frank laughed. 'Memoirs. You see, I've had an interesting life so I don't need to make things up.'

Madelin smiled.

Vince shook his head in dismay. 'The war reporter memoir is a particularly pernicious little genre.'

'Now we're getting to the heart of it. Genre envy. Because the world is such a dangerous and interesting place, books about the world are stealing attention from parochial bits of fiction.'

'If I may say ...' It was time for me to make a contribution.

I felt the warm encouragement of Madelin's gaze.

'... I do think there's a bit of a post 9/11 crisis of relevance for literary novelists. What's happening in the world is so exciting and disturbing and morally problematic, it's like there's a huge canvas which novelists ignore at their peril.'

'That's a good point,' said Frank.

'Yes ... indeed ...' I continued. 'British writers face the risk of irrelevance if they don't contend with the world at large, and the problem of authority if they do.'

'Totally agree,' said Frank. 'How does a postmodern novelist whose authority extends to a tiny fraction of the overall reality write about Britain today, let alone the world? He can only contribute a pixel in a photograph.'

'Precisely,' said Vince. 'Reality, in so far as it exists, can only be mediated by multiple perspectives. But fiction is not in servitude to some map of the real. Fiction reconstitutes reality, and the only thing that counts is the genius of the writer. God, this is boring.'

Frank looked down, and then at the rest of the table. 'I rest my case.'

'Absolutely delicious lamb,' said Helena.

'It was very good,' agreed Valerie. 'Is that an Iona Simpkins recipe?'

'Nigella, actually.'

'Good local meat,' said Johnny.

'Would anybody like some more?'

'I'm fine, thank you very much, Madelin,' said Frank.

I shook my head and smiled.

'Can you explain why war reporters are such bores?' Vince asked Frank. His expression was pleasant, but the question was meant to give offence.

'Oh, for God's sake!' said Madelin.

Frank gave Savage a square look. 'Drunks, yes. Bores, no.'

'I can tell you.' Vince was sitting back in his chair, his head pitched to one side.

'I'm sure you can,' said Frank. 'You seem to know all about everything.'

'It's you that could do with a bit more self-knowledge.'

'Oh, really? Is that so?'

'War reporters are sensation seekers who treat human suffering like a form of extreme sport. Get there, get the story, chopper out, do the cool-to-camera piece with those see-saw BBC inflections before shipping to the pub or the brothel. If you can take a bit of shrapnel in the backside and bullshit through a checkpoint you can be on the News at Ten, manfully despatching from the heart of darkness, while your family squirm in front of the TV set. It's a macho pose for people too hollow to reap interest from ordinary life.'

'You really did get out of bed the wrong side this morning.'

'I was fine till I saw you.'

'Come on gents, this is a dinner party,' said Valerie.

'My colleagues care about what's happening in the world,' said Frank. 'They care passionately. War reporting doesn't do enough, but it sure as hell forces governments to admit the reality.'

'That's the cover story,' said Vince. 'Typical war reporter is a shiftless fornicator with a short attention span whose perceptions are confined to the clichés of reportage, and whose inability to help the wounded and dying he parasitises for blips of infotainment sends him into a spiral of drink-sodden self-pity. In print, they are bores to a man. They devalue the events they cover, and obtrude their own egos and petty crises into the spectre of tragedy.'

'Verbose, but wrong.'

'Oh, come on, Frank,' Vince's voice was raised. 'If it didn't suit you to be sniffing around Mozambique after bits of pussy, getting a hard-on from all the murder and mayhem, you wouldn't be doing it out of good conscience.'

'I never ...'

'Good conscience would have made you marry Julia after you banged her up, but that didn't suit!'

'Oh, really!' said Helena.

'Vince, put a sock in it,' said Madelin.

Frank was goaded at last. He was eyeballing Vince, who darkly returned the look – unafraid to be nasty.

'I see. You're a moraliser as well as a snob.'

'But I'm not a fucking hypocrite.'

'You complete tosser!'

'Frank!'

'You eat my food and take the piss,' shouted Vince, 'but you can't get away with everything.'

'This guy's boiling in his own urine,' yelled Frank, jabbing his thumb. 'You've no right to cast judgement just because your lousy manuscript got rejected by six publishers.'

Vince rose violently. 'Fuck off. Jesus!' He threw down his napkin.

He stormed past me and went to the door, and then turned and shook his finger violently. 'Don't come back, cunt.'

We heard him crashing around in the hall. Seconds later the front door slammed.

Madelin looked down at her plate.

'Well, really …' Helena placed her hand on the table and glanced around.

Frank shook his head.

Johnny was gobsmacked. An awful silence followed.

Madelin concentrated with glowering intensity on her side plate, a brooding, flushed, stoppered look.

Gradually, we got up, chatted aimlessly and cleared the table. Frank took it upon himself to wash dishes. I dried up and put away.

Madelin kissed us goodbye with a glacial composure. Frank's offer to go and placate Vince was firmly turned down.

'Sorry, love,' he said.

Out on the drive, in the thin pall of light from the porch

lantern, Frank tugged my sleeve and drew me to his car. Before I knew it, he had given me a copy of Damon's dossier. 'No pictures, just the text. Please read it.'

He patted my arm and smiled gratefully, and then he slipped into his car and was gone.

I glanced at Vince's cabin and at the cottage before getting in the Peugeot. It seemed wrong to be leaving them to whatever dismal scenes would follow our departure, but Madelin had wanted us to go, and I, for one, was only too happy to oblige.

I drove home carefully in the steep darkness, but as I negotiated the narrow lane that led back to my cottage, I couldn't help thinking of them up there on the mountain, Madelin smouldering in the house, Vince stewing in the cabin.

They had a long night ahead of them.

Chapter 10

Madelin waited for Holly to fall asleep. She sat in the barn, sipping brandy, mood intensifying, mounting to a pitch, and then she rose and slipped through the front door into darkness.

The chill was like a warning. She could see her breath condensing in the frail lantern-light. At 2am, his desk lamp was still visible through a window in the cabin, an unwelcoming beacon. She crossed the drive, cradling herself. He was awake alright, but hadn't come back to say sorry or clear up. He had abandoned her to the embarrassment and the chores. Her hurt she had to cope with dutifully, uncomplainingly, or that seemed to be the idea. For five nights he had slept out in the cabin, turning his back on them both, and now as she approached, with a pantherish desire to disrupt whatever it was he found so compelling that he was prepared to risk their marriage for it, she thought Vince's dream of having a cabin had done his writing no good and positively harmed their marriage. This building, so stand-offish, so aloof, she had begun to loathe. It incorporated some God-given right to ignore her. This cabin could merrily be burned to the ground, and this was a resort that now appealed very much, because if Vince wanted war, she would give him war.

She drew close along the wet brick footpath, arms clasped. She would knock on the door and wait. But still, as she stood there huddled, and felt the wind assailing her in damp gusts that came off the edge of the hill, the remorselessness of his concentration became palpable, like a rejecting force-field. Some furious mental activity raged beyond that door in the light of which she knew her feelings and needs were non-existent, because nobody could do this night after night without the will to shut out everything, and as she stared into the darkness, the idea drilling into her, transfixing her with the sense of something recalcitrant and immutable, she was frozen by a foreknowledge of powerlessness. She hovered and waited. She seemed in contact with her fate.

Clustering in her mind were countless resentments. They intersected as random barbs: Vince's claim that his intellectual time was more financially valuable than hers, so it was her role to run the house and manage Holly; his refusal to talk about child-minding and Holly's education until he could think about it clearly, earliest six months, when the book was put to bed; his non-interest in summer holiday plans; his refusal to deal with the builders; his acknowledgement that this was difficult for her and not great for the marriage, but his blanket response that there was nothing he could do about it. His novel had imploded so the rest of his life was on hold. Sorry. She was to accept that she would get nothing from him, no help, support, no warmth, no sex, no companionship until he had fixed the book, because he simply lacked the resources to meet any other demands when his creative life and maybe his career was blowing up in his face.

This was not good enough, not by a long way. This subordination of wife and daughter to the writer's mission was pathetic, and she had to restrain herself from outright contempt. Madelin felt sharply that life was for living and that she deserved better than this pitiful performance in a husband. It was not for her to accept Vince's travails as part of her lot: it was for Vince to realise his priorities and come to his senses and dig himself out of the hole and be *gallant*. Somehow he must save everything – her respect, her love – by realising how bloody valuable she was. He must wake up. The onus was absolutely on him because he had made her suffer too long. What maddened her now, as she stood in this trance of impotence, was her evident failure to control him. What self-respecting woman cannot manipulate her husband!

She raised her fist, ready to knock. Why was she going to him? He should be coming to her, starved and needy, remorseful, contrite. If she was always the peacemaker, or worse, the supplicant, he would never learn. And yet it was her role to insist, it seemed, bossily, on the emotional support she expected from a husband. She was forced to be the one who broke first, and this she resented. She deserved considerateness, not to mention fucking chivalry, because she had thrown away her previous life to be with Vince, and that was a life of many possibilities and lovers and a certain glorious power, and the woman that commands such attention deserves to be served properly by a husband. This arrangement here, with her standing in the cold, hesitating, half bitter, aching with need, this was crap. Here was she: a neglected waif; inside the hut his mistress, the book. A book! Just words, notes, imagined things, made up. For this he shut her out. For the mirror of his own mind! And here was the crux, because whatever was unravelling with the book, he would not discuss it, wouldn't let her in. He and the book were in collusion: a vicious spiral. As the book crisis sucked life from the marriage, so her readiness to try and understand the crisis – in order to help, or share, or simply to sympathise – shrivelled; and instead she began to loathe his impotent preoccupation with a thing that didn't yet properly exist in priority to an ailing marriage that did.

Madelin rubbed at her cold hand and wrist. She was covered in damp, her face, her neck. Her eyes pierced the darkness like a night creature. Christ, it was exposed up here. The weather just blew in, unmitigated, absolutely fresh off the mountain.

She hesitated. Maybe she was complicit in this alienated set-up, because she, too, needed space, time out to get on with her work – a dangerous pact. It just pissed her off that he always needed more space and time than she did, though somewhere in her heart she had the steeliness not to care; except that, without care, a wasteland was in prospect. Couldn't he see this, too? Wasn't it obvious what lay ahead if he refused to compromise? Was he aware of the danger and just unable to do anything about it, or was his behaviour a cold calculation that she would not leave him? Vince had certainly started as he meant to go on, and the implicit deal was that any partner just had to wrap herself around his life mission on a take-it-or-leave-it basis. A souring thought. She must be careful with such thoughts. Such thoughts impacted into a hard sooty anger, instantly malign, and around the mean tightness of the idea that, as yet, Vince had not tasted her infidelity.

She gazed at the door, listening for signs of life within, and then turned and walked back through the fog to the cottage.

***

He had trudged, steaming, across the forecourt towards the cabin, the ringing crunch of the front door in his ears. His rage

139

was a kind of escape velocity, a burst-out energy, uncontrollable, a hot gush that made his ears burn and narrowed his vision and left the sense of damage behind, but at last that feeling was in *their* hands now. This acrid pent-up stuff inside him they would all be tasting now, not that he expected a shred of sympathy. The only solace was the insulated warmth of his cabin as he came in, shoving the door shut behind him, and the glow from the anglepoise, and the colours of his books. This was his sanctuary, the desk by the black window pane, the rugs, the divan, the knackered old armchair in which he would listen to Sibelius's symphonies 4 and 6, as his head uncluttered, and the thread of his attention was caught by vistas of sound, orchestral chasms, vibrant surges that cracked open his soul. Here was a place to escape the carping present. He moved about, switched the heater on. He clicked on his laptop. He ordered sheets of paper, but still his mind was swirling with guilt and resentment. Why had she subjected him to a dinner party? How was he supposed to produce a social front from the epicentre of bedlam? Yes, the fracas was her fault. Let it teach Madelin not to trifle with his feelings, not to trample on him, as though his writing were just a day job, or some self-indulgent habit or shed hobby that he had to snap out of whenever she wanted to exercise her fundamentally bourgeois instinct to entertain. Her lack of respect was so public, so flagrant. A part of him was twitching to go back and drag Frank out of the house and duff him up for his impertinence. Why was he always assailed by chancers? All those old pretenders, chippy wankers, who just didn't get it.

Madelin had obviously told Frank about the rejections. That was loyal of her!

Mike de Vere: Holy Christ!

Work was impossible, of course. He was too agitated. Things

would flow from this crappy little contretemps. There was danger hereabouts. More pressure. Necessary battles with Madelin would follow, exhausting.

He collapsed into the easy chair, his rage decaying. Walking out was like smacking the phone down on someone, momentarily gratifying, but rapidly regrettable because it left the hurt and the moral advantage with the other person. Until Madelin responded he could only stew in a horrible brine of guilt and righteous indignation, and all this seemed so unfair when he had been trying so buggeringly hard. Anyone else would admire his determination, his grit and bloody guts to keep hacking away at this intractable novel. Nobody else could tolerate the uncertainty or produce the effort. Even he was grimly fascinated by the baffling succession of setbacks and breakthroughs that accompanied every day's work. This was rollercoaster madness. So many times he had stood back from it, sweated out the logic again, the themes, made new connections, new solutions, and found himself returning to this or that locality of the draft with inspiration, a eureka feeling, as if the music were now at last on call; but these spates of conviction would last as long as the dream of composition and the very next day, after a thick night's sleep, he would roll awake knowing something was still wrong, that the plan didn't gel, and that he could go on busting a gut to reconcile the irreconcilable for ever. Then he would panic. A kind of seething despair would set in. He was a writer. It was his job, his gift to get it right. He should have blazed out three novels in the time it took to murder this one. The Henry Jameses of this world had seen off *The Wings of the Dove* and *The Golden Bowl* in as long. Being stuck was an indictment of his talent.

Many times he had filled himself to the brim with the ambition of the work and then delegated its swarming possibilities to his unconscious, knowing the unconscious to be the true assembler and creator. But it now looked very ominous indeed that his unconscious had passed the buck, handing the miasma back up to the executive brain to sort out properly, which his blasted conscious brain had done umpteen times already, endlessly remixing a cake that refused to rise. How could he pull out now? He was gestating a child he could no more terminate than give birth to. So much nutrition had gone into this creature, so much craft and care. The idea of abandoning it left him more bereft and desolate than the pain of perseverance. Was this mutant effort the proof of a perished creativity? One read that in the arts and sciences you need a breakdown to get a breakthrough. Was he being harrowed by a notion so vast and original that it needed to unhinge his mind in order to enter it? Was this frustration and distraction the reconfiguring havoc of genius? Should he squirm out the cosmic storm, like a literary King Lear, submitting to the whorls of mania radiating from his shed, or take the whole fucking thing, drafts, memory stick, notebooks, laptop and all, and incinerate them at the bottom of the garden?

Vince's forefinger rested on his head, creasing the temple skin. These questions were a kind of torment. Certainly, for sure, he was in new territory as a writer. He felt very different; and he felt the near impossibility of translating this vertiginous anxiety and perturbation into a form that Madelin could understand and relate to. What he was, or had become, had no social presentability. He could not get outside it, or around it, or leave it in the shed.

He heard voices, the slamming of car doors, engines starting up. One by one the dinner guests were driving off. Soon there was quiet, the impenetrable silence of a night on the Black Mountains.

142

He gazed wearily at the shelves of books around him. So many tasks ended. So much toil consecrated between covers. He was impressed by the ubiquity of this desire to write books. Books were such a commonplace, such a casually handled and read feature of the everyday, enormously taken for granted and so arduous to produce. How remarkable that the thoughts and feelings of people across the ages and from continents apart should huddle so availably on these shelves: Dante, Thomas Mann, Balzac, Hawthorne, Macaulay, Homer, Austen. The bustling proliferation of such voices and such production belied the miracle of conception underpinning just one successfully executed novel. That miracle was evading his clutches. Never again would he take for granted the creative spark that led to a book you could write with conviction and discovery.

Many times he had flipped through his old notebooks hoping to be inspired. Something of his essence as a writer might rub off on him. For hours, he could be held by the spell of what he had written before, and then his eyes would sting with the sense of expired fecundity. He was overcome with solicitude for the hope inscribed in such writing. There was such patiently manoeuvred precision here, such nurturing of detail, such aspiration. Even in his recent notebooks he preferred the little extracts of description to the novel he was writing now. There was purity in simple description. He wondered, should he dispense with fiction? Should he find a more direct way to convey his experience?

He fumbled through his notebooks for half an hour and was vaguely comforted. There was a kind of tenderness here, a better self, a kind of love, something restorative.

He should go back now. It was the right thing to do. He should make peace with her, say sorry, give her a hug, but still he lacked the harmony and hope to express tenderness, to reassure her. He would end up gesturing around something hollow and temporary, though he loved her. The bubble in which their love flourished seemed impenetrable now, like a glass egg. He could not constitute himself as a husband in this implosive state. He was ontologically vaporous, indefinite, unshaped, weak. He could just about manage the default position of misanthropy with people, because the pressure of their company irritated him into a kind of mental hardness, but this was not really anything to do with him anymore: this was a T. Rex hologram that sensitive souls project as a proxy self to contend with the world's knaves and dunces.

It would get worse, he was sure, before it got better.

He sat ossified in his chair, mind drifting. He felt almost too tired to sleep. Constructive thought was impossible now. In this suspended state he needed some kind of absolution, perhaps human contact. Unresolved conflicts in the back of the mind generated wakefulness. Through this mess he would have to continue.

He checked his watch around 2 am. A noise outside roused him, the crunch of gravel. He waited, listening. There was a footfall on the brick pathway. For a moment he felt the balm of an intense relief, almost gratitude that she had made the effort, cared enough to come over, as though she knew he needed to be rescued. He was ready for her now. She had come to him, and this made it easier.

He waited, tense, willing her to throw open the door and find him there, tortured, sleepless and in need of her. He felt like a sick child waiting for its mother.

The door remained shut.

Silence resumed.

Vince stared through gated fingers, brow furrowed, teeth set.

***

Mike lay in bed, Damon's manuscript on his lap.

His eyes were tired, but he had read for two hours now, page after page, in a groove of concentration that would not let up. Damon's was the kind of writing that forbade sleep.

'... *The long run across a cityscape, buildings collapsing, sinking to the stumps of their legs in skirts of mushrooming dust, window glass bursting, a skittering shingle, deserted cars taking a hide full of ammo; the whoosh of a hand-held missile released from a doorway, the bird shadow of a 'copter chasing its own parallel, spattering bullet tracks across a street. More running, more heart-rush and double-take as explosions converge, here, there, right, left, as he legs it, a blinding flash, magnesium white, a nest of men behind an upturned truck gesturing him to back off ... Attack and defence are locked in crenulated strongholds of advance and resistance, the enemy behind, danger overhead; he is sprinting to get on the right side of a line that fluctuates like a rippling rope. This was the ultimate game of risk-taking because you saw a reticulation of lethal movement from inside the labyrinth, everything in play, gunships, tanks, the streets screaming with a horizontal cross-section of fire, a lattice of projectiles, a total chaos of unleashed munitions and machine menace. Hardly anybody was visible. Men were present by implication of the flaming mini-cab or the shell shudder, or the echo of gun snap, or the pluming dust from the façade of an apartment block, or the light flickering from the underbelly of a helicopter – sending out death in different directions to the arc of its path in the sky, defying anticipation, which concentric circle would catch you; its thwop and jagger emerging in surges through the clouds, blown into ominous closeness through a gap in the roofline, receding to a remote thunder-rumble, a patchy monotone, then rearing up close, and all the downward violence of the choppers threatening you personally.*

He loved the kinetics and choreography of destruction even as he hated the killing.

145

Chapter 11

Madelin, I suspected, was most herself when alone. Certainly, she was not afraid to be alone. She had spent so much of her working life alone in a studio, or hiking across landscape – the bleaker the better – or sitting in an Indian restaurant in Archway engrossed in a book, scanning a paper, or gazing, as now, into the middle distance. In solitude she could resume intellectual control over daily life and the inconveniences inflicted on her by matrimony.

She summoned me mid-morning – a toneless exchange on the phone: pub, directions, time.

Even as I approached, wending my way around the curved settle that partitioned the saloon bar, her concentration persisted. She looked intense, but somehow composed. A pint of bitter sat before her. She wore a fluffy, black, polo-neck jumper that absorbed into a frame around her face the fall of her black hair. She seemed marginally reduced from a distance of twenty feet, a black cat blending into the shadows around her, but as I came forward, pleased to have found her, I could see her mouth was freshly lit by lipstick.

'Oh, hi!'

She un-nestled herself and rose. Her arms were like tendrils as she draped into my hug of hello. Always at such moments she was giving; a reflex.

'Can I get you a drink?' she asked.

'I'll get myself one.'

It was twelve thirty. The place was empty, except for some local groggins at the bar.

'Marion's around,' she said.

Marion and indeed Xenia were coming and going, Mum on the bar, daughter in the kitchen, all adding to a sense of plenty and welcome. Marion was a cheerful lady, with a plump, pretty face and a broadly plattered, booming bust; and Xenia was the next generation, eighteen or twenty, with russet curls, a well-stocked T-shirt, six inches of bare midriff and a Best Pub of the Year type backside, captured in cellophane-taut leggings that even Egon Ronay would have paused to notice before tripping into the Gents. I stood here, fingering my change as the mother/daughter time-lapse criss-crossed in front of me, conjuring a world of juicy sirloin steaks and buxom service, of girthy arms hauling beer levers, of chunky satisfactions taken with ale and best scratchings, double portions everywhere, and bend-over bounty as Bitter Lemons were grabbed from low shelves.

I had not slept well.

Madelin took care not to seem preoccupied when I returned with a pint. The pub was situated on the edge of a cattle-drovers' trail that in olden times had crossed the valley floor and passed across a stone bridge, still standing, before heading up the hills again. We talked about the walks that led from the trail. A spur of the droving route crossed the lane near my cottage. I explained where the cottage was, at the limit of the valley, and she knew it well. I did my best to conjure the view from the summit of Pen

147

Cerrig-calch and as I waxed lyrical she listened bright-eyed and intent because, of course, she could conjure it to mind so easily.

For a few minutes the shadow of the previous evening disappeared. It was pleasant to talk about this lovely area, to exchange tips about walks and places. After a couple of sips of beer, the raw, scaly feeling I had endured all morning began to smooth away. It had taken three hot hours in the middle of the night to burn off the existential rancour in my mind, the searing realism of night-thoughts that pin you to the truth, everything from one's essential mediocrity to the amazing scandal of mortality. I had wept for Nadia, too, at some point. Not the Nadia who got engaged to James. The Nadia who once loved me and was nowhere to be found in all the world.

For reasons that were not entirely clear I had called my solicitor at 10 am and told her to close the deal with Colin and the agency. I wanted out. Now I sat in someone else's skin, caring only for the present. It was a huge relief to have Madelin's company.

She kept a pack of Camel Lights under her hand, just for the reassurance. Like me, she had slipped of late and needed to soothe herself with drink and smoke.

'So you can see what I'm up against?' she said.

I had known that we were going to talk about Vince.

I had to be tactful.

'He's overwrought,' I suggested.

The traces of a bitter amusement played in her eyes. She swigged at her beer and set her glass down carefully. 'I have absolutely no compassion.'

I nodded.

Certain knowledge of her feelings pleased Madelin. Certainty was an inkling of power over fate.

'I'm not sure how helpful that will be,' I said.

'I'm not sure I care.'

'Really?'

'Are you surprised?' she said.

'Not exactly. But this is your marriage!'

For a moment she looked downcast. 'He's parked the marriage. Suddenly his wife and daughter have no claim on him.'

'He has no resources to meet the claim.'

'So he's either indifferent or weak.'

It was no mission of mine to defend Vince. I owed him nothing and associated him only with painful emotions. Somehow I felt that marriage itself, the ideal, the institution, was owed a chance against Madelin's hardening of feeling. Of course, her statements were rhetorical purges and I should have let her get more off her chest before offering another perspective.

'Listen,' I sighed. 'He's having a major creative crisis.'

'Don't make me vomit.'

'Madelin!'

'Crisis for Vince is a form of egomania: "I'm so important ... my failure to crack this book is a threat to cultural history." Negative feedback never causes him to doubt. Every reality check is twisted into some fantasy of cosmic struggle between a creative titan and the gnats of mediocrity.' She smiled brilliantly. 'There's a kernel of arrogance that I find absolutely breathtaking.'

It was very strange (and *almost* amusing) to hear this coming from a man's wife, but still sad that one had to agree. The world was indeed obliged to buy into Vince's vision of himself as a great writer, forcing good-natured friends into the role of shareholders in his success. Enthusiastic readers became outriders in a great cause: his next novel. The fan was not some necessary validator without whose taste and imagination the novel could not have life. The fan was a grinning crowd-face in the ego's palace

149

of fame. Meanwhile detractors were screened out, editorial criticism banished. Vince had put himself in a well-defended citadel immune to those doubts, influences and uncertainties whereby writers widen their sympathies and broaden the scope of their work. It was not difficult to see what such a stance could mean for his marriage. So absolutely concerned with fortifying his own reality, he would find it impossible to experience Madelin's and even harder to act on it. Manifestly, Vince's creative credo was not delivering the goods for his work or his relationships.

I liked to believe people could change. Maybe Vince *needed* failure. Possibly *in extremis* he could be made to see the error of his ways artistically, and if artistically, then by implication, as a father and husband, too.

'Listen, earning a living creatively is a head-banger at the best of times, and it's not just the work, it's your whole wonderful set-up that's at stake. That's *real* pressure.'

She shrugged, as if to disassociate herself from any attempt at sympathy.

I persisted. 'If Vince was some hedge-fund crookster firefighting a liquidity crisis that could torch his fortune, you'd be more sympathetic.'

'Certainly would,' she smiled. 'I'd be bathing in goat's milk and choosing colour schemes for the yacht.'

'And making erotic installation art on huge budgets.'

She burst out laughing. 'Where are these poor handsome bankers and hedge-fund heroes? I want to get myself one.'

I smiled, a little thinly. Nadia had got herself a hedge-fund 'hero'.

I halted awhile, suppressing unwelcome thoughts.

'Have you really tried to talk to him?' I said.

Here I was again, caught in the pastoral mode, being the good

Christian. Vince had done nothing for me and yet I was pleading his case.

'Yes,' she said. 'And always I become part of the problem, another set of demands, a selfish dependent, a parasitical spouse who wants to drain him emotionally.'

'Have you no solicitude for him?'

She frowned, as if measuring the last drop of her fellow-feeling for a recalcitrant husband.

'Mike, I'm beginning to see the whole relationship in an unflattering light.'

I could guess what she meant. 'You feel dispensable?'

Her eyes narrowed. This called up something very deep.

'I feel like having an affair.'

She smiled at my reaction.

The shock of this statement dislodged something from the back of my mind. I was thinking of Frank Jones.

'Have you *been* unfaithful?'

It was odd to be able to say this – but I felt I could.

She looked away, raised an eyebrow, dead casual. 'Not yet, but I'm planning to.'

'Blimey!'

'If you don't like the answer, don't ask the question.'

'Playing with fire.'

'I can handle a bit of fire. Bit of what you fancy does you good.'

'Holly?'

'Mike, you only live once, and I didn't push Holly all the way through the birth canal just to be ignored by a man whose sworn duty is to be my sexual worshipper.' She laughed a skyrocket laugh.

Madelin had travelled a long way to be in this frame of mind.

I knew she was being provocative and of course she was angry.

'It's mainly about sex, then?'

'Who's writing your script?' she said. 'I hear better dialogue on the box.'

'OK. Try this line. Would you like another drink?'

'Much better.' She clapped and smiled. 'BAFTA winning. Half of Butty Bach.'

I collected her glass and drifted off to the bar. Marion was sailing around, moving from pump to till in a graceful glide of stalwart boredom. A pair of Welshmen, huge-backed fellas in their manly mid-forties, were elbowed against the bar, leaning face on to each other, one of them pinching a tenner, the other clasping his pint.

'Xenia,' called Marion, and soon enough Xenia bounced through the doorway into the service area.

'Hello there!'

'Ay gorgeous,' said one of the men, chucking his chin up in general appreciation.

'You boys OK?'

'Could be worse.'

'Need another?'

'Very good for the moment.'

Xenia tripped over my end of the bar. 'Hi, Madelin,' she called, giving me a smile at the same time.

'Hiya,' waved Madelin, staying in her seat.

'What can I get you?'

She was all freckles, the hair coppery. Could this be Madelin's model, I wondered?

'Oh ... um ...'

'Same again?'

She turned to grab a pint mug. Xenia was a handsome

handful in both departments. It was as much as I could do to answer the question.

'And half of Betty Buttock.'

She laughed. 'Butty Bach!'

'Oh, sorry!'

'I can see what's on your mind,' said one of the Welshmen.

Xenia pretended not to hear this, but smiled to herself as she pulled the lever.

'You a friend of Madelin's then?' she said, confirming the obvious.

'Yes.'

'Madelin loves her bit of Betty Buttock.'

'Oh, right!' I smiled like an idiot.

'That'll be four seventy-five ta very much.'

She swung off to face the till, perhaps a little self-consciously, and then twisted back and dropped the change in my palm.

'How's your sex life, then?' said Madelin, as I brought the beers back to our table.

I nearly ducked. 'That's a bit personal.'

'You ask 'em, but you can't take 'em.'

'Well, it's not great, but I can survive for a few days without a fuck.'

'You call this survival?' she laughed.

'Are you trying to tell me something?'

'Who knows? Maybe we'll come on to the market at the same time.'

If this was some kind of backhanded compliment, I let it wash over me.

'Frank Jones is quite a character,' I said.

She gave me a sharp look, as if to put thoughts out of my mind.

'I read his friend's manuscript last night. Amazing.'

153

'Tell me about it some other time.'

I laughed, sipped my beer. 'OK.'

'Can I ask a question?'

She looked at me in a certain way, coiling in my attention, preparing me. A broad smile blossomed on her face. She seemed to flush.

'You can.'

Madelin hung her head to one side.

'Did you ever fancy me?'

I couldn't help laughing. I was wonderfully embarrassed. I reached for my glass and had a good swig. There was no very cool answer to this question.

'Come on, Madelin, everybody fancied you … fancies you … and well you know it.'

'I don't know it. How should I know it?'

'You're one of the world's most attractive women.'

'Mike!'

'Honest to God.'

'You don't really think that. You always fancied upper-class Lucinda types.'

'Well, I was … in love … with Nadia.'

'So, if there'd been no Nadia and no Vince?'

I chuckled uncomfortably. 'I would never pay you a bland compliment.'

'Any compliment will do. Pay me a non-bland compliment.'

Her question was disingenuous because she knew I fancied her, but it made me think, yes, of course she was still attractive. She had glamour, beautiful lips, a Gallic sexiness, all of it time proof, and indeed, the mere idea of her was sexier for all the years she had lived on in my thoughts. But if I had paid her the compliment of taking an interest before Vince wrecked everything, I wasn't

154

going to flirt with her now. My heart had been mangled by Nadia, and I had decided that attractive women were to be regarded as something life enhancing but very much at arm's length (particularly married ones).

I shrugged urbanely. 'You are one of the iconic sexpots of the era.'

She looked only moderately satisfied with my declaration. She was seeking reassurance more than anything. Vince's preoccupation must have injured her narcissism.

'What you can know from me,' I said, 'is that ...'

She was like a cat rising to the touch.

'You have a great future on TV.'

'Mike!'

'An artistic Nigella.'

'Stop it.'

'The Channel 4 tenders are going in. You know everybody. You have the voice, the brains, the buns.'

'You're a reptile!'

'And pretty soon the notoriety.'

'How did we get on to this?'

'Listen, if Marinda Beeton could do it ... Marinda's got crinkly hair and oily skin ... think how much more the camera will love you.'

I was and I wasn't teasing her. The diversion was tactical but also inspired.

'This is Melina Fukakowski's rep talking,' I said boldly. '*Female Bodies* could be a hit series, through-the-ages nudes and commentary, culminating in a leading contemporary artist's pictures and installations, sexily presented by herself.'

'I don't want to be a TV presenter.'

'This is your problem, Madelin. You're an asset-rich, highly

155

articulate woman of integrity and sex appeal …'

She looked at me with gimlet eyes.

'… who refuses to exploit her talents, when her talents are what the *Zeitgeist*'s crying out for.'

'You are such a bullshitter!'

'It's true.'

'How *did* we get on to this?'

I smiled broadly, sipped at my beer. 'I suppose … I just love talent.'

She gave me a crooked, suspicious smile, and then a richly knowing look. 'Your problem is that you feel the compulsion to manage talent when you'd be a lot happier just fucking it.'

I had to breathe in deeply. I looked away, dredging up some kind of riposte.

'Where fucking is concerned, I try to follow my heart.'

'Such a good boy.'

'Don't always succeed.'

Madelin did not know whether she was reassured by this exchange. She had pushed. I pushed back. The trouble was, you had to go the whole hog with her, or she might lose interest, and although I had no intention of giving her any signals beyond the tactically parrying compliment, I needed her friendship for my sanity.

'Madelin, you're beautiful. OK?'

She gazed at me testingly. Behind the humour simmered another emotion – was it regret, or a ruthlessly checked sense of despair?

'Great. Well, I'm glad we've cleared that up.'

'But that's not the issue.'

She started to bite her fingernails. Her knuckles were red. I could see a patch of eczema on the underside of her wrist. The

156

bubble had burst and suddenly she looked hounded and forlorn.

She knew I saw this.

I patted her wrist.

Her expression was desolate.

'Vince is a human being,' I said.

'Holly says she doesn't want me and Vince to split up, and she hates it when we argue.' She inhaled jaggedly.

'There's got to be a way through all this.'

'You want to save our marriage, you bloody talk to him!'

I mulled this over. It was a peculiar suggestion.

'The emotional and the creative problems are maybe the same,' I said.

'That's what I find so completely fucking irritating. His wife and daughter are just a subset of his creative agenda.'

'If one could challenge the creative agenda, it might have a knock-on effect on his relationships.'

As I saw it, Vince's literary credo had taken a toll on his emotional development. He couldn't do people – on or off the page; and if you don't much like or care about people except as fictional pin-balls, real people at some point stop caring about you. Vince's hollow-hearted vision of human nature had become a zero-sum game leading to dwindling sales and mental collapse. Soon the only virtue of his fiction would be the strangeness of its autistic self-sufficiency. Someone had to get inside his psyche with a hand grenade or two. It suddenly occurred to me that the situation might be crying out for intervention and that I might have the tools to help him.

'If you can edit the work, maybe you can edit the man!'

She looked at me sourly.

'If you can edit the man, just maybe you can edit the marriage.'

'Good luck to you,' she said with contempt.

I cleaved to my train of thought. 'You see, there *is* no division between the writer and the man. The writer is more completely the man than the man himself. If you hate his writing and resent his obsession, what is there left to love? You hate the essence. If Vince's writing has gone up the Khyber Pass because of psychological problems that writing masks, he's in double jeopardy. His means of coping isn't working and he's still the victim of forces that made him a writer. He's facing his inner demons, the usual bogeys and goblins that drive writers, *and* the collapse of his livelihood. Beneath the bloody-minded arrogance there's a man in meltdown. At the moment we could only reach him through his writing crisis. That's where the drama's being acted out. Madelin, if you can bring yourself to participate in that crisis he will feel your love. The moment he feels your love, you'll unlock his.'

She looked at me impassively. I think she was baffled by the perspective of an outsider on her marriage. She might have wondered why I cared. My speech may have revived a turmoil she was trying to escape. Because even as I held her gaze and watched her tap the cigarette and stretch slightly, as if she were winding down or withdrawing into a more everyday mood when nothing major was going to happen, I sensed a boredom with analysis of this sort, and it seemed as though she had no more energy to understand Vince's crisis than to face her own problems; and this made me ponder. Always, in the past, she had been the deserter. She left men. She bolted. Usually things were going off the boil, but Madelin was the one who shifted first, as if her investment in a relationship had always been contingent. It fascinated me to think that she might ditch Vince despite years of marriage and a child and a busy life together, because the marriage's DNA was compromised by her shallow model of relationships, always starting in a flurry of sex and laughter and

158

potent contrasts that never really blended into something new and shared. Were Vince and Madelin symmetrically maladapted to the task of understanding each other?

I gazed at the soft grain of the table-top and the brickwork behind her pew.

'I've quit the agency,' I said, abruptly.

This caught her attention.

'Why?'

I shrugged. There seemed little need to explain.

'Because I'm single. No kids. It suddenly struck me that I'm free.'

'Wow!'

'Had enough.'

It was her turn to be impressed.

'I'm planning to rent the London place and buy somewhere round here.'

'Oooh, I could help you house hunt!' She seemed cheered at the prospect.

'Yeah, and I can come to your life-drawing sessions.'

'We could go horse riding.'

'Antique shopping.'

She was all of a sudden lit-up, delighted. 'Mike, that would be fantastic. So are you around for a bit?'

'Yes, I think I am.'

'What a treat!'

'You can help me recover from the Nadia holocaust.'

'I will. D'you need lots of tender loving care?'

'A change of scene. A change of direction.'

'Ahhh.'

It was so soft and tender, that tone of hers.

'Upwards and onwards, I say.'

'Let's have lots of upwards,' she said, rising from the table. 'Got to collect Holly in an hour. Shall we drive back via your cottage?'

'Sure.'

'I want to see if it's the one I think it is.'

'OK.'

On that carefree note we strolled out of the pub into the mild afternoon air and the pleasant, cloud-chasing breeze that made the aspens behind the car-park flicker. We got into our cars and drove in train along the road back to Crickhowell and then up and over the massive flank of the mountain, high on the pass, with the view across to the Blorenge; and in fifteen minutes or so we were parked in that wooded crotch by the stream and she was looking at the cottage, and tripping up the path to see through the windows. We had a coffee on the garden bench and talked mainly of walks and places, and by the end of twenty minutes I was so grateful for her curiosity and eye for detail I felt better in myself than I had done in weeks. Perhaps, at last, I was living life on my terms.

Later, as she clambered back into the four-wheel drive, she seemed almost happy. It was back to the usual, the school pick-up, the fetching and carrying, a routine which, in this landscape, was perfectly life-enhancing. Perhaps a good talk in the pub had somehow eased her and put things in perspective.

She strapped herself in and clunked the door shut. The window rolled down.

She hardly glanced at me as she said the words: 'Talk to him.'

I nodded, and without further ado she drove away in a gust of exhaust.

Chapter 12

Inside the cottage, I tidied up. I had an afternoon and an evening on my hands. I was rinsing dishes and tying up bin bags, shelving cruets and wiping surfaces, stoking the wood-burner and brushing dead leaves from under a vase, all this in the lee of a decision I did not understand, but which left me feeling very different. The impulse had risen up without meditation. Kate was willing. She took my instructions efficiently. I asked her not to negotiate, but to get the paperwork ready for signature as soon as possible. That morning, after a desolate night, I knew I could never return to Acbe Agency. Reconstructing my career as an agent seemed too demoralising a prospect to entertain seriously. If I had failed with Sheila, why should I succeed elsewhere? I needed now to become someone different, do something different. Nothing tied me to the past.

The decision, though resolute, was unsettling, and at 6 pm I opened the diary on my laptop. I needed to work things through a little, as if to reinforce a chain of reasoning.

Settled at the table by the warm circle of light from a lamp, and with a penseur's cup of tea on the go, I opened a file in documents named 'Me'. Various thoughts trailed in half sentences on the screen, little blips of half-cut self-knowledge, rhetorical questions that seemed utterly pathetic, like ray-of-light exclamations followed by blankness. In the last few days I had churned up some rum stuff indeed: 'The screaming need for significance' stood boldly on the screen; as did 'What's available without this set of illusions?' and, hanging mid-page: 'I am not *necessary*!' I scrolled further down. 'How can you wait for all these millennia to have life on earth and then bow out as a nonentity?'

I sipped my tea. That line was certainly on the money.

I read on.

'Ordinary isn't an option. Is it an option for anybody? Ordinary means contented achievement of quotidian goals related to linear survival. Ordinary treats the world as a theme park, a set of lifestyle formulae designed by others for profit, or laid on by the accretions of social history. Ordinary navigates what is already there, tries to prosper, and then declines before the embers of mass entertainment and discount supermarket bargains.'

Did I really write that? I read another chunk.

'Most people instinctively seek self-worth through the indices of power or money, arriving in a middle-aged culmination of comfort and routine. These people get the culture as consumers. Why the hell couldn't I have been like that! That kind of ordinariness (quantifiable happiness linked to owning and spending power) has after all become the benchmark for success in the literary world. Unless your client's novel is in the Costa Coffee Best Reads Book Club Choice promoted at every rail terminus and in every airport, you and your clients must consider yourselves failures

162

because excellence without promotion and ad spend means nothing. One cannot enter the culture without endorsement from corporate sponsors. There is no opting out any more.'

From the point of view of someone newly retired from the book trade, these musings seemed mildly deranged. But then, I suppose, all careers trap us in a mini-climate of obsession that we mistake for some vital dialectic.

'There are so many meritorious careers driven by a simple desire to help one's fellow man and improve the human lot or relieve suffering: medicine, aid work, education, even politics. Why was I never driven to help my fellow man when everywhere there is so much need? Was I too selfish? Too solipsistic? Because the Christian mission – making the world a better place for other people – is so obvious, so satisfying. I could have done countless good things in the fifteen years I have been selling literary novels into oblivion and watching bestsellers fell the world's trees. Many are called (including Father), but I was not. That must be a black mark against my character; and here again, I see the secret reason why – the terror of insignificance. No sooner have you saved a Rwandan refugee from starving than God sends in a tsunami or an earthquake, or a war. One person is saved, millions more die. You can never get to first base …'

I started to type.

'No. I saw my role in the field of endeavour as a humanist not a humanitarian. What is the best that people can hope

163

to achieve if there isn't a holocaust or a famine or terrible housing? If we get past these ills, what then should we expect?

The arts.

For those involved in the promoting rather than the producing of the arts there is an underlying assumption that we help the dissemination of something people really need; and yet if you ask a successful book agent how he sees his life's work, what motivates him, what brings satisfaction, the answer will probably be those triumphs of agency (selling a title in a thirty-fourth territory, screwing a hundred grand out of a publisher) that are a function of an agent's role in the structure of the industry; things that only an agent can do well and which are more about effectiveness than a great love of literature or interest in the cultural value of the novel. The agent wants a measurable result and adjusts his sense of self-worth to the attainment of that result. More generally, he is pleased to be involved in the business of fiction and working in a field where the value of fiction is a given. And yet, when you ask him to say what has he personally contributed, pointing out that Joe Bloggs who won the Booker would have won it whoever was representing him, and that the title which sold thirty-four territories was a perfectly commendable *Da Vinci Code* derivative with a great premise and utterly banal writing; when you ask him to define his contribution to the human lot, he will probably sigh and shrug and say that it was an honour to have discovered Frank Fanatapan on a slush pile and got him published and nursed him to glory, and when you point out that it was an intern who first brought the manuscript to anyone's attention, and then a rather annoying assistant who read it and endorsed the recommendation while the agent was on holiday, and that Fred Fanatapan is very good but no Gabriel García Márquez or Saul Bellow, when you point this out he will probably grimace and nod and just say he loves the work or the lunches, the cut and thrust, because he has long since dissolved his individuality in an industry that subdues intellectual ambition to the vagaries of the market and private passion to a craft of informed gambling about what will sell. The agent is not concerned about legacy, but about a sustainable lifestyle where biz is conducted around an agreeable subject matter.

Was this enough?'

I gazed at the screen, suspended by a train of thought.

Chapter 13

Back at the farm, things had got worse.

Holly was behaving atrociously, spurning her food, defacing her homework, dialling random telephone numbers and saying 'stupid idiot' to whoever picked up the phone. She wouldn't go to sleep, couldn't get up, misbehaved at school, and produced hysterical crying fits whenever Madelin finally cracked and lost her temper. She wanted to see her dad and couldn't understand why he never came to the house, or read her a bedtime story, or showed any interest when she fell over in the garden and screamed for help.

Vince, meanwhile, was a week into his cabin exile. He was not eating properly. Madelin left sandwiches or bowls of pasta on a tray outside his door, usually neglected, and Vince was only fleetingly seen through a window when he came outside for air and passed across the garden stretching his legs. Contact between him and Madelin had shrunk to a sharp knock on the cabin door every time she left a tray. They were three days into official non-speaks, and Madelin had traversed several phases of anger, resentment, helplessness and despair before arriving in a state of black calm, an equilibrium of frustration and rage that was almost liberating. She sensed, perhaps, inevitability. Things had got so bad, so 'fucking unsatisfactory' that she had to stop resisting and succumb. Let feelings take their course, and if Vince couldn't change, she certainly would. Almost, she was past caring. Frank had been round with flowers and a bottle of vodka, and after charging himself up with a few drinks and Madelin's inflammatory talk, had taken it upon himself to venture over to the cabin for a man-to-man, which Madelin had shrunk from as she watched him entering the cabin through the kitchen window, like someone ducking a bomb blast. She opened the casement to hear better the raised voices which soon shook the cabin, and before long there were shouts and the sound of breaking glass, and then the door swung open and Frank bailed out, hurling abuse back into the cabin, and then Vince loomed in the doorway and jabbed a long middle finger before slamming the door.

***

I arrived at teatime in my Peugeot, with no idea whether this was a good or bad time to 'talk' to Vince. I felt like some unwelcome outreach social worker or dynamic parish priest called in for an exorcism. As I stepped out of the car and looked over to his cabin I began to have misgivings. Madelin might well have confided in me, but as far as Vince was concerned, his marriage was none of my business.

I found Madelin and Holly sitting at the kitchen table engrossed in Holly's Egyptian studies homework.

'Thought I'd go and see him,' I said.

'Are you armed?' she replied.

'I ... ah ...'

'I think he's starving himself to death,' she added, matter-of-factly.

167

'Oh.'

I had no wish to disturb Holly's homework.

'Shall I just pop my head in?'

'Don't bother knocking. He won't answer.'

I nodded. 'I just open the door and go in?'

Somehow this didn't feel right.

'Either that or you dynamite the whole fucking cabin.'

'Mummy!'

'Sorry, darling.'

There was a tense silence. I was parched for a cuppa, or something even stronger.

'Is Daddy going to commit suicide?' said Holly.

'No, darling.'

'I don't want you to get divorced,' she pleaded.

'I know, Holly.'

'I mean,' I was floundering. 'Do you think we should call in a mental health professional?'

'What, and feed some poor idiot to the lion!'

'Maybe Vince's clinically depressed, or God knows, borderline psychotic?'

'Shall I colour in this bit red?' said Holly.

'I could use a tranquillizer, that's for sure,' said Madelin.

'You can get addicted to pills, Mummy.'

'Nice pills, Holly. For relaxing. For going to sleep.' She looked up at me. 'Are you going then?'

'Ah … No time like the present.'

'You do know, he won't be thrilled to see you.'

'What? Me?'

'You.'

'Why?'

'Just be warned.'

168

'Why?'

'He's off agents.'

'Agents are smelly and stupid,' said Holly.

I smiled involuntarily.

'It's like Hitler's bunker in there where agents are concerned,' said Madelin philosophically. 'And the Führer is not amused.'

'Thanks for the tip, but I'm not an agent anymore.'

'You don't have to do this, Mike.'

She seemed genuinely beyond caring. She looked depressed, flat, inexpressive. Either she was so beside herself as to be in a daze of exhaustion and apathy, or she was growing accustomed to the crappiness of her lot and just hacking through what must have seemed like an endless bad dream.

'I *want* to.'

'Go on, then. Go and save my marriage.' She smiled villainously. 'Get it over and done with.'

'I have your permission?'

She gave me an 'are you mad?' look.

I took this as a yes.

***

It was an extremely long walk to the cabin, which seemed to crouch evasively beyond the drive and down the slope. When, eventually, I reached the doorstep I found an untouched meal from the previous night: three sausages and a dollop of mash on a plate.

I stood there for a few moments composing my thoughts. As I loitered by the shut door, hearing nothing from inside, feeling the sun's warmth on my face, I could sense how unsavoury my appearance would be to Vince, with what distaste he would regard me, with what contempt he would treat this marital

169

mediator who had presumed on his patience and trust. I was but a genial duffer in his eyes, someone whose professional services he had gleefully spurned and whose credibility as go-between was nought. My sole recommendation would have been a parish priest ilk of pastoral sincerity and long years of friendship with Madelin (actually, a disqualification, since many of her old friends were presumed to have bedded her). My only chance in this bomb-disposal-like situation was one of surprise, a left-field question so thought provoking that Vince's brain would engage before he blew up – even as he recoiled from the sight of my caring entrée into his lair with its gnawed bones and chomped carcasses and detritus of writerly angst.

I had to be like some Presbyterian minister paying a house-call to a village delinquent or fornicator. I needed the power of the Lord behind me: a desperate initiative.

I pushed into the cabin and found him at his desk. A monitor glowed in the corner. His elongated torso crouched forward, his fingers hovering at the keyboard. The air in the room was fuggy, sweet with sheet tang and trapped breath. I saw the withered sack of a sleeping bag on his divan, the used coffee mugs and clutter on the floor. The old armchair where he rested between blasts at the keyboard had a dented seat and shiny arms.

Vince glanced at me, expecting some quick message or bidding. The gleam in his eye was less fierce than frightened.

I halted, struck by this scene of fevered incarceration. Vince had shut out the world in favour of some half-compulsive activity conducted in semi-squalor.

He kept staring at the screen, hand on mouse.

'We need to talk,' I said.

I stood there, just within the door.

I heard the tap-tap of a foot. He was hypnotised by the text on his screen.

In here, it seemed, I was as nothing.

'You can ignore me, Vince, but you cannot ignore your wife and child.'

The light of the screen flickered in his eyes.

I drew the door shut behind me.

His breathing was measured but intense. He was royally blanking me out.

For thirty seconds at least I remained silent as if politely acknowledging his need to finish a sentence. I viewed the side of his face, feeling quite detached from the scene, as if I were not indeed here, not intruding, and not in the room; and after a while, the sensation of non-existence (and complete unimportance) was rather liberating. I wasn't here. So nothing I could say would matter.

'Colin's just sold your novel.'

He shot me a glance.

'Don't let me interrupt. I can see you're busy.'

'Sold my book!'

'Oh!' I said. 'I have your attention now?'

He breathed heavily, glaring at me. There were great saucers of black under his eyes; his hair was ruffled and greasy.

'I tell you Madelin's about to walk out on your marriage, you ignore me. I mention a non-existent book deal, you're all ears.'

'You fucker!'

'Listen to yourself. You're turning into a monster!'

'You tricked me!'

'Madelin is actually thinking of having an affair.'

He stared at me.

I had not meant to say this.

'That book's destroying your marriage right before your eyes.

You don't see it. Well, I do and I know for a fact that Madelin loves you but is so angry she's lost the ability to talk to you. You've locked yourself in, locked them out. It's none of my business and not my marriage but I have to speak because although you've never done anything for me I AM A DECENT HUMAN BEING,' I shouted. 'D'you want me to walk out, or d'you want to talk SO THAT SOME GOOD CAN COME OF THIS MISERABLE SITUATION?'

Vince stared at me, mouth agape, hand shaking.

I pointed at the computer and tried to recover my breath.

He covered his face in his hands and groaned.

'TURN IT OFF!' I bellowed.

With a few quick taps the work was saved, the file closed. The screen blipped and blanked and he gazed down at the floor. There he sat, his long legs furled under the chair, his arms cradled protectively. There was moisture in the corner of his eyes, though who could say whether this was the weepiness of exhaustion or the seepage of despair.

I glanced around the cabin, almost at a loss. Vince breathed in and exhaled fitfully, shedding a heave of tension.

'I don't want to intrude,' I said. 'I just want to help.'

He attempted a gesture, some kind of expiatory hand rotation.

There was a long pause.

Slowly, I moved towards the armchair. My heart was beating violently. I sank onto the seat and placed my hands on the shiny arms. I was all shaken up. I could hardly believe how vehemently I had shouted at him.

'Sorry,' he said.

I gave a nod.

Vince shook his head: a kind of guilty plea.

'I'm sorry.'

Chapter 14

'The need … to create …'
There was a lengthy silence.

He cleared his throat.

I looked down at the floor, hands meshed together on my lap.

'… somehow …'

His voice was level, slightly nasal.

'… rel …'

I nodded.

'… relegates …'

Vince's eyes were glassy, searching.

We sat at right angles to each other in the shadow of a room lit only by a table lamp.

'… motherhood …'

He hesitated, and then continued in a monotone. 'A husband who breeds his own babies … Not good. We're supposed to be hunter-gatherers. Not the makers of children.' He turned marginally towards me, as if appealing to my understanding. 'These literary offspring are an affront to the female reproductive agenda.'

Even in extremis, Vince managed weighty thoughts.

He glanced into his palms, as if sounding some further lamentable verity.

'In his fiction the writer reveals himself to be more dimensional than he appears through the bilateralism of a relationship. This unsettles partners. They feel peripheral.' He cleared his throat. 'No question about it. Being married to a writer is a tall order.'

I nodded, not agreeing, not resisting.

'But Madelin always knew I was a writer and that my life was writing. From day one this was a given.' He shook his head.

After the first minutes in which he felt powerless to speak and simply sat before me holding his chin and leaning on his elbows and sighing at the effort of somehow starting this conversation, he had begun to try phrases, gnomic little offerings which coalesced into a confessional. I listened with great care and concern. His candour was enormously surprising. The only thing more alarming than hostility, I realised, was utter frankness and honesty. What struck me was his ability to be both depressed and analytical at the same time. He was aware of Madelin's feelings, cognisant of his responsibility for them and yet strangely detached. He seemed split between some eye-of-God, writerly consciousness looking down at the world from great height and 'Vince Savage' the family man here on planet earth, suffering, getting it wrong, muddling through, doing his best with one hand tied behind his back because this particular member of the human race (with washing-up and child-rearing duties) was also a *writer* and thus destined to short-change wives and under-serve offspring, because such failings were a by-product of the writer's mission. This seemed to be his thrust, one which I found curiously circular: to be all-understanding and perceptive *because* one is a writer, and then be unable to do anything about it *because one is a writer*!

174

I felt I just had to break in. 'Madelin is a successful artist. She has her own need for withdrawal and creation and the same need to strike a balance. We're surely talking about a practical problem based on mutual needs that has to be worked out.'

He was thoughtful for a moment, as if testing this objection against some inner sense of the truth.

'Artistically we are symmetrical. As man and wife we are asymmetrical.'

I must have looked uncomprehending. I wondered if this was code for Vince's dismissive view – never voiced, and only suggested by his behaviour – that Madelin's artistic talent was minor.

'The burden of motherhood,' he nodded.

'Are you saying no woman should marry a writer?'

'I'm spelling out the occupational hazards.'

I nodded judiciously. 'Sounds like a charter for complacence.'

'It's a charter for *realism*.'

'Isn't realism a false god where love and happiness are concerned?'

'And there you have another problem. Illusion is the bread of marriage. Reality the grist of writers.'

'Vince, are you resigned to marital failure?'

'No!' he said, forcefully. 'But at times I feel powerless to compensate Madelin for what my writing appears to subtract from the relationship, because despite all the insecurity my vocation inflicts on her, I already love her as much as I can.'

'You do love her?'

He looked at me directly, his eyes penetrating. Sincerity for him was a risky business, placing immediate and unaccustomed power in his interlocutor's hands.

'I love her very much,' he said.

I nodded slowly. This was an immense relief. This was the

heart speaking. Suddenly, I wanted a lot more of the feeling man and a lot less of the cerebral writer.

'Knowing that implicitly,' he continued, 'I find it hard to understand her perennial insecurity. I don't love anyone else. I only love her. My heart belongs to her. That is ... or should be self-evident.'

I thought about this for a moment. 'You love her ... but you're not prepared to do anything about it?'

'I've committed my love and life to her as best as I'm able. That is objective.'

'Vince, you're an exile from the house. You live in this cabin.'

'Yes, I have an office. Yes, I work here.'

'And sleep here.'

'Sometimes I write till three in the morning.'

'She lies alone at night.'

He stared at me bleakly.

'She needs you but you don't come.'

'It doesn't work like that.'

'What?'

'You can't always just give somebody what they want!'

'When it costs so little to give?'

There was silence.

Vince's face hardened. I sensed a kind of bedrock obstinacy. This I had to confront.

'A woman needs a man in her bed.' I spoke as a perfectly reasonable man of the world with his eye on the priorities. 'Your wife is a passionate woman.'

He shook his head vigorously. I waited for clarification: was this denial, contradiction, some kind of candid qualification of an incontestable fact?

Vince, apparently, had nothing further to add.

176

'If she can't get love from you, she'll get it elsewhere.'

'You can't ransom arousal.' He looked at me sharply.

'Um ...'

'You can't leap-frog the issues, the hurt, the alienation just by ...' He scowled and blinked. 'Madelin's sexual taunting isn't what it seems. It's not a come-on. The sexual gauntlet's a booby trap, not an invitation. This "give me a stiff cock any day" talk, "a woman's needs must be satisfied" – that's not a passionate woman desperate for love and affection. It's retaliation for the hurt to her pride. I mean, have you ever contended with that level of female hostility? It's not Viagra. And I don't share Madelin's penchant for strangers, and right now we're strangers to each other.'

Vince's candour was breathtaking. The intimacy of these revelations put me on the back foot. Suddenly there were too many questions to ask and clues to gather. In leaping to Madelin's defence I had obtruded upon a marital crisis in which truth was a shifting point of view, where feelings were cauterised and unbiddable on the one hand, and fiery and unmanageable on the other; and in the midst of it all I was offering what? The lame duo of decency and common sense.

Madelin's sexual past evidently haunted Vince. When first they met, her reputation had probably not reached him. She probably underplayed that side of her character in the early days of courtship, though session one in her flat with its futon and oriental lanterns and blinds that conferred an aura of oiled, softly lit sensuousness on the theatre of her mattress, those Kama Sutran initiations must have seemed pretty potent to Vince. If what really fitted, then, were the minds, a rare event for the cerebral wordsmith, Madelin's arousability and amatory flare would have beguiled a man for whom sex had previously amounted to

177

so many fumbled shags with punk Cinderellas and wacky blue-stockings. Gradually, of course, he would have picked up the back-story: the statistics. If lovers from the past, her past, popped up at gigs and dinner parties, in pubs and in supermarket aisles, and if Madelin's emotional history revealed itself during week-end lie-ins when they chatted about former love-life, Vince must have hoped that he alone could arrest her waywardness; and indeed he did – because Madelin went monogamous after that. The recent crisis, however, must have revived the past in Madelin's fantasies and in Vince's fears. Once demand exceeded supply, the spectre of her legion lovers would unnerve him. I could see this, and I could understand the vehemence of his last speech, and I could easily sympathise with a man having to satisfy Madelin's demands, but however intimidating her needs might seem, he had the power to break the deadlock by showing he cared.

'If, as you suggest,' I crossed a leg, flicked some fluff off a trouser, 'there is a fundamental well of deep love between you, can't you go back to first principles and build it up from there?'

Vince stared into the middle distance. He wiped his nose with the back of his hand and settled his chin on his hand.

'There is love between a version of myself and a version of Madelin. Current circumstances have eclipsed or altered those selves. My preoccupation is to change the circumstances.'

I drew myself up in the chair. 'You want to finish the novel first?'

He nodded.

'The distress signals are going out now!'

He seemed to digest this. There was a period of intense contemplation.

'She's *thinking* of having an affair?' he asked.

The appalling directness of the question shamed me. 'I wish I hadn't said that, and I expect she does, too. It's the sort of thing people say when they're desperate.'

There was an unendurable silence.

'I don't believe it,' I said, to reinforce the point.

Vince closed his eyes for a moment, as though he were wrestling with a familiar form of grief.

He looked at me with sudden inquisitorial power. 'Did she say who?'

'There is no one!'

'Frank Jones?'

The face of a man contemplating his wife's infidelity is a dismal spectacle. It was awful to be privy to such intimate agonies, especially as Vince was hardly a friend.

'Vince, I asked Madelin explicitly: "Have you been unfaithful?"'

He could hardly bear to watch me, though he needed to see the truth in my face.

'She said "no".'

He inhaled deeply and grasped his forehead, turning away from me. Whatever he believed, he had to contend with the disturbing reality that Madelin and I had been discussing the possibility and that such conversations were at least symptomatic of something being wrong. What did that tell him? It told him a great deal about his capacity to be hurt by her infidelity.

We sat in silence for several seconds. I was unable to generate any kind of sincere reassurance.

'You know,' his voice was frail, 'writing's an amazing discovery when you're young, a possibility you explore with such excitement. Gradually it supplants anything else you might do with your life. It taps you into literature. It provides this extraordinary form, the novel, to investigate. It forces you to think, research, imagine, craft, refine. To fashion a book that will hold an intelligent reader's attention and add something to the value of their lives, that's a challenge; and it seemed to me at the time, a noble ambition that fills you with purpose.

'And then you get published, and a deep aspiration that comes from way inside you is validated by the world. A great moment. Literature, by which I mean the current of influence that runs through our heritage, has spoken through you, because whatever you do, minor or major, it draws on all the reading you have ever done. And that sense of belonging to a bigger club, of being a practitioner who has really nailed his colours to the mast is as satisfying and hard-won as qualifying as a doctor. You've joined a profession, but on your terms. It has taken talent, but mostly it's taken hard work and self-belief.

'When I first met Madelin,' he looked at me momentarily, 'she understood all this. She was doing something similar. We talked about books, painting, the creative process, and what I loved was her originality. She's the most cliché-free person I've ever met. I found her unbelievably stimulating and it mattered that we could talk about our work. She was a fantastic person to link up with and it pleased me to bring her into the heady world of literary London, because I knew she enjoyed it and could hold her own and, besides, all the dirty old goat novelists and poets I knew really fancied her. She could dazzle and network and flirt and get stuck in with Grenadine James, for example, or Boris Hogarth and Hannibal Chisolm, and still belong to herself afterwards. She never lost her independent-mindedness.

'That was back then. Still I'm a writer, still I'm trying to do good new work and pay bills, and it's a lot tougher because there are too many other cunt writers out there and the supermarkets are sending up the whole fucking racket, and because it takes a lot of stamina to keep going year in year out writing these beasts.

But we're not broke. We have a million pounds worth of London real estate paid for with my earnings. We have this place here. We have Holly. Madelin has a studio. She has friends. Over the years we've been to some pretty splashy parties and she's met some interesting people. As a spouse I haven't done badly. I've provided. And I've managed to write some good books along the way. The glamour's rubbed off a bit, and it's a long haul, and there are new phases in life, but I'm the same hard-working, committed person she married, doing the same thing, doing my damnedest to get this fucking book sorted, except that a "book" sounds so pedestrian these days, and "sorted" sounds so practical when it isn't. When a book goes wrong it takes your sanity with it. But we keep on keeping on because I'm a writer, and writers write because they can't do anything else. When the going gets tough and suddenly publishers throw the work back in your face, and you think "Christ, I've taken a wrong turning here", there's no safety net, no day job to crawl back into. Your whole identity's tied up with being this thing: a writer. Mini-cab driving just isn't an option. It's too late to retrain. Our generation is already over the hill job-wise. There's no going back and thinking "that was fun, I'll try something else". I'm in it for the long haul. But the nature of the problem is not easily resolvable either. The snag can be quite mysterious. It involves everything. A creative problem or block is total. You can't manhandle it and you sure as hell can't walk away from it, because you have nothing else and nowhere to go. You think, is this it? Am I a spent force? Is my time up?'

He sighed deeply, bathed his face in his hands.

'For Madelin, all this angst and mayhem is like an adulterous affair. I'm in it up to my neck with this sodding novel and she thinks I'm turning my back on her. But really, my back's against the wall. This is my sanity. For me, writing has always been a bulwark against depression. I don't know why, but that's the case. I thought she understood this. This is something I have to do, because that's the way I am. And sure, I'm in a state. I don't know whether I'm coming or going, and it's actually very hard to reach out to a woman who doesn't care about all this, doesn't give a damn about what I've given my life to achieve as if it were just incidental. How can I appease a woman who hates this venture?'

'She's fine with the venture, Vince. What she can't take is the loneliness. You have to find a way of doing both: Madelin and the book.'

He stared at me with a semi-deranged look.

'Without the book … there *is* nothing.'

I looked him dead in the eye. His tongue touched his lip.

'Vince …'

'Except an abyss.'

I nodded slowly.

He moved his head. He was looking very strange.

'Not writing?'

He swallowed.

I could only guess what he meant. 'A feeling of emptiness?'

'A void.'

I racked my brains. 'And writing chapters can save you from the void?'

He gazed at me keenly. 'I exist only by virtue of writing. I can't just *live*.'

This seemed both alarming and ludicrous. 'How come I'm alive, then? How come everyone who doesn't have a novel on the hob is alive?'

'Part of the problem is that just about fucking everybody does have a novel on the fucking hob.'

He was going mad.

'Christ, Vince there's a slush pile out there Everest high. But several billion people still consider themselves alive without having got near page one of a novel. Are they the walking dead?'

'That's several billion people who could be reading my books. Bastards.'

For a moment it seemed that Vince had snapped. I frowned back at him, gathering my thoughts as best I could.

His demeanour had changed. He was not himself.

'The abyss is a spectre that needs to be rubbished,' I said, forcefully. 'Step outside, there's a world going on. It's vastly interesting. Your cure is a change of scene. Your creative wellspring will come from outside of yourself.'

He looked at me sharply. 'Is Madelin … in love with Xenia?'

My heart beat hard. I was responsible for these outlandish suspicions.

'No! Of course not.'

He blinked and averted his gaze.

I glared at him insistently, as if to outface the notion.

Vince's eyes drilled at the vista I had opened for him. His writer's imagination took over, turning insinuation into haunting cameos of infidelity. His expression was as much computational – a fraught envisaging of what might have happened, or could be happening if he compared knowledge with suspicion – as it was pained. Such crazes of introspection show a person's dire capacity for suffering.

'Give me something to read,' I said softly.

He did not react at first.

'I'm a literary agent. It is … it *was* my job to help writers.'

There was never an 'idea' that Vince liked not to have been the first to have, but now he shifted, moved slightly, and this movement was an admission.

'If I can help, you'll feel better. If you feel better, there'll be space in your mind for Madelin.'

He could hardly risk looking at me.

'Perhaps there's another factor ... Madelin may need to be reminded that her husband is special.'

His hands were trembling.

I glanced away. My compassion had destroyed his self-control.

'Why not give me the draft Colin submitted?'

Vince shook his head, fending off distress.

'Or a couple of chapters, a segment?'

'I can't believe you're being this decent,' he shouted. 'I avoided you as an agent. Now you're offering to help.'

I was taken aback by the admission.

'I made a fucking huge mistake. Sorry. I'm sorry I didn't sign with you. Sorry I squandered your interest and good faith. I misread you, probably had some stupid ideas about Colin. But Colin doesn't give a shit, and you do. And now you're going so far beyond the call of duty that I feel absolutely humbled and completely ashamed.'

I nodded. It was quite something to hear this. 'There's got to be a way back,' I said calmly, after a moment of quiet acknowledgement.

'It's a mess. An assembly job. The Colin draft is history. I could ... I could maybe ... maybe I could ...'

He leaned forward and pulled a clutch of papers from his in-tray.

Even in this movement there was an energy that had been lacking before. Vince wiped his face and flicked through the pages, then shuffled them together. He sighed, reached another segment of manuscript off the floor.

There was no eye contact to be had with him. Even when he

placed a folder full of pages in my hand he was looking a few degrees to the left. His infamous ironic stare had melted away. His speech of remorse, I realised, changed everything between us.

'Thank you.'

A few weeks ago I was the last person in the world Vince would have asked for an opinion.

'When can you read it?' he asked.

'This evening.'

'I'm more grateful than you will ever know.'

I shrugged.

'I mean, there's stuff I need to change. I know it's not ready yet and I ...'

I nodded.

It was strange, the sense of power passing into my hands.

Vince's concentration faltered: the material, after all, would have to speak for itself.

'The great thing is, I'm coming to it fresh,' I said, rising.

He gazed at me in earnest acceptance of the point. Now that I held his manuscript he was keen to reinforce sensible verities.

'I'm glad we've had this conversation,' I said, moving to the door.

He seemed to assent, in muted fashion, to the positive note, though he did look distracted.

There was no need for any further exchange between us, so I opened the door and made my exit.

***

I knocked on the front door of the cottage and went in. There was nobody in the kitchen and nobody in the barn. Mother and daughter were not at home.

Upstairs, in the bathroom, I had a long pee and gazed through the window to the cabin. Vince's intensity had absolutely drained me.

Back outside it was cooling down. I stood in the middle of the drive, scanning over the property, the orchard, the outhouses and sheds beyond the cottage, the stretch of nobbly grass running up to the hedge. A swing straddled weeds. A child's bike lay on a pile of builder's sand. Beyond the plot, the hill rose steadfastly, a green flank pressing up to the level summit of the mountain.

I walked to the back of the house, along the path outside the kitchen. I saw an oil tank, a lean-to greenhouse, a rickety old barn with a tractor's nose poking out.

I glanced over a shoulder, thinking I heard a voice.

A dry stone wall backed the property. A roll of barbed wire was propped against it. Beyond the wall, a wilderness of bracken and gorse rambled away.

The voice came again, caught in the wind. Involuntarily, I gazed at the high branches of an ash tree from where weighty crows took it in turns to kick off and wheel about and land back in their nests.

At the head of the drive stood a creosoted barn. I walked towards it, snooping from one building to the next.

The padlock was clipped, but it hung on the ring behind the latch. I pulled on a screw standing in for a knob and the door swung open. Inside was a velvet screen, draught-proofing the space beyond. Though my entry was concealed by the screen, I could see a halogen lamp angled from the rafters above. The door fell to.

'Like this?'

'Yes … um …'

My ears strained.

The air was warmer in here.

'Sit up a bit.'

I could smell oil paint, and feel warmth from the lamp.

There was a concentrated silence.

Somebody sniffed. A chair creaked.

Madelin was in mid-session.

I stared at the curtain of material that hung before me.

'Xenia ...'

I listened.

'Hold still.'

There was a flash.

'Oh.'

Someone giggled.

'Whoops. Flash off.'

'Again.'

'Yah ... Maybe you can ... can you make it stick out more?'

There was silence for a few seconds.

My heart was picking up a few beats. I should either have declared myself or withdrawn.

'Just sort of relaxed, offering.' Madelin laughed. 'But couldn't give a fuck. You just *are*.'

'Like ...'

'That's lovely. Great boobs.'

A shutter clicked. There were footsteps. Madelin seemed to be moving towards me.

I stood back, reached for the door; as I reversed, I saw a chink of light where two sections of the curtain had parted.

'Now, if we turn down this lamp ... Are you warm enough?'

Very slowly, I moved towards the opening in the curtain. I stood with parched breath inches from the material. With my fingers in the fold where the gap opened I was able to part the

187

curtains a fraction more. As the aperture widened, the slice of light before my eye resolved into a view of a studio floor with a pair of easels and a trestle-table cluttered with paint paraphernalia, and as I manipulated the curtain to tilt the angle, I could see five feet away Xenia's bright naked body leaning back with Godiva-like ease against the props of her arms, Madelin behind her, her black hair trailing as she pushed her hand into the small of Xenia's back.

'As if launching yourself into a sort of massive bedroom bathed in morning light …'

Her voice was amplified by the empty resonance of the barn.

I swallowed, momentarily transfixed.

'Here. Let me …'

Madelin drove her hand into Xenia's curly hair, lifting, mussing it, and Xenia's head rocked loosely.

I gazed at her white thighs, at the dent of her navel, at the pendant liberated breasts, at the flop of hair driven forward by Madelin's grasp; and at Madelin's veiled look as she reset Xenia's head and returned to the tripod to check the pose.

Xenia welcomed the camera lens, the black eye pointing at her body. She yielded more, moving her shoulders, expressing her physique for Madelin's silent capture, chin raised, thighs grazing each other, breasts reasserted by the arch of her back.

I stepped back from the curtain, heart palpitating.

Moments later I sat in my Peugeot, Vince's folder of work by me on the passenger seat, and with a dry mouth I started the car, got into gear, and as quickly and deftly as I could, let the car roll down the drive and out through the gates, as if I had stepped from his cabin and left without further ado.

The ruts and bumps of the track, unavoidable and jarring, I hardly noticed. Not even the sight of little Holly, playing between stinging nettles and the spokes of some rusty piece of farm machinery perforated my distraction.

She ignored me as the car passed, and it was only a sudden coming-to that made me wave at her.

Chapter 15

Ipoked around in the cottage doing this and that, making tea, lighting the fire, plumping cushions, emptying groceries onto shelves, drawing curtains, attacking the smell of mildew with various air-fresheners, and readying the laptop on the side-table in the living room. Vince's manuscript sat on the coffee table. I had pulled out a pack of streaky bacon and a baking potato for dinner, and there was at least the prospect of a fireside read to get me through the evening. I fought the mild sense of claustro-phobia and switched on as many lamps as possible to warm the place up, and after the bachelor ritual of dinner – potato skins scraped into the bin, dish washed, pan in soak – I took my coffee mug next door and headed to the armchair where I slumped in the seat with a pencil and Vince's book.

I had absolutely no interest in reading. I was 'Vinced' to the gills and far too preoccupied to grant his demanding intelligence yet more attention. I put the manuscript back on the table and glanced around with a mounting feeling of distraction and impa-tience, crossing and uncrossing my legs, rapping my fingers on the chair arm and then looking forlornly at the wall opposite.

Later, it seemed as if I had been in this frozen introspective mode for upwards of half an hour, just staring at the wall, as if cruelly skewered by a mood that I can only describe as an impaled sense of injustice. I was riven by an emotion I could hardly define or source until the thought came to me that I was desperate for the love of a woman, and completely disturbed by the sight of Xenia in Madelin's studio, and even more deranged by the idea, triggered by Vince, and not exactly disproved (but hardly confirmed) that Madelin and Xenia were somehow intimate. As I sat, staring at the wall, digesting the impossibility of this but sounding its logic, then dismissing it as a preposterous twist in Madelin's well-attested heterosexual career; as I countenanced the thought much as Vince might have done, and recalled the way in which Madelin ran her fingers through Xenia's hair and moved her into a position that was so beckoning, so careless, so available, it was impossible not to imagine searing fantasies that clingily conjoined Madelin's sylph-like form with the edible globes of Xenia's booming figure, a feasting and repast that drained my face of colour and put steel in my trouser fronts; leaving me with an ache I could hardly bear: a raging sense of arousal and frustration, of exclusion and need that brought back thoughts of Nadia, of hair spilt on the pillow, of rising ribs in the cage of my hands, a whole cataclysm of harrowing memories that tortured me with desire but could never happen again; and then the tristesse welled up, as did an aching certainty that I was missing out on life and love and happiness, and truly doomed, and then I heard footsteps and a knocking on the front door.

'Who's there?'

Moments later the door was wide open and Madelin was in my arms and both of us were floodlit by the lamps of her Land Rover.

'What's wrong?'

She held me fast and tight.

'Get me a drink,' she said, releasing me and heading back to the vehicle to fetch something.

Infected by her urgency, I grabbed a tumbler and whisky bottle from the kitchen and came to the front door in time to see her huddling back from the darkness.

She leaned against my chest and I tried to embrace her. For a few moments we were almost fused.

She pulled a bit of paper from her trouser pocket and moved ahead of me into the living room. She rubbed her arms and held herself tightly as she went. It was not warm in the cottage.

Madelin collapsed on the sofa by the wood-burner. 'Read this,' she said, handing me the note.

The first thing I recognised was Vince's signature.

For a moment I felt struck with adrenaline, a sickening ache in the chest that felt like a heart attack. Fighting through the panic, I read the note and experienced a wash of toxic relief.

I nodded appreciatively, trying to seem collected.

Madelin sat crumpled and tearful.

The letter was an unequivocal and heartrending threat to commit suicide if Vince discovered Madelin was having an affair. Obviously, it implicated me as the source of the idea.

'Oh, fuck!'

'That just about sums it up,' she said, shaking her head.

'Madelin, I'm sorry …'

'Holly read the note.'

There was a shocked silence.

'She … Where's Holly?'

'In the car. Doped to the eyeballs.'

'Shall we get her? I can make a bed.'

'I've spent two hours talking her down. I don't want to wake her up. She'll go ape all over again.'

192

I pulled my fingers across my forehead.

'Fancy that. Fancy handing your daughter the note in which you make that declaration. "Give it to Mummy," he said. She opened it. She *read* it.'

Madelin began to shiver. Her brow furrowed in response to a surge of anguish.

I tipped some whisky into her glass, and went upstairs to my bedroom to get a tartan rug from the cupboard. My only concern was to make amends by whatever means possible.

'Here,' I said, arranging the rug around her and then giving her the whisky tumbler.

Her expression was vacant. The glow from the fire reflected on her face. I took my coffee mug and sat down next to her.

There were too many questions. Any comment could so easily backfire. The whys and wherefores were beside the point in some way; Vince's letter escalated the crisis without admitting the issues. I actually felt angry with him. I had spent ages in that smelly cabin trying to convey Madelin's point of view and build bridges. His retort was destructive as well as disproportionate.

'Madelin, is the car locked?'

'What father would inflict that on a child?' She was teary-eyed.

If it was chilly in the cottage, it would be colder in the car, and besides, I didn't like the idea of Holly being out there on her own.

She gasped. 'If I leave Vince, I'm responsible for killing Holly's dad! Vince wants to control me, shackle me to his will.'

There were so many issues here, not least whether Madelin was having an affair.

'He's sleep deprived.'

'He wants to trap me in a marriage that doesn't work.'

'He says he loves you.'

'Bloody blackmail.'

'Madelin!'

'I don't care.'

She gazed at the fire, her face fraught with emotion. 'Cowardly emotional blackmail!'

'This suicide thing … it's … it's a stupid negotiating position. He's afraid you'll jump ship before things can be worked out.'

'How dare he constrain my freedom? What right does he have! I never see him. He never helps. Offers nothing. What difference does it make if I want to fuck half the truckers in Swansea? Vince couldn't care less about my sex life.'

She picked at the rug, displacing misery with fidgety fingers.

'Where is he?' I asked.

She stared helplessly at the flames in the stove.

For an icy moment I had a vision of him alone in the farm, convinced that Madelin had absconded with Holly, fleeing to the arms of some lover. Panic seized me. What if he topped himself tonight?

'Is Vince …?'

'It's Holly I care about!'

'What did you say to Holly?'

'Nothing that made her feel any better.'

'Vince has to retract the …'

'He bloody well does.'

Contain Holly, soothe, explain, sedate further; disarm Vince, get him to sleep, apologise, quit the cabin, ship him into a hotel or hospital; then do my bit with the novel; then attend to the marriage, draw up ground rules, bring in a counsellor, get some orderly sessions where people are actually talking to each other, run through the history, the grievances, front up to the issues. Christ, the road to normalcy was long and barren and ridden with potholes and booby traps. Somehow or other I was

194

implicated in this thankless process because, as of now, only I could talk to both parties.

I poured whisky into my coffee. Marriage guidance counselling, it seemed, was a lot more onerous than agenting.

Madelin slowly picked herself up from her huddle by the fire; she rose with her back to me, and then she turned, letting me see her tear-stained face and look of dejection, the face of a miserable child. There was a kind of appeal in her eyes, an expression that said 'Help me. Do something', a look beyond exhaustion and anger, as though she lacked the reserves to go on, and so naturally I said 'Madelin' and with a fluid motion, a flop really, she landed on my lap and put an arm around my neck and her head on my shoulder and I reciprocated with a hug and a pat.

After a few moments I took the coffee mug off the sofa arm and offered it to her.

She sipped at the hot beverage. I could smell whisky and hair conditioner.

There was something fitting about the way she folded into my lap, and to be perfectly frank I was at ease with the weight of her body against mine, because just as she needed physical reassurance, so I needed the warm closeness of another human being, the sense, lost for months, that I could be some kind of haven or protector for a woman, a man at ease with affection and in no hurry to deny whatever it was that Madelin could beneficially extract from this improvisatory hug; and when I felt the light pressure of her almost vine-like adherence to my chest and neck, her hot breath and the moisture from her tears on my cheek, I became almost stupidly relaxed, as if this moment of togetherness was a release and we could just be bound by affection.

After a minute or two I did worry about Holly, but it was too soon to break the spell, and as Madelin rested against me, her

195

breathing more even, her tears drying, I found myself absently calling to mind scenes from the afternoon, Vince's bowed face, the sombre horizons around the barn, the deserted house, the pong in his cabin, the equestrian four-wheel drives surmounting the yard, the homely smell in the kitchen, the seemingly compatible nature of these everyday details of people's lives, the grey-weather ordinariness of it all which seemed to diffuse and disperse all the conflict, making it seem impossible that a slight ripple or reconfiguration could not restore harmony to the farm, so there came to my mind the stolen glimpse of Xenia rising from that divan, as though dipping her foot in a pool, launching herself into some scene of Madelin's imagination that one couldn't help witnessing without heat in the solar plexus and magnified longing, like a kick in the senses that ran its hands across belly and breasts, and around buttocks and between thighs until suddenly I felt a tightness in my trousers.

I gazed at Vince's manuscript, attempted an adjustment, a shift. Madelin's weight bore down on the area in question. As I arched my back she moved in response, and suddenly it flared.

I clenched my teeth. My pulse soared. The erection was so obvious, right under the seat of her trousers. No matter how I tipped my hips, the groove of her bum seemed almost to adopt the hardening knoll.

Desperately exerting mind-control measures I thought of obvious turn-offs, countermanding vignettes, anything to douse the fire below, but then Xenia's straddling midriff would pop into view – muff flaring, boobs dancing, hips grinding – and my blithering wick shot like a burrowing cosh under the groove of Madelin's arse.

'Hold me,' she said.

I felt her hair on my face, a tickly sensation.

196

She seemed to breathe more deeply.

I thought of Vince suffering in his cabin, of poor Holly in the car.

I clasped the coffee mug, as if steering a plummeting aircraft with a bust joy stick.

Madelin was panting; her lips had parted. Slowly her mouth raised itself towards mine; her hips were responding.

'Oh.'

My penis surged.

The coffee spilt on my hand.

'Ah! Oh!'

Her lips were on mine.

Suddenly I was trapped in the most adhesive and passionate kiss and Madelin's hand was at my trouser button and with many an awkward tug, and bucking, and much furious, docked kissing, I was suddenly at large and in the hot grip of her hand.

***

It was a startled awakening, a bleary, where-am-I type awakening, in which the ringing phone seemed explosively magnified and disorientating, a drill by the bedside, and pillows and bedcovers became surprising obstacles and the stuff of delirium.

Daylight flooded the bedroom through half-drawn curtains. I blinked and swooned and walloped my way up against the headboard, nervously double-taking the floral wallpaper and sloped ceilings.

I grabbed the phone. 'Hello,' I rolled half-beached, half-gaping to the edge of the bed.

His voice was frail. 'Have you read the pages?'

There were a confused few seconds, a near blackout of sense and direction.

197

'I … what?'

I felt drugged, hauled from the depths of sleep.

'Have you read the pages?' he said, desperately.

'Sorry … just …'

Where was Madelin? I looked at my watch. 10 am: frig.

I came awake with a startled flail in the bed.

'Oh, the manuscript!' I had promised to read it last night. 'I'm finding it … excellent … enormously enjoyable.'

There was a huge gasp of relief. 'Thank fucking God!'

'Uh …' I swept my hair back.

'What plot point are you at?'

I bounced around under the duvet, trying to get a grip. Something caught my leg – a piece of paper.

'Are you in the khazi, then?' he said, in a weak attempt at levity.

It was a note from Madelin.

'Can we talk later, Vince, when I've finished?'

I turned the piece of paper around to read a message: 'You're the talent, Mike. See you four thirty in the barn! xxx.'

'When's good for you?' he asked.

I couldn't take a meeting with Vince.

'Four thirty works for me,' he said.

'No!'

'Three thirty.'

'Can't do it.'

'Three pm, then. Thanks, mate. See you later.'

***

Somehow, I flipped the phone onto its cradle and lay back in a swoon. My first clear thought was that Vince would not have called me if Madelin had been found out, or told him.

The night before was a dream. Daylight made it uncanny and fantastical, a deniable felony, unwitnessed, to be cancelled from moral memory. I wasn't going to bother with remorse. Remorse was not of the essence when you've fucked the adultery taboo to smithereens and come into a heap-load of forbidden knowledge. I had been hauled, dick first, through a rollicking initiation of the sort you can't cleanse with guilt, or quarantine with excuses. Better to park it like a waking dream that a few hours of daylight reality will hose down the drain. Park it and evacuate.

The bloody phone rang again.

'Hello.'

Helen from the office. I pulled myself up against the pillows, as if to assume some kind of authority.

'Yes!'

Helen was really sorry to interrupt my 'break'. There was an urgent message to relay. I supposed she was under instructions to field calls and keep clients ticking over until the management revealed my fate.

'I'm having a lovely time, thank you.' I said.

She asked if I would call James Moyle.

'Moyle?'

'He's very keen to talk to you. I did say you were on hols, but it seemed urgent.' She read out a telephone number which I jotted down on Madelin's *billet-doux*.

'He called around ten minutes ago and wants to hear from you today.'

'Thanks, Helen.'

Moyle: an agent, late fifties. I had spoken to him maybe three times in twenty years. He was one of the great doyens of the business and it was an act of vertiginous condescension on his part to call me.

I dragged myself into a sitting position against the mounted pillows. My skin felt unfamiliar, stretched, somehow spiced. In retrospect I could hardly credit what had happened. Both the transgression and the acute sexual intimacy of it seemed unreal. Such a coming together between people who have known each other for years injects a potent strangeness, as though not we, but avatars of our social selves had made love, people that I hardly knew. There was no question in my mind that it must never happen again. A line had to be drawn sharply and this probably meant seeing Vince once more to create a post hoc impression of innocence, and then beating a retreat to London.

The phone rang again. Jesus!

I plucked it dartingly.

'Yes?'

'You were storming,' she said.

'Madelin, I …'

'You got my note?'

I swallowed.

'Nice to get a good review, eh?'

'Is Vince …?'

'He's great. Never better. We've all made up.'

'What?'

'I told him you just couldn't get enough of his marvellous novel,' she laughed.

'What?'

'I saw it on your table last night. Listen, Mike, be there at four thirty. Gotta go.'

'Madelin!'

She rang off.

I picked up the phone to redial. I needed to tell her never again, but as I jabbed at the ring-back numbers, and hit the wrong ones, I found myself slowing down, as if sapped by the unreality of the situation.

I lay in bed, quite still, my gaze trapped by the pattern on the duvet cover, or the flicker of sunlight across the ceiling. Leaf shade nodded on the wall by the window. It was fresh and bright outside and the insistence of birdsong from trees outside grew louder and more celebratory.

***

When first I became an agent, years ago, there were still a few upper-class types in the biz: courteous old boys with Garrick Club memberships and the finest vowels. Such figures lent a patina of class to our profession. Nowadays, just one of those great doyens remained, the grandly languid James Moyle. All life's snobs flocked to James. His patrician manner and profile, his aura of breeding and instinct for form, his dry humour, his flawless manners and elegance of phrase were immensely attractive to authors with professional standing but negative personal tone. Even his famous clients looked up to him. They envied his connections of course (he knew everybody), his association with the old elites (cabinet ministers, branches of the aristocracy, Oxbridge dons); but most of all they admired his derivation from a class that sighed with a natural sense of its own superiority, particularly now hierarchy was dissolved in the arts. Moyle's patronage bequeathed social grace on wannabe authors. Join me, he seemed to hint, and you'll belong to an elect. Join me and my reputation, both forbidding and formidable, will elevate the rude business of dealing with publishers. Join me, and you will belong not merely to a club of distinguished writers, but to something above merit: you will attain the upper classes.

In fact, Moyle was as pragmatic as the next agent, and as callous. The gentleman act was just the ossification of received conformity. Like most successful agents he had a knack and had done very well; and like most Brits redolent of class, his provenance didn't bear scrutiny. He was nonetheless an imposing figure and on the few occasions I had dealt with him I sensed a role model.

I had no great wish to speak to Moyle of course, just as one has no desire to speak to the Queen or the Archbishop of Canterbury (but if a monarch calls, you tend to call back). The phone had rung while I was on the loo, so he was obviously keen to reach me.

I took Vince's pages back to the armchair in the sitting room. I fingered the manuscript, as if trying to induce some kind of concentration, but then I would see the sofa opposite (where things had got going last night) and dry heat would cross my chest, my heart would flutter, images would slide into memory like a pop-up on a naughty website and it was all I could do to clench my teeth and grip the manuscript. I sat like a fighter-pilot dive-bombing in some rickety Spitfire or throbbing Stuka, yanking on my joystick for dear life as the casing and fuselage of one's personal integrity got rattled to fuck by the vertiginous recall of Madelin's gliding lips and mewing pleasure.

I breathed out, a heat in the heart.

Vince's font was rather small. The document was printed on single space with narrow margins. The dense column of words rose like a locust swarm or some sky-blackening tower of chemical smoke. There were pages of this stuff, not a shred of dialogue in sight. I had to read fifty sides of the fucker by teatime.

The words skated in front of me. The first sentence, it seemed, was one, no two, no three, no five lines long! Like a trainee lawyer bamboozled by the text of a statute I read, and re-read, and read again, until I realised that this sentence was in fact grossly unintelligible. Were we in the mind of a mental patient? Was this some kind of Joycean parody? Had my concentration so flipped that the sane and the lucid now resembled the ravings of a madman?

I picked a paragraph at random. Yes, there seemed to be a subject to this sentence. I followed closely, dutifully; I made it down to the bottom of the page – something about a boy, a bus, a person called Jude. I stifled a yawn, my eyes flicked back and forth. One had to work so hard as a reader; you had to bring so much, a preparedness to be led, and appreciation of the means, an appetite to be interested. After five minutes of suffocating effort I nearly screamed in boredom. It was like water-skiing on concrete.

Why was I doing this? Why was I reading this wretched book?

I felt persecuted by the sentence structure, by the endless proper names, the nebulous point of view, the absurdity of the situation; but then, being fair, being professional about it, I had to admit that very few writers' prose can compete with the shattering aftermath of Madelin Farrell's love-making, and maybe now was not the smartest time to be reading a turgid novel; except that, unfortunately and inconveniently, I had promised a distilled, critical reaction to the man whose wife had straddled me to Bangor and back again the night before.

This was stark.

I had to see Vince; I had to beard him about the suicide note; I had to offer constructive and fair advice on his novel, and then vanish. Whatever happened, one could not be implicated in the break-up of his marriage. It was not too soon for me to withdraw, and if the writing was on the wall for Madelin and Vince, at least I had done my best.

I grabbed the pages, sipped my coffee, and dived in again.

Three minutes later, I sat in the armchair, eyes staring wildly, my cock like a stove pipe.

Chapter 16

Vince stood in the doorway of his cabin, welcoming me in. I will never forget his expression.

A look of almost pastoral solicitude warmed his features, a welcoming, newly humbled, but somehow vital look that said both 'thanks', and 'we have work to do'. It was an expression I had never seen before, like a strange sharing of happiness. Of course, he was tentative, a little nervous. For him, this was a big moment, and yet one which he hoped to relish. Despite a sequence of terrible days and sleepless nights, and the pallor of domestic exile, I could already see that Vince was lit from within by new self-belief. Someone, at last, had entered his world, joined in the struggle, understood his purpose. He had the air of a boy praised by mummy for good work. One could almost discern in this fluffier, perkier Vince a likeable human being.

'Can I get you a coffee?' he said.

'Thank you.'

Before entering his cabin, I had glanced over the drive to the barn. The building was solidly there, dark against grey sky. The three members of the family had withdrawn into private worlds. There was no sense of a community or homestead to be had from the look of those buildings.

I was extremely uneasy.

Soon we were sitting on the usual seats. There was more light in the cabin and the place seemed tidier than before; piles had been neatened, the floor cleared. Vince wore a burgundy V-neck sweater, jeans and Doc Martens. He ranged around, tipping coffee granules, wielding the kettle and moving books off the side-table by the armchair. He was scene-setting for my comfort, so that I could devote my thoughts, my undivided attention, to the grand theme *du jour*: his book.

Yes, now that I had worked in my own free time on his pages, I was entitled to real hospitality: a mug of Maxwell House and a slug of longlife milk. I had really made the grade.

'Everything OK at the cottage?' he said.

'Yes. Fine.'

That was the extent of his interest in my life.

'Great. OK. So ... um ...'

I placed the pages on the corner of his divan.

Vince's demeanour had really changed, and as I sat there, looking at him, making him wait for the first pronouncements on his 'magnum opus', I found it extremely objectionable that only the night before he had threatened suicide.

'So ... what do you think?'

I stared at him hard.

He met my eyes.

For an instant, I saw vulnerable warmth in his look; he knew absolutely that he was at my mercy. He was open to the truth and hoped, from what he had heard already, that the truth would be bearable.

'I thought the suicide threat was a bad idea.'

His face changed colour.

'I …' He had turned grey. He looked away. 'I was desperate. Completely mad.'

His note, I realised, had been a betrayal of me. He had blown apart my efforts at mediation. This could not be papered over.

'The trouble is, you see, Vince. It makes you look weak.'

This he had not expected. 'But I …'

'Women find weakness a turn-off. "I'm going to kill myself if you don't love me" has a particularly feeble ring to it.'

He was as fazed by my take as my tone.

'But what if it's true?'

'True?'

'Yes!'

'True that you were feeling that terrible twenty-four hours ago?'

He missed the implication.

'I was.'

'Then it proves you're deranged.'

'I was deranged!'

'Which is equally unprepossessing! Suddenly you look like a bad loser and an emotional weakling.'

Vince hung his head, as if in despair of my understanding the simple reality – that his feelings were his feelings.

'I mean this threat suggests to me … we're beyond marriage guidance into the realm of the psychiatric. If Madelin were wise, she'd call in the guys in white vans with the straitjackets and hypodermics.'

'I just wanted her to know that actions have consequences,' he blurted.

'What actions? She hasn't …' I drew myself up. 'She hasn't done anything wrong!'

I felt myself colouring.

206

He exhaled. 'She's expressed intent.'

'Out of terminal frustration and despair. It's the rhetoric of acute unhappiness. Of which you are the cause.'

'Can we talk about the book?'

'Vince!'

'Yes!'

'You need to rescind the threat. You need to amend that tactical gaffe.'

'I feel better now anyway.'

'You have to command respect. Not incite pity or contempt. The ultimatum game is a bankrupt strategy.'

'OK. OK. I get it. Let's change the subject.'

I stared at him in astonishment.

'What subject would you prefer?' I said with heavy irony.

'My book.'

'That makes a change.'

'You said it was good. Tell me more.'

I nodded.

'What you don't seem to understand,' I sighed with intense frustration, 'is that your suicide note is an invitation to have an affair.'

He looked at me incredulously.

'You top yourself … she gets the house in London, the cottage, control of her life, the full train set, she gets to frolic with lusty hikers and Welsh landlords. As a bargaining chip "I'll subtract myself from the scene and clear the way for you to replace me" is not great.'

Vince's eyes drilled into me; his irises seemed glaringly reflective, as if the inner eye were lost to thought, as if his visage had been frozen at the point of catastrophe, like the image of an astronaut's face on the event horizon periphery of a black hole, a ghostly halo of light after the physical body has been snatched into an infinity of compression.

'What you don't realise,' he said at last, carefully, patiently, 'is that everything Madelin and I say about each other relates to a context that you as an outsider cannot penetrate.'

'Penetrate?'

'Penetrate.'

We looked at each other. I nodded.

'You're not like either of us and you're not privy to the hidden workings of our marriage. You can judge the form but not the content. The form is a rhetorical crust. In the light of a history you don't see and can't understand, my note to Madelin was not quite what it seemed. Yes, I was desperate. But the note was instinctively targeted at the command-control centre of her recklessness.'

'What!'

'A pre-emptive strike. You see, I felt bad, yes, but not completely impotent.'

I stared at him incredulously.

'I am ... still stronger than her. Why? Because, mentally, I'm less of a fuck-up than Madelin, and she knows it. She needed to be hosed down.'

I shook my head in utter bewilderment. 'You're a pillar of strength?'

He gazed at me with expressionless certitude.

Was I being very dull and slow-witted, or had Vince gone round the bend?

'I don't see how your fear of the abyss and your suicide threats are obvious signs of strength in adversity.'

'What kind of state was she in?'

'Oh!' This was more like it. 'She was ...'

'Tearful?'

'Yes …'

'Distraught?'

'Very distraught.'

'Angry?'

'Particularly about the fact Holly read the note.'

He nodded.

'Volatile?'

I cast my mind back to the previous evening. 'Desperately, desperately upset.'

Vince seemed almost satisfied by this account of his wife's sufferings, as if the list of responses were precisely calculated. Was he telling me that the suicide note was a ruse to contain or cauterise her impulsiveness? Was the desperate *cri de coeur* an attempt to arouse sympathy from some checked part of Madelin's heart – because it showed how much he cared?

I gazed at my hands in grim-faced confusion. Whatever the justification for his note, it had backfired disastrously. Madelin was now more alienated than ever.

I felt hot around the collar.

'I see. Your suicide note was a bluff?'

'I don't know. Maybe. I am an author. I see things with a certain detachment, see them coming, their plot value, if you like. The author can play a card with a kind of cold calculation. It doesn't mean to say that the man is unsuffering.'

'Your marriage is not some melodramatic Mills and Boon yarn written by an overwrought spinster on half a bottle of sherry!'

'I'd agree with that.'

'Vince, snap out of the ironic detachment mode. In the real world you can't offer to commit suicide as a plot-point scene twister.'

'As a way of evincing emotion. You can. And people do.'

'Madelin may very well call your bluff.'

'She will. But Madelin seems quite chirpy this morning.'

'You've spoken to her?'

'She knows it's a game. She runs the gamut of emotion winding you up, gaining your succour and support, and when that ruse hits a brick wall, she switches tack.'

I swallowed. 'She's in a good mood?'

'Very bright and fluffy.'

I nodded.

'My threat cleared the air.'

I stared at him. If he seriously believed this, he was not only cuckolded – in effect by his own rash actions which had sent Madelin to my cottage – but deluded. Of course, I was hardly best placed to put him right. It shocked me the extent to which Vince's vision of reality was impervious to question or contention. No wonder he had been editorially unreachable.

'She said you really enjoyed the pages.'

Vince looked at me with burning clarity, the look of restored confidence.

He had certainly changed since yesterday. Yesterday he was sallow-faced, exhausted, deeply fraught, on the edge of breakdown, or so it seemed. Was it conceivable that one fib about the quality of his novel had recalled him from the edge of the 'abyss', brought him back to an almost complacent stability and the illusion of marital harmony? And where did Holly stand in all this tragic-comic mood switching? Was she now satisfied that her dad's threat to top himself was a suave move on the political chessboard of marriage, blocking the queen's errant desire to fondle pawns and straddle knights, thus restoring order to the court: the queen back in her turret, brushing locks and reading

210

bedtime stories to the princess? Was militant little Holly also caught up in the familial *folie à trois*?

So Madelin was chirpy?

Momentarily, my close concentration on Vince's devious logic faltered, as images from the night before obtruded, welling up, barging into the sensible reality of the moment, so that what had seemed grainy and dreamlike a few hours ago, like the vestiges of a fantasy, took on a heart-stopping immediacy, a horripilating intensity, that connected some base order of my being to a carnival of delights assimilated as much through tensile yearning as through touch, a vision as surreal in retrospect as it must have been earthy in the doing.

'So what did you think of my book?'

I felt the edges of a headache, a twinge in the corner of my eye. The book, it seemed, was utterly inescapable. I let out a slow gasp of air and reclined in the seat, rubbing my eyes and composing my thoughts.

I gazed at the floor as if in a trance.

'Style, voice, tone. It's dense, it's allusive. Real writing.'

He nodded.

I looked at him solidly.

'It's nice to hear that.'

'A lot of work has gone into those pages.'

'Telling me.' There was a quaver in his voice.

'And this is not ... pulp fiction.'

Vince nodded. 'I'm afraid not.'

'So it's dense, allusive. You have to pay attention. You've got some long sentences in there.'

He waited, as if sensing a criticism.

'The vision is striking, clear, magnificently uncompromising.'

'Not the easiest sell, maybe.'

I smiled tightly. 'That cannot be your consideration.'

'It's great to hear someone say that.'

'You pursue an ideal relentlessly and hand it to the world. Without any doubt, you've executed your vision, even in this fragment, with meticulous attention to detail. I have no problem with the writing at all.'

'You like it?'

'I admire it.'

'You enjoyed it?'

'I acknowledge your artistic goals and your steadfast execution.'

He looked at me curiously. 'I'm getting some withhold here.'

'Very tough sell,' I said. 'In the current market. But that's not your concern.'

'Well, it *is* my concern.'

'No. I don't think it can be.'

'What?'

'On the evidence of these twenty-five thousand words you've shown not the slightest concern for the ordinary reader.'

'Oh, that cunt. Who is this bore who keeps dumbing things down?'

'Which is fine.'

Vince looked at me strangely. 'I'm sorry, I'm not getting you.'

'The readership for this book is extremely elite.'

'I detect a reservation.'

'I think you've achieved what you set out to achieve.'

'That's a tautology.'

I was beginning to feel really angry.

'I mean, do you like it, or don't you like it?' he said.

'I don't like it at all.'

He frowned. 'Sorry! What!'

He looked at me darkly, uncomprehendingly.

I lurched forward in the armchair. 'Read on its own terms it displays the hallmark qualities of your earlier fiction. It belongs to a corpus. One, I would suggest, that has run out of steam and always owed its success to fashion rather than substance.'

He looked at me with raised eyebrows. 'You're not serious?'

'I don't like the vision. I think it's superficial, limited, self-conscious and heartless.'

Vince looked at me with a deadpan absence of reaction or expression, as if my verdict was such a *volte-face* that response was impossible.

'I don't think your artistic agenda has been broad enough to sustain a readership beyond the initial splash of success. And the fate of your last book supports my case. This book has found no passionate advocates. It is honed and wordsmithed to within an inch of its life, but the effect is deadening.'

He covered his face with his hands. I watched out the silence.

Obviously, I expected some kind of backlash, or worse, an explosion. Maybe the way I just solidly sat there confused him.

In due course, he glanced up at me with a creased expression. 'Very odd to be hearing this from someone who wanted to represent me.'

This was tantamount to a charge of hypocrisy.

Vince had every reason to close the conversation and bundle me out of the cabin. Instead he regarded me with a kind of confounded amusement; it was not so much the sheer surprise of what I said, which caught him unawares and on the wrong foot, nor its audacity given the circumstances; it was the unprecedented totality of the criticism. I had gone beyond the local, the technical, the respectfully editorial and questioned his whole project in the teeth of enormous critical success and against conventional wisdom. My broadside, which annihilated his entire fleet, had one outrageous virtue: acute novelty. The proposition was, on the face of it, so cataclysmic (if true) that Vince travelled beyond the reflex of self-defence into the mode of ironic amazement, and thus his leery question, dealt with staring eyes and a forefinger against his temple: 'What standards should I have set for myself? Where exactly did I go wrong ... oh Master?'

There is a time in any relationship when it becomes a sham without a venting of the truth. Few relationships can take absolute candour, but I would not have felt 'real' if Vince hadn't heard my views. If I could no longer puncture his delusions about Madelin, I could hold up the mirror to his writing.

It took, I suppose, ten minutes to expand my view of the novel, and my difficulties with his literary project.

I started with the single proposition that the cleverness of Vince's novels strangled the life of his characters. The characters were *homunculi*, figurines, whose fate had not been lived through. Thus plot could deliver nothing profound about human nature because circumstance in his fiction was not real enough to evince a satisfying depth of psychology. His outcomes were fictional play, not meticulous representations of the human condition in which painstaking attention to causality underpinned a sense of truth. It followed, alas, that in Vince's work sophistication couldn't signify because all other values – ear for dialogue, set-piece management, street cool, PC quotient, pop-cultural savvy, sense-of-author chic, New Man palatability, urban contemporary vibe, anti-establishment attitude – all generously present, were not attached to a credible set of events. Savage had not read Henry James's stricture that no fictional narrative that fails to transect the centre of its protagonist's moral consciousness can be of substance.

214

Oh dear. That *was* an oversight.

He stared at me with a resistant frown as I spoke. Nobody before, no critic or reviewer, had ever questioned his project. Both the angle and the argument trapped his interest, whilst dismantling his oeuvre stone by stone. It must have been horribly fascinating to be dissected by a mere agent.

I argued that what happens in a novel, to be significant, must be in the nature of things; a revelation beyond the thrall of narrative. Richness of characterisation, I stipulated, demands a vision of the human psyche that has depth, and moreover the perspective granted by a near-ideal intelligence. For a novelist to defend his reedy characters as accurate reflections of a generation depleted by shallow education, bad TV, computer games, instant gratification, internet porn and Class A drug culture, as I believed Vince had done, was not good enough, in my view. To compound a fast-food consumer reality with an equally superficial mimesis was to turn fiction into a lifestyle accessory, and superficiality cannot be allowed to win the day after the miracles of the Renaissance and the glories of the Enlightenment.

'People need more than postmodern detachment and formal conceit. They need to connect with the meaning of their own lives.'

I looked at him squarely, like a plain-speaking Quaker-type who knows his onions and won't be persuaded otherwise. There was nowhere we could go with this, obviously. At the most, my observations were food for thought: more likely they repelled him intellectually and temperamentally.

He looked at me with an unreadable expression.

I had a sudden sense of the fatuousness of this kind of exchange, as things could only be what they were, and Vince's only mode of becoming lay within the maze of his mind. Very likely, he was spent as a writer: an idea I could countenance with ease. Who cared if one novelist ran out of steam and petered out? Another would rise in his place. It's a breed that keeps on coming.

At first he started nodding, as if somehow reckoning the whole crazy exchange; maybe he was experimenting with the look of an idea, the quite interesting notion that his life's work had been power-hosed off the forecourt. I could see him imagining invalidity, toying with the look and feel of complete irrelevance. No writer could be expected to walk into that idea. That message he was bound to repel. And yet, as he sat there, hands clasped together, his gaze turned down to the floor, he had the last six months to acknowledge: the publishers' rejections, the ordeal of revision, the chronic uncertainty. In his heart of hearts he had surely lost the plot, and my more general arguments, my tanks on his lawn, the shock and awe of a comprehensive critical trashing were harder, much harder to oppose with energy; and suddenly, I realised, mine was the straw that had broken Vince's back. My objections, which a stronger Vince might have wrestled to the ground and rubbed viciously in the dirt, were the *coup de grâce*.

His face seemed ghosted, wan. In the corner of his eye something glistened.

'It's just a view,' I said.

He looked away, but his cheeks were crazed with tears.

'Vince … I …'

He shook his head. He was crying copiously.

'I …'

Something curdled inside me.

He drew out a hanky and wiped his face. He shook his head back and forth, beyond the power of speech.

The room was hot and oppressive. I glanced around at the symbols of his trade, the shredder and printers, the computer cables, the mug of pencils and pens, the bookshelves snug with glossy hardback spines, the proof copies and foreign-language editions of his work, the slanting dictionary. These objects seemed to concentrate the sense of endeavour. This den was a writer's cockpit, the nodal link between inner and outer worlds; and now in the dim afternoon light it seemed like a last redoubt, some rickety lair or retreat, where ambition and energy sagged in the knowledge of defeat.

I felt a mild urge to console or retract. What was the point of cheating him of a raison d'être? Vince had done so much to live and work and earn within the remit of his imagination and, by any standards, he had succeeded for a while. Feistily, deter-minedly, he had done it his way – made something where there was nothing. But just as his project was fiction, so in the end his perceptions were fictional, his vision partial, his importance a conceit. Fawning critics and early celebrity had placed a chrome crown on his head, a false anointing which boosted his status above his achievement and wreathed confidence in hubris. My outspoken anatomy of his work, which I admit was polemical, had coincided with an inner weakening of conviction. At some level, Vince knew he was a fraud. At some level, only the writer himself can truly judge the calibre of his work, because only the writer can attest to the profundity of his plans, his inspiration, his insight in the process of creation. If Vince was unable to rage now, it was because he could no longer be sure of anything.

His voice when he spoke was toneless.

'So now you've got your own back.'

I frowned.

'Revenge ... served cold.'

217

'Excuse me …'

'Enjoy it, Mike. Putting the boot in when a man's down.'

'What?'

He smiled an ugly smile. 'Restoring your self-esteem by trashing mine.'

'But …'

'Enjoy the Schadenfreude.'

'There's no sour grapes.'

'Oh, come on. Have a little self-insight.'

'I'm sorry, Vince. I don't belong to your fan club.'

'But you wanted to represent me, or was that just hypocrisy?'

I stared at him steadfastly.

'When you offered to read those pages I believed in your good faith. I thought you were sincere. But now that I know you always detested my work and doubtless envied my success, I see your presence in this cabin as a fraud. You're here to gloat, to get your own back.'

'I wanted to represent you,' I said fiercely, 'until I realised you were the emperor's new clothes to the power of ten!'

He regarded me darkly.

It was like facing a baited animal.

'You're up a cul de sac, Vince. I can tell you why.'

He eyed me with hostility, wanting to bite back but needing to hear. Vince craved confrontation, a clash of realities. Harsh resistance orientated him.

'You need to control *everything*.'

He gazed at me unsociably.

'And it's left you with *nothing*.'

His queer half-smile was the perfect analogue of checked animosity.

'How can readers be interested in the artifices and conceits of an author who ignores the suffering on his doorstep?'

He looked away, his mouth pursed, and I realised then how gauche were the signs of real emotion. Vince was so far beyond any elegance or eloquence of riposte that he had descended to soap opera grimaces and displacements.

His eyes remained tight shut, a period of boiling over, and then he turned on the chair and pulled open a drawer in his desk. He lifted out a mickey of vodka and looked at me lugubriously. Efficiently he twisted off the screw cap and raised the bottle to his lips. He took a hit of the spirit, a dispassionate slug, and then replaced the cap. He offered me the bottle. I declined.

After a few moments, he resumed his earlier Rodinesque posture, chin on hand, elbow on leg. I saw his neck muscles working. He seemed to be negotiating some crisis of expression, a threshhold of pain it was necessary to push though.

I waited tensely and watchfully.

'The book is a fucking disaster. I know it. Forget what I said. You don't grasp …'

I waited.

His mouth hung open. He stared into space.

'Yes?'

He sighed profoundly.

'I don't grasp what?'

His eyes were round and searching.

He appeared momentarily to have lost the thread.

'Vince,' I began. 'If we …'

'Why do you think she …'

'She?'

'Was so … Madelin was so …'

He looked at me directly.

'So what?'

His nostrils vented and he took in a great heap of breath. 'So unbelievably promiscuous?'

'When was she promiscuous?' I said, blushing.

'For Christ's sake, Mike! She fucked Canonbury and Islington to rubble and dust!'

I gazed at him painfully.

'Let's call a spade a spade. Madelin was no virgin bride. I took a big risk marrying her. What she got up to ...' Vince's eyes searched from side to side. 'Off the fucking dial.'

His eyes flashed, an upwelling of emotion, the first indication I had seen of retrospective jealousy.

'Back then I thought ...' Vince ran his hand through his hair. 'Girl power. She's highly sexed, why not? Men do. Why shouldn't women? Let's not be prudish.'

His jaw jutted.

'But sex is never only about fun, or having a good time. Sex is psychological.'

He gazed at me with searing candour.

'In Madelin's mind sex bought attention, the sense of being needed. The men she fucked weren't her equals. Why? Because Daddy was an absentee father who travelled a lot, and probably had a lot offshore nooky, and Madelin knew very little of what good to expect from a man. She was starved of paternal affection and constantly seeking it from lads whose evasiveness resembled her dad's and who fell into bed easily, but inevitably fell short. I delivered her from that merry-go-round. I was the first man who was more than some token representative of the sex.' He sighed and reopened the vodka bottle. 'And for a while it worked. We were happy. Madelin was a sweetly monogamous partner, a new woman. But then Holly came along and with it an era of aspirational domesticity, the whole *House & Garden* panto.

Madelin falls into the trap of thinking a successful novelist is no different to an investment banker, and suddenly I'm the blank cheque book for whatever four-wheel drive, yummy mummy, Farrow & Ball fantasy she wants to act out, and the serious Madelin, the artistic Madelin, takes a holiday, whilst lifestyle Madelin goes to baby showers and hires expensive nannies and sashays at media parties; and suddenly it's no longer Mimi and Rodolfo, bohemians against the world, but Lady Macbeth and insomniac husband trying to pen them quick enough to pay the bills.'

He wiped his face, a gleaming, waxy prospect, side-lit by the desk lamp. I listened, hands tightly folded on my lap, mutely absorbing the husband's story. It was almost incapacitating to hear the woman I had made love to described from the far side of her own marriage.

'And when hubby hits the buffers and can't deliver, and is no longer the infallible success story, but a very worried, cracking up,' he sniffed, 'blocked, basket case, who doesn't know which way to turn, she begins to feel rejected, or second fiddle to what has always been a fairly obedient muse, and gradually the insecure Madelin comes back again, the flighty Madelin perks up with threats and taunts as if I haven't kept my part of the bargain which, if you're married to Madelin, is mission impossible. How can I reassure her that our marriage means everything if the reassurance she wants from me requires a kind of sanity to accept it?'

His speech impacted painfully. It made me feel shitty and shabby and taken down a peg or two, because who could not recognise a kernel of truth in this summary, and if Vince was correct about the causes of Madelin's behaviour it was doubly sleazy of me to have got carried away last night. I had let it happen, yes, as though impulse were an excuse. Perhaps there was some kind of unfinished business which kicked in, and maybe there was a modicum of animal frankness about getting naked after so many years, and maybe I needed it more than I was prepared to admit, and took more of the initiative than Madelin once things steamed up, but whatever the 'truth' of such encounters, it seemed trivial compared to the years of good faith that had gone into the only relationship that enabled her to transcend her past. In the riot of their marital disharmony, I was like a looter, stealing from another man under cover of darkness.

'Vince, you need to reach out, through the anger, to the woman you love. In the end …' Emotion was welling up. 'Love is the best any of us can do.'

For several seconds I was unable to continue. Even clichés strike home at times.

'… As for the writing, I believe that if you abandon that novel, you'll get a creative surge. I only plead that you write about something you love. You're living in beautiful landscape. You adore Sibelius, the music of landscape. Write from positive experience and surely you'll connect with a readership that has the same need for those positives.'

He looked at me in astonishment.

I had to get back to my own life. Instead of trying to fix bust marriages and broken writers I needed a mission of my own. I needed to walk for hours across the Beacon wilderness. Somewhere in that hinterland of western light there had to be the clue to a future beyond vicariousness, where I was no longer an intermediary or a salesman of others' talents, but a force in my own right.

'I've got to go.'

'Please …'

'Vince …'

'What you just said …'

He was staring at me oddly. He seemed momentarily confused.

I was desperate to be off. After this meeting, there was no question of seeing Madelin. I had to run, get clear.

'Vince, I've really got to go.'

'I *have* written something … About this area, the hills.'

He was meek.

'*And* Sibelius.'

'Well, there you are!'

'What you said is an incredible coincidence. The thing is,' he tongued his cheek, frowned awkwardly, 'if I … could I …?'

My heart sank.

'Would you read it? I'd really welcome your judgement.' He gazed at me forlornly.

My eyes misted over. I wanted free of all this. I never wanted to read a manuscript or talk to an author again.

'Colin's useless. There's no one else.'

I could hardly suppress a gasp of ennui.

'Please!'

'I'd be delighted to,' I said.

'Oh thank you. Thank you.'

Vince's finger was instantly working the mouse, clicking open files with new alacrity, and before long my deadened senses received the sound of the printer chugging out sheets, two, five, fifteen, countless pages; and before I knew it, he was handing me the hot swatch, a sheepish look on his face. How could he offer me more reading after my last reaction? Wasn't I the last person on the planet to show some tender piece of new prose? Oh God!

'Great,' I said.

'I won't chase you for a reaction.'

223

I smiled weakly.

A minute later I was outside the cabin, standing in the breeze and gazing at the view.

My car was parked a few feet away, its windscreen symbolically facing west, the stirring panorama of Beacon summits and mountain foreground, of dark ridges and baroque cloud and raked peaks, and the hammock of the valley that fell from the heathered heights around me to the verdant cradle below, all clustered oaks and luminous fields and arcing hedgerows, before ascending again in a rush to the solitary stanchion of the Sugar Loaf, poised and graceful in its skirted symmetry, its benign pre-eminence, its timeless facing of the hauling winds and the ceaseless dapple of cloud-light that raced across its cape.

Kate had called me before I left to see Vince. She had posted signature copies of my share-sale agreement with Colin. I was to sign them and return them immediately. Very soon now, I would be shot of the past.

I was about to step into my car and head home, when I glanced back in the direction of the studio where Madelin was waiting for me.

My departure, I realised, had to be unambiguous.

I relocked the car and walked across the gravel to the barn, composing myself.

Doing the right thing felt easier. Friendship was something you had to protect. She was a friend and we were going to keep it that way.

As I came to the barn door, the moment was strangely charged. I had dodged the consequences of transgression, but transgression leaves an indelible aftertaste.

I glanced at the yellow light of the cabin window, and pulled open the barn door.

Chapter 17

'Frank's dead,' she said, turning.

We were standing in her studio. She had been organising paint tubes.

She wore a blue jersey, jeans.

She glanced away, continued her sorting.

I stood there, dumbfounded.

'In Afghanistan. It's been on the news. He was doing a research trip in Helmand. They got ambushed and killed. I didn't even know he was out there. I thought he was in Llandrindod Wells.'

Her face was pale in the side-light, dignified, thoughtful.

'I really banked on him not getting killed,' she said, without emotion.

I sat down, stunned. I was completely unprepared for this.

'Everything gets worse,' she said.

Staring at the floor in respect for Frank and mortified by the news, I realised that if Frank had ever been Madelin's lover, she would have been tearful. But she was calm and beautiful as she sat on a wine-bar chair, knees together, hands on thighs, lost in her measuring of the moment.

This news: even before one escaped the crushing sense of pity, it seemed like a wake-up call.

My imagination ran out to a scene of harsh terrain in bleached light, the arid Afghan landscape, all rubble and dust, and the panic of a unit caught unawares: rifle crack, bomb blast. In what state of mind had Frank lost his life? The sense of his turn come round at last? Heart-pumping terror?

I gazed at the floor.

I had no special way to be with her at such a moment.

'Madelin ...'

'You don't need to say anything.'

'I know he was a friend.'

The silence was gridlocked and inarticulate. After a while the gloom in the barn became oppressive. She picked up a cigarette pack and lighter from the edge of the trestle table.

'Certainly puts things in perspective,' she said, almost brusquely.

I nodded.

'We only live once, Mike.'

She delivered the cliché with a searching look.

My task was not made easier by this news, though, in the light of Frank's death, other concerns seemed trivial.

'I guess he knew the risks,' I said.

'He lived the risks. He embraced the risks. Risk was a proof of good faith. He saw terrible things but remained kind and sweet-natured. I'm sure – in a way – he was prepared to die.'

I recalled the dinner party and wondered what that dreadful row would have done for Madelin's view of Vince, now Frank was dead.

'Fuck, what are we doing with our lives!' she said.

She sat there, her legs outstretched, her hair full and thick, and it seemed that she and I were on parallel planes of unhappiness,

226

and that neither of us had much to do with each other's lives and realities, and as I sat on my chair, stayed by the news, I had an overwhelming sense of futility. What was the significance of all this busying ourselves with lives constantly afflicted by setbacks and disappointments and tragedy barging in from left and right to belittle our hopes and plans? Earn a living, stay alive, grab happiness where you can? It occurred to me that if I died now, my contribution would be pathetic and my behaviour unworthy, and perhaps the only lodestar to follow as you buggered around making a mess of things was simply to do the right thing by other people – to do unto others as you would have them do unto you – and not add to the sum of the world's miseries. And yet, and yet ... misery and damage are out there in constant domino action and people cannot easily duck the current of woe that swings through the system, that kinetic booby-prize, or pass-the-parcel aggro that is only survivable if you let it out of your system and shove it on. Frank's misfortune was that instead of being the lightning conductor that pinged history's bolts into the earth of the world's media, dispersing damage, he became the chimney stack or lonely oak tree that takes it in the neck. His was nonetheless a significant death and a humblingly engaged life.

'I am going back to London,' I said.

She looked up. 'Why?'

'Get out of everybody's hair.'

'You're needed here.'

'I don't want to do more harm than good.'

She was alarmed. 'You've done nothing but good.'

'I'm in a rather impossible position.'

'Please don't go.'

I shook my head.

'Don't go now!'

It was like a declaration. I found this so difficult.

'We both need your support,' she said.

'I'm flattered.'

'Why should Vince's welfare take priority over mine?' she smiled.

'I don't think it does. You're my friend, Madelin.'

She considered this for a moment. 'More than a friend now, perhaps?'

There was a silence.

'I ...'

She lit a cigarette.

My heart was beating hard.

'You seemed to be having a good time,' she said, fingers at her lips, drawing on the cigarette.

This was so frank. It seemed like a challenge.

'I did ... It was ... I ...'

She let the smoke exude from her mouth.

'I did,' she said softly. 'I had a good time, Mike.'

I made an enormous effort to concentrate.

She looked at me intently.

'I have to get back in any case,' I said.

Her chin jutted.

'Biz.'

She seemed to find this faintly ridiculous.

'I have ... well, you know, I have a life.'

'I'm sure you do, Mike.' She tapped her ash into a dish.

There was a long silence.

'Madelin ...'

'What are you going to do?' she said.

'Do me a favour.'

She knew what was coming.

'Don't tell Vince,' I said.

She puffed on her cigarette. This didn't please her. When I should have been yielding I was trying to cover my back.

'For his sake. Not mine.'

'Are you still in love with Nadia?' Her eyes were large.

'Don't know. Probably. I have a heart.'

'Why on earth would I tell Vince?'

'To disillusion him about my good faith. To punish him.'

Her look was strange, and then she glanced away.

Several moments passed.

'This has nothing to do with Vince,' she said carefully. 'I just want a life. I want to feel alive!'

'Have you …' I had to ask. A lot seemed to turn on the question. 'Were you … having some kind of fling with …?'

'With?'

'… with …'

'Yes?'

I stared at her. 'Frank?'

She seemed to relish my discomfiture, whilst staring me down, as if to prove that of course she wasn't having an affair with Frank, and why would she, a married woman, a respectable mother, who had remained faithful and unimpeachable through seven years of marriage until the middle of last night?

There was brilliance in the light of her eye. Now that Frank was dead, of course, she had deniability.

'Of course not, you idiot!'

'What about Xenia?' I said stupidly.

She laughed brilliantly, a scandalised laugh that seemed to take equal pleasure in my prurience and naivety.

'What a wonderfully foxy idea! Mike, you do surprise me.'

'I wasn't foxy enough to anticipate last night.'

'I'll try not to be too offended by that.'

'I do have some respect for the marital ties of others.'

'I'm sure Vinnie would've been thrilled to see the marital respect you were lavishing on me last night.'

I looked away.

'You're a dark horse, Mike de Vere.'

'What's that supposed to mean?'

'All kinds of intriguing things.'

It felt very uncomfortable to be the subject of Madelin's searing insight into men, more raw data on the male sex, its characteristics and propensities. She had a lot to compare me with. My instinct for boundaries was certainly not her scene, of course. That was one big difference between us. Wise limits, forget it.

'Xenia's got a boyfriend,' she said. 'Frank's dead.' She rose and came towards me, holding my eye. 'Whereas I'm a novel widow and you're a single man.'

'But Vince and Holly!'

Her eyes searched mine before she spoke. 'Need never know.'

There was insinuation in her upward gaze as I took in the closeness of her mouth, her parted lips. She inhaled, as if readying herself, and then she moved, like a ripple, a stretching and loosening. Her eyes closed and then opened again, gazing into mine.

'I want you to kiss me,' she said quietly.

She placed her hand lightly on my arm.

My heart was hammering away.

She drew close, reaching up and around my neck.

'I want you to fondle my breasts,' she whispered.

I swallowed. I could feel her breath on my cheek and then her lips brushing my face.

'I want you to fuck me from behind.'

230

Chapter 18

I stared at a tree: a massive oak with zigzaggy branches and the thickest trunk.

It seemed to hold up the sky. Its limbs waggled before a distant yonder: remote valley depths and faint peaks observed from the edge of a steep incline where the Peugeot was parked and silent as I gazed through the screen, mobile in hand.

Mobiles come alive at this altitude. Bleeping pent-up demands, urgent *communiqués*, making you real again.

My eyes travelled across a panorama of distances. I felt half drugged in the driving seat, fingers on the steering wheel, great draughts of hill and sky streaming into vision.

Madelin had returned to the kitchen and a conversation with Holly, as I went across the drive to the car and made my exit. Out here on the hill, a quarter of a mile down the track from the farm I could will into nothing, into some unwitnessed crevice of time, what had happened in the barn, as if just being here was an alibi. Throughout the duration of what we did Holly played in earshot, Vince worked yards away; the risk of being caught infected every concerted second, and the sheer hazard of taking that risk was a kind of revelation.

I sidled away across the drive trying to seem innocuous, some-how in continuance of an earlier state. Get out, off the plot, move it. Just drive away casually, don't look around. Let the heart calm down at a distance. I could feel myself escaping from recall, from the hailing figure of Vince, from the last clutches of the place. Then, of course, I get Moyle on the line, Zeus striking from the clouds, a mobile-phone arrest just as I am bumping down the track in low gear. I talk to Moyle, head clearing fast, a multi-tasking triumph; and the Moyle call done, I phone Steve at the agency; and after the two calls, conducted on the roof of the world, everything is a little bit different.

Moyle first. The car was in low gear, so I pulled over when the ringtone went, and took the mobile off the passenger seat.

***

'Mike de Vere,' I said.

'James Moyle. Sorry about the telephone tag. I have a very simple proposition for you.'

As ever, Moyle was confident of his pleasing voice, his uniquely privileged way of coming to the point, as if I had been loyally awaiting his call for years and there existed an unspoken bond between his sense of prerogative and my fealty to excellence.

'Oh yes?' I was staring at a sheep's skull.

'Lunch.'

My cheeks bunched. Seagulls, blown inland by high winds, mewed overhead.

It was assumed that one would be flattered by such a proposal without needing to know its purpose.

'I'm in Wales at the minute.'

'I'm sure we could make a time.'

'Was there something you wanted to discuss?'

Moyle cleared his throat in the conventional innuendo-bearing way. 'Shall we say, matters of mutual interest.'

I waited.

'It's always a good idea to have a chat. Nothing ventured, nothing gained.'

Such calls come rarely in the life of an agent (Sheila's was the last) and when they do, the need for discretion engenders a kind of euphemistic over-familiarity; just as, for the purpose of this call, Moyle's tone suggested old acquaintance: a community of experience that implied we were equals.

I was more amazed, really, than pleased. Fortune's sense of timing was extremely perverse.

'Well … I … I'd love to …'

'Angus Gilmore speaks highly of you.'

One of Sheila's clients: old school.

'Angus is a dear friend,' he said.

Moyle's world would abound with 'dear' friends.

'Uh …'

'There's a little restaurant round the corner that's useful for these purposes.'

'You're in Kensington?'

There was a pause.

'I hear Sheila's not been well,' he said casually.

There was an enduring silence, as if Moyle were inviting me to offer information.

'Angus is quite concerned,' he said, at last.

This was news, indeed, and it took me a moment to recover my presence of mind.

'What day would suit you?' he said.

I was thinking fast. 'What about Thursday?'

I could picture Moyle studying his calendar on the computer screen, looking at appointments with higher-status specimens than myself and probably finding an existing booking for lunch on Thursday (at The Ivy or Le Caprice). It must have been a measure of something very urgent that he was prepared to meet me instead at a cheap local restaurant.

'Very good,' he said, snappily. 'Trattoria Bruno, 5 Bell Lane, 1 pm. See you then.'

He rang off, pleased to seem slightly brusque. Agents are always keen not to be too warm or human, retaining the right of instant dissociation if things turn out not to their advantage. The personal tone one took to be purely instrumental. Charm was a function of efficacy, to be used intensely and economically where required. In this way Moyle showed himself not the least brought down to earth by dealing with me.

***

I sat still, looking through the windscreen. Then I started the car and drove carefully down the track to a point where the Peugeot could not be seen from the farm. I pulled up next to the oak tree.

Minutes ago I had been fucking Madelin on a mattress in her office. I breathed in deeply.

It was time to call Steve at the agency. Moyle's call had a compressing effect, a focussing effect. It cleared away the cobwebs. It concentrated the mind.

Steve would get quite a surprise, which was good. A little disorientation can ventilate the truth, and where truth or privacy was concerned Steve was the original sieve. He had turned indiscretion into a lifestyle. The man responsible for such caring nicknames as 'Professor Fuck' was my nearest

234

thing to an office ally. I should have called him before.

I let the number ring. Jasvinder picked up.

'Mike de Vere, for Steve Bartholomew.'

***

The twang in Steve's vowels and the gravel in his voice (he was a die-hard smoker) were in some measure a stylistic counter to the pomposities of the book department. He liked to debunk, to chuck a line of cockney into the proceedings. Demotic chic, he called it. Let's ground the fluffy vestals of literature, the Sloaney work-experience girls and pleased-with-themselves book agents in the wider reality of contemporary culture, which he served as a TV agent. Vending scriptwriters to TV soaps, of course, had a warping effect on one's intellectual 'integrity'. The telly audience, Steve respected – ordinary folk wanting decent entertainment – but shows these days were so naff and on-the-nose and coma-inducing that even brazen populists like Steve were dismayed by the end-product of an industry he so coolly serviced. That said, with wall-to-wall crap everywhere, it should have been the case that gigs came easy, that clients could pile in, that a maturely cynical agent could earn plenty of commission shunting scribes on to *Ladette Circus*, or *Boyfriends*, or *Ibiza Mon Amour*, whereas in fact these series were so synthetically bad that getting to write for them was bewilderingly difficult. As a result, the mud-to-wall ratios and judgement-to-bullshit gearings were such that a queering mixture of undeserved luck and demented frustration had turned Steve – and his colleague Danny Shyter – into superficial breezers with oodles of scuttlebutt to throw at clients, and zip integrity.

Steve had two accents: East London for the trade, i.e. fag-bitten story-liners from the soaps, and Surrey posh for broadcasting's lady executives. He'd have made a great cabby. He wore Trotsky spectacles, closely shaved hair, and liked to tuck a fag behind his ear. He also had a stud earring. This added up to a metrosexual street cool that would leave him absolutely nowhere to go in about five years' time.

I got through to him after a single ring.

'Fuck! Mike!'

'Can you talk?'

'Let me just ditch this.'

I heard quick speaking. He was wrapping up a call on his mobile.

I waited tensely.

His voice was suddenly immediate on the line. 'Where are you?'

'Wales.'

'Wales!'

'What story are you getting about me?' I asked.

'Um …' Steve took a split-second to come clean. 'Rehab.'

'Rehab!'

He grunted confirmation.

This I now found very annoying.

'Rehab from what?'

'Oooh … um … alcohol dependency, violent temper, personal shit, general crack-up.'

'Says who?'

'Are you OK?'

'Of course I'm fucking OK! According to whom?'

'Your best friend.'

I inhaled mightily, trying to bottle it.

Steve started to laugh.

'It's total rubbish!' I said.

'I know, I know.'

'I'm fine. Never better.'

Steve kept his voice low. 'So what is *really* going on?'

It was like a lid had been flipped. For a moment I found it hard to speak, I was so aggravated. Everything about the Colin fiasco was so irksome.

'What are they telling clients?' I said.

'Hang on a minute.'

He went off to close the door of his office. He was suddenly back, his tone more urgent, more on my side.

'They're saying you're on leave. Personal reasons.'

'Just personal?'

'Yeah.'

He was sifting a diplomatic line, trying to keep me cool. Even Steve had to be cagey, it seemed.

I composed myself. Now was not the time to lose it. Of course there was a campaign of personality assassination going on behind my back. Of course!

'So what's the real story?' he said more sympathetically.

'Is Helen holding it together?'

'She's varnishing nails and making long-distance personal calls, as per usual.'

'Aren't these Oxbridge graduates just the best!'

'You picked her, mate.'

'Melina?'

'Getting her fanny tanned in the Azores.'

'The professors?'

'Going down on each other in a manor house in Berkshire.'

No change there.

'What's the deal, Mike? You and Colin have a wingding?'

237

Steve was not the safest repository of dangerous confidences but it served me to come a little clean. He needed to see enough of the big picture to be helpful.

'Colin's suing me for slander.'

He gasped, a harsh sound, as if here were the final jaw-dropping proof of Colin's idiocy. 'What slander?'

'I told Patrick Dooley and his new assistant that Colin was a liar, a cheat and a wanker. The assistant is Colin's sister-in-law.'

Steve started laughing outright, a moisture-in-the-eyes type laugh. 'You are my absolute hero.'

'And you're a corpse if you tell anyone.'

By now his laugh was more of a wheeze, a need for breath. 'That is so bad.' There was a cough, a clearing of the throat. 'I am the grave.'

'Steve, listen …' I tried to sound casual. 'Is Sheila OK?'

He gave this a dutiful moment's thought. 'She's fine.'

I paused, wondering if Sheila could be seriously ill without people knowing.

'That's not what I'm hearing.'

'Who's telling you what?'

'Has she been in?'

'She comes in once a week. I haven't seen her in a bit. Is something wrong?'

It was too early to start any kind of rumour mill.

'She's usually working from home,' he added. 'There's an awful lot of "working from home" in the book department. Divan time is important if you've got dozens of manuscripts to read and lots of late nights to catch up on. Mike, this is terrible about Colin. Can't Sheila weigh in?'

'I have to assume that Sheila no longer cares about the consequences.'

Even Steve would have been concerned to hear this. Sheila's lack of mediation I had certainly found disappointing. What I hadn't considered was that her reticence might have been illness rather than a tacit siding with Colin.

'Fuck,' he said, thoughtfully.

There was little more I wanted to share at this stage.

'And how is dear Turd-Face getting on?' I asked.

'He's jumping on everyone's tits.'

Steve felt a degree of immunity to the rivalries of the book department. His client list was highly exportable, and at the same time he was a competent flogger of film rights and handler of TV presenters. He could afford to be more who-gives-a toss than I.

'Cozzer's driving me berserk with this *Gormenghast* clone tome, which is as saleable to film as a book about grannies. I really don't care how much girly publishing tara it's had. It ain't visible, ain't brand enough, and actually the writing's crap. Oh, hi, Colin!'

Colin had just walked into Steve's office. I nearly ducked.

There was a bump as the receiver hit something.

I heard a voice in the distance.

'What can I do you for, mate?'

Steve's voice was clearly audible.

There was a rumbling response, which then grew clearer – as if Steve were angling the telephone mouthpiece in Colin's direction.

'Have you seen Christina?' I could just hear Colin say.

'Nope.'

Christina was a work-experience girl.

There was more from Colin which I couldn't hear and then: 'Could you ask her to come and see me?'

Colin's disagreeable tone had gained in assertiveness. With

Sheila absent he was trying to sound like the firm's boss.

'She's not under the desk,' said Steve perkily.

'We need to talk about *Quirk Castle*.'

This sounded like the *Gormenghast* clone tome.

'D'you mind, Col? I'm on the blower.'

There was a pause.

'Cunt's left the room,' said Steve in a low voice.

I found myself gazing distractedly at the dashboard. Colin's manner was like a dawning truth. He had got his way at last. The little cuckoo had usurped me, yes, but now it seemed Sheila too, and nothing would stop him. Once the day-to-day running of the firm was in his control he would stamp his authority on everyone and everything. He would be pushing for results, haunting the corridors, settling scores, confronting, bossing, shaking up, scaring the place into a percentage mill for his profit and glory. I was sickened by the thought of it.

'You heard that?' said Steve.

'I'm afraid so.'

'He's on Christina's case big time.'

My thoughts were elsewhere.

'Hardly surprising. My eyeballs are actionably harassed every time she reaches a book off the shelf. She's heart-attack hot!'

'Christina?'

'Yep. Colin's onto her. Being very generous with his time, nudge nudge. It's rather shocking the way he monopolises the pretty interns and ignores everyone else. And there's the cheesy acts of chivalry – making her a coffee, helping her on with a coat, giving her a lift into town ...'

'Are you saying ...?'

'I'm saying Colin's got the horn for every decent-looking chick that checks in the building. Molly ...'

He broke off.

'Molly?'

'Hang on.'

Once again, he went off to press the door shut.

He picked up the phone again.

'I've had a thought,' he said. There was a strange silence.

'Steve …'

I heard an odd vocalisation marking some breakthrough in Steve's train of thought.

It was a kind of mirthless laughter, a detached glimpse of future joy – truly antic.

'Well, hey hey, this is very interesting.'

'Steve, I'm running out of juice.'

'Molly, remember her?'

You couldn't forget Molly; she was a leggy fine-featured girl with the sweetest smile, excellent posture and graceful arms. She read English at Oxford, *adored* books and added a considerable touch of class to the office.

'You know why she left?'

'Why?'

'Templar became a little too fresh.'

'What?'

'There were gropings in a taxi on the way to the Simon & Schuster party. She told Tom in accounts. Apparently Templar had been trying it on, little remarks, flirtation, a grazing hand …'

'Sexual harassment!'

'Well …'

Steve told me how Molly had regaled Tom and Steve and Carla Venables, who worked at another agency, with the tale of 'Templar's Tentacles' as she humorously called it – hints at job offers, lunches round the corner, side-by-side editorials on his chaise, glasses of wine – a catalogue of ingratiating ruses and dubious favouritism, which she handled as deftly as possible, whilst trying to discourage him. Molly was smart enough and witty enough to deflect and sidestep most of the time, but she did admit to a certain fascination. 'He's like a frog,' she told Steve laughingly, 'but so determined you sort of give up and give in,' and thus Molly had allowed flirtation to run too far in her determination not to let Colin's enthusiasm spoil an excellent placement, but when Colin got friendly in the black cab ('suddenly his hands were everywhere,' she told Steve, half hysterically, half in horror) she decided it was time to give in her notice and move somewhere safer. Later, when a position came up at the Acbe agency and another intern got it, Molly felt angry that Colin's antics had diddled her out of a job.

'My God!' I said. This was breathtaking information.

'You should have called me before now, man. I would have thought of this. And there's more.'

'You're not making it up?'

'It sort of washes over me,' said Steve. 'Colin's a minger. Why be surprised? Molly said one of the work-exp girls had actually shagged Colin.'

I was aghast.

'Veronique! Royal Cumberland Hotel.'

The information was electrifying, and strangely stunning. Such revelations were dense with meaning but also depressingly logical, because, of course, Colin would be like that. Ambitious, ruthless, driven: of course he would cheat on his wife! Power had gone to his bollocks. Success was in the bag and now he wanted some pleasure for his pains.

One by one the engines of a colossal anger switched on in my mind. No way was Templar going to get away with this.

'I guess that's rather useful,' said Steve. 'You want me to find Molly?'

I would have to think very carefully about this information and the light it cast on things. It was crucial to control the agenda and not let Steve run ahead of me.

'Don't compromise your position.' I said. 'I need to figure the angles, then let's talk. Steve, I'm really grateful. You're a true brick in time of need.'

'This conversation has not taken place.'

Even as I clicked off the mobile and gazed at the western sky, through the serpentine might of an oak tree, I realised that call would register on the agency phone bills, and from now on my contact with Steve had to be untraceable.

I twisted on the ignition and revved the engine before releasing the handbrake.

Tomorrow, London.

Chapter 19

He might be driving, Mike, or parking outside his house, or buying a carton of milk, and in she slides, like a sudden heat, flustering him.

What he experiences in these moments is the converging of two kinds of knowledge. In his mind already is everything he knows about her, Madelin from outside, Madelin as a friend, Madelin through laughter and conversation, the dark chocolate social version of Madelin. Blending with this is the secret, ardent Madelin; Madelin as body-heat, embraceable Madelin, a soft-centre Madelin that yields and kisses and rises at his touch. The two Madelins merge disturbingly, causing a sense of revelation, something almost heart-stopping. He has moments thinking of this other Madelin in the corner shop, moments which make him draw breath, turn away, and look madly down the aisle.

This is new and uncanny, never sensed before, 'biblical' knowledge of a *friend*, inerasable: the forbidden fruit and the unique taste of the forbidden fruit. Did Madelin know she was like this?

Chapter 20

Trattoria Bruno was, as expected, a cavy little place with cellar arches and textured plaster, framed photos of Amalfi, dangling bottles in baskets, a sweet trolley veiled in gauze, subdued customers at tables tucked into the wall, ceremonial delivery of such steaming bog-standard staples as Spaghetti Bolognese and Frito Misto on trays sped forth by glum waiters, the kitchen door yawning and shutting. There was a 'Good afternoon, sir,' and 'Your coat, please, sir' and 'Would sir like to come this way?' the 'sir' always ironic, and a familiar plod past pepper mills and racks of Chianti and polished mahogany counters to a cloistered alcove where, under yellowy light, I saw James Moyle rising from his seat to greet me, his legs uncrossing, his long back straightening, his hand furrowing towards a shake that was firm and appraising.

Moyle was much taller than I remembered. His was an elegant, bony tallness, a hawkish height, slightly stooped. His face was superbly aquiline and enquiring; his nose an Elgarian creation, handsomely bridged, that helped him peer at you with irresistible attention. His hands reminded me of some *fin de siècle* aesthete: long, tapered fingers that could wave so elegantly at a passing waiter, and rest so spiderishly on the stem of a fork. His eyes received me with benevolent courtesy as if already we were mischievously conspiring and had known each other for years. Moyle was older than I remembered; a face hewn with experience, the hair grey-black, but still a lush lock sprung forward across his brow that he intermittently drew back with outstretched fingertips. Class was deeply bred in his features yet Moyle was also a man of the world. Easy in the grandest drawing rooms, a father figure to world famous authors and discreet agent to ex-prime ministers, he could afford to mix it with commoners like me and despatch business in dingy trattorias. His time in the army had developed a tolerance for unvarnished basics. He could do as the natives did without batting an eyelid. Moyle's magnetism, I realised, derived from the flattering fullness of his interest in the person before him, whatever their rank.

'Wales OK?' he said, with a slightly amused smile, as he resumed his seat.

I nodded.

'Nice to get away from the cut and thrust. How's business?'

'Business is very good.'

'You've been there what … some years?'

'Fifteen years.'

'Sheila is a remarkable lady. I've got a lot of respect for Sheila.'

I waited.

He flounced his napkin on his lap. 'Colin Templar any good?'

'Colin has his merits.'

Moyle broke bread, nodded encouragingly.

'We have a working relationship,' I said neutrally.

There was no need to be indiscreet at this stage.

'That's the main thing,' he said, looking around. 'Sergio?'

Sergio appeared from behind a pillar. 'Mister Moyle, what can I get for you?'

'Pair of dry Martinis.'

'Very good, sir.'

Though reasonably composed, I was not quite myself. This meeting so bristled with ambiguities that it was hard to know how to seem. Candour might be premature, but pretence was pointless. The safest tactic was to mirror Moyle's style as best I could, following not leading, and playing with a straight bat until I knew where I stood.

He looked at me reasonably. 'Quite a bulldog, Colin.'

Moyle was wasting no time with pleasantries.

'Colin's ambitious.'

'And you're more the diplomat, I'd have thought.'

'Well, it takes all kinds.'

The Martinis arrived and Moyle raised a glass and an eyebrow. 'We should have done this before,' he said. 'Your very good health.'

I nodded and sipped my drink: *molto* dry. Moyle regarded me amicably. His demeanour was both well-meaning and evaluative.

'Certainly hope your health is better than Sheila's,' he nodded.

'You are very up to the minute.' I was trying to sound cool.

'Yes,' said Moyle, considerately. 'It's quite possible that the news hasn't got very far and that very few people know.'

'I actually know nothing.'

He frowned, clearly troubled by this. 'One of Sheila's clients is a very close friend.'

'Angus Gilmore?'

'Keeps me in the loop. He speaks very highly of you, by the way.'

I nodded.

'Colin he thinks rather tricky.'

Moyle glanced at his menu and rolled a piece of bread between long fingers. 'Angus is quite worried, actually, about what will happen to the agency when Sheila departs.'

'Departs?'

He gazed at me with clear grey eyes.

'I dare say you've given that some thought.'

'I may well have done.'

'And now her departure is liable to be sooner rather than later.'

I looked at him searchingly.

'I'm very sorry, Mike.'

I swallowed.

Moyle's lips moved before he spoke. 'Cancer of the pancreas. Really sorry to break it to you.' He buttered his bread. 'Probably better that you know.'

I was absolutely stunned.

Moyle exhaled stoically. 'I can understand her wanting to keep it under wraps, and I suppose we should, too.'

Even through the daze of astonishment, I sensed something beyond chivalry. Moyle was telling me that Sheila's condition was commercially sensitive information.

I was about to speak when he anticipated me.

'Inoperable and aggressive.'

'Oh, God!'

'Three months.'

I looked down at my placemat. I felt many things, terrible pity for Sheila, acute sadness, and the diminishing effect that fatal illness casts on all of us. Sheila's friendship and the rock-like stature of her career had been facts in my working life for so

248

long. It seemed unthinkable that she might, soon, leave us all behind.

There was nothing Moyle could say to diminish the impact of awful news. When the waiter arrived, he greeted him affably, not breaking the mood, but moving to the next stage with minimum fuss.

'Sardines fresh?'

'Of course, but also today we have meatballs. With parsley, a little lemon juice.' Sergio twiddled his fingers. 'Very good.'

'Sardines and meatballs it is,' confirmed Moyle.

'And for sir?'

'The same.'

'Bring us a bottle of Chianti,' said Moyle.

'Arturo,' shouted Sergio. 'Table 4!'

Arturo sped out of the gents like an express train.

Moyle looked sombrely at the red tablecloth.

'I have a notion that goes like this,' he regarded me candidly, as if gaining permission for a little hypothesising. 'Sheila, bless her, passes on. Colin raises finance towards a management buy-out, taking the lion's share of the company. With some shoving and barging he finds himself in control of a firm with significant client assets and solid cash flow. He moves quickly to bag Sheila's most valuable clients, cherry picking the best, giving bread and butter names to younger agents. Much as he envies your relationship with Sheila's old guard you do not figure in his plans. Colin is not a sharer.'

Moyle raised his chin shrewdly. With his right hand he twiddled the stem of a wine glass. He considered me with a level gaze. It wasn't a look that invited comment or qualification; it was a look that seemed to read my mind, as though he were helpfully articulating something it would be quite indiscreet of me to mention.

'Your position becomes increasingly uncomfortable. Colin's style is a far cry from Sheila's. Gosh, he's bumptious enough as a colleague! As an employer …' He let the word linger. '*Ghastly.*'

I listened, fascinated. Moyle was remarkably well informed and perceptive.

'You decide to leave. Some other agency welcomes you. Sanity returns. But over your shoulder you look back at a famous agency now entirely controlled by Colin. By any standards this is a travesty. And there's worse. You see, Colin, for all his ambition, is too ruthless. His need to service buy-out debt cuts everything to the bone. Agents depart. Unhappiness descends. Before you know it, a once distinguished agency has become a shadow of its former self.'

Moyle let it rest there for a moment.

'An asset that in more capable hands could have prospered fragments and dwindles, donating its client portfolio to rivals.'

He looked at me gravely.

It was very odd to hear this scenario from Moyle. Were his predictions hunches based on what he heard and what he surmised; or was his depiction of a probable future a dressing up of actual knowledge? It hardly mattered. His reading of Colin, and his vision of my fate were bang on. I couldn't be bothered to protest for the sake of appearance. On the contrary: his lucid exposition had a reinforcing effect.

The sardines arrived, gliding into place.

'You don't believe Colin can hack it?' I said curiously.

The end of a giant pepper pot hovered readily, and a succulent pop signalled the oncoming Chianti. Soon Moyle's long fingers levitated a glass lightly splashed with wine.

'I do not,' he sipped.

I raised my eyebrows. Here was acumen indeed: concise, peremptory, unflinching.

'Wine's good,' he nodded to Sergio.

Moyle tucked into his sardines with a sense of urgency. The fish were eaten whole, eyes, spine, tail fin, the works; bits of salad and tomato were scooped efficiently. Within a couple of minutes the plate was cleared. He dusted his lips with a napkin and reached for his glass.

'From where you are standing, not a pretty prospect.'

I listened carefully, biting a thumbnail.

'If Angus Gilmore is concerned about Colin taking over, so will be Frances Gish.'

Another of Sheila's clients.

'I can't see Madeleine Letts or D. S. Henson *loving* Colin.'

'He's a useless editor,' I said.

'Not a nurturer. And, to state the obvious, not Sheila.'

He dabbed his bread in the juices of his plate. The discussion gave zest to his appetite.

'Those sorts of clients will be looking around. They'll be less loyal to the agency after Sheila's death.'

The word, *that* word – so shocking. Moyle's realism was pretty brutal. He was evidently testing my ability to face the facts like a man – and face them on the double.

'And the younger guns – people like Carl Phillips, Jane Kale …'

I nodded, trying to concentrate. I was struck by his knowledge of her list.

'None of these bright sparks are going to welcome regime change. If you've been represented by Sheila, you've been associated with the best.'

This was a good point, an observation with edge.

'There are other agencies you could go to.'

He let the point linger.

'Besides which, there is a limit to how many clients an agent

251

can handle. Colin will be overwhelmed unless he hires very quickly.'

We had now advanced to a scenario where I was out of the agency. Moyle's presentation was getting very close to the truth.

'Once clients begin to jump ship … a question mark will hang over Colin's stewardship.' He looked at me with urbane regret. 'The result: a feeding frenzy. Dear Sheila's legacy will be thrown to the four winds.'

He watched on neutrally as the sardine plates were swept away and the meatballs arrived.

A rather rank smell hovered over my plate. I glanced at Moyle, but he seemed indifferent, oblivious to the odour. Indeed, his appetite intensified as he launched his cutlery into the meat. He chewed, ran his tongue inside his gums, swallowed with little bows of the head, and masticated purposefully.

'I have an idea, you see.'

I waited.

'The Great Client Rescue.'

Although I had an inkling of what was coming – our lunch presupposed the idea of collaboration – I had not seen the beauty of it from Moyle's perspective. He and I might get on reasonably, but as a player he outranked me by several leagues and amalgamation between us made little sense. It was only as he expounded his 'idea' that its logic became seriously convincing. His plan was that I should leave Acbe Agency as soon as possible and join Moyle Associates. I would secure my clients, circumnavigate the non-solicitation clause in my employment contract, and bring them with me. Moyle would offer free housekeeping and staff support as I got my thighs under the desk. In return, I would tell him all I knew about Sheila's clients: an inside-track briefing that he could put to good use. Together, he and I could offer them the winning combination of excellence *and* continuity.

'Once Sheila's off the scene, we make an aggressive play for half a dozen top names on her list. If we time it right, we spring a wholesale defection before Colin knows what's hit him.'

Moyle deposited the last meatball in his mouth and ground at it effectively. He settled his knife and fork, touched his napkin, and gave me a look that was precise and dangerous. I realised later that he knew – he *must* have known – that he was offering me the vista of revenge.

Many powerful feelings crossed my mind as I sat there, dusting my lips with the napkin and gazing a little to one side. I tried not to let the emotion show. In the last few weeks I had been boxing and coxing with depression, veering from distress to denial, resignation to detachment, feeling like a loser one minute, a victim the next. Not wanting my fate I had tried to ingest it, as if there was a higher truth in the whole miserable business that I could manfully stomach, before lurching on to pastures new. But now, sitting in my suit, stiffened by tie and cuff-links, I felt a flush of feral excitement, a surge of pride that was always my fucking due. Moyle's plan was like a steroid jab. It proved that my professional life was real, could be rescued and vigorously prosecuted and that Colin was an adversary who could be shafted by those with the right kind of friends.

It was crucial to say nothing which might shake his confidence in me – or the plan. I could reveal nothing about the deal with Colin, my selling out, the non-compete clause, my banishment as an agent. This little fly in the ointment would have to be pondered carefully before I came clean.

'Does that make sense?' said Moyle, raising an eyebrow. He had certainly laid his cards on the table.

'It does.'

There was a pause.

'It is timely,' I said.

Moyle nodded.

Only days ago I had wanted to give up and walk away from it all. Why walk away on somebody else's terms? Why let Colin dictate the final scenes of my career? For agents, success was the only raison d'être. Moyle's overture stirred a passionate desire for vindication and self-respect.

Moyle rewarded himself with a top-up of wine. He did the same for me.

Now that his cards were arrayed there were tactics to discuss. Here was a busy, successful man taking a punt. He wanted the most value he could get from our lunch. I might be awash with powerful emotions but he had neither the need nor the inclination to service the human dimension of a business idea.

'You and Sheila go back,' he said, pinching his septum. 'I think a bunch of flowers and a nice note can hardly go amiss.'

I caught his meaning. 'You think I should go and see her?'

He looked at me expressionlessly. 'Phone one of her children and ask if there's anything you can do.'

I nodded.

'Little touches of kindness and sympathy may be remembered.'

I nodded again.

'Some kind of blessing might follow. You know … deathbed recommendations to distressed clients – "Oh, you'd be very happy with James and Mike",' he smiled evocatively. 'Not that I want to seem cynical. But life goes on for the rest of us and we may as well get it right.'

I was suddenly struck by Sheila's illness. For years we had been a part of each other's daily life. Whatever she thought of my efforts as an agent, she had always treated me decently. One could see why the poor woman had not ridden to my rescue. She was beyond the hassle of placating Colin, and probably beyond caring. What Sheila faced was a challenge from a higher realm, one that had a humbling effect on agents in particular, engaged as we were with temporal obsessions and vicarious campaigns.

'Anything else I should do?' I said, after a moment's distraction.

'What would be ideal,' Moyle toyed with his dessert spoon, 'is a high-profile defection from Colin's list.'

Moyle's absence of hypocrisy was pretty bracing. I was let into the workings of a mind that freely countenanced the need for ruthlessness. To will the end one must make love to the means, he seemed to enjoin.

'One thing to raid a deceased agent's clients,' I said, carefully. 'Quite another to poach them from a Young Turk.'

'"Poach" is a misnomer. This is a *rescue* mission.'

He looked as though he believed that. Moyle was too sophisticated to acknowledge truth over spin until it became presentationally unavoidable.

'Why would any of his clients break ranks?'

'Because somewhere else looks better.' He tongued at a molar: this seemed to democratise a thought process. 'Sheila dies. Her sorrowful clients consider their position. They consider Colin. Or rather, Colin invites their consideration. "I'll look after you," he says. "I'll build on what Sheila's done. I'll do more. Sheila trained me, but I'm younger and know the ways of the world better than she. She was the past. I am the future. Stay with the agency and I'll lead you to greater things."' He was thoughtful for a moment. 'We need to make that little speech seem *fatuous*.'

This kind of talk was closer to conspiracy than tactics and I might have found it off-putting. Between a readiness to shaft

255

commercial competitors and the will to stiff an ex-colleague lay a very thin line. I was on notice of a cunning intelligence that might not always have my best interests at heart.

'A defection from Colin's list would be dreadful PR,' he concluded.

'Embarrassing.'

'Anybody come to mind?'

Poaching from Colin was more hazardous, particularly for me, and represented a line I wasn't keen to cross. It was too early to let Moyle in on the terms of my deal with Colin; but if my plan banked on breaching that agreement after it was signed, after I'd been paid, and somehow blocking Colin's enforcement of its non-compete terms, it would be mad to provoke him excessively.

'It's important, you see, to strike first,' he smiled lustily. 'With deadly force.'

'There are probably legal issues.'

'Let him issue a writ. Against whom? Me?'

Against Moyle, Colin could have no cause of action. If Moyle represented whoever left Colin, as well as Sheila's ex-clients, and came to an arrangement with me behind the scenes, Colin would lack an obvious target. Moyle had thought this through very carefully.

I considered this for a moment. Between the blueprint of his plan and its successful execution lay the major uncertainty of how Colin would perform under fire. Canniness would be essential, and a yen to lay the first punch. Or kick. I could understand my own motives for wanting to hurt Colin. What intrigued me was Moyle's delicately controlled hostility towards him. Had Colin offended him, or pulled a fast one? Was Colin the disagreeable face of a younger, thrusting generation who played by different rules and showed no respect for reigning monarchs?

'I've got nothing against Colin personally,' said Moyle, as if reading my thoughts.

'He's a wanker.'

Moyle liked this very much. It was my first unguarded remark, and it told him a great deal.

'Wankers must be bested,' he declared.

A thought rose up, glaringly obvious.

I hesitated. It would be a mistake to raise expectations. On the other hand, I sensed a pressure to deliver. In exchange for levelling with me, Moyle wanted something back, something solid. Cards had to be lain on the table for a plan to become a pact.

'Vincent Savage,' I said.

He looked at me sharply.

I felt a rush of excitement. This was a gamble.

'Ah!'

I returned his look as blithely as possible.

'Quite a piece of work!' he said.

'Yup, he is difficult,' I swallowed. 'The question is whether his defection would damage Colin.'

'It would!'

I waited.

'Savage is a prominent client of Colin's. His defection would be visible and compromising,' said Moyle.

'Savage is a handful.' I didn't want to seem naive.

'But here, Savage is firing Colin. Not vice versa.'

'Yes, and if you see fit to represent Savage, the presumption is against Colin.'

Moyle stroked his lip and then looked at me with clear blue eyes. 'Can you get him?'

I forced a smile. I had to be confident.

'Yes.'

Moyle's pleasure in the answer showed in an expressionless look of reckoning. He gazed unblinkingly at his side plate, at his wine glass, as though the blueprint of a battle plan had become the battlefield itself.

'That would be a very handy start. If you bring in Savage, we can do a nice little deal.'

I nodded meaningfully. A nice little deal would be pretty damn crucial and a revealing process, to boot. Moyle's offer to me would have to strike a balance between personal avarice and a tactical generosity, the exact calibration of which – to satisfy both of us – would need to reveal the hand of a master.

'You're an admirer of Savage's oeuvre?' I asked. It seemed wise to check the extent, if any, of Moyle's good faith towards a prospective client.

'Another drop?' he said.

'Thank you.'

He filled my glass and then looked at me with a stony absence of feeling. 'I would be delighted to represent Vincent Savage. And you can tell him that.'

'And the work?' I persisted. 'You admire his work?'

Moyle knew he was being tested and took rather kindly to my professional thoroughness.

'Oh yes,' he said, smiling, as if it were the most obvious thing in the world.

I gazed at him, trying to evaluate the obvious lack of sincerity. Perhaps he shared my reservations about Vince's writing. Perhaps he had not yet sampled our great contemporary bard.

'In your opinion what's the best course for him?'

If I went to the trouble of persuading Vince to join Moyle's agency, I would be responsible for the *bona fides* of the recommendation. I was putting Moyle on notice of his duty to me as an intermediary, as well as his obligations to a possible client.

'What is he?' said Moyle casually. 'Five, six novels in?'

I nodded.

Moyle leaned impressively forward, fingers linking over his plate, hair flaring in leonine splendour. 'He seems to have arrived at the stage in a career when I always tell a writer, write your war book.'

'War book?'

This sounded very glib.

He smiled serenely. 'No matter how good a writer is, it's impossible to break out without a war book. Imagine McEwan without *Atonement*, de Bernières without *Captain Corelli*, Barker without *The Regeneration Trilogy*, Faulks without *Birdsong*.'

I frowned.

'Then there's *Suite Française, Stalingrad, Life and Fate, War and Peace*. The list is endless. Epic accounts of human suffering do the biz, time after time.'

He regarded me with solid self-assurance. One did not rashly call Moyle's bluff. His assertions were like riddles impregnated with a logic that feebler minds could decipher in their own time.

'I couldn't go very far along the road you suggest without having an arrangement,' I said.

'I wouldn't expect you to. I've already thought of that.'

I nodded.

He looked at me carefully. 'Bring me the head of Vincent Savage and I'll make you a proposal.'

Later, on the street, the Albert Hall behind me, I felt different. If somebody takes you seriously, you take yourself seriously. Moyle's overture reinforced what I had always wanted to believe:

that I was actually quite good. There was much to think about now. As I strolled along the pavement, I was determined to be very clever indeed. I had interesting plans for Colin. Vince would be a load trickier. Our relationship was a conversational knock-about plotted by uncontrollable subtexts and suspicions, but at least I had an honest pretext for return: his latest set of pages.

As regards Colin, I must sign the severance deal and get the money in. His thousands would give me purchasing power, and thus my final question to Moyle:

'I don't suppose any of your clients would know of a good private detective?'

Moyle played this with a very straight bat. If he was curious, he concealed it.

'Yes, there's somebody I could ask. Want me to get a number?'

'I'd be very grateful.'

I rose with a smile.

Already I was beginning to sound and speak like him: the sincerest kind of dissimulation.

***

I watched the traffic rush past and gazed at the Albert Memorial with its tracery of pigeons spanning in arcs against the blue afternoon sky. I had arrived at the point of no return. In my case were the severance contracts, now signed by me and ready for Colin's signature. I decided to get on with this momentous end to my years at the agency and suddenly had the mobile out and dialled. I asked for Colin's assistant and told her I would drop the agreements off in an hour. 'I'll be in a cab, so perhaps someone could come down and collect them?'

I continued along the pavement, feeling buoyed, dangerously focussed, ready to act.

I turned to hail a taxi, but my eye caught a familiar face across the street.

The cabby pulled over, rolled down a window.

I stared at him blankly.

'Where to, guvnor?'

'Sorry,' I said, rooted to the spot.

He seemed to get this, and pulled hard on the steering wheel. 'Make yer bleedin' mind up.'

The cab drew away, leaving a view of a woman turning into Blenheim Crescent.

Nadia.

***

Nadia walks towards him, holding hands with a man in blazer and chinos.

James Woodruff, her fiancé: sandy hair, clear jaw, medium height.

They are in a world of their own – where every street is Paris, every expensive shopping arcade the future, where old people smile at the sight of them, lovers, their hands garlanded, in a dream of happiness as they halt and linger on the kerb.

Now he leans in and says something to her. She smiles, eyes adoring, and he raises her knuckles in his hand and kisses them, and she flings her arms around him and they embrace like a couple in the movies, the city swirling around their love.

Mike freezes. He is a predator of this scene. His eyes feed on the spectacle, absorbing everything. He cannot budge. He cannot evade them. He expects to be spotted across the road but he won't look away, because the information is transfixing, about Nadia, about the pair of them, about the sight of your ex in love with your successor, giving him the smiles and the embraces and the melting looks she once gave you, and the information you get about yourself when you see it all, a diffusing hot river of mortification and sorrow that runs in through the eyes and turns your innards to jelly.

Chapter 21

The hill bobs in the foreground of his vision, jarred by each tread. He tries to *see*, to notice, to absorb. There is a moment when seeing catches at words, when sensation levers metaphor, when the overwhelming multitude of figures and particles in vision focusses down through the straining of an impression, the saturation of an impression, to form phrases, similes, word patterns that begin to reconstitute the miasma in language; but the miasma swirls now, intoxicates, brings forth terrible emotion, the fringes of divine madness; so now he must concentrate, each forward step moving the lens over the landscape, the teeming of the present.

The grass is sheeted with water. Water seeps down the slopes. The rills are busy. Ditches are guttering. Water moves everywhere. The hill bleeds water. Laid hedgerows follow the footpath. Half-crippled birches stoop at the field's edge.

Sunlight now, heat on the neck. The clouds are still gaseous, gliding in misshapen disarray against rising ground. Distances clear, valleys are revealed. Thunderous black turmoil hovers over the crests and peaks. But the sunlight flows across his path, greening up the field, etching tree bark, sparking wetness into foil-like

263

sheets of glisten, and when the warm light travels up the hill ahead, its coat of bracken glows like eczema, like great patches of inflammation. From the heights of Cwm Du he will see nymph-like birch trees, arms aloft and tapering like ballerinas bound in white.

Vince hears the subdued thunder of an aeroplane, suddenly blotted.

He climbs, almost robotically, a ritual of ascent, of leaving the flat world behind, an acquiring impulse, get higher, see more, be on the roof, gain equality of vantage with those mighty personages that dominate the landscape, those immemorial fells and peaks.

A white van hundreds of feet below moves like an insect along the road. Lanes fall like ribbons across the foothills.

Turneresque cataclysms of cloud-light hang in the west, rays streaming through breaches in the canopy, dazzling forests, floodlighting the green breast of a hill. The sky is an extension of beacon drama, a vaporisation of mountain menace into vaunting cumuli and black escarpment and orangey chasms that mass and move like some predatory amoebic monster trailing over a beautiful reclining body.

He trudges upwards, hearing the music, an inchoate straining of violins, the upper reaches, swarming urgently, a gathering of forces, movement below, tectonic shifts in harmony, profound adjustment in the basses and tubas, a gradual revelation of some awesome vista, the dead drop of a canyon, harmonies strained and still evolving out of some central contortion, patches of light, triadic chords that transiently combine, shining reassurance in the murk, and now the big progression, brass in the centre, coarse, majestic, ripping, everything stretched on the vertical rack, tightening here, squeezing there, like a rearing figure roused

264

to an agony of awakening by a vast organ-like crash of C major, the radiant crisis, coalesced ineluctably out of discord and mayhem, a glimpse, a first glimpse of transcendence, a soul-harrowing, breathtaking transcendence.

And then silence before the alien clarinet note.

He would walk for hours hearing Sibelius.

He would come down off the heights, stalk through woods with twisted trees and noisy streams, cross road and field on determined bee-lines, the mud gathering on his boots, his hair wet, his lungs tingling; and as he traipsed onwards, delighted by the rainbow arcing over Crickhowell and the opening continent of blue sky and the gloss of the pastures, he realised this would always be available; this beauty, he possessed it; everything he loved was here, and if this was available when he needed it, then nothing that counted could be taken from him, and his mission seemed different: to appreciate, to be grateful, to cherish the living world. He was blessed really. He could be happy, he could find peace. What more was needed than to give thanks, and to tend and nurture what you had, because already this landscape renewed him?

There were tears in his eyes as he went up the lane to their house. He felt the love rising within him. Love for Holly. Love for Madelin. What a beatitude it was to have a wife and daughter! What more did a man need, except to make them happy and look after them and help them get the most out of their talents and dreams? He was surrounded by dapple and motes of blue sky in the overhead branches and clarity of form in all things, and nature's plenty, and it squeezed his heart and made him sorry for what he had done to them, sorry and ready to be kind, loving and selfless, ready to set aside everything for them, to show he cared.

He walked along the farm track past the old machinery; he felt light-headed; a kind of euphoria washed over him. He opened the gate and strode up the drive. He had to act on this feeling. He was bearing something within him. He saw his long shadow on the lawn; heard his boots on the pathway, saw his hand on the doorknob, the door swinging inwards, the floor rug, the sofa; he heard her in the kitchen; went through the hall, saw her at the sink, leaning into suds, hair falling. He came forward, treading closer, his looming height filling the corridor, and as he passed into the kitchen, a tower of remorse, and she kept on at her washing, and he saw the resistance he faced, he sank to his knees and put his arms around her waist and said: 'Forgive me, Madelin.'

***

He held on to her.

Her body was stiff.

Her hands continued to work in the bowl.

He released her. She moved away, pulling off her rubber gloves. She opened the door of the washing machine and pulled the wash into a basket.

He remained on his knees, head cast down.

'I'll get a job. Look after you and Holly.'

She brought the laundry basket over to the counter, lowered the rack over the Aga. She pulled out white school shirts and kids' trousers and hung them. She worked away in front of him, unwinding, draping, sorting.

The floor was hard, but he needed to abase himself.

He could hear her breathing, little sighs of effort. She had not wished to face him.

'Where do we start?' he said.

The silence, her silence, seemed interminable. Still she kept working.

'Don't let Holly see you in that ridiculous position,' she said, suddenly.

He adjusted his knee. Rising would have been a kind of defeat, a return to the familiar postures of marital compromise.

She moved a bowl roughly to the sink.

'Madelin …'

'How am I supposed to take pity on someone who has been utterly ruthless to me?'

He bowed his head.

'That was someone else.'

'So who are you, then?' she said, mockingly.

'I don't really know. I only know that I love you and Holly and want to make it work.'

He could sense her anger, but also her unpreparedness for this. He had surprised her and this she resented, too. Reconciliation was not quite on her shopping list today.

She drained the sink, cutlery clattering.

'Madelin. Sorry.'

'I don't feel like having a row at this precise moment,' she said.

'It doesn't have to be a row.'

'What else would it be?'

'An explanation.'

He stared at her fervently.

'It may be too late for explanations,' she said.

'I hope not.'

He would have to keep turning the other cheek; a penance would be required.

'You can't just walk back into a relationship you've ignored for weeks.'

'I know. I'm not expecting to.'

She carried on. Her movements were jarring, noise-making.

'I know what you've been through,' he said.

'I doubt it.'

'I want to make it up to you.'

'Well, you can start by washing the dishes.'

'Yes. OK.'

She moved across to the table, mopping off crumbs, splashes of tomato sauce, a vigorous wiping.

Slowly, he rose, knees aching and cold from the floor.

'Madelin, could we …'

'This place doesn't just run itself. There's work to be done.'

'I'll help.'

'Good. Because I don't need words. I need actions. I'm not ready to forgive.'

He stared at the back of her head. It was possible to love somebody through a barrage of hostility.

She walked past him, drying her hands on the kitchen towel, and out into the corridor. Moments later, he heard the hinge of the front door as it opened and shut; and then the sound of a car engine revving, which faded as she drove off.

***

Vince stood over the sink, hands in gloves, sponging clean a knife. He stared at the turquoise tiles behind the sink. The dots of colour in the glaze seemed to intensify; the different shades and hues were moving, aqueous, composed of swarming particles. The suds were iridescent. Droplets on the steel sink captured light. Hot water in the tub warmed his hands through the glove rubber. He wiped and rinsed, soaked and rinsed. Water jetted from the tap, a steaming spurt, and cascaded off plates. He set a glass in the rack and stared at a tile, held by its ambiguous tonality. Colour and time seemed at one. This reflected light was a section of spectrum repelled by its surface. The extraordinary beauty of this unstable merging of green and blue was itself a miracle. He looked closer, frowning. You became the thing you observed. It saturated vision, thought, and feeling.

***

He was in the kitchen when she returned: seated; rubber gloves still on, eye trained on the view through the window.

'Let's go on a holiday for a couple of weeks,' he said.

She set down a shopping bag.

'Maybe we need a holiday from each other,' she replied.

'It's over. I'm through with it.'

'I don't know what you're talking about, but it doesn't change anything.'

'Writing.' He looked at her squarely. 'It's madness, a disease. I can live without it.'

She avoided his steadfast gaze, glancing over to the sink. He had not finished washing up.

'Mini-cab driving for you, is it?'

He refused to look away. His eyes followed her across the room.

She put potatoes on a rack, rice in a cupboard.

'Vince, it's not the writing that's the problem. It's you.'

She folded a teacloth over the Aga rail and left the room.

His eyes fell slowly, resting on levels of things: spice rack, wall calendar, the back of a chair, the yellow mesh of conjoined gloves on his lap.

Holly is spellbound.

It is the first time that Vince has read to her in weeks and she cleaves to him tightly, her little hand clutching at a fold in his jersey as they sit on the bed. Today, Holly kidnapped the school hamster and brought it home in her pocket. The hamster was let free to navigate around her bedroom before getting trapped behind the radiator. When Madelin heard Holly's cries, she called Vince and told him with a look, and he charged upstairs to the rescue. Holly was wailing and the hamster was shivering and it took a lot of crouching around and delicate finger-work to extricate the creature. They made a home for it out of a shoe box, cutting in air-holes and putting in a carrot. He soothed his daughter and sat her on the bed with a book while Madelin got tea ready downstairs. Holly needed him more than the hamster, he saw from the way she worked her head into the crook of his arm. During tea Madelin sat at the end of the kitchen table avoiding his gaze. They both ministered to Holly, talking to her, but not to each other.

His eyes become tearful as he realises what he has done. He is emerging from a realm of insanity, and the pressure of her little body against his great torso rings out his compassion for her. He sets down the book, squeezes her to his side. His throat is tight.

'Sorry, Holly.'

There is silence.

'It's all right, Daddy.'

He nuzzles her hair with his chin.

'Daddy's better now.'

She holds on to him even tighter. He must be explicit, must allay her fears.

'That note was just me being stupid. Don't worry. Everything's OK now, and we're going to have fun.'

He could hear her breathing and see her little chest rise and fall. She is holding on to him for dear life, desperate for him not to go.

He cups Holly's hand in his, squeezing it.

***

Madelin sits at her desk in the barn office. The windows are dark, uncurtained. Her shelves of artist's material (paint tubes, pots of acrylic, rolled canvas) and the detritus of memorabilia (postcards tacked to the wall, earthenware jugs with opalescent glazes, aerial pictures of rainforest and river delta torn from pages of *National Geographic*, a photo of Frank on a hill, hair slanted by the wind) are garishly lit by a strip bulb. She holds a mug of coffee and sits pensively.

She sees the hamster episode as a devastating indictment of parental failure, and a warning. Holly wanted something to love and pet. She had to steal it. The neglected child is impelled to love even as she craves love for herself and neither Mummy nor Daddy have let love pass freely in the house. Love has been bottled, even Madelin's for Holly: a grave admission. She feels such solicitude for Holly, even as she sees the truth. And yet, failure compounds failure. She stayed downstairs while Vince did the comforting. He ran to the rescue and she withdrew into domestic autopilot because that was all she could manage. Holly's misdemeanour was a rebuke. Vince rose to the challenge but Madelin catered it. During tea she felt incompetent as a mother. She did not have it in her to sustain the soft, dove-like mother noises of reassurance or

271

even go through the motions. She detests herself for this and hates Vince for his melodramatic personality transformation which she cannot respond to. She cannot yield to his remorse. Holly and Vince are now cuddled on the sitting-room sofa watching a film.

Is it too late, she wonders, to focus on Holly, to do what Holly wanted just so that later Holly would believe she had had enough from a mother who in reality was too unhappy to vest some life-giving part of herself in a child?

Madelin occupies herself in the studio office amidst the aromas of white spirit and charcoal. She is easier here where her pictures are; she feels that the best of her is stored in portfolios and drawers: paintings, lithographs, mementoes of a past life, of art school and the early years in London, those footloose Archway days. Was she meant to be single always? A free spirit, consorting with men for amusement and delicious interludes of sex, and then shooing them off so she could be alone and get on with it? Was marriage her undoing? Such thoughts tighten the heart.

Now come on, she says, get out the pictures, have a look at what you've done. She lifts out a group of canvases and sets them on the counter: a triptych of oils, clay colours, hints of pink, heavy brushwork, irksome to behold at first, but already the eye is reading colour and form into what is not fully realised, as if the pictures were talking to her, and inviting their means of improvement. She gazes with the slack expression artists manifest when regarding their work, as if all sense of the outgoing personality has been syringed from the countenance. These paintings of Xenia's headless torso are little dreams of jealousy, she realises. How Madelin would love a jouncy young body like this with those buoyant breasts and that taut tummy and the gorgeous bumper of a bottom (so relished by Xenia's biker boyfriend, the handsome Nick). With what pleasure she had coaxed those sexy volumes into paint, an act of erotic appropriation. Her images of Xenia are a means to arouse and disarm: one woman's tribute to another's nubile body: decapitated.

The artist was a kind of vampire in the end; though what she needs now is not blood but wine.

The young Nicks of the world have an awful lot to learn, she thinks, as she pulls the cork off a bottle of Sauvignon Blanc and stares at the canvas.

***

The hallway is only a door's width and hems Mike in as he enters. Dim window light stands in the living room. The still air traps a grey silence. He gazes in a trance. His furniture speaks to him of solitary routines; the wing-backed armchair; the footrest his mother gave him. Pictures and prints greet him with washed-out familiarity.

He drifts through the flat oppressed by its sameness. What pains he had taken back then, all the wood-stripping, and shelving, and curtains, to make the most of his home. How pleasing were the cornicing and alcoves that you got in these tall Victorian terraces. How stale and pointless it seems now.

***

He lies on the double-bed. He can only lie. He is injured and has no mind for anything else. He never expected to feel so much pain, such physical misery, and can only succumb, letting it take his thoughts where it will. Yet lying down is almost worse. Lying

273

adds the suffocation of inertia to the agonies of the spirit. Lying lets it get to him, the storm of emotions, in his chest and belly, in the neck and the temples.

He had known his own unhappiness before. What he had not reckoned on was the effect of Nadia's happiness. It overran his defences. Before he could deflect or somehow dodge the blow, her happiness had cut him in the heart. She was in love with James. She was beaming with love for him, and the sight of it was killing.

The revolution of emotions in his chest is an unwelcome reminder of the unprotected self that exists beneath the person that he has tried to be in the world. He is all turmoil inside. He cares. He is tortured. He feels as badly as ever, worse actually, and the feelings are like an aching boil in the entrails.

Mike has no choice but to suffer the cruellest paradox: that his perception of what he took to be Nadia's lovable essence has not enabled her to become the self she wanted to be. Another man excites her more; and Mike's love is powerless and without value. He holds no sway with any woman who wants a future, and a man with a future like James is much more of a man. Life with Mike was a cosy flat. Life with James is a mansion with children's voices and rolling lawns, and staff.

The hope and promise of the years have led to this.

For hours he lies as the windowpanes turn black and the room darkens. At times his thoughts are so miserable he feels a physical pain. In the throes of bereavement his face crumples up. He thinks there is no moral framework to this suffering, because what sententious life lesson could gainsay the hurt he feels?

He will remember hauling himself up against the pillows and rubbing his eyes and clicking on the table lamp and thinking that

274

he has to do something to crawl out of this state. He glances at the briefcase on the floor. Wearily he rises from the bed and grabs the case and pulls out an *Evening Standard*, and a swatch of pages: Vince's.

He reclines against the bedstead to read the pages. He has no energy or interest, merely a kind of dumb will to do something.

***

Many times over the years Mike has known that curious moment when office work brought home – yet another manuscript or outline to get through – seeming like a chore or tax on spare time, becomes engrossing, a gift to the listless or tired. He holds Vince's typescript and feels that he has nothing to offer this piece of work, and nothing to take from it. He is deadened inside and he lies – head on pillow – like a recumbent stone lord on a cathedral sarcophagus. His eyes track the lines of print, his chest rises and falls. Later, he will remember the indiscernible progression of his interest in the pages before him from zero goodwill to a kind of numb passivity – let this take me where it will – to a moderate absorption (during which the critical daggers are wrapped and set aside) to the inklings of enjoyment, as in: 'OK, I'll go with this if you don't muck me about'; and from qualified approval to a sharp quickening of interest in response to a beautifully apt sentence, and thence to a new, intensified involvement that he later marked as having occurred on page 32. It is the last time he will feel in a position of superiority to the material. From here on his attitude elevates from respect to admiration to enthralment. By page 60 he is sitting up, fully engaged, physically revived, and the fairy lights are twinkling, the set of responses that have literary agents on alert. This, he realises, this, he declares, is the real thing; the manifestation of a level of talent that is newsworthy and towards which he owes an exciting duty. This piece of work redeems its author. These pages are glowing evidence of a humanity and artistry that Mike would never have suspected. This he can respond to with all the partisanship and selflessness in the world. He has been granted the privilege of a first look, and the opportunity to deliver to its creator a ringing endorsement.

OK, he realises, getting up and slipping into his shoes and padding about the bedroom in a state, this 'Sibelius' fragment, with its majestic evocations of landscape – unlike anything Vince has written before – is merely a trailer of the brilliance to come. He can sing its praises wholeheartedly, enforcing Vince's new-found direction, but the problem of form and direction is open-ended. Vince has the kernel, how does he develop it? God, what a rollercoaster! Nothing to live for, and then something to live for, and all of it coming from outside himself, as though he were just a very emotional instrument played on by other people. He flops back onto the bed, dazed. He must call Vince. Vince needs a shot in the arm. He is aware of the pleasure of bringing good news to a man who has suffered and kept on going through the drizzle and bird shit. This literary agent job enables you to reinforce the endeavour of another human being. To give praise is certainly better than to receive it and bonds people across the trickiness of personal relationships. Mike's brain is active now. He is tingling with purpose and intimations of opportunity.

Impulsively, he picks up the phone and dials a number. The voicemail kicks in, so he leaves a message for Vince to call.

Madelin rings immediately.

276

***

'Are you coming back?' she says.

He is not ready for this. This catches him out. He is absolutely unequipped to meet this.

'How's tricks?'

'Fine … Fine!'

'You sound different,' she says.

He is sitting on the bed, a hand at his temple.

'I'm fine.'

'Vince has gone mad. He's been washing up and saying that he loves me.'

Should he tell her about the manuscript? Not her scene.

'Don't say "how marvellous" or I'll be offended.'

Mike has to gouge something out of another part of himself.

'I suppose you *do* want your husband to love you?'

'I think it's rather inconsiderate of him under the circumstances.'

Her tone presumes a kind of casual, gossipy betrayal of Vince which now seems inappropriate. A lengthy silence follows.

'I need him back in the cabin, Mike.'

'Yes, well, obviously, he's got to get writing. I've read his latest …'

'He's given up writing, by the way. Vince is quitting the literary life. He wants to devote himself to Holly and me and grow vegetables and do housework, and minicab driving for pocket money.'

He sits forward on the bed, a displacement.

'Your marriage guidance counselling seems to have hit the spot.' She hiccoughs.

Mike's mind swarms. 'Um … So … How do you feel about that?'

She laughs. 'Your bedside manner is truly soothing. I don't have any feelings. I'm a feeling-free zone where Vince is concerned. He systematically destroyed my feelings, except rage and hate, of course.'

'Hate might be evidence of love.'

'Whose side are you on?'

'Nobody's. I want the best outcome for all parties.'

'Yeah, well that isn't going to be possible, I'm afraid. Are you coming back here to amuse me?' she says in a huskier tone.

His heart is racing. 'Obviously, it sounds as though Vince needs some bucking up.'

'We could all do with some bucking, Mike.'

He blanches.

'I hope you're still up for a bit more adultery.'

'Madelin!'

'Is that a "yes"?'

He cups his forehead, worried.

There is a hiccough. He thinks he can hear her swigging.

'Are you drinking?'

She laughs. 'Of course I'm drinking. I'm on the bottle pining for you.'

Madelin drunk and denied is a wild card.

'I have an errand for you,' she says.

He reaches for a glass of water with the sense that complications are multiplying and that he no longer has the stomach for it.

'I want you to buy me a lads' mag or three. Xenia has set her heart on modelling and I'm putting together a portfolio of glamorous body shots.'

'Xenia?'

'Delectably nude.'

The wanton streak in Madelin was never manageable or subject to reason. He grimaces, panicking. 'Try the internet.'

'We need to see the fashionable boy mag positions. But we're too shy and well brought-up to go into a shop and reach something off the top rack.' She bursts out laughing.

Mike has no idea what tone to strike and his hesitancy will doubtless offend her. The line runs for a while without either of them breaking the spell cast by his not having anything to say.

'D'you know what's really pissing me off?' she says.

'I don't know, Madelin.'

'What's really pissing me off ...' She was beginning to sound slurred.

'Yes?'

'Sorry, am I boring you?'

'No, you're not boring me.'

He waits, infected with unease.

'Why did Frank have to die? I can't stop thinking about him,' she said. 'He was such a fine man and now he's dead.'

Mike sits back against the pillow. It all links to grief. Her dependencies are jumbled, he realises. She latches on here, there, a bit of this, a bit of that: Frank one minute, then Mike, then Vince, an insecure ranging around, not properly differentiated. Is she grieving for Frank, or herself?

'I know ... I know ... you've lost ...' It is enough to go through the motions. The motions are an acknowledgement. He can be emollient. He has always done emollient well with clients: it never goes amiss and only costs time.

Madelin is unable to proceed beyond her last statement.

'Will there be a memorial service?' he asks, not caring. It's all in the tone anyway.

'Get here, Mike. There's nothing left for Vince in this marriage. Please come back.'

Before he can answer, she rings off.

***

Mike sits on the chair by the fire, reading under the ivory illumination of a standard lamp. On his lap rests a sheaf of loose pages. This dossier has survived the death of its compiler, Damon McCabe, and the death of his best mate, Frank, and now it reposes in Mike's warm hands. He turns its pages carefully, invoking the outlines of an idea. He is so intrigued by the possibilities of a novelistic transformation of the dossier that he questions its ethical rightness. Here, for sure, is Vince's war novel.

James Moyle would have no problem with this notion, no problem at all.

Moyle has been an education. The great agent's view of writers was different to Mike's in that Moyle felt no need to identify with the writer's struggle. For Moyle, literary excellence was a commodity. If Excellence would keep its part of the bargain and deliver, Moyle would keep his: get the Money. Everything else was just good manners. Moyle's self-esteem drew nothing from associating with novelists. He was too snobbish to depend on the reputations of mere scribblers for a sense of worth, and thus his clear-sightedness about how the trade worked. He exercised the kind of detachment which in times of yore would have reconciled itself to months of boarding school or service in distant colonies, or the giving of wartime orders that would let thousands die for a strategic goal. He had figured the publishing game for what it was, and would act to his own advantage (and others' ruin) if the rules permitted.

Is this the way forward, thinks Mike: an espousal of ruthlessness?

McCabe's dossier is for ever source material now its author has died. There need be no theft or infringement. A novelist can duly credit his inspiration. Vince has a conscience and, if Vince sees what Mike sees, his gratitude will be consuming. Mike's hunch amazes him. He knows that McCabe's hyper-real description of war will impress Vince and he believes that Vince's imagination will kindle through knowing Frank; that Frank's death will haunt him as he reads this account. Vince has the Brecon Beacons in his soul and at his pen's tip, and thus a route into Frank's Eden and place of retreat. The dossier gives him a landscape of war to match this peace, and thus the key to a juxtaposition that might, just might explode in his mind. And thus the glimmerings of a book that could transcend all his previous work, a book Mike can edit and Moyle sell.

Mike is like a tennis player facing a powerful opponent's serve. Aces have flown past. Weak returns have been volleyed at the net, depriving him of control or advantage; but now he is reading the serve and his reflexes are doing the work and the ball is cracking back low at an angle, and control is returning and with it the architecture of fluent rallies that he cuts and shapes as much as his opponent, bringing self-expression, the exuberance of kinetic force marshalled to thrilling effect.

The way forward for Mike is to liberate intuition and use his hunch to unite for Vince, and himself, countless seams of emotional energy. It won't work for him to be cynical. The cynic's circus is not for him because nothing real can succeed without wholeheartedness and it is better to have loved and lost and lost and lost if you can come up with this feeling again. The way forward is to believe in his hunch and triumph or die in the cause. Here the means are first class, the timing propitious. He can see the wood for the trees at last – a matchmaker's blaze of insight into the normally vexed relation between art and commerce. This is what he has been waiting for.

He sets the dossier aside. Mike knows what he has to do now and believes in it furiously. Madelin, he must conclude, is not for him.

Chapter 22

The next day, I wheeled the car into Vince's drive and parked beside the lawn. My return was unheralded: there being no requirement to inform Madelin in advance. On the lawn Holly was larking about in a scene of her own imagination, and Vince stood at the ready in jeans and T-shirt. He glanced my way, but kept an eye on his daughter's feverish movements.

'Holly and I are playing,' he called, as I got out of the car.

'Take your time,' I said.

I held McCabe's manuscript under my arm and strolled over to a bench in front of the farmhouse. I sat down, glad of the fresh air and sunshine. It had been a long drive back from London, full of rumination. I was well prepared for this return, but nervous, too. It was maybe a good sign that Vince and Holly were able to disregard someone who had become a familiar figure about the place.

Vince fell to his knees and roared impressively. Holly roared back with raised fingers, clawing the air. I pretended to ignore them so they could get on with it unselfconsciously. The glorious view was my distraction, the view that Vince had described so well in his pages. Sun poured from the wide sky, warming brickwork, shining grass, filling the garden air with heat. Beyond the garden, the panorama glimmered with backlit rims of incandescent green as hillcrests took the light and diving woods became lava flows of emerald.

'Nice to have you back,' said Madelin, crossing towards me from the barn and carrying a tea tray.

'These two are having a fine old time,' I said.

She smiled and looked calmly away.

Holly and Vince's game seemed to intensify as Madelin passed to the front door.

'Tea soon, Holly,' she called, passing into the house.

There was some tussling on the ground between Holly and her father. Vince was certainly making an effort, but I sensed he enjoyed it. I was fine about the fact that in Vince's new scheme of things Holly's entertainment took precedence over grown-up business. What I had to say was impervious to a few minutes' delay, and far better that Vince's attention, when I had it, should be completely undivided.

Holly rose from the grass and ran past me into the house, an uncoordinated rush of arms and legs. Vince remained on his back. He was gathering the energy to haul himself up. After a moment, he upended himself into a lotus position, as though testing the suppleness of joints that had not been exercised in a while. He threw back his arms, stretching, loosening.

'Vince,' I said.

Suddenly, he shot to his feet, an athletic burst, and took off down the lawn towards the shed. There were noises off as he rummaged in the shed, and then he emerged, dragging a rotor-bladed mower. He thumbed the lever on the handle, yanked the chord and the mower bellowed into life. Soon he was nosing away at a patch of grass and driving stripes across the upper

284

lawn. There was something almost iconic in his wielding of the machine: a vision of the paterfamilias tending his plot with virile purpose.

I was happy to wait. I would adjust to the rhythm of the household and let them get things done. The ordinariness of the scene was a kind of reassurance that things between Vince and Madelin were at least civil. The ordinary, of course, was deceptive. Vince's embracing of fatherly deeds and doings, his gardening efforts and horseplay belied an ever more fissile creativity in the reactor of his mind.

Madelin emerged and perched beside me on the bench. Her hair was coiled in a bun, and she wore a cardigan and jeans. She was sipping at a mug of peppermint tea and vaguely smiling, as if in the middle of some benign train of thought. There were no special looks between us. Already we were practised dissimulators.

'Vince's going great guns,' she said.

'Isn't he just!'

In the golden afternoon light Vince's physique seemed manly, indeed. He had a way with wheelbarrows and mowers, a rangy, long-limbed propelling strength that Madelin might have admired in happier times.

'I've found him an agent,' I said.

She gave me a glance. She wasn't sure whether it bored her or not to learn this kind of news.

'Someone good?'

'The best. The top of the tree.'

'Was that your business in London?'

'That and bumping into Nadia.'

'Nadia?'

Vince was upon us, striding across the grass at last, drawn to

285

his wife more than me perhaps, now that she was taking a break.

'Mike's got news,' she said.

He looked at me blankly.

I glanced at her, as if to triangulate their attention for an important announcement. Before I could speak, she had stood up and walked off.

'Where are you going?' called Vince.

'I've got some work to finish in the barn. Can you clear up the tea things?'

She moved smartly off, tea cup in hand.

He frowned.

I watched her departure closely. She was cutting both of us: Vince on principle, me for mentioning Nadia.

He sat beside me at the end of the bench, tugging his trousers as he levered down. Once seated, he stared hard at his boot. Just as Vince had been too big for literary London, he now seemed too big for this bench. His long limbs indicated a military level of exertion incompatible with the round-backed sedentary life of the writer. His active, ceaseless mind had made a prisoner of this huge body.

'I thought you'd peeled back to the Smoke,' he said.

His little jerks of distraction transmitted through the bench.

'I absolutely had to come back.'

He worried away at his temple with a forefinger.

'*Sibelius* is superb,' I said.

Vince blinked.

'The best thing you've written. Magnificent, actually.'

He turned his face towards the soothing heat of the sun.

'I know it's a fragment,' I said. 'But it lassoes the reader's heart.'

'She's ignoring me. It's like I don't exist.'

I was staring at the side of his head. 'I've found a leading agent who wants to take you on.'

'I've done shopping and housework for days. I'm getting on very well with Holly. I'm doing everything I humanly can to show good faith, and I can't even get a bloody conversation with her.'

He turned to face me, an attention-securing look that discharged a thunderbolt of anguish. 'I say to her, come on, have a go at me. Say what you've got to say, get it off your chest, because then we can talk. There's two sides to every argument. She's entitled to slag me off and I have a right of reply. Because I want to get beyond this. I want to get back to something more real than this rancour. But she won't. She ignores and avoids me. I might be ready to talk, but she isn't, and if she isn't, well then tough. Her attitude is not good.'

I nodded carefully.

'May we talk in the cabin?' I asked.

'I don't do the cabin any more. I'm through with writing.'

'We can just sit there. Have a coffee.'

'I'm going mad. I had a career. I had a marriage. Now it seems that both were an illusion.'

'Vince, a new chapter of your life is about to begin.'

'On the contrary, I think I'm about to tip myself off one of the Brecon Beacons.'

'Don't be silly.'

He shook his head, upset all over again.

I waited for a moment, letting it wash over him. This was going to be hard work alright, but the best ones always were. Without emotionality there is nothing of value in a writer.

I had to compel perspective, find a way of taking Vince outside of himself. 'You know Frank died last week?'

'You're joking!'

'Shot by the Taliban.'

Vince flung his head in his hands. 'Fucking hell.'

'He loved these hills, you know. Frank would have been moved by *Sibelius*. He would have been amazed. This is not something you can just let go.'

Vince's face was creased with pain. His brow was furrowed; he had a poisoned look.

'Madelin is grieving the death of a friend. Give her time.'

I could hear his breathing building up in powerful intakes and exhalations. His eyes grew large as his gaze switched about. His hands, spread tensely on his knees, now clasped at each other.

'Frank reminds me of one of those war poets,' I said, 'who came back to England to say goodbye, because he had to return to the front. Once your comrades have died, survival is dishonour. After all that carnage, who could enjoy life without feeling he was betraying the dead? Frank's brother-in-arms was Damon McCabe, and Frank gave me McCabe's war memoir. I've been reading it all week and can't get it out of my mind.'

I brought up the plastic bag and set it next to Vince.

His eyes flickered warily at the package.

Whereas before he had been fidgety, he now seemed checked by humiliation and shock.

I spoke as calmly and evenly as possible. 'I have a major agent who wants to take you on. He would like me to work with you on your next book. With my help and his clout we can get the best deal for the best novel you've ever written.'

The drip-feed into Vince's mind would take its course. The ideas would become psychoactive eventually because that was their nature. 'There is something providential about this dossier.'

He seemed like a stone. His energy of being had all but diffused.

'How can I … How can I … How can I …?'

With steepled piteous eyebrows he regarded the undulations of the view. Then he managed a glance, indirect; enough to reveal the tears in his eyes, a brave demonstration.

'Without Madelin I have nothing. She's the only woman I ever loved.'

I remained attentive, but said nothing. I wanted him to know that I understood implicitly what he meant by this declaration. The telling of it was sufficient. It stood between us like a hard object in space.

'If I go back into that cabin now, without … some sign from her,' he shook his head despairingly '… we'll both know it's over.'

It was clear what I had to do: back Vince to the hilt. We were at the bottom of things and there was no other way.

'OK,' I said. 'If you read that,' I handed him the Damon dossier, 'I'll talk to Madelin.'

'Do some good in the world. Save a career. Save a marriage.'

I heard his sucking in of breath, a powerful sound, and then he turned towards me and crushed me in his arms. I submitted in surprise, accepting the pressure of his relief and recognising in its force a passionate simplicity of heart that I never would have suspected a few days ago.

I patted his back lightly and watched him spring up and depart across the lawn, knowing he could not bear to look at me after that.

Chapter 23

Xenia was captured in a pose of frontally nude recumbence, sitting on the edge of a divan and leaning against the props of her arms. It was a pose that said: 'Here I am. Aren't I mouth-watering? Wouldn't you like to …'

We heard the chunt of a printer.

In the corner of the studio was a counter with a laptop on it. Madelin stood by the screen clicking away at a picture of Xenia. She moved the cursor from toolbar to image and back again, troubling over tiny specks of light.

Half a dozen prints were propped against the wall – conventional poses for the male readership. The two women had had a fine old time cooking up saucy poses and getting the goods, and in Xenia's sultry deadpan gaze was an implicit mirth: the risqué aspect of getting her lady bits out before a member of the same sex, and really going for the poses. Xenia had the gear, no question. She brandished and arched, pouted and pursed with consummate physical self-love, as though the session with Madelin was the climax of a thousand hours before the bedroom mirror.

Madelin guided the shiny photograph onto the desk.

'Please try couple counselling,' I said. 'Relate have a very good service.'

She frowned, attention elsewhere.

'I don't fancy talking to Vince.'

'I understand that, but if you loved him once and he's willing to try, maybe you could love him again?'

'What do you make of these?'

I remained silent.

'I think they're pretty good,' she said.

'There are issues you need to thrash out because you are man and wife.'

'What if I were to fondle you while you looked at these pictures?'

She was trying to make a point: that she had power over me; that I could not resist. This was not the case.

'You asked me to help. I'm helping.'

'I like a man with a sense of purpose. Just as long as it isn't marriage guidance counselling.'

'You seem remarkably sanguine if what you're implying is true.'

She shrugged reasonably. 'I know my heart, thank God.'

I stared at her intently. 'Don't you find it frightening that your husband is dying for love and forgiveness and you don't give a damn?'

'I accept the reality.'

'You two have a history. Two halves of a shared life.'

'No.' Her voice was raised. 'For Vince the most important thing was always his work.'

'Which he's now abandoned for you and Holly. Don't you see? Things have changed. Vince has made a sacrifice. He really loves you.'

She looked at me with disbelieving amusement. 'So how come you want to get him writing again?'

I hesitated.

'What are your plans, Mike?'

She pulled out a photograph of Xenia kneeling against the divan and shot from behind.

'Look at that. What an amazing arse! It's so arousing and demanding, like a great beckoning target. The female body is such a masterpiece of provocation. Makes me wish I had a willy and could prang her myself.'

I breathed in deeply.

'God, the things I say!' she laughed gleefully. 'Must be something in the tea.'

'Madelin …'

'You really believe Vince has given up writing to save his family?'

'He's changed, and you are punishing him by ignoring it.'

'It's a pose. He's acting out the great drama of the artist renouncing literature for love. He wants me to feel so touched and so moved by his sacrifice that I take pity on him and say "Don't worry, darling. Everything's tickety-boo. You go back to the cabin and do what you love doing and Mummy will be ready for you in the kitchen when you want supper."'

She set Xenia's picture on the pile.

'Since when has Vince ever sacrificed anything for anyone?'

The truth, I felt, was different, and she hadn't caught up with it. Her view of Vince was right until a few days ago. A few days ago everything changed. I was there when it happened. It was like the Soviets going nice under Gorbachev – sudden, bizarre and real. These things build up for ages and then just happen. Of course, Madelin might have her own reasons for not wanting to recognise this, and for not yielding easily. I found it hard to believe that I was part of the reason. My head was not into the reality of having an affair with her. And if my head wasn't, hers could hardly be.

'What d'you really want?' I asked flatly. I had to try something different.

She laughed nervously. 'Freedom.'

'And I'm just part of your entertainment plan?'

'I want to be selfish for a bit. I invite you to be, too. We can have more fun that way.'

'It's reassuring to hear you don't have any feelings for me.'

She laughed. 'I might have feelings for you.'

'It's all right. I know I'm dispensable.'

'You hypocrite! You're still in love with Nadia.'

'Nonsense.'

'You are! And I like that. I like a challenge. I was always rather offended that you fancied her instead of me.'

'Oh, for God's sake! I always appreciated you.'

'I hope "appreciate" means wanted to fuck the first moment you saw me?' she laughed.

'Of course! Like everybody else on the planet. But you could never work me into your schedule.'

'Ooh!'

'And then I fell in love.'

'And then *you* were unavailable. Which is not the case now.'

'Why now? Why me?'

She seemed genuinely mystified. 'For a man with a readily satisfiable penchant for fellatio you do ask a lot of questions.'

'Stop play-acting! What will you do? Watch it break Holly's heart?'

Madelin stared unflinchingly at the laptop. 'Oh, I'll keep

painting, and I'll look after Holly. She'd probably be a lot happier if Vince and I separated.'

She was clicking away at the screen again, moistening her lips as if in preparation for some new forbidden delicacy.

'I grant you your power over me,' I said, wearily. 'Please stop trying to prove it. It doesn't mean anything.'

'I don't want power. I want you to resist. I want you to chastise me with lots of moral high ground …'

'And then succumb to your wiles because you are so irresistibly gorgeous …'

'Forbidden fruit is the juiciest. Who else could I have such naughty fun with? And anyway,' she said with some feeling. 'You need it as much as I do. I can tell from your face when we're doing it.'

Yes, of course, I did desire her. I did like her. Yes, my heart fluttered when she switched it on: all that keen pleasuring just a touch away, more than pleasure because she was so gifted. She naturally swam in foamy erotic waters, a sprite in silky, swirling arabesques. A dream that haunted, but a dream only, and more was at stake. Other priorities were compelling. Besides I did not want to get caught with my trousers down. I wanted to be making love in ideal circumstances and these were not ideal. Madelin knew she was playing with fire, anyway, without acknowledging inconvenient realties and without acknowledging me.

'Vince understands you because you are both creators. He saw the artist behind the enchantress and he loved what he saw. I don't think his remorse is self-pity or self-dramatisation. It's the bearing of a man who, in extremis, lost sight of what he most values and has always recognised: your peculiar genius.'

Madelin glared at the monitor. Her mind was swarming with

a barely containable drama in which primordial rage was compressed by inordinate self-control.

'Tell him it's OK to write at least,' I insisted. 'Give him permission to do what he needs to do. Everything else can take its course.'

She looked up at me suddenly. Her eyes burned. 'Why should he?' she shouted. 'Why should he get off after three weeks when he's made me suffer for years?'

I stared at her. The vehemence was ugly. Its force dismayed me. Such anger had a long bitter half-life ahead. Already a post-separation rancour hung in the air.

'I should have married you,' she said suddenly.

Sounds familiar, I thought. Everyone should have done something with me and didn't.

'To think that marriage has become, in the end, just a job.'

'He is committed.' I said. 'I rate commitment.'

'Would you have married me? Just say yes.'

'Sure.'

She laughed. 'I believe you. That's nice. I think you would have cared for me.'

'Oh, Madelin, the hypothetical past is full of cheap regret!'

'What a fuck-up, I can't believe it, marrying the wrong man. How could I have been so careless?'

'Vince was a famous young author. I'm sure it turned your head.'

'It did!'

'But he's someone else now and there's a bigger picture. Sorry, it's hard work this.'

'I just …' she turned to look at me without front, with a lovely smile, '… it's just happening, isn't it?'

'Madelin,' I said gently, with some feeling. 'The man in that shed is desperate to get his wife back. He values and loves you. It's not my role to piss on his love and hope.'

'Nice phrase.'

'I … Well.'

I shrugged.

She sat down on a chair. For a moment, she didn't know what to say.

She is in a stew. I am thwarting her. She is maybe incredulous that a new lover should develop the moral will to resist her after she has opened herself and let go, yet she can see, perhaps reasonably, that she was the one who brought me into the vexed space between her and Vince. She has surely lost the patience for such unfortunate complications. Impulse is gathering against the stalemates and compromises. More and more she rages against Vince and the traps he continues to set for her: if not the writing then the penitence for being a writer, if not the writer's block and distress, the rebirth of a love that she must kowtow to. He keeps coming back, like an insatiable pet, demanding attention. She doesn't like any of this, or want to reinvent the wheel of their relationship only for it to run her over again. Sex is alive for her now. Such revivals of the libido do not grow on trees. It's something about Mike. Mike she can get through to. He is contiguous. He is present, without being over-intense. She feels all this, I know it in my bones.

'Maybe you're right,' she said. 'Relate is something we should do.'

'What?'

She shook her hair so it fell on her shoulders. 'For Holly's sake.'

It was strange to hear this all of a sudden. 'For Holly's sake,' I nodded in agreement.

'I'm sure there's some nice, kind person Vince and I can talk to in Abergavenny. Poor sod.'

'I'm sure there is.'

She seemed tranquil and self-possessed. She seemed different.

'So we just forget it?' Her look was indescribable: a mixture of regret and appeal.

She was offering what I had come for, but confirming it was not easy.

'I won't forget anything, Madelin.'

'That's nice to know.' She smiled bravely.

'I don't want to be ... I would like ...'

'Come here. Come here,' she said.

She took my hands in hers and held my eyes, a look of leave-taking.

'I'll go to Relate with Vince. I'll do it. I have to do it, I know.'

'It is the best thing.'

'Kiss me then. For my pains. A last kiss.'

She saw my reaction – an expression of uncertainty.

'What does it matter now? I won't be kissing anyone like this for ages.'

Why not, indeed? I hesitated of course, but she squeezed my hand and her touch was tender and appealing and it seemed fatuous to resist. Why not, then?

Our faces drew slowly together and before I felt the brush of her lips, when her eyes were glassy close, she said quietly: 'You're not who you pretend to be, Mike.'

I knew that a kiss would be hard to end. Kissing Madelin always seemed like a renewal as the memory of heavenly sensations took over. All sex was in that soft, vulval kiss of hers, the full invitation, and I tried to hold back, to be moderate, but knowing it was the last, couldn't bring myself to break off. Five seconds became ten seconds. Ten seconds thirty seconds. The soft delicious labial pressure sent darts around the back of my neck. Its delicacy held us in suspension. Every moment I took in as though it were the last, or the one before last, thinking it was time to break away, but what was the point of breaking off at this moment, as opposed to the next? Why leave the nectar when the nectar was still plentiful and giving? Why break this tender contact that would be my last ever sexual kiss with Madelin? Submit a little longer, draw it out, even as the fairy lights come on, the whole erogenous party, the heave-ho downstairs, the tug that wants to move things on fast and forcefully.

'ok, I'm going,' I said, touching the side of her face.

She held my hand tightly.

Her brown eyes seemed to swim in sightless dilation. She was floating away.

'Please,' her hand went between my legs.

I detached her hand and reversed and made my way to the door, head fogging up.

'Please stay,' she called after me.

***

I could hardly believe I was leaving the building, but I was, I was, I was walking away and it seemed utterly bogus to be bursting off like some Victorian lord in a third-rate TV series, turning his back on temptation with a tool like a crowbar and testicles thrumming, but I was, I was because this is the sort of thing I was apparently obliging myself to do, to keep on my feet. What utter balderdash, I thought. What nonsense! What cant! To be turning from a kiss like that, striding off towards the inside of my grubby car and an evening alone in the cottage with the rest of my empty life before me. Doing the right thing again. Right was such a pain. Right was going to hurt lots if I wanted mastery rather than dependence, success instead of intoxication, integrity not compromise, and so, fucking hell, here I was striding away from the whole wind-up, the whole vexatious piss-take. I had to move it, get clear of this marital madness, and as I did, I felt more and more furious. I mean, what member of the idiotic penis-led breed could pass up Madelin's charms without vengeful self-castration? What red-blooded male could deflect her entreaties when given the chance or the choice, except by running for it, which I now was as I gunned across the drive determined to put this misery behind me. I was just a plaything, here to be teased and twitted, my protests muzzled; my will sultrily sapped. Those of us lucky enough to fuck Madelin became androids, in that such forbidden pleasures were addictive to the point of idiocy. Her kiss was never a farewell. It was a declaration of power. 'There's nothing you can do or say to resist me because I reach the parts that other girls don't even think about.' I'll bet her line about Relate was a lie, damn her.

My ears burned as I crossed in a bee-line towards the Peugeot, willing Vince not suddenly to spring up, please God, from a bush or cabbage patch. As I grappled the keys in my pocket, I saw the afternoon's shadow stretching away from the ash tree, and the breeze that raked its crown, and the glancing radiance of the sun on the front of the house, its flashing windows.

I got into the driving seat of the car with a nauseous feeling: anger and curdling lust. If Vince had come onto the drive I would probably have run him down in panic and then reversed over his carcass in sheer annoyance.

The car bumped down the farm track leaving them behind,

bringing me into the light of the everyday. Everything unravelled, a huge shedding, fluttering away in the breeze from the rolled down window. Let it all go, please. Abandon them. Forget Moyle, my career, everything. Be shot of the whole barking apparatus. Whatever moves I played, Madelin would get the better of my good faith and sooner or later Vince would find out, and Madelin would pull the rug, and all my efforts would blitz up in smoke and hubris. Why should it be my role to chivvy a novelist to write a novel, for Fanny's sake, or stop a delectable woman having sex with me? I could feel myself combusting with preposterousness, like a skyrocket stuck in the ground, fuse fizzling fast till it blows up buggeringly and bangingly.

***

Steep slopes reared around me as the car came downhill. Great hangars of beech and sycamore swallowed the lane momentarily and then released it into the wonder of a panorama that spread nature's huge society of hills and bluffs before the eye like some fabulous new territory or promised land. Arching oaks reared above, driving their limbs to snaggled destinations. Gaunt chestnuts with spiralling bark dignified pasture with venerable imperviousness. As the lane sank and sank into deep dell-like places towards the intimate bed of a valley, its neck crushed by abundant verges and the collar of the hedgerow, I sank with it into the calm of a distilled resolution that would see me drive without a backward thought to the cottage and make me gather my things and pack and get the car ready for a homeward drive to London. The charade was over. Henceforward I would mislead no one.

I was about to turn into the cleft of the valley when I heard a buzz. I pulled over and fished the mobile from my jacket.

'Moyle' read the screen.

This was the moment of truth, then.

'James,' I said.

'Hello, Mike.' His tone was clear and immediate, as if Moyle hovered benignly in the skies, invisibly watching the Lord's toiling idiots.

'I'm sorry to report that Sheila died in her sleep last night.'

He allowed me a moment. I gazed at the failing blue of the mountain sky.

'My condolences. She was a very distinguished lady and a dear colleague to us all.'

I found it impossible to speak.

'I can't tell you about the funeral arrangements. I'm sure you'll want to come.'

A scattering of sheep and their shadows stood on the panel of a green field across the valley from the car. It was a picture of absolute stillness and clarity.

'Speak soon.' He rang off.

***

I brought the car to a sharp stop outside my cottage and jumped out. The sooner I could absent myself from these hills and get home, the better. I whipped around the house gathering my things. Drawers and cupboards were cleared, wardrobes emptied, suitcases readied. Perishable food I reclaimed from the kitchen. Rubbish I bagged and put out. Sofa cushions and side tables were knocked into a semblance of order, sheets stripped back and blankets folded. My feet stampeded downstairs, my fists worked hard on counter surfaces rubbing stains. The Hoover got driven like a mad thing over the threadbare carpet and vegetable waste was bundled and bunged. Only the laptop remained in iconic solitude on the desk table, its cables plugged and pilot light winking, and out of a kind of reflex I tapped the screen alive and saw three waiting emails.

The first was a confirmation of the money transfer, sent by my bank.

The second was a copy of my farewell letter to clients, apparently drafted by Colin and forwarded by Steve secretly.

The third email, headed 'get this', also from Steve, contained no text but carried an attachment. The attachment I clicked and soon was looking at a photo forming. There was a wall, a bit of sky, and in the last materialising section of the image, a couple kissing. I looked closer. The man was short and broad, clad in a leather jacket; the girl wore a coat and seemed familiar. I zoomed in and saw Templar's fop fringe, the bar of his specs, the engulfed mouth of a girl.

For several minutes I scrutinised the picture. I searched it as Colin might, hunting for get-outs. Steve had caught them behind a pub or in an alley – careless.

I sat down on an armchair. This 'proof' was a like a gun in the hand. The clarity of opportunity had a sobering effect.

Was I this ruthless, I wondered? Was I up for the course of action implied by the picture? How strange to have sinister power over Colin. I sat pondering, knuckles rubbing my chin, dark thoughts creasing my brow.

Strike capability conferred a choice, and Christian forbearance might well have been one of the options. Ignore your persecutors and turn the other cheek. 'Vengeance is mine, saith the Lord.' Colin's fate needed no help from me as conniving runts get their comeuppance when the world's decent people shun them in disgust, and the ambitious little creeps are marooned by their nastiness, their final fortress the falsely deferential corridors of the workplace. Colin's fate – to be loathed by his colleagues – needed no help from me. Already he belonged to the legions of the lost, holding no kindness in his heart. But damned though he was, onward Christian soldiers might yet have a duty: to liquidate Saracens, the careerists and tosspots who besmirch the temple, sullying the divine, lowering the tone, applying the bottom line to a vein of experience too fine to abandon to false prophets. Colin reduced publishing to vanity and lucre and we could not have a world run by people like that. Bigger souls were required if literature was to survive: agents who could recognise arduously wrought achievement and harnessed sensibility in the work of writers – even writers like Savage, God help him. To treat this noble vocation as a fast-moving consumer goods sub-economy, to see agents as profit centres, and agencies as units of cash flow was a heresy that poisoned the literary life and debased its *raison d'être*. That was Colin's crime and anyone presented with the chance should put down the little cur, before he did even more damage.

I suddenly felt shot through and feverish. Sheila was dead. The omniscient Sheila: gone. It seemed unreal, this news. I dwelt on the fact of it for long salutary moments, a private, sedentary, reflective tribute in which all that Sheila was, and the sense of all that had been taken from us suffused me. Hers had been an honourable life, and it is as truly sad to lose a role model whose talents have been fulfilled as it is to lose someone younger with much life ahead of them. Every fine person that passes is the realisation, in death, of a unique humanity. We mourn our own short lives at their passing, but the real loss is to see our small universe of friends and colleagues, the only reality we ever really know, picked away at by the inevitable. I would never again be the young agent and Sheila the doyenne. Her life had passed. Mine was passing, too.

***

The phone rang.

'Hello.'

I could hear deep breathing.

'Hello?'

There were little panting sounds and then a sniff.

'Who's that?'

I discerned the strains of orchestral music.

'Mike!'

I cradled the receiver under my chin and gazed bleakly through the window.

'Vince!'

'We're going to Relate. We've had a talk. I don't know what you said to her. I can't … It's like …' He was caught up in the emotion of it. 'We had eye contact for the first time in weeks.'

I drew myself up in the chair.

'So … I had the feeling we were just one mood switch away from being happy again. There's a kind of honesty that's possible between us and it's taken a crisis to bring it alive. We both have to listen and understand. It's about the will to forgive. I think she wants to find a way.'

'Was Madelin … was she different?'

'I believe she honestly wants to try.'

'You're sure?'

'I'm not sure of anything these days. We're in the process, I suppose, of some kind of reinvention.'

There was a lengthening silence, Vince stalled by reflection, my thoughts elsewhere.

'I don't know what you said, Mike, but I am so really terribly grateful I can't tell you. Madelin is like … she's like another person. I know there's a lot of hurt there, and maybe like me, she just wants to stop the cold war, can't bear it any more. I know this. I have to give her what she wants. Her happiness has to become a rule with me. I'm not going to negotiate anything. I will give her what she needs unconditionally. She wants to move to London, we move to London. She wants a holiday, we take a holiday. I'm determined to become a bearable husband again. I want to be a force for good in her life. Give her something she cannot get for herself. We need to recover the romance and become each other's best friends. If she wants to go to a counsellor and say it all in front of a third party as a way of getting stuff off her chest, I will take that as my due. I have made her suffer and I will atone for that. I'll give it everything because I love her. Listen, if there's anything I can do to thank you ...'

'There's nothing, Vince.'

'I don't think I ever appreciated what a ...'

'It's fine.'

'... remarkable person you are.'

'Not at all.'

'We should talk,' he said. 'She's given me the green light.'

'The what?'

'To write. That dossier. I haven't read it ... was there some kind of idea you had? Maybe we could squeeze in another session? I didn't really react to your praise for the *Sibelius* partial.'

'I ...'

'Obviously, I'm not going to be working 24/7 in the cabin.'

'I'm returning to London.'

'When?'

'In five minutes.'

'No! Can I bribe you to stay?'

'We can communicate by email.'

Suddenly, there was a loud rap on the door.

'Please don't go.'

I couldn't see anything out of the window. This seemed like the perfect excuse. 'Can I call you back?'

'You must!'

I rang off and passed through the corridor to the front door. With a tug I opened the door and there before me, in blue jeans and T-shirt, was Madelin.

***

Madelin's hair was in beautiful condition, somehow fluffed and enlivened into a quintessence of debonair glamour. She wore lipstick; her eyelashes seemed longer, darker. There was a lilt in her carriage as she stepped indoors, a sexy sense of arrival, heightened by heels and the line of thighs and hips. Her smile encompassed my reaction; she was daring and amused and excited and high on adrenaline, and ready to engulf my disapproval with sensual momentum.

All this travelled through my astonishment like an oncoming wave.

'So, here I am,' she said, with a hint of self-consciousness.

'I've just been on the phone to Vince.'

Her look appealed to a modicum of gallantry, as if to say, don't labour the point, don't spoil the mood.

I fell back against the kitchen counter. Instead of advancing towards me, she sauntered over to the window. After a moment she cast me a glance, picking up on my mood – disapproval, amazement – and then she came back towards me. Each step closer was a proposition, the effect of which she followed in my eyes. She was like a weather front, a passage of body heat, breath and scent, and static current that reached my skin before she did. She knew how to touch, and the imminence of her touch charged the air.

I inhaled deeply. 'Vince is *overjoyed* that you're going to Relate.'

She stared at me blankly. 'You asked me to tell him that.'

'He's convinced you're serious!'

'I am.'

'Then why are you here?'

She was about to answer, but then thought of a better reply. 'You can despise me all you like, but you can't blackmail me into loving Vince.'

She glanced darkly away, but then recovered her poise, and turned again towards me, as though a front-on stance would be more persuasive. She hovered momentarily between a sense of injustice and a desire to resume the cabaret act. Suddenly, she smiled, like a victorious Miss World contestant, with radioactive self-confidence. 'Relate gives me an out. He still doesn't understand what he's done to me or how I feel about it. If we talk it through in front of another person it may help him come to terms with the inevitable. Then I won't be deceiving him.'

My face must have fallen as I digested this.

'You're irrelevant,' she said.

I looked at her, puzzled.

'You are not the cause.'

I nodded. 'Great. Then how come I feel so shitty?'

She had used my recommendation against Vince, and Vince had misconstrued her completely.

'Is guilt the only emotion you really enjoy?' she was incredulous. 'At least have the bloody courage of your convictions.'

'What convictions?'

'Well exactly. I'm beginning to see why Nadia moved on. Mike, my mess is going to be a lot bigger than your mess. It's going to be horrible, and all you're concerned about is how you'll come out of it, as if sleeping with me were just about moral hazard. How can you be so utterly bloodless! You typical fucking agent.'

'Madelin …'

'Stop patronising me.'

There was a shocked silence. Momentarily, she seemed consumed with anger.

'Madelin, I had the best intentions.'

'Am I so utterly uninteresting or what?'

Her eyes glared with defiance.

'Shall I just go? Find myself a pig farmer. Somebody who knows what's good for him? Shall I? Walk off into the sunset leaving you twiddling your thumbs and brewing Earl Grey, or are you going to show some care?'

I shook my head, as much in hurt as disagreement. 'I'm sure I don't deserve you.'

'Here we go. What is this cap doffing, lowly humble servant …?'

'I was being sarcastic.'

'Don't take me for granted whatever you do.'

'Oh, for God's sake! Getting into your knickers was never going to be that difficult.'

'You bastard.'

'Sorry, Madelin. My self-esteem doesn't go into orbit just because I've been dick number sixty-seven between your legs.'

She looked at me in baited astonishment.

'Pleasurable though it certainly was.'

'Pleasurable! You arsehole!'

'I have no illusions I mean anything to you just because we had sex.'

This seemed to take her breath away. 'Mike you're a real cad. A filthy beast in the bedroom, and a sententious prick out of it.'

'Fine. Let's just be frank.'

She raised a finger. 'I've seen frank. You with your boxers round your ankles. That was frank.'

She stood there, arms at her sides, welcoming the next chance to strike at me.

This was about honesty, and all I could do was raise the stakes by being more honest.

'How on earth could I ever trust you?' I said, suddenly.

She had not expected this and reacted with a look that modulated from aggression to a kind of exasperation. 'Mike, you'll only get out what you put in.'

'That's a very trite life lesson which I've learnt not to be true.'

'Then risk a little, because you've nothing to lose.'

'I'd be so dumb to fall in love with you.'

She smiled at this, as though it were an admission of weakness. 'Yes, but men always do. I can't help that.'

'Listen, you want my soul? It's already been ripped out of my body and fried in garlic by Nadia.'

'And even when you have nothing to lose, you're cautious. What is it with you middle-class English males?'

'We're entirely generic to you. Just a phalanx of tasselled twits at the entrance to the bed chamber awaiting your queenly summons.'

She laughed coarsely.

'Why not skip the human beings and buy yourself a box of plastics?' I said. 'You'd have more fun and less trouble.'

'Good idea. Shame I've already had it.'

She gave me one of her looks and laughed triumphantly. 'Shall we just cut the cackle and go to bed?'

I felt myself tensing. Her eyes swept over me.

'Absolutely not.'

'You want to.'

'How can you be so sure?'

'Oh, come on.'

I held on to the edge of the kitchen sink and felt a wall of heat rising up my chest.

'Don't you want to punish me for being such a harlot?'

'No, I don't.'

She came closer. Her eyes switched from my eyes to my mouth. I was unable to move.

'That's the face of man who's beginning to have an erection.'

'No it isn't.'

'Yes it is. Shall I check?'

'It doesn't need to be checked.'

'It needs to be checked. I'm good at checking.'

I flinched.

She had put her hand on my fly. Her touch sent a tingle through me.

'Oh yes,' she smiled smoothly. 'Oh yes, it needs to be checked.'

I stared at her as she drew down the zip.

Her lips pursed as she felt inside, her small hand exploring sensuously, and quickly she reacted to pressure with a deft rummage that produced me in one scooped out motion.

I exhaled jaggedly.

'There,' she said, soothingly, her cool palm around my hot skin, her other hand loosening the button of my trousers, which she hauled to my knees.

My body tensed at her touch. My heart was thudding.

'Shall I go now?' she said. 'We could call it a day if you want.'

I stood there with my back to the sink and hands on the counter edge.

She worked away, with her slender wrist.

I was unable to move. I was trapped between a riveting pleasure that went in through the root, and a paralysing sense of the forbidden, as though I could not respond without complete hypocrisy, a passivity which Madelin took for an encouragement that made her work more thoroughly and enthusiastically, quickly maximising the jut of my hungering bone till it craned between us like some villainous latecomer to the scene.

'That's a full English breakfast if ever I saw one,' she said, sliding down my legs and up-tilting her face into nuzzling proximity.

'Hmmm. Nice.'

I gasped.

She enjoyed me for about thirty seconds.

'See you later.'

'What?'

'We've wasted so much time talking, I've got to rush.'

She sprang up with a light bounce, full of beans.

'Oh, for God's sake!'

'Listen, tasty boy, see you soon.'

She was out of the kitchen in a flash. I followed her but got snagged on my trousers and lost balance. I tripped to the ground with a thud.

'Ow!'

She rushed back into the kitchen.

'Bloody hell!'

I was lying on the kitchen floor, elbows smarting, thighs against cold lino.

'My God, Vronski.' She burst out laughing. 'You look wonderful in that position.'

'Don't go.'

'Bye now.'

She shot out of the room.

***

I caught up with her in the car. She was buckling up, but I pulled
the door open and reached across her lap to release the seat belt.

'Hey!'

'Come on,' I said. 'Don't be ridiculous.'

'I've got to go.'

'It's five thirty.'

'Oh, my goodness me! We've got a plumber in.'

'Don't leave!' I said.

'A woman's work is never done.'

I tried to kiss her but she ducked away. 'Excuse me, pardner, I
have a job to do.'

'Madelin!'

'Are you obstructing a housewife in the execution her duty?'

'Please!'

She allowed me to kiss her, a hot nuzzling kiss.

'Really, no, I can't. I'm a married woman.'

'Come back,' I said, my arms around her.

'No, no,' she said.

Five minutes later we were on the mattress in my bedroom
swiving energetically between zippy bags and the corner of my
packed suitcase.

Chapter 24

In the days that followed I divided into two functioning but utterly compromised beings, my time split schizophrenically between working with Vince on a new novel and the escalating affair with Madelin. If, at first, I had been tentative with Madelin, with each new tryst I became more reckless and impulsive. Conscience? Oh, Jesus! Once the proprieties were in shreds at our feet, once the guilt was knifed and bundled like some unwitting crime-scene witness, there was nothing left but to get on with it, nothing left but the crudest abandon, which Madelin spurred with relish. She saw through me, somehow, through my caution and care, to the viagran verve that middle-class males harbour beneath well-brought-up, sensitive demeanours. My ejaculations became tumultuous events, bovine and appalling, a parody of pornographic prowess. 'A lot of seed around,' she said after one epic, extravagant, bewildering, copious climax that left me the charred ruin of incandescent lust as I keeled on the mattress. I couldn't tell whether she was flattered or dismayed by the hot film all over her skin, the produce of our love-making, which must have seemed a morass of teeming life.

'I'm infertile,' I said.

'Really!'

'Yes.'

She laughed. 'How can that be? With all this?'

I could tell what she was thinking: 'Safe sex. How very convenient. Wonder what Mike thinks about that? Don't go into it now.'

To be honest, I couldn't deny Madelin's hint that some essential part of my nature had always craved carnality, that the veil of well-meaning vicarishness in my character masked an infantile aggression probably engendered by my mother. Was it the goody-goody pact of a churchman's family, mother's attachment to form for form's sake that made me so stifled at heart; or was it her neurasthenic lapses when things didn't go her way, forcing her sons into a role we never wanted to play: eunuchs of sympathy and attentiveness? Should I always have been more direct and uncompromising in getting what I wanted, and more ruthless in defending my patch?

I couldn't see into Madelin as we lay side by side after those sessions. Our Janus-faced relationship, I came to realise, was a way of looking back at the worlds we were contending with, not a contemplation of new togetherness. Madelin's emotions were not for my benefit, though I could sense her state. The emotion she revealed was not exactly sorrow for the wastes of a marriage or a disappointed heart. It was for the fiasco of having your life caught up in the wrong marriage, a rage for vanished time, an emotion that boiled painfully in the space between lost hope (she was too disillusioned) and an intractable sense of the truth, i.e. that Vince's 'love' was never more than a rhetorical trap set for her by a man who fundamentally wanted to be alone. In that light, her love-making was a release from the tension of knowledge. She had earned abandon. She deserved it; and afterwards, as we thought our thoughts and contact held strange ambiguity

314

(was tenderness allowed?) it seemed there was a limit to what she could give me, that sex was an activity beyond which Madelin had little to say and less to feel and that our intimacy was fulfilled once the sex was done.

We did it in a croft by Offa's Dyke. We did it in a picnic rug in the Llanbedr valley beyond a grove of stinging nettles. We had quickies in the barn when Holly was at school and Vince shopping. The only times that really worked for me were the sessions on my bed in the cottage, but even then I wondered if some local farmhand might spot the Land Rover and start a rumour. I worried about Vince finding out, about the violence of his reaction, the danger to Madelin, the instant obliteration of our friendship, his pain, how his fury would shrink me into something that would taint my view of myself once I saw it in his eyes. I dreaded this, but an affair becomes its own reality, spontaneous and consuming, so compelling that other concerns fall away and seem unreal. An affair like this happened because it had to happen. It blocked the pain of Nadia like a lumbar puncture and led me into a combustive relation with a woman I knew but didn't know.

Daily I sat with Vince in the cabin talking about the dossier and the 'Sibelius' partial. We were fermenting the structure of a novel. Vince was profoundly grateful that I had postponed my return to London and I was suitably gracious. As we knocked ideas about I almost forgot I was having an affair with Madelin. I was so intent on helping him that I found it impossible to conceive that I was betraying him. Madelin was being kinder to him now and he was doing his stuff about the house, and living on the right side of the law, and there were days when all seemed OK with the world. People were getting what they wanted and living harmoniously. With Vince I forgot Madelin. With Madelin

I almost forgot Vince. As the days passed and the alibis stood in place and our love-making happened when and where it safely could, I came to believe that Vince would never discover us because he would never suspect. The hypothetical spectre of an adulterous liaison between me and Madelin was eclipsed by my earnest presence in his cabin.

Perhaps I relaxed a little, after a week or so. Then I found more passion in myself, as though the opportunity of Madelin's loveliness opened a space for the passion that an improbable relationship calls into being as a reason to secure what cannot be secured. And in those moments, it was impossible to believe that Madelin wasn't also caught up, and that her distance afterwards was not evasion or withdrawal but the vacant satiety of one who has got everything she needs from a man and is free at last. Yes, I wanted more from her, and couldn't quite believe Madelin lacked the need for love. When I beheld her in unguarded moments, in a trance of reflection, or in the capture of my arms after love-making there was a nobility in her loveliness, an endearing innocence of mien that tugged on my heart, arousing protectiveness, the special coils of affection one reserves for very few people; and yet, these vistas of tenderness she blocked with her wit and her sense of reality. After all, what could proceed from this stalemated triangle of relationships?

We made love heroically, with filmic abandon and zest. And yet, even so, when I turned her, and buried her face in the pillow, and marshalled my straining loins into a great welling that seemed to bury ever deeper inside her, and felt the tight gather of sensation that coursed up, I was sufficiently aware, through the rictus of painful pleasure, to know that these Centaurean sirings were not just grandly virile performances, but an eroticised desperation, an almost bestial need to make someone pregnant and join her to me indissolubly.

Sex is a portal. The rooms it unlocks are strange, unsettling

316

rooms full of ghosts. No longer could I keep up with myself. I was living faster than I could reckon. Even my dreams became hectic and alien.

One night I dreamed of myself as a befuddled, tiny sperm jigger-jaggering between confusing targets, hammering tinily up one blind alley and then haring back desperately, recalled, thwarted, endlessly willing, but somehow hopeless as I swum in the blind warmth of a bifurcating delirium, my strength failing, my hopes dimming.

***

Things blew up with Colin a few days later. By then Vince and I were well away. He had absolutely taken to my idea of a novel that followed the consciousness of a Frank-like character though contrasting landscapes – the hell of a war zone and the peace of the Black Mountains, a book about impossible concurrencies of suffering and beauty, Eros and Thanatos, duty and love. McCabe's descriptions and photographs gave Vince a series of short, sharp prose shocks. Frank's death had changed him. He was sympathetically steeped in the being of a man whose conscience could not for a minute forget tyranny and injustice, whose busy life had been focussed on the lives of others, and who had paid a terrible price in solidarity with the fallen he had reported all his life.

Was it Vince's fragility that made him so receptive? Or was Vince a new artist? I liked to think the latter. We sat in his cabin talking around plots and narrative arcs, the psychological motors and set-pieces, the task of realising war in convincing detail, and the need for a love story back here in the Black Mountains that would define 'Frank's' dilemma: the urge to follow his late colleague back into the heart of darkness versus a craving for restorative love.

317

I helped him sketch a treatment. We talked about the war novel as a genre. Now and again the old Vince flashed back, like an interfering radio station, lambasting the books we discussed. I had to be very careful responding to these outbursts because they tended to bring out the literary snob in me. With two literary snobs in a cabin in the middle of nowhere cooking great cauldrons of vitriol about Vince's literary rivals we would get absolutely nowhere. Sometimes, when he sensed me overstepping the mark, or when the project looked too mainstream, he would toy with me, and then a playful but dangerous exchange would threaten the venture.

'Why do I have to write a war novel again?'

He was sprawled on the divan, hands behind his head, Doc Mart soles up. For once I was sitting on his chair.

'Well, you have to be tactical.'

'I know, I know. But why a war novel? Why not chick lit, or a boring old crime series, or God, fuck it, a children's book?'

'You're a literary novelist not a hack. The war novel is singular in being almost the only kind of literary genre that sells big time. I'm talking break-out success. It would be a grave mistake not to notice that.'

There was a long pause.

'Break-out success, Vince!'

'Like it.'

'So let's have some.'

'Maybe I should write a Lolita-type thingy.'

'No!'

'More fun than a war novel.'

'Please be serious.'

'All right. What do I do? Bog off to the Novotel in Helmand province?'

The discourse had to change. Vince had to hear it and sign up, because new levels of humility were required. 'Listen ... war is a crucible of the human condition, all narratives intensified. Its themes bring out the best in a writer. The writer puts his great talent at the service of human suffering, and proves he can take on something bigger than his own ego.'

'Oh, not the human condition again. You can run but never hide from the human condition.'

'There's no point unless you offer something with the DNA for greatness.'

Vince was appalled. 'The DNA for greatness?'

'Do you have to repeat everything I say?'

He looked at me with sudden openness. 'You're actually quite funny, Mike. Did you know that?'

'Vince!'

'Maybe I should stick you in a novel. And Lolita. Pop the pair of you in a war zone and I'm laughing all the way to the bank.'

I looked at him glumly.

'I'm joking,' he said. 'Where's your sense of humour today?'

I smiled very patiently. 'There is no need to go to Helmand because the dossier has everything you need. Moreover, you know one foreign correspondent with plentiful insight because you managed to have a stand-up row with him only a few days before he died. If I didn't think you believed in the urgency of this material, I wouldn't be sitting here, taking the time and trouble to help you produce what I think could be an enormously significant novel.'

He shook his head. 'Sorry.'

'That's OK.'

'Having some light relief.'

'I understand.'

'I mean, this is serious stuff. This is, like, heavy sausage. OK. Where were we?'

Failure had humanised Vince. He could no longer forget his real nature. He needed desperately to find a literary focus. Detachment was a thing of the past for him. From now on he would be writing for his life.

***

I had just written Vince's letter to Moyle when Steve called. I was at the cottage when the phone went.

Steve said they were about to send the email that Colin had drafted to all my clients. Did I know about this, and had I seen the attachment he forwarded? He took care not to mention the Colin photo.

'They've been having some fun with your swansong letter. Better take a look.'

I rang off and booted up the laptop. I had overlooked this and now returned to it with concern. Apprehensively, I flicked the thing up on the screen and gave it the once-over.

The document was titled 'Draft retirement letter for M de V – confidential'. It read as follows:

Dear (client's name)

After many very happy years at Acbe agency, I have decided it is time ~~for a change of direction~~ to give up and I am ~~seeking pastures new~~ going out to pasture. As of the 21st of this month I will be ~~leaving the agency~~ falling on my sword and assigning the management of all clients to a wonderfully talented team of Dee Pocock and Bella Lumley who will oversee your business far better than I. Bella will be in touch shortly. I'm sure you will find them highly dedicated and efficient (makes a change).

I know this will be a period of transition. My consolation is that I leave the agency in rude good health under Colin's maestro stewardship, absolutely confident that Sheila's brilliant legacy will persist.
Yours,
The Loser

Moments later I had Steve on the line.

'They weren't going to send that out,' he said, in a bluff attempt to mollify me. 'Just having a bit of a laugh. Maybe a pre-emptive strike would quell the nerves. As in: get to the clients before Colin does. You're still networked,' he added, softly. 'There hasn't been an IT service day since you split. You can log on via VPN and send emails to all your clients.'

The letter was unbelievable. It filled me with hatred and despair all over again. The competition doesn't just defeat you, it humiliates you. Win the war and then kill the little children, rape the women, burn the villages. Leave nothing to rise up against you. Colin must really have detested the idea of me to want to write that.

I felt terrible. To be one of history's losers, mown down by somebody ambitious and inhumane – what an awful way to go! How dreadful to be trashed just for being in the way of someone's business plan. My soul rose up against this.

I was so enraged that anger had to be carefully stored and concentrated not to overwhelm everything. I moved about the kitchen in distraction, lost really, and then realised I had prepared for this.

***

It seemed odd to think that Moyle's private detective had been in my employ for a week. I called Mr Judd on his mobile and learned that he had been busy with the register at the Royal

321

Cumberland Hotel. There, Colin's visits with Veronique and Christina had been recorded.

'In the name of Mr Mike de Vere,' said Judd. His voice was level and laconic, full of smoky humour.

'That's me!'

''Fraid so. He seems to have been banging birds in your name.'

'Good God! The little shit.'

'Quite a card, your Mr Templar,' said Judd. 'Paid cash, obviously.'

I struggled to recover myself. 'How do we know it's him? I mean, it obviously wasn't me!'

'You wouldn't put a private dick on your own trail, would you, Mr de Vere? No, a friendly porter confirmed the ID off a dashing snap from the *Bookseller*. I can give you the times. Should tally with his office diary.'

I clutched the mobile, mind racing.

'In the lunching hour. Room 15 would be a favourite.'

Colin was supposed to be working for the agency during the 'lunching hour'.

'Lunch can be a busy period for the married man.'

'What about the girl?'

'Arrives later and leaves first. Nice legs, says the porter. Blonde.'

The evidence was so prejudicial I wondered whether anyone would believe it.

'Does the porter have an opinion on what they were up to in room 15?'

Judd sniffed. 'Several used condoms have been cleared from the en suite pedal bin.'

I pondered this unalluring detail. I suppose it gave some figment of pleasure to know that Colin had been obliged to 'rubber up'. He would have bulging pocketfuls of the things, of course.

322

He'd rubber up in a flash, Y-fronts at his ankles, specs steaming over, pupils flickering like cat fleas on heat.

'Used condoms?'

'Durex Featherlite and some flavoured brands,' he added.

'Oh …'

Judd cleared his throat, a hint of professional world-weariness.

'Flavoured brands, you say?'

'Yes, indeed.'

This was more information that I really desired to know, and probably more than Mr Judd cared to impart.

'May I ask, Mr Judd, what particular … flavour were these condoms?'

'Bear with me a minute, sir.' There was a brief pause as he conferred with his notes.

'Pineapple Passion,' his voice rang out like a town crier. 'Then there's Three Fruit Surprise.'

(I had to work hard not to let these details jade the palate.)

'And Banana Split, if I can read my own handwriting.'

'Thank you, Mr Judd. That is most helpful.'

***

Moyle was set and ready. He had an announcement about our merger lined up for the *Bookseller* and *Publishing News*, and had been gathering Sheila's clients' phone numbers. I told him Vince was nearly ready to share an outline for a war novel and, if Moyle liked the look of it, we could proceed. There was no need to go through the charade of his meeting Vince before signing him up as Moyle and I were partners, and Vince would be ever so grateful to have an agent.

'I'll take him to Claridges when he's next in town,' said Moyle.

'Take him anywhere but Trattoria Bruno.'

He laughed rather smarmily. 'I like that little place. Food's awful though, isn't it?'

'Yes. It is awful.'

Moyle agreed to check my draft letter to clients. It was hard to believe that I was about to send a torpedo in Colin's side, a breach of endless contractual clauses, and grounds for every lawsuit in the book. Thirty authors would receive it the same time as Colin. I would launch the message by group mail at around 8.30 pm, and hope to pack in calls to key clients before he saw it on his Black-Berry. Once Colin clocked the message, all hell would break loose.

I had coffee that afternoon with Vince in his cabin and made him email Moyle, which he did with terrible feverish anxiety, fearing rejection. I had to remind myself that Vince knew nothing of the plot with Moyle.

'Are you sure it's OK to send?' he said, miserably.

'Yes!'

It was actually me who clicked the 'send' button.

Vince covered his face in his hands, as if a new ordeal had started.

Writers!

At 8.30 pm I despatched my own little mail from mission head-quarters on the kitchen table. My forefinger rested on the mouse for long, nervous minutes as I read the letter time and again. Never had a pre-emptive strike been couched in such genial terms. Sending it would be like dealing a knee-jab into the ether that would only connect over a hundred miles away. I wouldn't see the moment of impact; but there was such sadistic joy in the little tap that converted two paragraphs of electronic text into a remote, painful groining. Somewhere out there, possibly in seconds, Colin would clock his BlackBerry and recognise an unloved name.

Doubtless he would frown, and then he would read, blandly at first, not getting it, and then in confusion, as though at some office cock-up, and then with a faint heartbeat and mounting alarm, and then with incomprehension, as if such an email were beyond any kind of reckoning on his part. Soon he would be panicked, apoplectic, furiously furtive. He would be chewing at fingernails and calling Shyter, calling his lawyer, looking for my number, wondering what the fuck, and swivelling sweatily on some media-club toilet seat where he had incarcerated himself to take in the crisis.

Dear Melina

I have some very exciting news. Forgive me for imparting this by email, but events have moved with speed, and I want you to be in the picture without further delay. After many fulfilling years at the Acbe agency I'm delighted to inform you that I'm going into partnership with James Moyle, one of the country's leading agents with an incomparable and highly prestigious list. One of my concerns in making the move was how better to serve my wonderful clients and I have no doubt that Moyle Associates will enable me to offer you world-class service with amazing contacts through all branches of publishing and the media. The agency is based in salubrious offices off High St Kensington and supported by a global network of experienced sub-agents and dedicated Film/TV staff.

I am delighted to report that my separation from Acbe agency has been conducted with immense goodwill on both sides and with the warm blessing of the board. Please feel free to phone me about this, but I shall be in touch anyway. I look forward to our first lunch in Kensington (which has some excellent restaurants).

Yours,

Mike

Chapter 25

I had almost forgotten Colin's voice: a reasonable baritone with a good depth of public school confidence behind it. He could always do the sensible sounds and convincing cadences. To the hopeful client Colin's manner was charged with educated frankness and excitable spin. Unusually for a book agent, he had an emotional commitment to getting results and therefore wanted what he wanted with aching, testicular need. His focus was so personal that his passion for prevailing gave him a human patina. Wishing to see himself as the pattern of success he was desperately on the ball. Without power he knew he was uncongenial, socially and physically. Only with power could he rule the roost over greater men and command a degree of female attention.

When I took his call, it was 10.30 am.

'Colin Templar. For you,' said his PA down the line.

I pictured his torso bunched at the desk. His concentration would be screwed tight, like a constipation-sufferer scowling blue murder from the bog seat.

'Hello, Mike.'

'Hi, Colin.'

'You know what I'm calling about?'

I said nothing.

There was silence on the line.

'You've just broken your compromise agreement.'

'Are you referring to the email?'

'I am.'

His voice was flat.

'Colin, you've got what you wanted,' I said. 'Live and let live.'

'I bought something for a price and now you're trying to steal it back. Have you gone soft in the head?'

I waited, glanced at the back of my hand. 'I'm fine, actually.'

'You can't be. You're wide open to a lawsuit.'

'Not advisable, Colin.'

'This is madness. We made a deal. You got a good whack.'

'Void for duress.'

'Oh, don't be ridiculous!'

I let the line run silent. I was better at controlling my temper than he.

'Don't patronise me, Colin.'

'You know what, it's hard, Mike, it's hard. You've just pissed on a done deal. To be frank, I've just about had it with your monkey business. I don't know what kind of boozed up mid-life crisis you think you're having, but if you believe I'm going to put up with any fucking about, you are wrong. My lawyer will sue the living shit out of you, and we'll go to war in other ways.'

'It's a shame your money is sitting in my account isn't it, Colin?'

'I'll get it back, every cent, and take you to the cleaners.'

'In my offshore account. The flat is all mortgage.'

'I can injunct your fucking clients.'

'I'll get round that.'

'OK, I'll sue you for slander. We can open that can of worms.'

'Now that *would* be a mistake.'

'Sorry, Mike.' His exasperation was overloading. 'This bluffing game of yours is the latest in a series of fantasies that has dogged your entire career. You've come unstuck from reality.'

'I'm blissfully unstuck from you, mate. Most of your client list will be, too, soon, if you don't take the hint.'

'What hint? I'm not afraid of your slanders.'

'You know, Colin,' I said, 'publishing loves a good, sordid scandal.'

'You're pissing in the wind. Let's focus on what you're going to do. You are going to email your clients …'

'But clients don't. Clients are averse to agents with squalid personal lives.'

He attempted a pitiful laugh, as though this were just another try-on.

'Mike, listen, I don't know what you're talking about …'

'A phrase which invariably means you do.'

'Oh, this is pathetic. This is clutching at straws …'

'You've been clutching at things, Colin. Very hands on.'

There was a momentary hesitation.

'So the question is … who else gets to know?'

His voice was raised. 'I have absolutely no idea what you're talking about …'

'Violetta may have something to look at shortly. Then you'll know.'

'Right. I'm terminating this call. You'll be hearing from my lawyers.'

'Colin! One squeak from your chicken-shit lawyers, I'll tell Violetta everything.'

I heard him catch his breath. 'Are you blackmailing me?'

'And then *you*, Colin, will be hearing from *her* lawyers.'

'Listen, what are you …?'

'There goes your house, your marriage, and your business.'

'For God's sake!'

'Back off, Colin.'

I crushed the receiver down on the cradle.

Thirty seconds later the phone rang. I did not pick it up.

***

I stood there, gazing through the window, teeth set, deeply breathing. The shock of adrenaline and anger blurred vision, compressing and darkening things. I grappled the back of the chair and snorted hard and strode to the kitchen, rubbing knuckles and blinking through a mist at the cooker, the fridge, the draining board, as if these forms were anchors, familiar bulwarks, steadying witnesses to some great psychopathic eruption, an almost blinding surge of hate. I flattened my palms on the counter, a bullying push, a spasm, as though I had to lock muscles against some force that was out there, something to smash my will against.

I exhaled in ratcheted bursts, stalked out onto the front lawn, chin up, fists tight. Here was blue sky overhead, pigeon warble, the cheep of a thrush. The fresh air cooled my face and neck. The dense leaves of the oak trees seemed crinkly and opaque, like a barrier, a muffling. The hills rose pacifically, swooping to summits on either side of the valley. I wiped my nose and rubbed my forehead. I could hear a bee amongst the lavender by the path.

Where was I? Who was this?

***

Vince received a delighted call from Moyle at 11 am. James found the outline 'admirable', and already had ideas for UK and US publishers. He imagined 'perhaps' fifty pages would suffice to get a deal and hoped to launch the project before Frankfurt, leaving Vince a comfortable chunk of time to get the work done. It seemed Moyle had 'reacquainted' himself with the earlier novels and was able to flatter Vince with a few quotes and references. When I stepped into the cabin Vince was strangely composed. He was adjusting to a recovered sense of normalcy, of things being on track. Moyle's cordial call attested to his perennial standing as a writer, someone who had weathered the ups and downs but was a stayer, able to secure another top agent without too much bother. Beneath the gratified sense of recovered stature was an immense relief. Moyle's endorsement now welded him to the outline and a hearty agenda of work. His life was back in focus.

'Let's celebrate,' I said, patting him on the back.

'I'm up for that.'

'But first, you better sign off with Colin.'

Vince had no problem with this suggestion. His draft resignation email ran to five words: 'I hereby terminate your representation.'

'Maybe a little short.'

'What d'you want me to say? Apart from "Fuck off, twat"?'

'I like "Fuck off, twat" very much. It has a certain ring to it. A certain *je ne sais quoi*.'

Vince managed a smile.

'Perhaps instead: "Dear Colin. It won't come as a surprise to

330

you that I am terminating the agency with instant effect. Please forward relevant correspondence to my new agent, James Moyle. I am grateful for your efforts but feel the need of a more editorially skilled type of agenting. Yours, Vincent Savage."'

He frowned at the text of this email, once it was typed on the screen. Such civility was not his style.

'We don't want any bad-mouthing,' I said. 'And the reason you give is fair and inoffensive.'

'Good riddance to bad rubbish,' he said, tapping off the email like a flicked bogey.

***

I felt oddly calm and in my own skin as I dialled Melina Fuka-kowski from their house (Madelin was out). She was attentive and quiet when I told her. She grasped quickly the shifting power at Acbe Agency, knew of Moyle, and was impressed that I had sewn the whole thing up. I said there would be garden parties with famous authors and much better networking opportunities. I had to explain in fairly tedious detail what would happen to her existing contracts. Whatever alarm she felt at the suddenness of the news, she was coerced into a reassuring 'yes' by something in my tone. I was a train that smart clients had to board quickly. 'Fabulous, Mike. When can I come to these posh offices?'

Moyle had detailed me to call six of Sheila's clients and explain the new set-up. I prepared my best Queen's English tone and hit the list methodically. Because Sheila's illness had been sudden few people had had time to consider the future. Nearly everyone I spoke to was interested, whilst admitting that Colin had been on to them with promises of lunch, as yet unfulfilled.

'James knows your work very well. Funnily enough, we were

talking about you last night and he was asking what happened with *The Light Fantastic*. He knows a German publisher on the look-out for a high-profile author to launch ...'

I made Moyle Associates sound like a rival dinner party where everybody was having great fun and expecting Sheila's clients to join them like late guests, prompting fresh champagne opening.

'I mean Colin's very good. But it rather amused me the other day when he said that he lacked the "attention span" for fiction.' I laughed. 'If you're a footballer's wife or a super-chef, he's the man. Can we get you round for a chat? Oh, good.'

I did this in the living room on a sofa facing the inglenook. I sat there, pen on lap, and felt a shape forming in the corner of vision, the sense of a shadow which disappeared when I glanced to the right.

All I could hear was the workings of the house; the fridge-freezer in the boot room, a clock ticking, a rumble that might have been a lorry in the valley, or just the sound of the mountains themselves. I returned to my list, but gradually the sensation resumed. This time I let it linger, something inchoate, like a figure in the doorframe.

If somebody was looking at me, let them look, I said to myself, as if to call the bluff of the very odd sensation of being watched; and then I turned, and once again there was nothing.

There was a clatter in the kitchen and a banging door.

Quickly, I rose, glancing along the corridor before proceeding into the kitchen. All I could see through the window was windblown grass and swaying poppies and a warming patch of sunlight as the sun made a hole in the clouds. The back door was an inch ajar. I paused for a moment, gazing at the expanding cone of window-light in which tiny particles rose and fell.

***

On Offa's Dyke, the wind clawed at my hair, England's glorious panorama spread to the east. Various messages beeped on my phone, including a text from Kate.

Pretty soon I would have to go back to London. Moyle and I had to meet, greet and trumpet the future.

I returned Kate's call first.

'I've just heard from Able Hardiman,' she said, clearly alarmed. 'They've got an injunction on us.'

'What's the claim?' I said.

'Breach of non-compete and non-solicitation ...' she read. 'What is going on?'

Colin was calling my bluff. This gave pause. He was trying to out-face me. Why would he do that? Was he too angry to back down, too contemptuous of my ability to hurt him? Would he risk Violetta finding out? Would he take a hit and try to patch it up with her? Was the deal with me more important than his marriage? Was the marriage already breaking up? Did she know of his infidelity already? I thought fast and with mounting panic.

'I'm setting up with another agency.'

'Mike! You can't ...'

'Quiet!'

I could hear her breathing hard. Mine was no way to speak to a professional advisor.

Violetta might know, or suspect, but Violetta would hate to know that others knew *more*. And Colin would hate to be exposed. Conceivably Colin might think he could weather the storm and achieve a kind of notoriety, and be on his way to so much dosh that he could let the marriage go, lose half a house, park the Violetta problem and fire-fight scandal. He wouldn't have been the first successful

333

agent to have ditched a wife and fucked his way around the block. He might even calculate that the bad publicity was good publicity.

You calculate the risk and then you take it. Nerve. Have nerve, I thought. Take the risk. Go in hard.

'This will be resolved out of court. Email Colin's lawyer and demand that the application is rescinded by 5.30 today. Ask him to confirm that my clients be allowed to join me at Moyle Associates and that Colin Templar agrees for a consideration of one pound to annul the non-compete and non-solicitation clause in my severance deal.'

Kate was typing this down as fast as she could. My strident voice had a galvanising effect, no doubt. I could tell she was offended, but I paid her bill, not she mine.

'Failure to confirm will result in …,' I pondered the choice of words, 'a counterclaim accompanied by full and frank disclosure.'

'What does that mean?'

'It will mean plenty to Colin.'

Kate completed her note-taking and then read it back to me.

'What if his lawyer phones me?'

'Say that the principals have come to an agreement and that he should talk to his client.'

'There's nothing dodgy about this, is there?'

'The email will go in ten minutes,' I instructed.

'Yes.'

'Copy it to Templar. Text me when the answer comes.'

Colin was calling my bluff. I would now call his.

***

I got back to the cottage, let myself in quickly, and went to the laptop. The first thing was to create a new email account. The user address I worked up carefully, to catch his eye. The text I fiddled with for several minutes. I had to land him a sharp kick in the crotch without using everything. I typed Violetta's address at *The Times* in the centre of the mail.

Fifteen minutes later I was glued to the screen. The constellation of words had a distilled neutrality. Only Colin would be exactly sure what this meant. I brought up the photo attachment and with a beating heart opened the file. I couldn't help a smile of relief as the image came alive. This was no polite peck goodnight. This was a flesh-eating French kiss – a cameo of passionate, hungry, brazen infidelity. It would turn Violetta to stone. I clicked the send icon and gazed at the floor, savouring irreversibility.

From:
Veronique.Room15@hotmail.com

Souvenir, ma chérie.
Shall I forward this attachment after 5.30 pm?
Violetta.Prittpen@TheTimes.com

No injunction. We can have more fun.

Kisses
Christina Loves Featherlite

Three minutes later the phone rang. I knew it was Colin.

After the ringing ceased, my mobile started.

There was a kind of desperation in these insistent attempts to communicate.

The silence that followed, empty afternoon silence, left me alone with intense impressions of light and shadow, the immediacy of mute objects, the unwavering peace of the cottage front room, and of a calm day outside. The solid quiet persisted indefinitely, like deafness. I sat on the edge of the chair, hands clasped together in a kind of attunement, a listening posture that felt like a fusion of attention and imperviousness, unbreachable.

Kate's call came earlier than expected. I listened dispassionately to her reading of an email from Colin's lawyer and the wording of a draft agreement, noting that Kate was curiously cool and business-like now that she had been put in her place and that Colin's lawyers were taking no chances with my approval.

The capitulation was total. I exhaled mightily, relief flooding through neck and chest, but leaving the sense of hard power in its wake.

I thanked Kate, asked her to expedite the documentation, and rang off without more ado. I had dared, and I had won.

***

At moments of triumph there can be a strange vacuum in the heart, as if all the strain of vanquishing enemies is simply defensive, returning one to the status quo ante, what should have been; and yet as Mike rose from his seat and made his way into the hallway and pushed open the front door into dazzling afternoon light that seemed to focus all its heat and solar glory on the front of the cottage, he was struck by a violent exultation, a fist-clenching moment of pure vicious joy that swelled in his breast to a bursting sense of command. He was triumphantly delivered. The future had lain down at his feet. The shackles of irony fell in a clatter about him. Somehow, he owned his life again, what he desired, what he wanted, what pleased him, including this view ahead, no longer tragically beautiful, but glowing with reward. The certainty of this pumped him, filled his breast, and tightened his neck muscles.

There was work to do now; an office to get going; advantage yet to press. He must seem like an incoming presidential figure. Staff would be needed, systems: a blizzard of work.

He would have to get back pretty much right away, to assert authority and pillory the waning Colin.

Mike stood on the pathway, staring up the high banks of the valley at the density of trees, the intersecting fields, the steep drama of the upper heights, and felt conviction rush to the edge of his skin. Everything had been taken from him. Now he was clawing it back.

He sloshed out a whisky in the kitchen and went outside to sit on the garden bench. He drank it in a gulp, shivered. With his fists on the bench he felt his eyes moisten. He was weeping – stress, relief, the sense of the bitter journey behind him, the resurrection from failure. He had come through a lot, and allowed himself a tear for the struggle.

As he brushes the wet off his cheek, banishing the sense of a childish collapse that purges so much crap, such tension, he thinks of Madelin – the only person he is near to – because you need to confess. Someone has to share this drama of the self. She owes him a heart to heart. This moment of triumph is really no more than the shock of survival. She must understand, please, how much this means to him. He has been reprieved of a death sentence, because there was never ever anywhere else to go. Life's push requires much fortitude and not a little ego. But the ego needs success to be healthy. The ego without success is a Nazi.

Madelin … he gasps … the drink and sunlight are wilting him

337

and so is the shock. Feeling rises, a slew of emotions, like a sky loading with cloud before a downpour. What does one take from sexual union? That one simply needs more? That it is good? That one's soul is transacted along with the seminal fluid? Obviously a homecoming of sorts, actuated by exquisite sensation, appetite, all that, but taking you somewhere not quite mundane. What were all these couplings but conversions of form into spirit? An affair always rises above its premise to some state of potentiality. She had privileged him as was her wont with men, quickly achieving the unforgettable, a diva-like distinction that made you want more, and then become addicted; but through the usual pattern, the sequence of erotic shocks, was a coincidence of minds and temperaments, a mesh that inevitably grew between lovers and which it was hard to ignore though easy to play down.

Now that he must go back to London, he feels a separation anxiety. He must see her. They have stuff to talk about, he thinks, that hasn't been aired before, but now pretty much has to be, because he will need something to take back with him. It would be trite to presume that either of them was emotionally inert, whatever the context.

He is shot through with feeling now, and knows why. He wants his life back rather passionately, and is not to be held at arm's length by anyone. He deserves what he desires. If it worked with work, it can work with love.

Love. The engines are running all right. That lasso of hers tightens every time. Need, desire, tenderness blaze away beneath the surface. For what was all that sexy choreography but the objective correlative of the deepest human need? Mastery over fate rouses him now. He has been brave and the brave deserve the fair. Or rather, he has rights in whatever affects him, whatever involves him, and Madelin has moved the agenda to a place

338

where he has ownership and must claim it. He is stirred by this, even as complications loom.

Vince.

He can't think around this yet. Vince is effectively a client. They are bound as agent and author. He smiles, almost mortified by the conflict of interest he now faces, and rather thinks this unethical Gordian knot the existential crux of his job, an occupational maelstrom awaiting agents that some avoid by chance and others flip into, because the middleman's essential propensity is to rise between principals like oil and get himself between both sides of a deal, playing one side off against the other, and that intimacy with the struggles of others, that is his talent. All the force and complication of recent weeks has flowed from his managing to be in the right place at the right time. The ethics are a mess, but the results are signal. What agent could deny the accomplishment, the breath-taking impressarioship, the élan and audacity of rehabilitating an author whilst ravishing his wife, of stinging Colin whilst joining Moyle, of counselling both partners in a broken marriage whilst benefitting from them both? Such protean multi-tasking was surely an apotheosis of the agent's craft, a *ne plus ultra* of ubiquity and dexterity. If talent and timing had contrived such an end, this gaudy Machiavellian come-back, Mike must ride the wave a bit longer, because when forces are aligned you see where they take you. Especially as now, sitting in the sunlight, hit by the whisky, shattered and emotional, heartbreakingly reprieved, he felt the upsurge of feeling and with it the recovery of his bearings. The discreditable fiasco behind him was somehow irrelevant now. Sure, things were complicated. Secrecy, dissimulation and hypocrisy were in the script. But sooner or later Madelin would leave Vince, and Vince somehow would cope, accepting the inevitable, perhaps learning from it, and even Vince might not care that Madelin and Mike had come together. Mike wanted to be around for that moment. He sensed possibility, a through-line to future happiness, the chance – his one chance in a lifetime. Madelin had a child and didn't want another. His infertility would never deter her.

With a lurch in the heart, he grasps the pressure of hope. The lineaments of unsuspected destiny are apparent and painfully compelling. All this is disorientating. The self springs these surprises.

***

Mike packs and gets ready to leave. Even as he does so things are developing elsewhere, emails are being sent, representation terminated, meetings set up. Moyle's patrician social manner is working a little harder and faster as he phones Sheila's clients with high-pressure salesmanship and lays the bait, fixing lunches, listing questions for Mike, getting in there like some jumbo-sized vulture whose wingspan casts its enormous shadow over the terrain blotting out sunlight and ominously deterring smaller predators from the richest pickings. Soon he and Mike will be side by side at Claridges or The Ivy with Angus Hitachi or Melina Fukakowski, nodding with acumen, smiling personably, ordering wine, flattering with a straight face, erupting with laughter at an author's wit, judiciously positing, peerlessly insinuating, cordially embodying a kind of pedigree and class that could never be acquired by meritocratic promotion, but could only come from an empyrean higher than publishing itself, some cloud-based, column-vaunted Olympus, where gods consorted and occasionally swooped to assist worthy mortals in their humble strivings. Thus Moyle's conceit: that writers and publishers were playthings of the gods, and the gods were agents.

Mike rushes to grab his things. Now he is about to return the light seems more beautiful than ever on the trees outside, the greens richer and more saturated, the slanting fields reflective of light, and the sky a grainy azure. He drives along the Llanbedr valley glancing through breaks in the hedgerow at golden meadows. Radiant sunshine soothes his face, drenching him in well-being.

Madelin will be alarmed by his departure. As he shunts down the lanes over dried sheep-dung and a gravel of beech mast, he can anticipate the leave-taking, the current of her touch, the rising pulse, a melting into something misty-eyed and purposeful which they must control because Vince will be across the drive and Holly back from school; and yet this charges him up, makes him headlong, all ajangle as he hangs a left and drops a gear and then begins the climb to the farm.

Chapter 26

Paintings everywhere, floor to ceiling, all walls covered.
They are leant against chairs and counters, hooked on
beams, propped against easels. The barn is a gallery packed to
the rafters with Madelin's work. The exhibition surrounds him
like a revelation. Madelin has dragged everything into view
from a back storeroom and from unzipped portfolios. She
has got it where it can be seen, an overwhelming display of
artistic plans and obsessions. He is ambushed by imagery and
by the energy of a style. There are charcoal torsos, strenuously
figurative, bodies twisting like taxed trees in a gale. The long
ridges of Black Mountain landscape become vast sea creatures, hump-backed whales riding the ocean gloom. A female
body is conjugated through straining arched positions rendered in section. A trio of line drawings repeat the textures of
a castle ruin in meticulous detail. He sees dark self-portraits
with shadowy eye-sockets and jet hair, bare necks and prominent collarbones. There are exuberant pastels; garden vegetables, flowers in pots. Raised and immense, a silhouetted nude
and mare, the woman bleached and irradiated as she leans
against the horse's side.

The evidence overwhelms him.

She stands in the centre of the room, watching his reaction, as if reading the effect of so much expression on an unsuspecting visitor.

What he sees reaches so far beyond what he knows of her that her face seems mask-like. He feels dispassionately regarded, an object seen through a viewfinder. She was not expecting him and now has to emerge from a contemplative trance. Her expression is soft, neutral. She is spellbound by the deepest thought or reckoning, like a pregnant mother. She sees him from the epicentre of self-communing that he cannot penetrate and she can barely disrupt.

Mike hesitates. A force-field holds him on the periphery. He suffers a fallopian confusion. Madelin is like a figure in a brilliant painting, fixed amidst crowding forms, present and unwelcoming.

'Hi,' he says.

Her eyelashes flicker.

There is something so absolutely strange about her quiet watchfulness and the way it makes him feel, that he forgoes small talk or any kind of introduction. It is necessary to come to the point, he feels, as she is preoccupied and not reacting to his presence.

'What's happened is ...'

She gazes at him neutrally.

'I've gone into business with Vince's new agent.' He exhaled. 'So I have to go back for a few days ...'

He looked down. Such direct accounting of plans and movements sounded ominous.

She followed his eyes.

'I will continue to edit Vince's work.' This seemed like an admission.

He risked her gaze. She was now in possession of the facts. These she might construe unsympathetically.

'It's just come about like that. I needed Vince, yes, but Vince needed me, too. So. The result's good for us both.'

He couldn't tell whether she accepted this.

'But I want to carry on with you. I mean … I …' He raised an eyebrow in appeal. 'Madelin … I'd like to carry on, somehow. Because I … I do …'

She seemed fathomlessly intrigued by his awkwardness. Her lips were parted, her brown eyes set with listening. She seemed ready to absorb his intent.

'I can get back here regularly. And maybe if things, well … with Vince …'

Their eyes met. She had never looked at him in this way before. She seemed contemplative and somehow receptive, ready in some way, ready to hear words from the heart perhaps. Her silence was an encouragement, he felt.

'I do actually care,' he said, 'what happens. I am whole-hearted, Madelin, and will continue to be.'

She smiled disconcertingly.

'Maybe there's a logic to what's happened. I'm not deserting you. I feel like I'm deserting myself going back to London.'

She smiled again, as though she were pleased, and happy to show it. Such declarations – the form of words, the manner – could be very charming.

'I wanted you to know.'

He reached towards her.

'Mike,' her face was up-tilted, available. 'Holly's found out.'

He started.

Her gaze chased him into himself.

'What?'

344

'She told me this morning. She said, "I know you and Mike are sexing".'

It hit him hard, a jarring shock.

He swallowed. 'How?'

'We haven't been careful.'

Madelin was mild but focussed. She was extremely collected.

He was shot through with embarrassment and the appalling feeling of having been caught out.

'She's going to tell Vince unless we stop.'

He was utterly mortified. That a six-year-old should have been exposed to their love-making filled him with shame.

'What did you say to her?'

'That Mummy and Daddy have not been getting on well. That Mummy's been lonely and you were comforting me.' She looked down.

The bubble had burst and now he was panicking.

'I'll get out of everybody's hair.' It was said on a reflex, and sounded too pragmatic and unprincipled, almost craven. Enforced retreat was not what he meant.

'I think we need to be very careful,' she said, subdued. 'Not really great for either of us if he finds out.'

He nodded in half-agreement. This was her problem as much as his, maybe more so.

'Perhaps we should call the whole thing off,' she said.

Her look was one of appeal.

Mike hesitated, a sort of double-take. She seemed to be appealing to reasonable common sense or moderation, which was something of a first.

He nodded: a registering, time-buying nod. His heart was hammering in his chest.

'I thought you were going to leave him,' he said.

She was silent. He waited.

'You said the marriage was dead.'

'Well, I'm not sure …'

'Not sure?'

She shrugged.

He was honestly surprised. There was a confusion of issues here and the ache in his chest told him how much was at stake.

She would not meet his eye. Her reticence was devastating.

'Madelin,' he drew a little closer. 'Vince is more in love with his last sentence than anyone in the world.'

'I don't deny it.'

'So how can the marriage not be dead? How can all the sex we've had be evidence of a living, breathing marriage?'

'The marriage was always a compromise. It's just that I want to work now. I have work to do. And so do you, for that matter.'

'Work?'

It sounded very hollow indeed, though, yes, he could see, she was obviously inspired and full of the joys of creativity. His mind raced; there seemed a lot of disentangling to do.

'You can't be dictated to by Holly.'

'Holly's my child.'

'Holly's the victim of a dysfunctional marriage.'

'Vince is different. You made him … change somehow. I just don't know if now is the time to blow the whole thing up.'

He felt run through. It was far too early to be sensible and pat and conservative like this. That kind of simplicity had long been defenestrated.

'Oh, I get it. I was just a pick-me-up.'

'No!'

'Thank you very much.'

'You're great.'

'Why are people always flattering me and then dumping me? It's not that easy and it's not that convenient, and besides, you're lying to yourself about Vince. He is what he is and will never change.'

'You were trying to save my marriage a week ago. Was that just to get Vince as a client?'

'That was a good-faith attempt to resist satanic temptation which failed.'

She smiled. 'But it's a bit close, don't you think? Having a lover who represents one's husband.'

'Things are already close, if you haven't noticed. Don't tell me you've lost your nerve.'

'As you rightly say, I've Holly's happiness to consider. The chances are she'll tell Vince anyway.'

She was almost unrecognisable. There was a measured calmness about her. She sat before him on the wine-bar chair with a maternal poise and containment. Her hair fell evenly and beautifully. She bloomed with womanly fulfilment, surrounded by paintings, her family of art works.

Mike moved around between trestles and tables, knuckles whitening, mind turning revolutions. He could not see sense if he tried. His heart churned. The violence of his emotions amazed him. He felt opposed by something unexpected and unacceptable. She had stirred up feelings. She could hardly step away. The excuse of rational self-interest was false, a self-betrayal.

'Sorry. I'm not like the others.'

She remained sitting, her head bowed.

'I know you're not. But if Vince finds out ...'

He turned sharply. 'Why shouldn't he find out? Writers understand these things. It's part of the human condition, fuck it.'

'Mike …'

'He can bloody well write about it. We should come clean, make a virtue of necessity.'

'Calm down.'

'I can't calm down, Madelin. I'm not a domestic animal.'

'Why destroy what you've tried so hard to achieve? He's back on the rails again.'

'This is the mirror image of what I said to you last week and you didn't give a toss.'

'I've changed my mind.'

He halted. 'Yeah, and so have I.'

She looked at him in alarm.

'Be sensible.'

'Sounds very weak coming from you. Was it sensible to be shagging on the floor when Holly might come in and spot us?'

'No! And now we've got to deal with it. Sooner or later you always have to deal with it.'

'Have you asked yourself what all that activity meant?'

She regarded him warily.

His gaze was unrelenting and painful to receive.

She frowned, not inconsiderately. 'It means something different to you, I think.'

He was crushed, crestfallen. His face fell and for a moment he was at a loss. He drifted back a few steps. When he spoke his tone was different, softer.

'I didn't know what it meant at the time … but now it has come to mean something.'

She bowed her head.

He waited. Nothing else seemed to matter. London, Moyle, the future, all had shrunk away behind some firewall of desperation.

348

'I don't deny …' she began.

'What?'

She afforded him one of her looks, holding his eye. 'It was good.'

'It?'

She shrugged, dismissing whatever distinction he was trying to make.

'What I needed,' she said. 'I mean, I haven't been unfaithful to Vince before.'

He nodded. 'Which only makes it more significant, don't you think?'

'Mike, it was impulsive! You knew it was bonkers.'

'But sustained and determined.'

'We do these things for ourselves until we know where we stand.'

'Now you're going to tell me you love Vince.'

'If Holly hadn't found out we might have had more room and time, Mike, but we have to react now, and at the moment I'm not ready to push the red button, and you're naive if you don't get that.'

'So I should never have believed a word you said?'

'Words are a game.'

'Know what? You're worse than Vince. He's a selfish bastard writer. You're a selfish bloody painter.'

'Can you very quickly get a life?'

'Well, as a matter of fact, no, because I'm infertile and not eligible for single women wanting a family, and much as I've tried hard to survive a professional *coup d'état* and reconstruct my working life, I'm finding it hard to get love and stay loved, and feel somewhat taken advantage of by people who should know better than to expect absolutely disposable convenience from the

349

person they have physical relations with!'

There was a long silence.

He stood his ground, looming in the after-shock of his speech, as if charged by his own rhetoric, which surprised him actually. He was hearing himself declare things that gave the game away, and yet this was his truth, and there came a point when you had to get it out there, in competition with other people's truths, because maybe yours was truer than theirs, because maybe others needed to be shocked into knowing what they were doing to you.

'I'm sorry,' she said. 'I didn't know till you said.'

She was alluding to his infertility, his handicap for which it was insinuated she would have made allowances had she known. He didn't want allowances. Who would?

'Yup, well you don't ask many questions outside your own agenda. You want to be at arm's length and under no obligation.'

'Oh, Christ, Mike ... Will you stop this! You were the one with the qualms last week. We were both being very naughty and knew it. I was hoping it did us both good.'

'Please, Madelin! Don't shut the door on me. I'm too old to be shut out. I can't take it, actually. I can't face it. We've made first base. Let's stay cool and not throw away something which ... which ...'

'Mike, isn't this all about Nadia?'

He shook his head, glaring at the floor.

'No!'

His eyes were round and searching – a mixture of defiance and vulnerability.

'It's all about loneliness.'

Madelin took this in steadily. She frowned: half consternation, half acknowledgement.

There was space in her thoughts for regret, and possibly confusion. Parallel realities certainly existed and Mike needed no reassurance, in her mind, of the kind of feeling she might have for him. She had been forthright, urgent, passionate, and it was not to be assumed this could happen with anyone. That, and its consequences, she could reckon well enough. Her responses to this were simply guillotined by supervening events and if Mike didn't recognise *force majeure*, she certainly did, and anyway things had shifted, because now she wanted to paint. She wanted her own time. Vince, somehow, had got back into a manageable place.

She sighed. 'I'm going to have to come to a deal with Holly. Holly's got to believe a promise I will never see you again. Please put yourself in my shoes.'

This he heard as ruthlessness. She would withdraw back into the home, closing shutters, bolting the front door, resuming propriety.

'It's a ticking bomb. If she hears me on the phone to you or gets suspicious, that could be it. She loves her father and wants us to be happy, and has been through a shitty six months like the rest of us.'

This is ludicrous, he thought. Holly cannot be the arbiter of my fate. Holly cannot be expected to keep a secret for years. Holly is not the reason. Reasons never stand in Madelin's way. She wants to paint. That makes perfect sense. Vince is being human for once, thanks to me. Call it quits, enjoyed the ride, back to business. I've supposedly leveraged a new career out of Vince's crisis, thousands more days in the office spinning plates and schmoozing clients and working like a bugger on heat to stay ahead, just to stay in a game nobody believes in anymore, forcing squares into round holes, waving off casualties with a smile, becoming a boringly familiar face in a cottage industry, playing my hunches, making money if I'm canny and don't get caught up in the treacherous integrity of my own taste, subjugating passion to pragmatism. That's what I get from this serviceable little encounter on the hills, whilst Madelin and Vince retreat to what they did before, into the solipsism of creativity, as if real life were just a pool you dipped your toe in from time to time, a sort of background myth beyond the main quest: to make an alternative world in which one has complete control and all the answers, because you can't change horses now. You can marginally improve, but destiny is writ in what we have already chosen for our lives. We are who we are, and our crises are not opportunities, but scheduled dramas in the inexorable voyage of the self that ploughs through repetitive waters with or without the consolation of legacy. Believe in that, she seemed to say. Sex decorates all that, but sex is no longer where the action is; sex can only mean so much at our age. Those grand romantic impulses are a trap. Hold the pattern, get back to your work; that's the real asset, that ontological cockpit with its headrest and joy stick and blithe ease of vertical take-off from the bore of people. That's what she meant, and that little paean to the wise and sensible I now found utterly detestable because what passes between two people in the crux of an affair, what erupts is not some pleasing duet, some trading of glandular ache and emission, but the compliment the abandoned self pays to another: an exchange of fundamental knowledge, inviting more; and when that passes there is hope, the space for love, the start of something new and perhaps the chance of a better self, a self you only discover with the aid of another, and with it the deepest happiness which sets you up in life, makes you generous and better for other people, a beacon of human warmth and constancy, not some black hole

352

into which sexual passion is vacuumed; and that beginning was there for sure beneath the lacquered hardness of Madelin's sexiness, behind the artist's abstraction, and the comic indignation of the thwarted housewife, undiscovered, unused, unfelt, invisible behind the executive rationalisations of a sexy but alienated woman I knew. Madelin was flailing around with the hassle of false being, making do with surface and strategies, constructing a half-restored Humpty Dumpty of a life, the brittle hysteric one moment, emotionally confounded the next. Was this bogus simulacrum of misalliance and compromise the life? Was that moody stand-up Vince her best way forward?

No.

And how did I know? I was just a lucky knob, the inveterate middleman, a membrane that slid between abrasive surfaces, Mike de Vere the good-natured standby with a beguiling mixture of humour and humility; on hand for females when it counted, but only as an intermittent compère to the damaged and deranged, the catwalk catastrophes of the fairer sex to whom I was fatally attracted as the one nice man they could touch base with before flinging themselves at more dangerous and hardened operatives. How could I know anything for sure if, as Madelin's behaviour implied, I was not real in the way men need to be real, too attentive and contingent, taking my cue from others and their talents, placed in the throng only to serve, and therefore a means but never an end, a confidant, life-coach, lover, but not the main thing? Was I not who I claimed to be? Was my entire persona an elastic labial sheathing of forces beyond my control, the rictus smiles and purses and gapings involuntarily forced on me by unresolved inner tensions?

No, it bloody wasn't.

'If you won't tell him, I will.'

She is scared now. 'You're mad!'

'Dare me.'

'Oh, Mike, for God's sake!'

'This whole set-up is a lie, a kind of schizophrenia. It's time for you to have the courage of *your* convictions.'

She gasps. 'Think of your own position!'

'I don't need Vince. He can get another bloody editor. He's hardly going to tell the world that an *agent's* been screwing his wife.'

'You don't hate him enough.'

'I hate the falsehood more. This is not you.'

'If you had a child, you'd understand. I can't account for my behaviour, I'm sorry. I don't want to do it anymore. It's over, Mike. Your salvation doesn't lie here.'

His eyes burn. 'Madelin!' Spit flies from his mouth. 'I'm not a piece of trash to throw out!'

'Tell him then!'

She stares at him.

'It won't get you anywhere with me.'

He stares back at her.

'So what purpose will it serve?'

He snorts. 'I don't care, actually. Revenge!'

She faces him with cold rage. 'Take your revenge!'

'I will.'

'Mike!' Her voice quavers.

'It's your turn now, Madelin.'

She watches him exit the barn.

He stamps out into the yard, Vince's cabin bobbing in vision, murder in his heart. Kill them and get out.

'Mike!' she calls behind him sharply.

Holly speeds from the house. He sees her fraught face.

Drop the bomb and leave.

His lips flare and spread around his teeth, brow notches, the cabin bobs closer through the rising mist of his anger, vision streaming.

'Mike,' she screams.

'Go away,' says Holly.

The door comes closer, the gravel scratches under foot, the cabin is before him. There's a presence inside. He reaches for the handle, but the door bursts open and Vince towers, aghast, shock in his eyes, amazed at the sight of him, a round-eyed gaping stare.

'Vince … you …'

Vince grabs him and twirls him about mightily, his balance gone as Vince tips him back and pulls him again into a muscular crush of chest and armpit.

'Mike, you arsehole.'

He is crushed.

'You fucking …'

'You know?'

Vince is necking him almost, a wrestler's body grip.

'Oh, my God.'

'Vince,' shouts Madelin.

He drops Mike as Holly closes in.

'What?'

His face is charged.

'Madelin!'

Her alarm is palpable. Vince is possessed.

And now Vince's long-legged sally up the slope to the barn where she stands waiting to be picked up and tossed by this lank, tall maniac, then madly spun round and set down. He yanks her back to where Mike is standing, frozen; grabs Holly, a chain of three clutching hands, Madelin breathless and terrified, Holly attached to his leg like a fanatically loyal pet. They stumble towards Mike, Vince's face pink with exertion.

Vince draws breath, kisses Madelin's head.

She looks at him tentatively, playing along, hopelessly confused but sheltered by his height and powerful forearm.

He stares at Mike now.

Mike is checked. Mike cannot move a muscle.

Vince recovers himself, breathing deeply.

'Moyle's just done a deal on the book,' he says, gasping. He leans down to get his breath back.

Madelin catches hers.

'One hundred thousand pounds.'

She gasps.

'Yihee!' Vince erupts in a warrior leap, a tomahawk dance, a jump for pure joy.

Madelin's face transforms with astonishment. She is smiling with uncontrollable delight.

Mike's face is blank.

She catches his eye. 'Well done, Mike.'

'Hundred grand for a ten-page outline!'

Now Vince is advancing towards him for the superhuman bear hug, the crunch of love and gratitude and brotherhood. Mike's nose and mouth is driven into Vince's chest and the humid warmth of his neck.

'Words cannot express …' says Vince, standing back. He nods manfully. 'I owe you everything.'

He feels his cheeks bunching meaninglessly.

'Champagne everyone? Let's get some bubbly. Let's get smashed.'

Vince revolves amongst his family like an excited Shakespearian monarch bringing high celebration to the court after bittersweet endings and recovered love. Madelin holds his hand tightly and gazes at him in admiration, and Holly hugs away for dear life, gripping her daddy's leg; and Vince gazes in joy at mother and daughter and keeps them tight bound, his big hands spreading and clasping; and Madelin's upward look becomes a beaming smile, a melting smile, which he reciprocates.

Mike stands there.

Slowly the family trio edges towards the house, united, slightly stumbling. Vince won't release them and they support him, and Madelin keeps her arm at his waist, drawing him on to the cottage.

He is empty. Mind blank.

The after-image of the family is iconised on retinal vision, a biblical grouping.

They have disappeared inside the house and left him on the drive. Minutes pass in the blink of an eye.

He breathes deeply, a sudden intake demanded, oxygen restoration, and stares blindly at the alien building and empty concourse.

That triangle of faces is engraved on sight. It dazzles. He has seen the circuit of a family's love in that twining of figures, a scalding X-ray; and the pattern of their affection in her upward gaze and blush of astonishment. How snugly she fitted against Vince's side. With what ease and feeling he hugged her to him.

He lowers his head.

The body is overtaken at such moments, like diagnostic aftershock, a weightless sensation. One shrinks to the periphery, the margins. The welling, the agony: shut down. Passion is dead-headed.

He has seen the truth again and fades before it. He is where the action is, but outside it.

Mike, shrunken now, gazes at the air – the day is grey, though the distant clouds have form and sit flat-bottomed over the valley.

He fondles his car keys in his pocket and heads quickly to the Peugeot. The middleman has done his job and must move on as middlemen do.

Acknowledgements

Great thanks to my stalwart and generous readers Katrin MacGibbon, Pip Torrens, David Sherwin, Mark Roberts, Mark McCrum, Rod Williams, Jo Willet, Tony Mulholland and Nina Killham for enjoying the tome in its various drafts and giving me wise comments. A special nod goes to David Miller for services rendered. I bow steeply to my editor Miranda Vaughan Jones, and graciously to my agent Isobel Dixon, and I blow a kiss to the author's wife, Fiona.

A Note on the Author

Conrad Williams was born in Winnipeg and lives in Willesden Green. Educated at Bedales School and Trinity College, Cambridge, he qualified as a barrister before becoming a literary agent and author. As an agent, he represents screenwriters, directors and playwrights, and works closely with book agents. He is the author of two highly acclaimed previous novels, *Sex & Genius*, and *The Concert Pianist*, published by Bloomsbury in 2002 and 2006 respectively, and is a keen amateur pianist and chamber musician. His short stories have been broadcast on Radio 4 and published in *You Magazine*, and he has written on musical matters for Pianist Magazine. He is married with two daughters. For further information www.conradwilliams.co.uk

BLOOMSBURY READER

Discover books by Conrad Williams published by
Bloomsbury Reader at
www.bloomsbury.com/ConradWilliams

Sex and Genius
The Concert Pianist